Praise for the Find

LIGHT IN TH

"Clay is probably one of the most complex, tortured characters I have ever read, but he has had such a profound effect on me. This is the type of book that opens up your mind and your heart."

—*Smitten's Book Blog*

"True love that you felt with your whole heart. . . . A beautiful, emotional, and unconventional love story . . . [that] will remain in my heart forever."

—*Aesta's Book Blog*

"Brilliant, amazing, gut-wrenching."

—*Shh Mom's Reading*

FIND YOU IN THE DARK

Picked for the "What to Read After *Hopeless*" List
by *Maryse's Book Blog*

"Emotional, turbulent, and honest."

—*Heroes and Heartbreakers*

"The characters jump out of the books and into our hearts each and every time. . . . Sweet and sassy with some sexy to steam up the pages."

—*Book Addict Mumma*

"One wildly bumpy ride. . . . Emotional doesn't even begin to cover it. The feelings were so raw and vivid that it seemed so real. . . . This is one story that I plan to follow to the end. It's going to be me and my tissue box all the way."

—*The Bookish Brunette*

light in the
the
shadows

A. MEREDITH WALTERS

GALLERY BOOKS

NEW YORK   LONDON   TORONTO   SYDNEY   NEW DELHI

Gallery Books
A Division of Simon & Schuster, Inc.
1230 Avenue of the Americas
New York, NY 10020

First Gallery Books trade paperback edition July 2014

GALLERY BOOKS and colophon are registered trademarks of Simon & Schuster, Inc.

For information about special discounts for bulk purchases, please contact Simon & Schuster Special Sales at 1-866-506-1949 or business@simonandschuster.com.

The Simon & Schuster Speakers Bureau can bring authors to your live event. For more information or to book an event, contact the Simon & Schuster Speakers Bureau at 1-866-248-3049 or visit our website at www.simonspeakers.com.

Manufactured in the United States of America

10 9 8 7 6 5 4 3 2 1

ISBN 978-1-4767-8232-4
ISBN 978-1-4767-8230-0 (ebook)

For those searching for the light . . .
Never stop.

light in the
the
shadows

prologue

Forgive.

Such a small word. Only seven letters, but they carried the weight of the world.

Seven letters between me and the one thing I wanted most in my life.

The saying goes: *To err is human; to forgive, divine.* As if it was so easy to accept. No word in the history of words was harder to give and even more difficult to receive.

But I needed it. Craved my redemption deep in my bones.

I still struggled with my doubts and self-loathing. I didn't deserve forgiveness or understanding. I didn't deserve the love of the girl I had destroyed.

But it didn't stop me from chasing after it.

And I wouldn't stop until I caught it.

Until I caught her.

And maybe then I could learn to forgive myself.

chapter
one

"You're cheating! There is no freaking way you can win six rounds of poker!" the scrawny boy across the table from me said, throwing his cards down in frustration. I chuckled as I scooped up the pile of red and blue chips, adding them to my pile.

"I warned you that there was no way you could beat me, Tyler. Not my fault that you didn't take my advice," I said. Tyler grumbled under his breath, but grabbed the pile of cards and started to shuffle them again.

I leaned back in the wing chair, waiting for my roommate to deal. I had been at the Grayson Center, a private facility for teenagers experiencing mental illness, for almost three months. I was enrolled in a ninety-day program and my time was almost up. Looking around the recreation room, I realized I would actually be kind of sad when I had to leave.

Which is weird considering how much I had fought coming here in the first place. Once I had gotten over my anger and resistance to treatment, though, I almost came to enjoy my time here.

I found that the staff and the other patients did something I never thought possible.

They showed me how to heal.

And that's what I was doing. Slowly. Not that I expected a perfect fix in three months. I realized my healing would take years. And there were days I never thought I would be able to leave and live a decent life outside the support of the center and the safety of its walls. But then there were good days, like today, when I felt like I could take on the world.

Like I could find my way back to Maggie.

"What's with the goofy smile, bro? You look like an idiot," Tyler said good-naturedly as he tossed out cards. I blinked, taken away from my happy thoughts, and picked up my cards.

"Nothin', man. Just having a good day."

Tyler smiled. Other guys would probably have given me shit for acting like an emo pussy. But not the people here. We were all here because we *needed* to have those good days. So we understood the importance of happy days for those who had them.

"Cool, Clay. Glad to hear it. Now, focus on the damn game. I want to win some of my chips back," Tyler retorted, concentrating on his hand.

I grinned before beating him soundly yet again.

◆

The group sat on the floor, kids relaxing on oversized cushions. Looking around, I could almost imagine this was just a bunch of friends hanging out together. Except for the two adults who sat in the middle asking them questions like, "Tell me about your relationship with your family," and, "How does that make you feel?"

Yep, group therapy was a blast.

The girl to my right, a dark-haired chick named Maria, was here to deal with her severe depression and promiscuity brought on by serious daddy issues. She was trying to figure out how to answer the question that Sabrina, the female counselor, had just asked her.

"Just think about your happiest memory with your mother. It can be something simple like talking to her about your day, or a time she smiled at you," Sabrina prompted gently. Maria's problems, like those of most of the kids in the room, were rooted firmly in her relationship with her parents.

Today's group topic was trying to acknowledge the positive aspects of our familial relationships. To say this was hard for most of us was an understatement.

I dreaded the groups when we had to talk about our parents in a more positive way. It was so much easier to vent about how crappy they were than to find something nice to say.

"Um. Well, I guess there was a time, I was probably like six. And my mom took me to the park and pushed me on the swings," Maria volunteered, looking at Sabrina and Matt, the other counselor, for approval.

They each nodded. "Good. And how did you feel then?" Matt urged.

Maria smiled a bit. "It felt good. Like she . . . I don't know . . . loved me." The smile on her face was sad and my heart hurt for her. I understood her need to feel loved by her mother all too well.

There was some more processing to help Maria identify and handle her feelings, followed by a period of silence while everyone allowed Maria time to get herself together. Then it was my turn. Matt looked at me expectantly. "Clay. What about you? What is a happy memory you have about your parents?" The group looked at me, waiting for my answer. Over the last two and a half months, this disclosure thing had proven difficult for me.

I didn't reveal personal details very easily. It had taken Maggie, the person I loved most in this world, a long time to get me to open up. And if it was hard for me to talk to Maggie, then it was nearly impossible to get me to open up to a group of strangers.

But over time, after lots of individual and group therapy sessions, I was able to loosen up and talk more about what I had experienced. The things I felt, my fears, my pain, and what I wanted most in my life. And I found that the more I talked, the better I felt.

I began to recognize that these people weren't here to judge me or make me feel bad when I talked about wanting to kill myself or how hard it was for me not to cut. Cutting had always been my form of coping. Comforting and familiar, it was easier to make myself bleed than to face the truth of my issues. And these people didn't look at me like I was crazy when I would break down after a particularly gut-wrenching session. This was the most support I had felt from anyone besides Maggie, Ruby, and Lisa in my entire life.

And it felt wonderful.

So, with all eyes on me, I thought really hard about my answer to Matt's question. And then, just like that, I had it. A memory that was actually good and not tainted by anger and bitterness. "My dad taking me fishing." Sabrina smiled at me. "Yeah. It was before things got really bad. My dad wasn't the district attorney yet, so he had more time for me. He picked me up from school early one day and drove us out to a lake. I can't really remember where. Anyway, we spent all day fishing and talking. It was nice."

I smiled as I remembered when I could be with my dad without wanting to rip his face off. Matt nodded. "That sounds awesome, Clay. Thanks for sharing that with us." And he was moving on to the next person.

The memory of that time with my dad made me feel pretty good. I was feeling that way a lot more lately. Less of the crazy depression and anger, and more of the happy-go-lucky thing that I never thought I was capable of experiencing.

I'm sure it had a lot to do with my new medication. After I came to the Grayson Center, my new doctor, Dr. Todd as we kids called him, put me on a new pill. Tegretol helped control my manic mood swings without turning me into a zombie.

It was pretty great. And even though I had moments where I strangely missed those energetic highs, which Dr. Todd told me was normal, I sure as hell didn't miss the crippling lows. The psychotherapy that I attended three times a week was also helping a lot. It was nice to not have to worry about hurting myself or someone else. To think that maybe I would be able to get my shit together and find a way back to where I belonged.

With Maggie.

I shook my head. I couldn't think about her here in group. That was something I saved for when I was alone. Because if I started thinking of her now, I would invariably remember how much I hurt her and how I fucked things up so royally. And then my good mood would evaporate in a flash. *Snap*. Just like that.

I must have zoned out for a while, because I realized that the other kids were getting to their feet. Maria grinned at me. "Earth to Clay!" She reached for my hand to help me up. I looked at her a moment as I stood. Maria had a nice smile and really pretty eyes. But she wasn't Maggie. I dropped her hand quickly. I tried to pretend that I didn't see the disappointment flash across her face. We walked together out of the common room and headed down the hallway to the cafeteria. "That was pretty tough today," Maria said as we joined the others, who were getting in line for lunch.

I nodded. "Yeah. It's kinda hard finding something nice to say about my parents. You know, considering they're a bunch of self-absorbed asses," I joked, picking up a tray. Maria giggled behind me.

"I know what you mean. My mom is a cracked-out deadbeat who refused to protect me from my dad because it got in the way of her next high. Thinking of the ooey-gooey times together is hard."

I took a plate of pasta and a salad and moved to drinks, getting myself a bottle of water. Maria followed me to our regular table near the large window overlooking the gardens. Tyler and our other friends, Susan and Greg, were already seated.

"Hey, guys," I said as I sat down. Greg scooted over to make room and Maria sat on my other side.

"How was group?" Tyler asked around a mouthful of sandwich. Maria and I shrugged in unison and we laughed.

"It was group. How about you guys?" Maria said. The other three were in a group for substance abuse while Maria and I were in ours. Susan Biddle, a short girl with brown hair and big brown eyes who reminded me a lot of Maggie's friend Rachel, snorted.

"It would have been better if loudmouth Austin hadn't decided to be a total dick to Jean." Jean was the substance abuse counselor at the center. And Austin was this place's Paul Delawder, the dick who had destroyed my MP3 player my first day at Jackson High School back in Virginia. The guy Maggie had jumped to defend me from. I smiled at the memory of my brave girl.

Maria elbowed me in the side to bring me back to the conversation. "Fuck Austin. He sucks," I said, smiling. Greg, Susan, and Tyler agreed and the conversation then focused on the movie the center was showing tonight.

Every week, if we had earned enough merits and were doing well in our therapy, we were rewarded with a movie night. We earned merits for completing various chores that the behavioral aides and therapists assigned us. This week my job was to keep the common room clean. I shared the job with three other kids. I had earned all of my merits for the week, which was pretty cool. I had lost a lot of them my first two weeks here. So getting to join in the fun stuff was about the most exciting thing that happened to me anymore.

It wasn't like we left the facility or anything. But it was nice to hang out with everyone in a nontherapeutic way and watch a movie without having to talk about our feelings. Everyone could just relax and remember for a little while that yeah, we were still teenagers.

Maria, Tyler, and I walked back to my room after lunch. We had an hour until afternoon sessions started. I had a one-on-one with the substance abuse counselor, Jean. The others had sessions either with their counselors or in groups. That was the thing about this place. It was one big session after another, with a tiny bit of school squeezed into the mix. We had two hours in the morning for schoolwork provided by the Miami School District, then the rest of the day was all about dealing with our *issues*.

Maria flopped onto my bed, making herself at home. I had gotten pretty close to her since I got here (in a purely platonic way, of course), and she often came back to the room to hang with Tyler and me. But it still felt weird to have her on my bed, even if she was just sitting on it. Because I didn't want to see any girl but Maggie May Young on my bed.

Even though I had written Maggie a letter a month ago telling her to move on, it didn't mean that I had moved on. I couldn't stomach the thought of being with anyone but her. No one else mattered. I had a feeling that Maria was starting to like me as more than a friend. And even though I hadn't done anything to encourage it, I felt like I was going to have to say something to her soon.

No way was I going to hurt another girl I cared about.

Tyler got on his computer and started typing out emails. I pulled up my desk chair and straddled it backward, resting my arms on the back. Maria leaned over and picked up the framed picture on my bedside table.

"She's really pretty," Maria commented with a twinge in her voice that I couldn't identify. Maria had picked up the only picture I had in the room. It was of Maggie and me from the Fall Formal. We were sitting beside each other at Red Lobster and both made faces at the camera. I didn't need to look at the picture to remember how things used to be between us. It was all I could think about. Every second of every day. All I did was think. About the good times. And the bad times. And all the messed-up stuff in between.

Maria gave a small sigh and placed the frame back in its spot. "Do you ever talk to her?" she asked me. I always felt strange talking about Maggie. Even though things had gotten ugly between us, my love for her was the one pure thing in my life. I wanted to keep it all to myself and not share it with anyone. She was the last thing I thought about before I went to sleep and the first thing my mind went to when I woke up.

I constantly wondered what she was doing, if she was happy, if she had started dating anyone. That thought hurt. A lot. Because I really did want her to live her life, even if that meant moving on from me. But that didn't mean I had to like it. "No. I don't think that would do either of us any good," I admitted, repositioning the picture frame so I could see it.

Maria frowned. "Why? If you love her so much, don't you think talking to her would be a good thing?" I gritted my teeth. Explaining anything regarding my relationship with Maggie made me defensive. But I forced myself to calm down, using those breathing techniques the counselors had been drilling into our brains for months.

"Because, Maria, the fact that I love her is the reason I can't go turning her life upside down anymore. I won't fuck with her like that again. She's been through enough because of me." I sounded so pathetic. Maggie's hold on me was as unyielding as ever.

Maria's face softened, her eyes getting that dewy look that girls get when a guy says something sweet (Maggie used to get that same look every time I told her I loved her). "She's lucky to have your love, Clay. I hope she realizes that."

I swallowed, getting a little uncomfortable talking about this with Maria, particularly with Tyler playing on his computer five feet away. Maria reached out and squeezed my arm, her fingers, I noticed, lingering on my skin. "Just keep doing what you're doing and maybe one day you'll feel like you can call her."

I smiled. Yeah. Maybe . . . one day.

chapter
two

maggie

This job was going to kill me. I wrapped a wet paper towel around the scald on my wrist and winced. Hot coffee and Maggie May Young clearly didn't mix.

Let me rephrase. Hot liquid shooting out of an espresso machine with more knobs than the space station and Maggie May Young were bad news. I removed the towel and glared at the huge red splotch on my skin. That would definitely blister.

"What the heck did you do?" a voice asked from behind me. I rolled my eyes at Jake Fitzsimmons, who put down the pastries he was loading into the display case and came over to check out my wound.

"I was on the wrong end of a mocha latte," I deadpanned, pulling my sleeve down to cover my wrist. I gave my coworker and friend a painful grimace. Jake frowned with concern and held out his hand.

"Let me see, Maggie," he told me firmly. I rolled my eyes again but held my arm out for him to inspect. I looked around the bustling café and knew I needed to get back to work. The place was slammed.

I had been working at Java Madness for two weeks. I had just been taken off of probation three days ago and here I was, nursing a nasty burn and ready to throw my apron on the floor and stomp out. For some reason, I was really struggling with coffee making and waiting tables. It wasn't brain surgery, but I had dropped more trays, broken more mugs, and gotten more orders wrong in the last two weeks than seemed possible.

The manager, Jacob, looked ready to can me last night when I had a table complain about how I screwed up their sandwich order, not once, but twice. I was trying. Honestly. But as with everything in my life these days . . . it was just a struggle. Nothing was easy and normal anymore, and it was difficult putting all the pieces together into a picture that made sense.

Jake had been working at Java Madness for a year and was trying to help me keep my job. I gave him a wan smile as he ran his fingers over the burn lightly. I tried not to rip my hand away from him, not liking him touching me in any way. But it wasn't like he was trying to cop a feel. He was just being concerned.

After a few more seconds, I couldn't help it; I wriggled my arm from his grasp. "I'll live," I muttered, turning back to the espresso machine that had already maimed me once. I glared at the shiny silver contraption. "Play nice," I said under my breath.

Jake laughed as I started to fiddle with the knobs. He reached from behind me and put two mugs under the spigots and turned it on. "Thanks," I said, giving him what I hoped was a sincere smile. I would seriously be lost in this place if he didn't continually rescue me from coffee-related mishaps.

"You'll get it . . . eventually," he teased, turning back to the display case. I waited for the drinks and leaned against the counter. Jake looked up at me, his eyes sparkling in that flirty way of his, and I had to look away. Jake was cute, and at one time I had found his boy-next-door good looks to be attractive. With his short red hair and pretty blue eyes, what wasn't there to like? But that was before I had been ruined for any guy who wasn't the dark-headed, tortured lone-wolf type.

Jake's smile immediately made me feel uncomfortable. Jake and I had an easy banter. Always had. Even if he had never been exactly subtle about the fact that he wanted more than friendship. But he hadn't pushed it since . . . well . . . since *the incident*.

God, I couldn't even think about it properly in the privacy of my own thoughts. I couldn't think about *him* at all, not while I was out in public. Otherwise, I ran the risk of turning into a huge blubbering mess. And I had vowed to myself a month ago when I had gotten *the letter* that I wouldn't become that person . . . ever again.

But I still felt strange being around people. Like they were all looking at me and talking about me and feeling—gah—*sympathy* for me. And I hated that. Because I didn't need or deserve their sympathy. But I was the girl who had run off with her mentally unstable boyfriend, only to be brought back to town after his suicide attempt and being subsequently institutionalized. Nothing was a secret in Davidson, so of course everyone knew the sordid details.

And boys . . . well, they were out of the question. Dating, kissing, maybe loving anyone else was so not on my radar. Not when every night I fell asleep with the picture of his face ever present in my mind.

And Jake. Sweet, good-hearted Jake. We were just friends. Would only ever be friends. But I saw the way he looked at me. I wasn't an idiot. I was just refusing to acknowledge it. Denial seemed to work for me, so I stuck with it.

I put the small, circular tray on the counter and loaded it up with drinks. "Maybe you should come back and get the rest," Jake suggested, indicating my full tray. His raised eyebrows made me laugh. And that felt good. I laughed so rarely anymore that I almost forgot what it felt like when it did happen.

"I think you may be right," I conceded, taking a few of the drinks off and going around the counter to take them to my table. I delivered everything and did a little jig when I got back to my station by the espresso machine. Jake came up and gave me a high five, grinning at me.

"You did it! That's four tables in a row without dropping anything! That *has* to be a record," Jake joked, squeezing my shoulder. I tried not to shrug off his hand and forced a smile.

"I have employee of the month written all over me," I quipped, and Jake just shook his head before going to tend to his own tables.

I looked up at the sound of the bell on the door, signaling another customer. "Hey, guys!" I called out as Rachel and Daniel came in. It was still strange seeing them together, holding hands. They looked up at me and in unison dropped their clasped hands. I frowned. They did that a lot. Made a point not to touch or act like the couple that they were. I worried that they were doing that because of me, which was ridiculous. I had told them time and again I was over the moon with how happy they were together.

Or maybe they were taking pity on my pathetic, loveless existence.

Daniel gave me a smirk. "What's the total?" he asked without preamble, making a joke out of the number of glasses I had broken that day. I shot him a look of pure death. He laughed as Rachel elbowed him in the gut, making him grunt.

"Shut it, Danny," she growled, and I smiled at her. Rachel had really grown into herself over the past six months. Long gone was the girl who was scared to speak her mind and stand up for herself. And I was the first person to be glad to see *that* particular girl take a hike.

I liked this Rachel a hell of a lot better.

Jake came up beside me and leaned across the counter to fist-bump Daniel and then to give Rachel a hug. He slung an arm around my shoulders. "Zero today, man. Our girl is on a roll," Jake said over a chuckle.

My stomach clenched and I instantly tensed up. *Our girl?* Uh, I don't think so.

I looked at Rachel, who was staring rather pointedly at the arm Jake had so carelessly flung around me. And it was obvious she was picking up on my discomfort with Jake's over-the-top familiarity. We were just friends. Then why did it seem as though I was committing a betrayal by even allowing him to touch me?

Oh that's right, because I still hung on to the hope that my broken knight would gallop back into my life and sweep me off of my feet.

I never claimed to *not* be delusional.

I wiggled out from under Jake's arm and he backed away a bit. He gave me a smile that barely concealed his disappointment. *Well, he'll have to live with a lot of disappointment, because I am not going there with him,* I thought harshly.

Daniel let out a whoop, pulling my attention back to my best friends. "Nothing broken in two hours? That's damn near amazing, Mags!" He ruffled my hair in that annoying way of his and I swatted him away.

"Enough about my less-than-stellar waitressing abilities and give me your damn order," I bit out, trying not to be irritated by his friendly ribbing. Rachel elbowed her boyfriend again and he grabbed her hand and pulled it to his mouth, kissing it softly.

They stared into each other's eyes and I wistfully watched the way they instinctively moved toward one another. Then as if realizing what they were doing, they simultaneously looked my way and backed away from each other.

And that made me feel like shit. I didn't want them to hide how crazy in love they were just because they felt sorry for me. Even if watching their obvious happiness was like a knife in my heart. A sharp reminder of my own loneliness and misery.

I plastered a smile on my face. "The usual?" I asked, looking between them. They both nodded. "Head over to a table and I'll bring your order in a minute," I said, pushing away the money Danny tried to put in my hand. "It's on me," I told him.

"Thanks, Maggie," Rachel said appreciatively and blew me a kiss as she headed toward a table by the window. Daniel grabbed a handful of napkins.

"Don't drop anything!" he joked and I threw a coffee stirrer at him. Jake made Rachel's tomato-and-cheese panini and I loaded up a plate with brownies and cookies for Daniel. For a guy in such great shape, he really did eat like a five-year-old with a sugar addiction.

"Are you going to Ray's thing tonight?" Jake asked. I darted him a look from the corner of my eye as I grabbed a macaroon. Peering down at the plate, I figured I might just put Danny in a sugar coma with this junk.

"Uh, I wasn't aware there was a *thing* at Ray's," I answered noncommittally. It's not that I was purposefully not invited; I just knew that a lot of people stopped bothering to extend their offers of parties and get-togethers anymore. As much as I was trying to have some sort of normal life, it was slow coming. Rachel and Daniel were the only ones I spent any sort of time with. Massive social gatherings felt like a panic attack waiting to happen.

I had never before been this kooky social phobic shut-in that I had become. But after everything I had been through this past school year and knowing that I was still the subject of so much speculation and gossip, I had no desire to mingle.

Jake let out an exasperated snort and I looked up at him in surprise. "What?" I asked defensively. He narrowed his eyes and looked as though he wanted to shake me.

"When will you stop hiding away like a hermit? Your life isn't over as much as you act like it is," he said with irritation. My eyes widened a bit in shock. And then they narrowed into angry slits.

What business was it of Jake Fucking Fitzsimmons's if I go out or not? I did not appreciate his insinuation or attitude.

"I don't act like my life is over! Pardon me if I have more to do with my time than to hang out with a bunch of lame-ass drunks who find beer pong to be the height of sophistication," I hissed, grabbing the plate with Rachel's panini from Jake's hands and sending potato chips careening to the floor.

I let out a growl of frustration and bent down to pick up the mess. I wanted to scream at Jake that he needed to back off. But I also wanted to scream at myself. Because maybe he was right. I *had* been in my designated hidey-hole for months now. I *did* act as though my life were over.

But wasn't it?

Hadn't I pinned all my hopes and dreams on a boy who ultimately ripped them up and threw them away? I had been a stupid, naïve girl. But I missed that girl too, because the one who had been left behind was bitter and heartbroken.

Jake knelt beside me and sighed. "I'm sorry, Maggie. I'm just sick of seeing you mope around over that guy. He's gone. He's not coming back. Don't you think it's time to start doing something more than what you're doing?" he asked me delicately, obviously not sure how I would respond.

Because we never talked about Clayton Reed. In fact, most people avoided the topic altogether. Well, at least to my face. I knew his name was whispered behind my back—a lot.

But Jake was just being a friend. And I was in short supply of those lately. And maybe he was right . . . I needed to let my friends off of my emotional suicide watch. And then I felt angry again. This time at Clay. For reducing me to *this*. For letting me go. For abandoning me when I had never, not once, abandoned him.

And that made me get to my feet and straighten my spine. "You're right, Jake. I'll go tonight," I said with a determination that I had been missing for a while now.

Jake grinned and pulled me into a hug. I tried not to push him away. But he seemed to be doing the touching thing a lot lately. I should probably put him in his place. Remind him that I was *not* interested in him like that. But it felt nice to be held. However briefly. So I let him. For a few seconds at least. Then I felt the weirdness and pulled away.

Feeling a little bit better, I brought Rachel and Daniel their food and drinks. Daniel didn't waste a moment before attacking the plate of diabetes I gave him. Rachel bit into her sandwich and looked at me with her all-seeing eyes.

"Well, things are looking awfully friendly in here," she remarked, and I wanted to snap at her to drop it. Rachel and Daniel had mentioned—on more than one occasion, mind you—that Jake was interested in me. You'd have to be blind not to see that. They never pushed it, knowing I wasn't ready. But I knew they held on to the silent hope that I would snap out of my Clay funk and give Daniel's friend a chance. Rachel had serious double-dating fantasies (something she probably wouldn't have convinced Daniel to participate in if I was with Clay). I was really sick of dodging this bullet. But for once I didn't smack down her comment. I just shrugged my shoulders and sat back in the chair, watching in disgusted awe as Daniel finished off the last of his food.

I saw the considerable effort it took for Rachel to suppress her obvious glee. She knew my lack of a hateful response was in its own way a small victory. And I let her have it. For now.

"I don't know whether to be completely impressed or ready to throw up," I whispered dramatically as I put Daniel's empty plate on the tray. Rachel shook her head and shot Danny a loving smile. The softness of her expression reminded me so much of the way I used to look at . . .

I jumped to my feet. There had been enough reminiscing for one day. "So, I think I'm going to head over to Ray's this evening," I announced louder than I meant to. Daniel and Rachel stopped making goo-goo eyes at each other and looked at me in surprise. Well, surprise was an understatement. They were staring at me as though I had suggested hitchhiking to California. And that just reinforced how out of touch I had become with my own life.

"You are? Really?" Rachel squeaked, and I set my mouth in a grim line.

"That's awesome. You need a ride?" Daniel asked, grinning at me.

I shook my head. "Nah. I'll drive myself. That way if you want to leave early, or stay later than me, it won't be a problem. What time should I head over?" I asked, ignoring the giddy expressions on my friends' faces.

"Uh, eight? But what made you decide to come?" Rachel asked me.

"I convinced her to grace us with her presence for the evening," Jake piped in, appearing by my side and taking the tray from my hands. I clenched my hands into fists and willed myself not to say something hateful. He really was all up in my business today.

Rachel's eyes flashed at me and I could see the wheels turning. I glared at her in warning. She wisely stayed quiet. "Well, thanks for the intervention. She needs to do more than work and go to the grocery store. She currently has the social life of a nursing home resident and even *they* play bingo," Daniel said.

I threw my hands up in frustration. "You guys act like I've been sitting in a darkened room every night. Give it a rest, will you?" I snapped. Rachel seemed contrite, while Daniel, damn him, just laughed at my ire.

"Not far from the mark there, Mags," he mused, and I shut up. Because he was right.

"Okay, well, I'll see you later," I said, giving up on the conversation. I left Jake to continue talking with Rachel and Daniel and headed back toward the counter. There was a line and Jennifer, the other girl working, looked flustered.

I hurried to help her and got lost in the chaos for a while. I found that being busy really helped keep my mind free of the dark thoughts. And I realized I was looking forward to going out tonight, being around friends. I was finally ready to take a step in the right direction and get things back on track.

"Maggie." I looked up and froze. And I wanted to run in the back and hide. Not because I didn't want to see the person who said my name, but because those dark thoughts that I had kept at bay all afternoon came rushing back.

"Hi, Lisa. How are you?" I asked, trying to sound happy to see her. And on some level I was. I really liked Lisa. She and Ruby, Clay's aunt and Lisa's partner, were two of the most loving people I had ever met. And I would always appreciate the way she had supported me during one of the bleakest times of my life.

But seeing her made me invariably think of *him.* And given my yo-yoing emotions, I knew that wasn't a particularly good thing.

Lisa's mouth raised in a hesitant smile as though she wasn't entirely sure of the reception I'd give her. I hadn't seen Lisa or Ruby since right after *the incident.* In a small town like Davidson, it was actually surprising that we hadn't crossed paths. But we hadn't. Until now. Until I was finally feeling ready to move on with my life and get it together. It was like fate or something.

Fate was a fucking bitch.

I felt bad seeing Lisa's wariness. So I came around the counter and gave her a hug. The much taller woman squeezed tight before letting me go. "You look great," she said kindly. I cleared my throat uncomfortably. Yeah, I'm sure I looked a hell of a lot better than the last time she saw me. I had been a complete wreck, so I was sure anything had to be better than that.

"Thanks. How's Ruby?" I asked, realizing that I missed Clay's wacky aunt. I missed her store. I had made it a point to stay away from my favorite shop, knowing it would be too painful to go inside.

Lisa's face softened at the mention of her girlfriend. I had always loved the natural and beautiful affection between her and Ruby. It was something I had aspired to have in my own life. And at one time, I thought I had it.

"She's Ruby. Wonderful as always. Still trying to force herbal tea down my throat on a daily basis." We both laughed. Ruby was formidable when it came to forcing herbal concoctions down your throat.

"She'd love to see you," Lisa said softly. I looked away, not sure how to answer. I'd love to see her too. But it was too soon.

"Yeah," was all I said, needing to end the conversation and get my ass out of there. But then, as if compelled, I spit out, "How's Clay?"

There was an immediate silence. I couldn't believe I just asked that. My heart started to hammer in my chest and just saying his name out loud was like a bomb going off inside me. My hands were clammy and I felt strangely light-headed. Jesus, I was a mess.

"He's . . . better," Lisa said. I looked back at her and she appeared guarded. As though not sure how much she should say. Not that I blamed her. Clay had made it a point to not let me know exactly where he was. He had sent me a letter, telling me to get on with my life, and not once did he mention ever wanting to talk to me again. Without giving me any say in the matter, he had cut me off.

Clay and I had been toxic together. I thought I was helping him but in reality I hadn't been. My denial and refusal to talk to anyone about what was going on with him had ultimately been his undoing. So, talking to the ex-girlfriend who had helped him walk off the cliff had to be awkward for her. It was a wonder she was talking to me at all.

My eyes zeroed in on my sneakers. I felt small. And vulnerable. "That's good," I choked out. I wanted to cry. I wanted to yell. I wanted to disappear. Damn, and I had been feeling so good too.

"Maggie, sweetie," Lisa said quietly, and I looked up at her again and wanted to cringe at the blatant sympathy in her eyes. I hated sympathy like I hated polyester. It made me itchy and uncomfortable. "I know things have been rough for you. I saw how much you loved him. Just know he's really trying to get himself together."

I swallowed around the lump that had formed in my throat. I couldn't deny the relief I felt at her words. I wanted Clay healthy and whole. I wanted him to get better. And I could admit that I hoped once he did that, he would come back to me. Because even as angry as I was at him for giving up on us, I missed him so much I hurt with it. So hearing that he was trying was the absolute best thing I could hear.

"I'm glad," I told her sincerely. I looked over my shoulder and saw that Rachel and Daniel were watching Lisa and me intently. The concern for me was obvious on both of their faces. I gave them what I hoped was a reassuring smile. I also noticed that Jake was paying close attention to my exchange with Lisa. I wanted to roll my eyes at the lot of them. Did they think I was going to fall apart just by talking to a person connected with my ex? Sheesh, they should give me a bit more credit than that.

"I should get back to it. It was great seeing you again, Lisa," I said, ready to put distance between me and the sudden reminder of my painful, not-so-distant past. I gave Lisa a final hug and started back toward the counter.

"Do you want us to give him a message? We're planning to see him next week for his birthday," she called out, just as I was about to make my escape.

The breath left my lungs. Clay's birthday. Of course it was coming up. I thought about the present I had worked on for him just after he had left. It still sat, wrapped in newspaper, underneath my bed. I squared my shoulders and shook my head.

"No, that's okay. Have a nice trip," I said dismissively, not wanting to talk about Clay anymore. Lisa seemed to take the hint. She picked up her to-go cup and with a last smile left the café.

I noticed that my friends didn't approach me. They knew I wasn't in the mood to discuss what had just happened and I appreciated their sixth sense when it came to my feelings. Jake gave me space as well and for that I was grateful.

Because right then, my mind was too full and my heart was too heavy. And that's all I could focus on.

chapter
three

clay

i stared down at the spiral notebook in my lap. The pencil in my hand was limp between my fingers and I couldn't focus on the chicken scratch on the pages. My breathing had become shallow and my heart was racing.

I was in the midst of a full-blown panic attack. Dr. Todd was looking at me with concern, which should have freaked me the fuck out. Because not much marred the good doc's placid calm. But I must be making a massive spectacle of myself if he looked as though he were ready to put a tranq needle in my arm.

"Breathe, Clay. In through your nose. Out through your mouth. Count backward from twenty. Slowly. In and out." Dr. Todd's words were firm, and I needed that right now because my mind had rioted against me.

I followed his advice and closed my eyes, concentrating on the numbers in my head. In through the nose. Out through the mouth. I clenched my hands into fists, trying to control the urge to scratch at my skin until it bled. I needed the physical hurt to erase the horrible goddamned agony in my heart.

Not once did Dr. Todd touch me, no comforting hand on the

arm or pat on the back. Which was good, because I would have punched him in the nose if he had. Instead, he sat in the chair opposite me, counting with me down from twenty. Reminding me to focus on my breathing.

After going through the countdown five times, my body finally started to unclench and my heart rate began to slow down. My breathing was less shallow and it felt safe to open my eyes.

"Better?" Dr. Todd asked me, the concern gone, replaced by his typical neutral expression. Some people might be bothered by the therapist's lack of emotional response. For me, it was exactly what I needed. I had lived my life being ruled by my feelings, worrying about what those emotions would do to the people around me. So having someone sit there, seemingly unfazed by my shit, was nice.

I nodded and put the pencil down in the crease of my notebook. I closed it without another look, knowing that what I had written on its pages was what precipitated the level-ten meltdown. New Age music punctuated the silence. It made me think of Ruby, and that was more crucial in helping me get my shit together than anything else.

"Man, I wasn't expecting that," I let out in a quiet rush. I ran my shaking hand through my hair, knowing it was probably sticking straight up. Good thing I didn't give a crap about things like my appearance.

Dr. Todd smiled in understanding. "You handled that really well, Clay. You're learning to manage your attacks much better. You should feel good about that." I knew the doc was trying to offer me something to feel positive about. But I didn't want any of it.

Just when I thought I had things under control, the reality of *who* I was smacked me squarely in the face. Being nuts was no fun, let me tell you. I was a far cry from being the lovable eccentric. The wacky dude who mumbled to himself and wore his pants inside out. Nope, my kind of nuts was scary and consuming.

Sure, my new meds were huge in helping me regulate my swings. Therapy had been instrumental in allowing me to work through the millions of ways I was sabotaging my life on a daily basis. Having been diagnosed with both bipolar and borderline personality disorders was like living with a ticking time bomb. I never knew when it would blow up in my face and decimate everything. So I was learning other coping skills, ones that didn't involve a blade to my skin, in order to survive the pain. I hadn't cut myself in over a month. These were all reasons to feel successful. I was a far cry from being the man I wanted to be. But I was getting there.

Then stuff like *this* happened. It was reality's way of smacking me in the face and telling me to wake the fuck up. Have I mentioned how much I *hated* reality sometimes? If it were a guy I'd beat the shit out of him. Because if I couldn't even write in a damn journal about how messing up things with Maggie had destroyed my entire world, I wasn't ready to see the outside of these walls yet. And I *wanted* to be ready so freaking badly.

Dr. Todd said Maggie had become my trigger. Can you believe that? The girl who had easily been the best thing in my life was now my greatest nightmare. According to the good doctor, I was projecting all of my anxiety, all of my shame and guilt, onto her shoulders. How messed up was that? After doing the "right" thing and letting her go, I couldn't even have the memories of her. Because now when I thought about Maggie, I wigged out. I couldn't breathe, couldn't think. It was way too reminiscent of how bad things became before I came to Grayson.

Dr. Todd was trying to help me work through it. I was seeing him three times a week and at least one of those sessions revolved around how I needed to learn to forgive myself. He said it like it was the easiest thing in the world. But you try to forgive yourself after you hurt everyone you have ever loved. It doesn't make you the most enjoyable guy to have around, that's for sure.

This process was painful. Actually it sucked balls. It was like forcing yourself to look in the mirror after you had been doused in battery acid. I felt ugly and raw. And I wasn't a fan of the guy inside me that I was getting to know. But Dr. Todd was trying to make me see that I wasn't the horrible person that I seemed to think I was. He was helping me recognize that I was taking control of my life. That person who had hurt Maggie so badly was only a part of the person I was and he didn't define me. The doc liked to tell me that I had to learn to accept all sides of who I was if I hoped to be healthy and whole.

Once upon a time I would have laughed off the psychobabble. But now, in this reality, I couldn't afford to do that. So I bit my tongue and drank the Grayson Center Kool-Aid.

Some days it worked. Some days I was able to talk about my relationship with Maggie without sobbing like a little bitch. There were times I left my sessions feeling like I was a step closer to being the person I wanted to be. The guy who would be able to show up on Maggie May Young's doorstep and tell her that his life would always begin and end with her.

Today was *not* one of those days.

Dr. Todd held out his hand for my notebook. I gave it to him, wishing he'd let me burn the stupid thing. Journaling had never been one of my favorite therapeutic activities. But the counselors here *loved* it. I had been told over and over again that sometimes it's easier to write down your feelings than to talk about them. That when you feel overwhelmed, just jot it down. What-the-fuck-ever.

I thought it was nothing more than an exercise in reminding me of my colossal screwups. Hey, Clay, sit down and write about how much of a jackass you are! Sounds like a fun day, huh? I'd hate to go back through that thing and read the ramblings of a guy who had messed up his life and spent an inordinate amount of time feeling sorry for himself because of it. I'd rather be kicked in the nuts.

"Do you mind if I read what you wrote?" Dr. Todd asked me. "I'd like to see what triggered your reaction." If I said no, he wouldn't push. Not about that. There were some things Dr. Todd pushed me about. Things he forced me to face even when I didn't want to. But the cool thing about him was that he understood when he needed to back the hell off. It's what made our dynamic work. Like Butch Cassidy and the Sundance Kid. Except that I was in a mental health treatment center in Florida. And I wasn't a gunslinging outlaw. Oh fuck it, never mind.

The point was that I had fought therapy for so long that our easy candor was pretty unbelievable. It was no secret that I didn't *like* people. I avoided them on a good day. But Dr. Todd was different. Maybe it was the fact that he didn't look at me like I was crazy. There was no forced sympathy or condescending advice. He let me talk. Or he let me stay silent. He'd push when he needed to but let things go when *I* needed him to.

So having him check out my journal didn't feel like a complete invasion of privacy. Something I had written had thrown me into a tailspin and go figure, my therapist wanted to know what that *something* was. Made sense, right? Plus, if I ever wanted to get out of here and get on with living my life, I had to figure out how to handle this new level of bullshit I had unloaded on myself. Why couldn't my life ever be simple? What happened to the normal teenage experience? Shouldn't I be making inappropriate remarks about girls' tits with my friends and devising ways to get my girlfriend to screw me?

Nope, I had been given the shitty parents and chemical imbalance card. Woo-hoo! Lucky me!

I nodded. "Go right ahead." My voice sounded thready and breathless from my most recent round with the crazies. Dr. Todd gave me a small smile before opening my lime green notebook. He thumbed through the pages until he stopped at the entry I had written. He had asked me to reframe a painful memory. He had told me to think about something that hurt, something that had been extremely difficult for me and to look for a positive to take from it. Reframing was hard on a good day.

Had I mentioned that today was *not* a good day?

When Dr. Todd had finished reading, he looked up at me. "Well, you definitely picked a doozy to focus on," he said in a way that made it difficult for me not to laugh. I appreciated his dry humor.

"Well, you know what they say. Go big or go home." My lips quirked in an effort to smile. I probably looked as though my mouth was spazzing out.

Dr. Todd gave me an answering smile and glanced back down at my notebook. "I'm glad to see that you were going in the right direction with this activity. Tell me what made you have the reaction you did." Ahh, so now I was going to talk about my feelings. I just loved when therapy became so clichéd.

"Well, I think it's pretty fucking obvious how I was feeling. I had a goddamned anxiety attack. I wasn't hearing the birds fucking chirp and seeing rainbows, okay?" I bit out angrily. Dr. Todd closed the notebook with a snap.

"No, I'd say not. Don't get defensive, Clay. Now please tell me, what were you feeling?" he asked me again. I took a deep breath and tentatively started to think about the situation I had just shared in my journal. I had to be careful. I couldn't lose it again. I had come too far; I would learn to deal with this shit or it would kill me!

"Angry," I said shortly, settling on the truth. I could have dodged the question, but after my little episode, I was too exhausted and way past hiding what I was thinking.

Dr. Todd frowned. "Angry, huh. At who?" I wanted to groan. That was a loaded question.

"Maggie. Me. Ruby. My parents. Take your pick." I was feeling petulant. I knew this wasn't earning me any therapy brownie points but I was so raw I could bleed. I wanted to bleed. I wanted the pain that only a razor could bring. It would be a hell of a lot better than facing the demons that raged inside me. The demons that on days like today seemed to never be far from completely obliterating me.

Dr. Todd didn't say anything. He just watched me as I processed what I had just said. "I'm angry. With everyone. My parents are easy. They fucking suck. They've never been parents. They just stuck my ass in here to rot." I gave a humorless laugh. "They wanted me to lose it. They wanted an excuse to get rid of me. Too bad for them, I'm gonna get out of here and live my life," I said vehemently, and I saw Dr. Todd try to cover his smile.

He nodded. "Your feelings are definitely understandable. But more importantly, you are seeing that you are in control of your life, not your parents. You having control is what will help you move forward." Sometimes Dr. Todd sounded like Gandhi or something. I could get annoyed by it, or I could hear his words for what they were. The truth.

"I'm mad at Ruby for making it so easy to deny what I was doing to everyone around me. If she had just laid it on the line, told me she knew what I was doing . . ." My words trailed off and Dr. Todd cut in.

"You would have gotten help? Stopped cutting?" he asked me pointedly. I arched my eyebrow, seeing what he was doing. He was trying to make me see how irrational that anger was. He was walking a very fine line. I could either get ragingly pissed or acknowledge the validity of what he was saying. It could go either way, really.

For the moment I ignored the delicate balancing act and continued with my train of thought. "I'm mad at myself for being such a fucking waste. For screwing up everything in my life. For not holding it together and letting my parents win," I ended softly. I ground my clenched fists into my eyes, feeling a headache start behind them.

"And Maggie?" Dr. Todd asked quietly, and I dropped my hands into my lap. Maggie. I *was* mad at her. Really flipping angry.

I gritted my teeth. "I'm angry at her for making me feel, for a few moments, that I could have a normal life!" I said too loudly. I took a deep breath and tried to calm myself down. When I felt I could keep going without blowing a gasket, I started talking again. "I'm mad at Maggie for giving me something that nearly killed me to lose when I invariably fucked everything up. For showing me what perfect looked like right before I destroyed it. I'm angry as hell because she built back up what I had broken, she gave me everything: a life, a future. And now it's gone." My voice cracked and I felt traitorous tears slip down my face. I wiped them away furiously. Damn it! I hated it when I devolved into *this.*

I took another deep breath, feeling my body shaking with emotion. Now that I had admitted it, I felt . . . better. See there, boys and girls, therapy *does* work.

Dr. Todd was looking at me, that impenetrable calm firmly in place. How I wondered what was really going on in that head of his. Was he really that serene or was he just as fucked up as the rest of us? What I wouldn't give to know.

"That was hard to admit, Clay. Thank you." He leaned forward so his elbows rested on his knees. "Your feelings about Maggie are intense. They are all tangled up with pain and loss. You can't separate the love from the hurt and that's what is triggering you. You say she was the best thing in your life, yet you have made her the focal point for all of your misery. We have to pull apart those two things. You *can* have one without the other. You have to keep working on your reframing. To recognize the positive where your mind wants to look at only the negative."

Thinking about the situation I had written about in my notebook, I wasn't so sure following that advice was possible. I mean, how the hell was I supposed to find the positive in trying to kill myself? It wasn't a trip to Disney World, for Christ's sake! It was me taking a piece of a broken mirror and cutting my arms open to the point that I had to have forty-five stitches on both arms. I had heard the doctor in the hospital tell my parents that I had almost hit bone. I hadn't been fooling around. I had wanted to die.

And for what? Because I thought, in my twisted head, that Maggie had betrayed me. I hadn't been able to see that she was confused and scared and had really only been trying to help me. And that is where the guilt came in. Because it started when I had been thinking about Maggie and how for a brief second it had been the two of us, together, ready to take on anything. Then my mind went to *that* night. And all I could see was the darkness. The moment when all I wanted to do was die. And I had lost it. The panic attack swept me away in its merciless tide.

My anger picked up a notch. Why couldn't I just think of Maggie? Why couldn't I simply remember her without all the other nasty stuff, like guilt and shame and the soul-sucking anguish? I only wanted to think of how much I loved that beautiful girl before I had turned our worlds upside down.

Maybe this was my punishment for being so weak and selfish. Karma was a vindictive jerk.

Because Maggie was my trigger. And it wasn't a good one. And I hated that my fucked-up mind had taken something so wonderful and warped it into . . . well . . . something ugly. Something that only served to remind me of what I couldn't have. Something that I was trying desperately to be healthy enough for but deep down worried I never would be. No one had ever accused me of being a Pollyanna. I was not a glass-half-full kind of guy. But Dr. Todd was hell-bent on changing that. And damn it, I needed him to.

I growled in frustration and tugged at my hair. I struggled to take a deep breath and loosened the grip I had on my scalp. I could do this. I could work through this maze of crap.

After a few minutes I sat up and let my hands hang limp between my knees as Dr. Todd spoke. "Tell me something positive about that event in your life. Think, Clay. Think really hard. The thing about the shadows is that they're not all darkness. You need to have light to have shadows. So just look for it," Dr. Todd encouraged me.

That was his mantra. Finding the light in the dark shadows inside me. He really should have T-shirts made or something. It made me think of a gospel choir raising their hands to the sky singing, "I've seen the light! Hallelujah, I've seen the light!"

But I got what he was saying. There were times it was impossible to do, with my natural pessimism and all. But I did as he asked this time. I thought hard about the good stuff.

"I guess if I hadn't bottomed out, I wouldn't be here. I wouldn't finally be getting the help I need," I said, feeling a bit proud of myself in being able to verbalize something good in that horrible mess.

Dr. Todd grinned, obviously pleased with my statement. "Exactly! The choices we make in our life don't have to define us. It's what we learn from them that's important. You made the decisions you made while you were in pain, and that doesn't change. But the outcomes are what you make of them. And you have to remember that you are making significant strides in your mental health. You are miles ahead of being the young man who entered this facility almost ninety days ago," he said with total sincerity. I could only nod my head.

"I have been hesitant to prescribe you any other medications, with your history of substance abuse. But given the severity of your panic attacks, I'm going to prescribe you a beta blocker, which is a mild tranquilizer that can be used to treat the physical symptoms of your anxiety. It isn't habit forming, but I would still only like them used as a last resort. I truly believe we can work on your triggers through therapeutic self-talk and relaxation techniques." Great, more drugs. Just when I wasn't feeling crazy enough.

"The staff will know you've been authorized to use them when necessary. But again, Clay, I urge you to only use them if all else fails," Dr. Todd said firmly, and I nodded again, knowing there was nothing else to say.

I was relieved when Dr. Todd said our time was up. Today's session had left me feeling wrung out. He handed me my journal. "Keep using it, Clay," he said as he opened his office door.

"Sure," I responded, tucking the notebook under my arm. I headed out into the hallway and stopped. I didn't want to go back to my room. It was after two and I knew Tyler hadn't left for his group yet. I didn't feel like company and I knew I wouldn't be any.

My feet started moving and I found myself heading out a side door into a tiny garden off of the common room. It was entirely fenced in with three benches in a semicircle around a stone bird-bath. Sure the space was small, but it was a nice spot.

It was the middle of March and in the mideighties. Perfect Florida weather. I sat on one of the benches, putting the notebook down beside me. Leaning back, I stretched my legs out in front of me, crossing them at the ankle. Linking my hands behind my neck, I tilted my face up and closed my eyes. The heat felt good. And the kinks that had knotted up during my session with Dr. Todd started to unravel a bit.

I could hear the television blaring inside the common room, but other than that it was pretty damn peaceful out here. The last hour had been brutal. I had been doing really well overall for the last four weeks. Sure, therapy and support groups got old after a while. Who wouldn't get sick of reliving the shit in your life day after day? There were times I wished I could pack it all in and just say screw this. But for the most part, I was glad I was here.

I was quickly approaching the end of my ninety-day stay. What the future held after that, I couldn't tell. I knew that Dr. Todd and the rest of the staff would like me to stay on for a full six months. I just wasn't sure how I felt about that. Then after that, I'd most likely be recommended for a group home to begin my outpatient treatment. Given the reason I was here in the first place, I should be thankful I wasn't in a straitjacket at a psych ward. I guess my parents' money was good for something. Because of their fear of public humiliation, I had been carted off to the secluded Grayson Center. And it had been the best thing they could have ever done for me. Even if their motives were purely selfish.

I hadn't seen or spoken to my parents since being admitted. They were supposed to be involved in my treatment. Which meant family therapy, regular visits, and the rest of it. I didn't know how aware they were of my progress. I was pretty sure Dr. Todd had kept them in the loop but I had yet to hear a peep out of them.

I didn't know if I should feel relief or disappointment. Because that little boy needing his parents' love still lived deep down inside of me. As much as I wanted to squash him, he was still there, waving his arms, wanting their attention. But then the almost-adult man was much more of a realist and knew that those two particular individuals brought nothing but a whirlwind of shit with them and it was probably best that they stayed the hell away.

I wondered if they would bother to show up for my birthday next week. I didn't even want to think about whether I would be gutted if they didn't.

I scrubbed my face with my hands and let out a noisy breath. Then without thinking, I picked up the notebook and let it fall open to what I had written. I propped it on my knee and stared at the barely legible words in front of me.

> *I remember your hair. The way it smelled when you woke up beside me in the morning. It's the best smell in the entire world. I lay in the motel bed and buried my nose in your neck. It was the most perfect moment of my entire life.*

I hated that such an amazing memory turned me into a panic-ridden freak. I wished I could just think of Maggie without crumbling. But the reaction was intense and instantaneous. I recognized the flutter of my heart and my breaths becoming shallow. Here we go again.

Goddamn it! *No!* I mentally screamed. I forced myself to think of Maggie's eyes. The way they crinkled when she laughed. My heart was pounding so heavily in my chest I could practically feel it rattling my ribs. *Keep going!* I thought harshly. *Stop being such a pussy!*

I remembered kissing her that first time, even after acting like a total asshole. The way she had melted into me. Cherries. That's what she tasted like. Just like her lip gloss. Was it weird that I bought a tube of it after that kiss and would carry it in my pocket, just so I could taste it? Yeah, that was most definitely weird; I wouldn't be admitting that out loud anytime soon.

I felt the dizzy light-headedness of my panic attack as I forced myself to revisit the memories. I was terrified that I would make myself forget them just because they hurt. And as painful as it was to remember what I had lost, it was much more frightening to think of my life without those memories at all. I needed them. They were my reminder that there was something for me on the outside. Something worth fighting for.

I took deep breaths as I concentrated on the memory of my girl. The thousands of tiny moments that flashed through my head like a movie. And after a while, my heart started to slow and my hands unclenched.

"Working on your tan?" a teasing voice called out. I snapped out of my head and focused on Maria as she stepped through the doorway and into the garden. I gave her a weak smile and lifted my shoulders.

"I was feeling a little pasty," I joked back halfheartedly. Maria narrowed her eyes and I knew she saw through my pathetic attempts at nonchalance. Maria had become a close enough friend that she was able to call me on my bullshit with the best of them.

"Well, you'd best get inside, group starts in ten. You look like you could use a coffee," she suggested, waiting for me to get to my feet. As I got closer, she tossed me something. I caught the package of Twizzlers and was finally able to give her a genuine smile.

"Figured you'd need them," Maria said lightly as though it wasn't a big deal. It had become our thing. After a session, Maria would bring me Twizzlers and I would give her a bag of unsalted pretzels from the vending machine. Stupid maybe, but it was the little stuff that made the bigger, terrifying stuff easier to stomach. Maria understood that those sorts of things were important to me. I needed those tiny, seemingly insignificant gestures.

"You have no idea," I muttered, tearing open the package. And now we were off to group therapy; fan-flipping-tastic. I took a deep breath and steeled myself for another sixty minutes of sharing my feelings. Maria looped her arm around my waist and leaned into my side. I stiffened, still not feeling entirely comfortable with her easy physical affection. I had never been the touchy-feely sort. Particularly not with someone whose name wasn't Maggie. So this felt wrong. Like a betrayal. Which was ridiculous. I wasn't with Maggie anymore. And even if I was, I wasn't remotely attracted to Maria.

But that didn't change the fact that I knew Maria *was* attracted to me.

I didn't move away. And I didn't respond either. I tried not to look as relieved as I felt when we reached the coffee machine and she dropped her arm. "Tough session today, huh," Maria stated rather than asked. It had to be pretty clear on my face that I was not in a tap-dancing kind of mood.

I grabbed the Styrofoam cup from the machine, opening the top in order to dump three packets of sugar inside. I stirred my drink and snorted. "Yeah, you could say that. It's been a pretty crappy day all around," I admitted, waiting for Maria to get her hot tea.

Maria gave me a sympathetic smile. "That sucks. But just make tomorrow better," she said. I swear, sometimes I felt like after we all left this place, we could easily get employed writing fucking fortune cookies. When life hands you lemons, make lemonade. The day is darkest before the dawn. It was a joke. If I didn't need to believe that stuff so badly, I'd laugh at how douchey it sounded.

"Right," I said shortly. Maria rubbed my arm and gave me a look that let me know exactly what her feelings were where I was concerned.

I cleared my throat. I had to tell her something, anything to stop her from getting too carried away. There was no way in hell I would ever be able to reciprocate her feelings. Not that she wasn't a great girl. But my heart wasn't mine to give away. It had been taken months ago and I didn't see myself getting it back anytime soon.

"Maria," I started to say, moving away slightly so that her hand dropped from my skin. Her smile flickered and died. "You know I think you're awesome, right?" I said lamely. I couldn't launch into *it's not you, it's me.* There was something fundamentally dickish about that.

Maria laughed without humor and gulped down her tea. "Yes, I'm awesome. And you really like my friendship, right?" she asked with a surprising amount of bitterness. Christ, had I led this girl on more than I thought?

"Seriously, Maria. I'm sorry if you got the wrong idea—" And then she cut me off again.

She gave me a strained smile. "Nope, no wrong idea here, Clay. I've seen the picture by your bed. I know the score. We're friends. Sorry if I made you feel like I wanted something else. Not my intention, I swear." She held up three fingers in the Girl Scout promise thing.

Damn it, this had the makings of epic awkwardness all over it. Maria Cruz was easily my closest friend here. And at this point in my life, friendship was in short supply.

I jammed my hands into my pockets. "Look, you're my friend. A damn good one at that. Have I fucked this up in some way?" I asked, trying not to grit my teeth in frustration. I was sick of miscommunication and mixed signals. Couldn't I have one uncomplicated relationship?

Maria must have sensed I was not able to deal with any sort of drama, because she backed off quickly. Her eyes dropped shyly and she started to chew on her bottom lip. "Sorry, Clay. I guess you're not the only one that's had a shitty day," she explained, tucking a piece of dark hair behind her ear.

She reminded me so much of Maggie just then. Down to the dark hair and total discomfort. It made my heart squeeze tightly in my chest and I just wanted to fix this tiny problem. I wasn't in a position to fix the greater messes I'd created, but this small thing, I could do something about.

I leaned down and bumped my shoulder with hers. "Hey, we're cool. We'll always be cool," I assured her. Her pretty green eyes blinked a few times, and then softened. Though she didn't touch me as she normally would have. No hugs or arm taps. I was fine with that, but I felt a little bad that she felt she couldn't do it.

"Thanks, Clay. After group, let's watch some TV. I bet there's a daytime soap calling my name," she teased. I made a show of groaning.

"Really? Come on, don't subject my manhood to such an overwhelming display of estrogen. I know you want to watch something macho like *American Chopper* or *LA Ink*," I joked.

Maria shook her head and I was able to fall into that small semblance of normalcy I had been able to create for myself.

chapter
four

maggie

"Why did you bail so early on Saturday?" Daniel asked me after he joined Rachel and me at the lunch table on Monday. I was making pretty little patterns in my mashed potatoes and not really in the mood to explain why I had freaked out and needed to be alone. I was sure that my behavior on Saturday wasn't a surprise to my friends. But it didn't stop me from feeling bad for not being able to pick up the pieces and become the "old Maggie" like they wanted me to.

I was trying really hard, though. After my lightbulb moment at work, I was more determined than ever to stop hiding in my room and to embrace my life. Moping around and writing really bad poetry (which *no one* would ever see) wasn't my idea of a good time. So I had gotten dressed. I even made myself a bit more girlie than usual. I amped myself up to engage in some good ol' teenage shenanigans.

I had gotten into my Corolla, which was still kicking, by the way, and headed over to Ray's. I knew I was in trouble once I had gotten there. There were a lot more cars than I had anticipated. I thought it was going to be a small get-together. But there were easily ten cars lining the driveway. Once I got to the front door, my suspicions were confirmed.

It was a full-blown party.

I really wished Jake had told me that Ray's parents were out of town. Then I sure as hell wouldn't have bothered to show up.

I used to love to party. I used to love hanging out with my friends and getting loaded. But that was "PC." Pre-Clay. Back in the days when I wasn't hypersensitive to the whispers and looks. The first few weeks after I had returned from my dramatic stint as a teenage runaway had been brutal. I had been miserable and depressed. Trying to go on with my life after losing Clay had been daunting, to say the least. And it was made infinitely worse by the rumors and the whispers and the blatant stares I received once I had returned to school.

I tried my damnedest to seem unaffected by it. No one had to know that every mention of *his* name made me die a little bit more. I wore a fake smile while I tried to become that *other* Maggie again. The one who would never jump headfirst off a cliff of teenage drama.

Sure, the level of gossiping had subsided a bit, but it was still there. And I knew people still looked at me as the girl whose boyfriend had tried to off himself.

So I had purposely avoided social functions as much as possible. Sure, I was moving on into my post-Clay existence. But it was slow going. And approaching that front door, I knew, deep down, that the party was a bad idea. But I had forced myself to suck it up.

And darned if I hadn't been right. While it had been great to see Claire (I had been a bad friend to more than just Rachel and Danny), the rest of it truly sucked a fat one. Jake had found me seconds after my arrival and decided to be my party guide. It was like he was my escort at a freaking debutante ball or something. Taking me around to groups of people I could give a shit about talking to. He was so persistent in me having a good time that it bordered on pushy and annoying. But I had gritted my teeth and suppressed the urge to tell him to back the hell off. I smiled, I made asinine chitchat. I was the belle of the crappy ball.

Rachel and Danny had been there, which always made things better. And for a moment I thought I had succeeded in salvaging the night. I had convinced my jangled nerves to take a hike and I was actually able to engage in semicomfortable conversation with people I hadn't talked to in months. That's right, one point for socially competent Maggie Young!

Then Dana "I wanted to bang your boyfriend" Welsh had pissed all over my quite enjoyable parade. That bitch was lying in wait to bring the smackdown.

She had sneered at me with Jake's arm slung around my shoulders. She had tossed her obnoxiously shiny hair over her shoulder and laughed. "Jake, I'd watch out if I were you. I hear crazy is contagious." Her evil henchman, McKenna, had giggled beside her like a deranged hyena.

Jake had tensed up and stared at the duo. "Excuse me?" he had asked, as though he couldn't believe what she had just said. As if her rudeness was surprising. Give me a break!

Dana had simply shrugged. "Well, she's already made one guy want to kill himself." Dana and McKenna had laughed as though that was the funniest thing ever. I could feel the blood leave my face and I had felt faintly nauseous. As much as I was trying to channel the old Maggie, the one who would have jumped their shit, I just couldn't summon her. So I stood there dumbfounded, my mouth hanging open with the snappy comeback that never came.

Jake had jumped to my defense, which I should have appreciated. But what did I do? Oh yeah, I just walked away. Miss I Hate Bullies took off with my tail between my legs. Maybe that was letting the mean girls win, but all I had cared about was getting my ass home as quickly as possible.

I looked up from my artistic potato mountains and rolled my eyes. "Sorry, just wasn't my scene." I brushed off my friends' very obvious concern. Daniel frowned and looked as though he wanted to say something else but Rachel cut him off.

"Well, you didn't miss much. Except for Ray puking all over the kitchen," Rachel said, shuddering.

"Yuck. Seriously?" I pushed my tray away and crossed my arms on the table. I watched a little wistfully as Daniel opened up a Snickers bar and handed it to Rachel. She took it and gave him a sweet smile in thanks. He ran his fingers up her arm, stopping to brush her hair off of her shoulder. Seeing the way his hand lingered on her skin made my throat close up and my eyes start to burn.

Their absolute love and affection for each other, while totally beautiful and deserved, still had me looking away before I succumbed to my tears. I hated that I couldn't just be happy for them. But it was really hard seeing such devotion when my life was devoid of anything resembling the contentment they radiated together.

"Yeah, I went over the next day to help him clean up and it was rank. Ray was so hungover that he spent most of the time dry heaving in the sink," Daniel shared. I pushed my depressing and lonely thoughts out of my head.

"You're a better friend than me, Danny boy. No way would I help anyone clean up vomit," I said seriously. Rachel tossed a napkin at me.

"Hey! You wouldn't help me clean up puke? Really?" she complained. I raised my eyebrow at her and shook my head.

"Is that a surprise? I have my limits," I told her. My attention was pulled from my friend to watch Paul Delawder amble into the cafeteria.

The school bully closed in on his newest target, a hapless

freshman who quickly lost his cell phone and his lunch. I almost got to my feet, ready to take on the nutwad again. But Mr. Kane had for once witnessed the situation and was intervening.

I was flooded with clear memories of that day last year, when I had rushed in to save a boy who really didn't want my help. A boy who ended up needing me to save him so badly that he forgot to save himself. I had let that boy down and now here I was a sad shell of who I had been.

I let out a noisy sigh and I turned my attention back to Rachel and Daniel, who wore almost identical looks of worry. I wish I could laugh at them. They were so transparent. They were scared to death I was going to crawl back into that dark hole I had disappeared into after I lost Clay.

But there was no way I would do that. Because I was going to move on, even if my heart rebelled at the idea.

As if on cue, Jake slammed his tray down onto the table beside me. I jumped slightly at the sudden intrusion. He slid onto the bench and quickly reached over to take my chocolate chip cookie. I let him, not wanting to engage in a fake protest about it.

I watched Jake out of the corner of my eye as he greeted Rachel and Daniel, who seemed genuinely pleased he was there. And I was overcome with some seriously intense déjà vu. This whole thing was wrong.

Jake sat in exactly the same spot that had been Clay's. He was laughing with my friends and taking bits of my lunch in a way that should have been reserved for Clay. I started to feel irrationally angry about that. I didn't want Jake Fitzsimmons sitting there, in a seat meant for someone else.

Why hadn't I just thought about moving on? Because right now, my body, my mind, and my heart weren't moving past the fact that the wrong guy sat beside me. I got to my feet without a word. I dumped my food unceremoniously onto Jake's tray. "If you're so damn hungry, just have it all!" I barked. Rachel and Danny, who had been in the middle of telling Jake about a movie they had seen, became instantly quiet.

Jake's mouth hung open in shock and he looked at me with hurt evident on his face. And that made me feel even worse. "Sorry," I mumbled and then walked away as fast as I could without actually running.

Of course Rachel followed me. "Mags! Wait up!" she called out as I tried to make my escape. There would be no getting away from her, so I stopped and let her catch up, resigning myself to a round of "What's wrong?"

But I should have known that Rachel would understand exactly what I needed. Because she didn't ask me anything. "Let's go to the library and study for that chem pop quiz you know we're going to have," she said, pulling on my arm.

I looked down at the petite girl and wanted to hug her. And I would have, if that were my thing. But since it wasn't, I just let her pull me down the hallway. And like that, my fantastic friend pushed me straight into that normal I was desperate to have.

✦

Though once the floodgates were opened, it was pretty hard to shut them again. Clay's memory taunted me all day long. Who was I kidding? Even as I tried so hard to get on with things, he was always there waiting to yank me back again. The ghost of him was almost more dangerous than the real thing.

After school I rushed home, giving my friends an excuse of a headache. They hadn't questioned me, even as I knew they saw straight through my bullshit. Luckily my parents hadn't gotten home from work yet, so pretending I was fine wasn't necessary.

I dropped my book bag onto the couch and headed upstairs to my room, taking two steps at a time. Once there, I closed my door behind me and fell onto my bed. I was tired. Bone-aching, gut-wrenching tired. I stared at the ceiling and wished for the millionth time that I could talk to Clay. I just wanted to know that he was all right. I wanted to hear his voice saying my name like it was the air he breathed.

Which was so beyond stupid. He had left me behind. Had sent me that awful letter telling me to move the fuck on. To get on with my life, as if forgetting about what he and I had been through was an easy thing to do. Maybe it had been for him. Not for the first time, I wondered if I had loved my sad, broken boy more than he was capable of loving me.

Without thinking about what I was doing, I slid off my bed and got on my hands and knees to root under my bed. Finding what I was looking for, I pulled it out. The heavy package wrapped in newspaper. I didn't do fancy gift wrap. What was the point when it would be ripped apart?

Why was I hanging on to this thing? I had gotten the gift in the first week after losing Clay. I had been desperate to do something, anything, that allowed me to hold on to what we had. I had wrapped it and put it under my bed, never forgetting about it, but not entirely sure what I was going to do with it either.

It wasn't like I could send it to him. I didn't even know where he was. And after getting the brush-off, I should have just thrown it out. I stared at the gift a bit longer and then made up my mind.

I tucked it into my messenger bag and went back downstairs to grab my keys. Fifteen minutes later I was pulling into a familiar parking lot. My heart hammered in my chest and my breathing was heavy. What the hell was I doing?

I found myself getting out of my car and walking toward the front of the store. The tinkling of bells indicated my entrance. Looking around, I was comforted by the familiarity of my surroundings.

I knew *why* I had avoided Ruby's Bookshelf, but standing there, breathing in the pungent incense and hearing the predictable strains of the New Age music over the speakers, I only felt peaceful. I wasn't hit by any of my newly acquired neuroses when confronted by anything Clay-related. No, this was a place I had loved before he came along, and I realized that I could still enjoy being here.

"Maggie!" I turned to the sound of Clay's aunt Ruby, who had come around the counter and was practically running toward me. Despite the initial gut twisting that accompanied seeing Ruby after all this time, she was still a welcome sight.

"Hiya, Ruby!" I said softly as I was enveloped in a warm hug. There was just something about this woman that made me feel safe. As if the bad memories could be washed away by her infectious happiness.

"It's been too long, my love." She squeezed my cheeks between her palms and I couldn't help but grin.

"You're right. It has been." I looked around the shop. "I think some new reading material is in order," I said, putting off the real reason for my visit. Ruby nodded and shooed me into the back where she kept the books.

"Take your time! I just got a bunch of new stuff. They're in a pile on the table there." Ruby seemed so genuinely glad to see me and I felt a bit guilty for not coming by sooner. I couldn't shut everyone and everything out. It was time for me to grow up and reintroduce myself to my spine.

So I did as Ruby said and took my time browsing the books. I even took it upon myself to shelve the items she clearly hadn't had time to sort out yet. It felt good to slip back into a part of my life that I had avoided for so long. And even if doing the mundane task reminded me of a dozen days spent doing this very thing with a boy I had loved and lost, it still felt good to do it.

After loading myself up with an armful of books, I made my way to the front counter. The shop was quiet; only a few other customers roamed about. Ruby reached out to take the books.

"Wow, you really stocked up." She dropped them into a plastic bag and handed it to me without ringing them up.

"Uh, didn't you forget the whole paying part?" I laughed, pulling my wallet out of my messenger bag. Ruby waved my money away.

"You are absolutely not paying for a thing. I've missed you, Maggie. Consider this a *happy as pie to see you* gift." Ruby's wide smile made it hard to argue. Though I made a good show of grumbling.

"I want to pay, Ruby. Come on," I urged, still trying to shove some cash into her hand. She curled my fingers around the money and squeezed.

"This is also my way of saying thank you," she said quietly. I swallowed thickly.

"Thank you?" I asked weakly, though I knew instantly what she was getting at.

"Yes, Maggie. Thank you for being the loyal, amazing girl that you are. And for loving my boy the way you did." Her eyes sparkled with the strength of her words and I had to blink rapidly or I would start crying.

I cleared my throat, feeling overwhelmed by emotion. Almost recklessly, I yanked my bag open and pulled out the wrapped package, laying it on the counter. I pushed it toward Ruby. "Here," I said abruptly.

Ruby frowned and picked up the heavy gift. "What's this?" she asked, turning it over.

My hands were shaking, so I shoved them into my coat pockets. I took a deep breath. "I ran into Lisa . . ." I began and Ruby nodded.

"Yes, she said she saw you," Ruby said, watching me, waiting for me to explain what I had given her. I started to panic. Maybe this was a bad idea. I was just starting to put Clay in my rearview mirror. But here I was dredging everything up all over again, trying like hell to hold open a door that had shut firmly in my face.

I was either an idiot or a complete glutton for punishment. I was beginning to think I was a mixture of both.

"Uh, yeah, well, that's a gift for . . . Clay. For his birthday," I let out in a rush. Ruby's eyebrows rose and I could tell I had surprised her. "Well, Lisa said you were going to see him and I've had that for a few months now and it's just collecting dust under my bed. And it's not like I even know where to send the stupid thing, so I just thought you could give it to him. You know, because it'll be his birthday and all," I rambled on nervously.

I stopped before I could say anything else. Ruby watched me silently as I bit down on my lip, feeling ridiculously embarrassed. Yeah, this was stupid. Clay probably didn't want a damn thing from me. I looked pathetic and sad and all the million and one things that I probably was.

I reached out to take the gift back. "It was a stupid idea. Never mind," I mumbled, but Ruby pulled it out of my grasp. I startled and then looked at her.

"I'll give it to him, honey. I'm sure he'd love to have it," she told me, but I saw that she was bothered by something. She tucked the gift underneath the counter and I had the impression that she wasn't entirely sure that she wanted to give it to her nephew. And that just made me feel even more foolish.

"Oh, well. Thanks," I said dumbly, wanting to get the hell out of there now that I had made a complete idiot of myself.

I gathered my bag of books. "I'll see you around," I said dismissively, ready to leave.

"Maggie. I'll make sure he gets it. I promise," she called after me, though now I wasn't so sure I wanted him to have it. But I suppose it was too late now.

I left Ruby's shop and got into my car. Why couldn't I leave well enough alone?

chapter
five

clay

It was my birthday. I wanted to be giddy. Excited, even. But I just felt numb. It had been a long time since birthdays really meant anything to me. I seemed to recall a party when I was five, complete with scary clowns and pony rides. Maybe it was the clowns that ruined me for all future birthdays. Because those fuckers are scary.

Despite my self-imposed birthday gloominess, this year was different. Because today I turned eighteen.

Yep, eighteen.

I was finally a socially mandated adult. Able to vote and buy to-bacco products and porn. I could join the military and open my own checking account. But these typically exciting rites of passage meant shit to me. Sure, it was great and all, but I wasn't going to rush out and buy a pack of Camels and a *Playboy* (not like I could go anywhere anyway). Nope, this birthday was about something even sweeter.

This particular day was all about *freedom*. Because for the first time I was free. Free to make my own choices. My own mistakes.

Free to live on my own terms.

For the rest of my life freedom would taste like birthday cake. And I was good with that.

Control was well and truly mine. I had never really allowed myself to think about what I would do when that magical day arrived. And here I was, minutes into my adulthood, and I felt almost overwhelmed with the possibilities.

This all felt like a dream. And dreams had a way of crashing down around you. So I always tried to stay away from dreams. They were nasty business for a guy with no future.

But there was a time not so long ago when dreams and a future weren't a ludicrous delusion. And that had led to something one hundred times more beautiful. And a thousand times more dangerous.

Hope.

Hope. That thing that got you up in the morning and made living that much easier. Hope. The indescribable emotion that had the power to level you when it was taken away. Because mine had died a tragic death at the hands of my own selfishness and fear. And even as I tried to reconcile my guilt and shame about ruining the one good thing I had, I still felt it like a sharp pain in the gut.

But today that pain twisted into something else and I recognized it for the amazing thing it was.

Hope.

It was there, hanging out in my heart with a polka-dotted party hat on, waiting for me to realize that perhaps it had never really left me.

I woke up to Tyler blasting the Beatles' "Birthday" accompanied by some of the worst dance moves I had ever seen. And coming from a guy with two left feet, that was saying something.

I sat up and wiped the sleep out of my eyes, trying to wrap my brain around the image of my normally shy and introverted roommate, gyrating around the room completely out of time to the music.

"What the hell are you doing?" I asked, laughing. Tyler pumped his fists over his head and jumped on the desk chair, singing at the top of his lungs.

Not thirty seconds later, there was an authoritative knock on our door and I shot Tyler a look as he scrambled to turn the music down. Jonathan, the aide on duty, poked his head in the doorway and gave us a stern look. Jonathan was probably in his late twenties and already balding, poor guy. But he was nice enough, in that I-still-live-in-my-parents'-basement kind of way.

"Guys, it's seven in the morning. You know the rules about music. I'd hate to confiscate your stereo." Tyler looked sheepish and switched the music off. The Grayson Center was all about rules, birthday or not.

"Sorry, man," my roommate mumbled, clearly embarrassed by the reprimand. I got out of bed and stretched, scratching the back of my head.

Jonathan gave us a smile. "Just don't let it happen again. I hate having to be the bad guy." The aide looked over at me and threw something in my direction. I grabbed it before it fell to the floor. It was one of those cheesy "I'm the Birthday Boy" buttons that you wear when you're a kid.

"Happy Birthday, Clay," Jonathan said, grinning as I stuck the pin into my shirt. I grinned back, displaying my button proudly.

"Thanks, Jon. Just what I always wanted," I joked as the aide left. I went to my dresser and pulled out some clothes and then gathered my shower stuff.

"Hurry up, Clay. The kitchen staff will make you whatever you want on your birthday. So unless you want to choke down a shit-tasting bagel with the rest of us, make it snappy."

I snorted at Tyler. "Yes, sir, I'll make it *snappy*," I replied sarcastically. But Tyler was right. I wasn't missing out on a Southwest omelet for nothin'. I couldn't get rid of the ridiculous smile on my face as I got ready for my day.

This happy stuff was pretty awesome.

✦

By around two in the afternoon I was officially in the birthday spirit. Maria, Tyler, and a few of our other friends made a big production of wheeling out a cake during lunchtime. Maria insisted I wear a pointed birthday hat made of cheap cardboard. I played along, not being able to help but enjoy the whole thing.

The counselors had gotten me a new journal—oh joy—and some books about loving myself or whatever. I didn't get hung up on the cheesiness of it and just appreciated the fact that they thought to get me anything at all. Louis, the center's administrator, gave me some coupons redeemable for different privileges, like extra TV time and a few "get out of chores" tickets. It may not seem like a lot, but to the patients at Grayson, those coupons were like gold.

Everyone was going out of their way to make me feel special. Which was definitely needed when by late afternoon it became apparent that I wouldn't be getting a phone call from my parents. I received the obligatory greeting card of course. It looked cheap, like something from the dollar rack. I was pretty sure it was something my dad's secretary had picked up at Walmart. It had only been signed "Mom and Dad." And I was almost positive that it wasn't even their handwriting.

It wasn't as though I was surprised by their lack of sentiment. But I had to seriously tamp down the hurt and bitterness that threatened to swallow my good mood. I really wished I could just turn off the juvenile expectation that my parents would for once act like . . . well, parents. Setting myself up for the disappointment was way past old.

I had met with Dr. Todd right before dinner. He had wanted to touch base with me about my ongoing treatment. He explained that he was legally bound to inform me of my rights now that I was of age. I technically had a few more weeks at the center according to the treatment plan my parents and I had signed when I was admitted. But now that I was eighteen, my treatment was my own. Given that I had made significant progress and no longer posed a threat to myself, I could be approved for discharge as early as the end of the week.

I cleared my throat, taken aback by the information I was just given. "What about my parents? Couldn't they fight that?" I asked. I couldn't imagine my parents sitting by and letting me discharge myself. Not without some serious legal wrangling. But just knowing that I could do as I liked was empowering.

Dr. Todd sat on the edge of his desk and crossed his arms over his chest. "Well, to be brutally honest with you, Clay, your parents wouldn't have much to stand on legally. Yes, they had you admitted, but they have been, well, less than involved in your treatment here, despite efforts by staff to engage them. You have made progress without their input. But I must say, as your therapist, that you still have a lot of work ahead of you. With the regulation of your medication, you've been able to focus on getting your self-injury and suicidal thoughts in check. But this will be a lifetime battle."

I nodded, not feeling defensive or irritated by his assessment. He was only stating facts. "And when the time comes for you to leave Grayson, we can discuss my recommendations for your continued treatment. Leaving in-patient is difficult and usually requires a transitional program, such as going to Langley's, the group home over in Miami Springs."

A group home? That sounded about as much fun as a freaking funeral. But I got what the doc was saying. I didn't want him to think that just because I was eighteen now I would forget everything I had learned since coming to the center. I felt the need to prove myself. To show him I *was* getting better.

"Doc, I'm not going anywhere. I'd like to make it through the rest of my stay and then we can discuss what comes next," I said confidentially, watching as Dr. Todd tried to control the look of relief that flashed across his face.

He got up and went to sit back behind his desk. "I'm glad to hear that, Clayton," he said, giving me that calming smile of his. After that, our session was more lighthearted. No delving into my gnarly past or reworking my twisted thoughts. Instead, we engaged in benign chitchat. Including an almost heated exchange about college basketball.

Yep, today was shaping up to be one of the good ones.

◆

After dinner, Maria, Tyler, and I were heading to the common room to watch some TV when Jacqui, the night administrator, asked me to come to her office. I shrugged at my friends, who looked at me questioningly. "I'll catch up with you guys in a bit," I told them, following Jacqui down the hallway.

"I didn't do it, I swear," I teased as we entered her office. Jacqui's normally sour face jerked into an almost smile as she patted my arm.

"Nothing to worry about, Clay," she assured me, waving me in so she could close the door. As soon as I was inside, I was enveloped in a set of warm arms and the pungent scent of patchouli. My aunt Ruby gripped me like her life depended on it. And I suddenly realized that I should have been more than a little suspicious when I hadn't heard from her yet today. As if Ruby and Lisa would ever miss my birthday.

I had never thought she'd travel thirteen hundred miles to see me, though. But that was Ruby. She had always loved me more than I sometimes deserved.

"Ruby," I said, smiling at my much shorter aunt. She beamed up at me. She was dressed in her typical gypsy getup, complete with flowing skirt and some crazy scarf thing around her neck. She even had tiny shells sticking out of her hair. Where the hell she got the ideas for her outfits, I had no idea.

Ruby reached up and patted my cheek, the way she had done since I was a little kid. "My Clay. It's so good to see you." Her grin was infectious. Ruby radiated a positive energy that was impossible to ignore. She had helped pull me out of more than my fair share of dark places by just being her. I would do anything for the woman who stood in front of me. She was the mother I wished mine could be. She had been down at least four times in the last three months. Lisa had come with her whenever she could, but work kept her pretty busy.

Four times, my aunt had been to see me and my parents hadn't come once.

"What are you doing here? And where's Lisa?" I asked as she hugged me tightly again. Ruby pulled back and gave me a mock scowl.

"As if I would miss your eighteenth birthday! Don't be silly. And Lisa would have been here but her work has been crazy," she explained, swatting my arm. She pulled me over to the small couch that sat in the corner of the office. Jacqui had left, giving us some time to visit. Ruby hefted a heavy canvas bag that she had with her.

"Are you carting around a ton of bricks in there?" I joked, watching as my aunt pulled out a squished cardboard box.

"Oh darn. It's all smooshed," Ruby complained, peering down into the box. She closed the lid and handed it to me. "Well, it should still taste good." She had brought me a freaking birthday cake. My name was swirled in blue icing and tiny paintbrushes decorated the surface. I felt my chest seize up. Christ, I was seriously turning into a mess. Crying over every tiny thing. What happened to being a *man*? I needed to find some shit-kickers and a Stetson. Channel some Marlon Brando or something.

But fuck me, I couldn't remember the last time I had a birthday cake. And today I had been given two. Even I wasn't immune to the warm fuzzies that brought on. Ruby then pulled out two plates.

I watched her as she cut me a large slab and I attacked it like I was starving. I was always a sucker for anything sweet. Ruby ate delicately around the icing, complaining that she should have gotten carob instead of chocolate because it was healthier. I let her grumble about white sugar being worse than rat poison and how ingesting white flour was like asking for your pancreas to shut down. I just listened silently and ate the hell out of some diabetes slathered in chocolate.

"I still can't believe you came down here. It really means a lot to me," I said after I was finished. Ruby's eyes started to water and I braced myself for the tear fest. Ruby was notorious for being overly emotional, and once upon a time I would have run for the hills at the slightest hint of the touchy-feely stuff.

I had spent a long time creating a very thick, impenetrable wall around myself. A wall that made it easier for me to live each day inside my own very screwed up head. If I didn't let people get too close, then I didn't have to feel the guilt of disappointing them later.

But that had been blown to pieces by a pair of beautiful eyes and a snarky attitude.

Can't go there. Not now. Not when I was feeling good. Otherwise I'd end up a blubbering mess alongside my already blubbering aunt.

Ruby wrapped her small fingers around my arm and squeezed. I covered her hand with my much larger one. I was learning to be okay with showing people that I cared about them. That it was good to share your feelings. That I didn't have to protect people from the person that I was. That, damn it, I was worth loving. This was drilled into my head every single day. I was told over and over again that gosh darn it, people like me. But it still stuck in the back of my throat. This insane notion that I was a decent human being.

"Clayton Reed, I would have moved into your room if I was able to. But something tells me they might frown on that here." I snorted. Even though she was joking, I wouldn't have put it past Ruby to try. "Lisa and I love you as if you were our own. We will always be here for you. No matter what," Ruby said, giving me another hug. My throat felt uncomfortably tight, but in a good way. A really good way.

"I love you guys too. I can't thank you enough for everything you've done for me," I told her quietly, proud of myself for being able to express my feelings in an appropriate way (thank you, Coping Skills 101). Ruby furiously wiped at the tears that leaked out of the corners of her eyes. She pulled a handkerchief from her pocket and blew her nose noisily. Nothing like a cotton wad full of snot to kill the heaviness.

"Enough with all of this crying. It's time for gifts!" Ruby enthused, giving me a watery smile before pulling three packages out of her bag.

"Ruby. You didn't have to get me anything. You being here is more than enough," I said, though I couldn't help but feel the anticipatory excitement that I hadn't felt in a long time. The kind of bubbling in your stomach that you feel only on Christmas morning. Or before you get behind the wheel of a car after getting your license.

Or before you kiss your girl for the first time.

Anyway . . . on to presents.

Ruby watched as I unwrapped the gifts. She and Lisa had gotten me a new charcoal kit, a ridiculously expensive set of paintbrushes, and a bunch of new sketchbooks. I couldn't stop the goofy grin that spread across my face. There was nothing in this world she could have given me that would have meant more.

Drawing and painting were everything to me. I had become almost obsessive about it. It was that indelible part of me that I refused to ever give up. I had lost so much already, but I would always have my art.

"I wasn't sure exactly what you used, but the girl at the art store in Charlottesville assured me these were the best," Ruby said a little nervously, as though worried I'd hate what she had gotten me. I ran my hand through my hair, a little overwhelmed by those prickly emotions again. But I didn't worry about what those feelings could cause. Medication, when done right, was a fantastic thing.

"They're great, Ruby. Thank you. I'll call Lisa later to thank her as well. This is just . . ." My voice trailed off and I grinned like an idiot at my aunt, who was equally excited about my response to the presents.

Then suddenly Ruby's mood sobered. The change in her demeanor threw me and I was instantly on edge. She reached into her bag and pulled out another gift. This one wasn't wrapped in the traditional birthday paper as the others had been.

Looking closely, I could see that this one was bundled up meticulously in the *Davidson Gazette*, the local paper of Davidson, Virginia. I looked at Ruby questioningly. She was staring down at the mysterious gift and I could tell she was uncomfortable. What the hell was hiding in that paper? A fucking bomb?

"More gifts, Ruby? You shouldn't have," I joked, already hating the seriousness that had overtaken my typically jovial aunt. Ruby clutched the object in her hands and held it out for me to take. Slowly I reached for it. It was heavier than it looked. I couldn't get a read on its contents through the thick paper.

I started to pull at the tape when Ruby covered my hand, stopping me. She looked at me with concern and I dropped the object onto the table. "What is it, Ruby? Just spit it out," I said, feeling annoyed by the evasive bullshit going on. What was so scary about a damn present?

Ruby sighed. "It's from Maggie," she said quietly.

Oh. Well, there was that.

I swear the air left my lungs and I felt like I was suffocating. My heart started beating in overtime and I thought I might pass out. It was nuts how just the mention of her name caused such an instant physical response. It was like my body reacted on a primal level to it.

Ruby and I never talked about Maggie. At least not in a very long time. I rarely mentioned Maggie at all unless it was within the safe confines of therapy. My memories of Maggie Young had proven complicated. My crazy, fucked-up mind had succeeded in twisting my beautiful girl into something that caused me complete and total anxiety. The darkness that lived and breathed inside of me, while kept at bay for the most part, still worked to destroy the one thing that I had wanted most in my life.

The girl I loved beyond reason. The one person who had been prepared to walk off the cliff with me.

And I had almost let her.

"Maggie?" I choked out, trying not to strangle on the effort it took to say her name.

Ruby nodded, her mouth tight with worry. I knew she was scared that mentioning the girl I had loved and lost would make me lose it. And part of me wanted to lose it. It bubbled there, just beneath the surface. The panic fluttered in my stomach and I struggled to keep it under control. I was tempted to get angry. To give in to the rage that I felt when I realized how I may have sorted some crap out, but in the process I had unleashed even more.

But I held on to that rational part of Clayton Reed who recognized the futility of my anger and panic. Knowing that it wouldn't accomplish anything but set me back even further. I needed to work through these tangled emotions and sort through the chaos they still created. Maggie wasn't the boogeyman. She was my light. My reminder of what I wanted in my life. Of what I strove to have again.

Holding on to that, I picked up the gift again and set it in my lap, fingering the creases in the folded paper. "She came into the shop last week," Ruby began, watching me closely. I worked hard to keep my face perfectly neutral when inside I was cursing the fucking cosmos, fate, whatever, for this goddamned tragedy that I called a life.

"Oh yeah?" I asked with the fakest attempt at casual that I had ever heard. It was laughable. I *would* have laughed if I hadn't wanted to cut my fucking skin until I bled.

Damn it! I would not feel this way!

So I took a deep breath and counted to ten. I found my shiny, happy-people place in my head and got my shit together. Because as much as it hurt, I had to hear about Maggie. I was starved for her. I craved just the sound of her name. So even though my body and mind labored under the turmoil she unleashed inside me, I would suck it up. Because nothing could keep me from finding out what she had wrapped beneath the newspaper in my lap.

Ruby took another deep breath and continued. "I hadn't seen her since right after you had come to Florida. Lisa had mentioned that she had seen her at that coffee shop in town. She's working there now." I nodded, encouraging her to keep going before I decided that I couldn't hear any more.

"She looked beautiful as always. Though I can tell she's lost some weight and she was already too skinny," Ruby rambled and I felt guilty about the possibility that I had anything to do with Maggie's weight loss. My hands clenched around the package until my fingers ached.

"Did she seem . . . okay?" I couldn't help but ask. Because if she wasn't . . .

What would I do? If Ruby told me Maggie was miserable and depressed, would I break the promise I made to myself to leave her alone? I didn't know. The only thing I *did* know was that I couldn't live my life knowing that she was unhappy. My refusal to contact her, the reason for sending my letter, was for her to have a clean break. To let go of me and to live her life.

But if she was as miserable being away from me as I was being away from her, then I would throw all of my foolish good intentions straight out the window.

"Yes, Clayton. She seemed okay. A little uncomfortable maybe, but she was good," Ruby told me and I hated the selfish disappointment that I felt. What sort of asshole did that make me? Did I want Maggie to be unhappy? Of course not. But if she was doing all right, then it confirmed I had made the best decision in leaving her alone. And that was hard to accept even if it was the right thing to do.

"Well, that's . . . uh . . . good to hear," I said, looking down at my white knuckles. I wasn't sure I'd survive this conversation. This was tearing me apart. Ruby eyed me again as if waiting for me to grow another head or something.

I sat up a little straighter and met her eyes. "That's great actually," I said more firmly and forced myself to smile. Ruby's face relaxed marginally.

"Yes, it is," Ruby agreed. She cleared her throat. "She came in to look over the new books. I told her it was good to see her but I tried to leave her alone. She didn't seem to want to talk much and I didn't want to push her." I could only imagine how awkward seeing Ruby had been for Maggie.

There was a moment of silence and I thought that was it. But I should have known better. Ruby was notorious for dragging a story out. You could find it either endearing or exasperating. Right now I was leaning toward the latter.

"She got some books and then just as she was leaving she

handed me *that*. She said it was for you. For your birthday. She asked that I make sure you got it because she didn't know where to send it." Ruby gave me a pointed look then. One that clearly said she thought I was an idiot for keeping my whereabouts a secret from Maggie. She just didn't get how hard that decision had been for me to make. How some days I questioned my judgment so intensely that it took everything in me to not pick up the phone and call her. Maggie was my weakness. My compulsive addiction that once fed wouldn't let go.

At one time, I thought she was the healthiest, purest thing in my life. And part of me still did. But now, with a clear head, I was able to see how the darkness had tainted so much of what we were. And Maggie needed more than what I could currently give her. The back and forth, tug and pull of my feelings about that beautiful girl had become a daily struggle. One that, no matter how much time passed or how much distance was between us, would never let up.

"I wasn't entirely sure I was going to give it to you, Clayton," Ruby told me, turning a startlingly piercing gaze in my direction. For all of her feigned ditziness, it concealed a sharp mind and an even sharper eye. Ruby saw more than I ever gave her credit for. And something told me that she knew all too well how hard I struggled, even with the strides I was making.

I grimaced in understanding at her hesitance. I got it. Really, I did. "It's cool," I assured her, hoping like hell she believed my pile of bullshit.

Not waiting any longer, I pulled at the wrapping and tossed it onto the floor. At the first glimpse of the dark, charcoal butterfly on the cover, I had to sit back and take a minute. Because this girl was going to undo me from a thousand miles away. She was getting ready to rip my fucking heart out.

You see, I recognized that butterfly. Because I had drawn it myself. For her.

For Maggie.

"What the hell?" I asked, pulling the leather-bound book from the last scraps of paper. Opening it up, I realized it was a scrapbook. Page after page, Maggie had carefully placed my drawings on plain mats. They were the ones from my bedroom wall in Virginia. And the ones I had given her.

Every single one was there. Every. Single. One.

Ruby was looking at the pictures over my shoulder as I flipped through. I turned to my aunt. "When did she do this? When did she get my pictures?" I asked in absolute disbelief. I was stunned by what was in my hands. Like a piece of me had been returned. As though, once again, Maggie May Young had swooped in to the rescue.

I couldn't put into words the way my heart opened up at seeing these pictures again. It was easily one of the most amazing and thoughtful gifts I had ever received. As if I could expect anything less from the girl who had made it her mission to save me from myself.

Ruby traced her finger along a picture of Maggie's face that I had drawn in pencil. I loved that drawing. I remembered the day I had done it. She had come over to my house to study and had ended up falling asleep. I loved it when she did that. The absolute peace that I would feel as I watched her deep, even breathing was indescribable. Yeah, so maybe it sounds a little creepy. But it wasn't. It was beautiful and perfect. And gave me the illusion that my life had made sense, if only for a little while.

So I had drawn her. I was compelled to try and capture that moment when Maggie was completely unguarded and open. Some small part of me recognized, even then, that I was hurting her. That as she swore that she was happy, I had seen the strain my crap was causing. Seeing her sleep helped me create this picture in my head that things were just the way they should be. Crazy how I had always been able to create the most fucked-up justifications for the equally fucked-up things I did.

My heart thudded in my chest at the weight of what this album meant. This wasn't put together by a girl who was putting a shitty relationship behind her. By an ex-girlfriend desperate to move on. No, this whole thing screamed at me. Yelling with a vengeance that I needed to wake up and see how much she still loved me.

And there was a selfish relief in that. I was glad to know that she hadn't forgotten me, even if I had told her to. I was such a dick. Because I wanted her to miss me, to long for me, to crave me the way I craved her. Which was 100 percent contradictory to the martyr act I had been playing for the past few months. The reason that I had sent her the letter to begin with.

I knew I would never be over Maggie. And knowing I wasn't alone in that, that she was feeling it as intensely as I was, made me feel unfairly happy. Unfair, because I shouldn't want that for her. But damned if I didn't want it all the same.

And I hated myself for feeling that way.

"She came over to the house, not long after you were sent here. She asked to go up to your room, that there were things she needed to get from up there. Lisa and I didn't see the harm. Not after everything—" Ruby stopped abruptly. There was no sense in her continuing that particular sentence. We both knew how much Maggie had been through.

I continued to thumb through the pages. Ruby and I remained quiet as I took it all in. These pictures that reminded me so much of the one bright spot I had during the darkest times of my life. Of the girl who had tried to save me even as I destroyed her.

Shit, I was going to fucking cry. I felt the tears prick in my eyes and I rubbed them away with the heel of my hand. I squeezed my eyes shut.

Deep breath.

One. Two. Three.

Deep breath.

I opened my eyes, lingering on Maggie's face in front of me. It had been so long since I had seen her that I couldn't look away. But then I flipped back to the front of the book. And then I saw something that I hadn't noticed earlier. On the bottom corner of the inside cover, a piece of paper was taped to the leather.

It was from Maggie. Christ, she had written me a note. I wasn't sure I could read it. Not when I was already feeling like I had been run over by an eighteen-wheeler.

But I did anyway. As if I could ever resist her.

And I was glad that I did.

There is more beauty inside you than in anyone I have ever met. These pictures don't lie. I won't ever forget you. Or stop loving you. You can ask me to. You can tell me to move on. But I won't. And I never will. Just don't forget how beautiful we were. How beautiful we can still be. Please.
  Maggie

Ruby had looked away, sensing I needed a moment. Another round of deep breathing and I made myself close the scrapbook and put it on the table. Looking through that book was like ripping a Band-Aid off a barely healed wound. Letting the blood flow without even trying to stanch it. I didn't know what to do with this fresh round of emotional turmoil that I found myself in. Maybe I should write about it.

And maybe I should start wearing a fucking tutu and take up ballet.

"Thanks for bringing it, Ruby. I appreciate it." I gave her a hug and I really did mean what I said. As much as it had hurt, it had been a kind of necessary pain. Because Maggie was entirely too necessary in every aspect of my life.

Ruby and I were able to enjoy the rest of our time together without any more drama. Jacqui came back thirty minutes later and let us know that we'd have to wrap up our visit. "Where are you staying?" I asked Ruby as she gathered up her bag and we made our way to the office door.

"I've gotten a room at the Comfort Inn over by the airport. I have an early morning flight," Ruby said, going up on her tiptoes to kiss my cheek.

"I still can't believe you flew down here for one night. You're crazy. But awesome. Definitely awesome," I said with affection as Ruby looped her arm with mine. Jacqui and I followed Ruby out. And after a few more hugs, my amazing aunt got into her rental car and headed to her hotel.

The scrapbook felt like a weight in my hands.

chapter
six

clay

I went to my room, forgoing the movie playing in the common room. I was hoping to avoid my friends, needing to be alone. I practically fell onto my bed and threw an arm over my eyes. I wanted to sleep but knew that with the way my mind was whirling, that wouldn't happen.

So I sat up and pulled out Maggie's scrapbook, taking longer to go through the pages this time. Lingering over every picture. Making myself remember when I had drawn them and why. Forcing the memories that both tortured and thrilled me.

There were dozens of drawings depicting Maggie's face. I had never been able to get enough of drawing her. She was, and still is, my favorite subject. My eyes followed the slope of her jawline, the small divot in her chin. The tiny freckle above her lip that I remembered touching with my tongue. Her hair, thick and heavy in my hands as I moved it away from her neck so I could kiss the sensitive spot at the nape that would always make her shiver.

I looked up at the clock on the wall, and without allowing any time to talk myself out of the crazy idea that had just popped into my head, I got to my feet and headed out into the hallway.

I headed toward Jacqui's office again and knocked softly. "Come in," I heard her say on the other side. I opened the door and walked in. She looked up at me in surprise. "Clay, didn't I just see you?" she joked.

I gave her a tight smile, gearing myself up for the lie I was about to tell. "I wanted to know if I could call Lisa, Ruby's partner. She wasn't able to make it down and I wanted to thank her for my gifts," I said, proud and a little disappointed with how easily dishonesty still tripped off my tongue. But phone calls were limited to immediate family members and those deemed "integral members" of my support system. So the lie was necessary.

Jacqui smiled. "Of course. Do you have your calling card?" she asked me. I pulled the small paper card out of my pocket and held it up. "Well, come have a seat. I'll give you some privacy," Jacqui said kindly, getting up to leave her office.

"Thanks," I told her, reaching for the phone. Once I was alone and the office door closed behind Jacqui, I took a deep breath and quickly dialed the number burned into my brain. It started to ring and I had to stop myself from hyperventilating. Shit, I was really doing this. Why the fuck was I doing this? Maybe I should hang up.

Me and my dumb spontaneity. Hadn't I learned that it wasn't always smart to jump into the water with all my clothes on? To hang up or to not hang up, that really *was* the question. And how long was I going to sit here and debate with myself about it?

Yeah, I should just hang up. Doing this now, after such a long time, would only dredge up a mountain of shit. My finger twitched and hovered over the end button. And then it was too late.

Because I heard her voice and there was no longer a decision to be made. She still had me firmly by the balls. There was no way I could hang up. Not now.

"Hello?" Maggie's voice was breathy, as though she had to rush to get to her phone. I didn't say anything, rendered mute, goose bumps breaking out over my skin. God, this was a mistake. What the hell was I thinking?

"Hello?" she said again and I knew she was about to hang up. And the thought of her ending the phone call put me into a near panic.

"Hey," I said quietly. I could hear her quick intake of breath and then utter quiet. The phone buzzed in the silence as I waited for her to say something. Anything.

"Clay," Maggie finally said. She didn't say my name as a question but as a statement. And I noticed that her tone wasn't a happy one. Not the reception I'd hoped to have, but not unexpected.

"I just wanted to call and say . . . thank you. You know, for my gift. I loved it." I couldn't get my voice above the barest whisper. As if by speaking too loudly, it would shatter whatever this was.

Again Maggie was quiet for a while and I wasn't sure she was still there. But finally, after a few moments she said, "No problem. Glad you liked it." I wasn't deaf to the bitterness in her words. I hated it. I loathed the fact that it was directed at me.

I cleared my throat uncomfortably when it became obvious she wasn't going to say anything else. "Um . . . well . . . how have you been?" I asked lamely. Christ, had I really asked that? Why didn't I just ask her about the weather? Because irrelevant conversation seemed all I was capable of.

Maggie's sharp bark of laughter let me know that she too thought my question was a total joke. "How have I been? Before or after your Dear John letter? Oh, I've been just peachy, I'm so glad you asked." Her sarcasm was laced with a very obvious anger. Not that I didn't deserve it, but damn, it sucked.

"About that letter . . ." I don't know what I was about to say. Maybe try to explain that I never had any plans to let her go. That I loved her just as much as I ever had, if not more. That there wasn't a second of the day that went by that I didn't think about her. But I never got the chance.

Maybe I should tell her it was a lie. That I didn't want her to move on. That the thought of her with another guy made me physically ill. That the dozens of faceless jerks I envisioned her with each died a very painful death in my head.

Because *that* would go a long way in proving my improved mental health.

"Save it, Clay. I don't want to hear whatever it is you feel the need to say. You have no idea how I've wanted to hear your voice. But now . . . I just can't." The anger was gone and now she just sounded sad, and I hated that even more. I couldn't fix this. There was no way in hell Maggie would ever give me the chance to. I had messed up too badly.

It's what I had feared. The scenario that kept me awake at night. That even after I was able to get my life together, I wouldn't have her to share it with. And here it was, smacking me in the face. It was the nastiest reality check I had ever had.

"I'm sorry," I said into the silence. No two words had ever been truer. Or so completely inadequate. "Please know that. I . . . I love you, Maggie. Always," I said in a rush of desperation. I needed to say it. Needed her to hear it. If only one more time.

I could hear Maggie sigh. "I know you do, Clay. But that stopped being enough three months ago." Fuck, that hurt. And there went my heart breaking all over again.

"Yeah, I get that," was all I could say. I couldn't argue with her. She was right. Love had never been our problem. No, the issues rested entirely on my shoulders. So we sat there, listening to each other breathe for another few minutes as though we were both afraid to sever whatever tenuous connection we had in that moment.

"I've got to go, Clay," Maggie finally said. I rubbed my fist over my heart, feeling the constant dull ache kick up a notch into an almost unbearable pain. The finality of her words couldn't be any clearer.

"Okay," I replied, biting my tongue on the millions of other things I wanted to say. Because I knew it was useless. "Well, I'll . . . um . . . well, take care," I stuttered.

"Thanks. And, Clay?" Maggie said quickly before I could hang up. "Happy birthday," she whispered and then I heard the click indicating she had hung up.

"Thanks," I muttered to no one in particular before hitting the end button on the telephone. I gripped the phone in my hand and had to suppress the urge to smash it against the wall. But I loosened my hold and dropped it onto the table. I leaned back on the couch and covered my face with my hands.

Well, that went way worse than I pictured it in my head. Yeah, I can admit that I had clung to the delusion that Maggie would want to talk to me. That she would be over the moon to hear from me. What a fucking joke.

Sitting up, I pushed a pile of papers off the table, watching them flutter to the floor. Then I noticed the pair of scissors that had been underneath. Picking them up, I pressed the tip of my finger to the sharp edge and winced at the sudden slice of pain. And just like every other time before, I felt like I was in a tunnel and all I could focus on was the physical sensation of the slice. Anything to take away the pain inside. If I could focus on the other, the heartbreak wouldn't feel so bad.

I pushed my finger onto the blade of the scissors until I saw a bright blot of crimson come to the surface of my skin. It was fascinating, the way the blood rushed out and dripped down my knuckle. So I pushed a little harder and started to slide the scissors down the length of my finger. All the way to my palm. A straight line of perfect red. Pain, real and constant, flooded through me and for that brief time, it brought relief. It was only a shallow cut, barely bleeding. But it was enough.

"What the hell are you doing?" a voice called from the door-way and I dropped the scissors onto the table. I pulled a tissue from the box and deftly wrapped it around my finger, pressing into the cut, trying not to enjoy the bite I felt at the contact.

Maria was frowning, her arms crossed over her chest. She was staring pointedly at my hand, which I hastily shoved into the pocket of my jeans as I stood up. Now that my moment of weakness was over, I felt the shame and guilt that always accom-panied my cutting. I felt my complete failure for giving in to the urge.

"Maria. Hey. I just called Lisa—" I started, proud of how steady my voice sounded, but my friend cut me off.

"Cut the bullshit, Clay. If you were talking to Lisa, then I just got off the phone with the Pope. I'm not stupid." She glared at me. I walked over to her and nudged her playfully with my shoulder.

"It's all good," I said as convincingly as possible. Maria rolled her eyes in a way that was entirely too reminiscent of Maggie. I swallowed hard and clenched the hand in my pocket until my hurt finger started to throb again. Once I felt the pain, I felt the tightness in my chest ease up a bit.

This was so screwed up. Maggie used to be the one who kept me from cutting, and now she was the very one hurtling me toward it. I wanted to pull my hair and scream. I was so beyond sick of being this fucked-up guy!

Maria must have recognized my deadened expression because she didn't push me to explain what had happened. That was the cool thing about her; she had enough of her own darkness to know when to leave me alone with mine.

"Come on, let's go watch the rest of the movie. Nothin' like a little Will Ferrell to make things all better." Maria wrapped her arm around my waist and pulled me in the direction of the common room. I wasn't really up for company right now, but I let Maria pull me along anyway.

And the truth was I was sick and tired of living this fucked-up drama I called a life. Watching some stupid comedy might have been just the thing I needed. The thing to stop me from obsessing about Maggie May Young for the rest of the night. Because God knows that would only mean more cutting and more shame.

I had been doing so fucking well. Just when I thought I had turned a corner, I hit the wall at a hundred miles per hour. Enough of this shit! I forcibly put Maggie out of my mind, convincing myself that it was high time I moved on. Isn't that what I wanted for her? To have a normal life full of normal relationships? Something that made her happy?

Well, it was time I started wanting the good stuff for myself as well. And while I would never give up on my love for the girl in Davidson, Virginia, I had to try and learn to live my life without her in it. Because tonight's conversation made it very clear that a life together wasn't in the cards. Particularly while I was still far from being the person I wanted to be.

That phone call had been the ultimate test. And I had failed big-time. There would be no do-over. This was it. I had been obsessing since leaving Virginia about talking to Maggie again. How would she react? How would *I* react? Well, I had my answer. And if it wasn't the one I wanted, it was the one I was stuck with.

I could either wallow and whine about life not being fair, or I could suck it up and find something else to live for. And maybe, for once, it should be for myself.

A bunch of our friends called out greetings as Maria and I entered the common room. This was good. This was what I needed. I wrapped an arm around Maria and gave her a quick squeeze before letting her go.

She looked up at me and smiled. "I think you could use some leftover birthday cake," she said seriously and then laughed when Tyler and Greg piped up, stating that they wanted their own slices. Looking around the room, I was happy with this tiny bit of life I had carved out for myself at Grayson. I just wished I could take this with me when I left.

Because I wasn't so sure the life I had waiting for me on the outside was one that I wanted.

◆

"So you cut again," Dr. Todd said, steepling his fingers under his chin. It was the day after my birthday and I had come clean with my therapist. I had thought seriously about not telling him. About keeping it my nasty little secret.

But then I would be backsliding even more. And last night was all about revelations. I was through with sabotaging myself. Even as I had thought I was getting better, my ugly subconscious was lying in wait to fuck it all to hell. So I was taking this bitch by the horns and dealing with it.

I laced my fingers behind my neck and leaned back on the leather couch in Doc's office. "Yep. I did. And it felt good for about thirty seconds and then . . ." I trailed off, pulling my hands apart so I would stop stroking the scabbed cut with my thumb.

"Then . . ." Dr. Todd prompted. I blew out a breath and pushed my hair out of my face. I forced myself to make eye contact with the man who waited expectantly for my answer. There was no judgment there, no disappointment that I had relapsed. Only patience and understanding. Damn, this guy was good.

"And then I felt horrible about it. Mad at myself, you know?" I started to bounce my knees up and down. I was agitated and edgy. I had already gnawed the skin off around my fingers and had begun to pick at the hole in my jeans.

"Good," Dr. Todd said forcefully. I blinked at him in surprise. Huh? Had he just said it was good that I felt like shit? That didn't seem right.

"Excuse me?" I said a little angrily. Dr. Todd leaned forward, his eyes intense as he looked at me.

"I said *good*. I'm glad you felt like crap. That you were mad at yourself." I opened my mouth to say something that would have definitely been dickish, but Dr. Todd kept going. "Because if you're feeling horrible about it, then you're not feeling good because you did it. Yes, you felt the euphoria at first, but the fact that you started to feel the shame and guilt afterward proves that you are starting to rework the way your brain responds to the pain. That it's not the escape it used to be. You've reframed your feelings about cutting and that's a huge step, Clay." Dr. Todd smiled and I sat there sort of dumbstruck.

"But it doesn't change the fact that I cut. That I felt like cutting after talking to—" I stopped, realizing that I had yet to tell him about my late-night phone call last night.

Dr. Todd narrowed his eyes. "You called Maggie," he stated. I nodded. No sense in denying it. So I waited for the expected chastising. The millions of reasons why it was a bad idea to contact her. If she drove me to cut, I wasn't ready to communicate with her yet. Blah, blah, blah.

But damned if the good doc didn't surprise me once again.

"I'm glad." My mouth dropped open. I was extremely confused by this turn in things. Dr. Todd chuckled at my reaction. "I'm not going to berate you, Clay. I think you need to learn to face obstacles, not avoid them. You've been dealing with a lot of complicated emotions when it comes to Maggie. And for the first time, I feel like you're really taking charge of your life. You're finding your control."

"Uh, but I cut myself afterwards. Isn't that . . . I don't know, counterproductive or something?" I was looking for the punch line. The "Just kidding, you're a royal screwup." But it didn't come.

Dr. Todd picked up his notepad and pen and started writing. "Yes, you did. And you had a right to feel the anger, the hurt, the pain. Those emotions are *okay* because they're *yours*. You don't have to explain to anyone, let alone me, why you feel the way you do. And you met those feelings head-on, Clay. In the past you attempted to avoid any and all situations that elicited a strong emotional response from you. But you went headfirst into something that you knew would be hard for you. That takes courage. And you should be proud of the fact that you fought hard not to let your fear stop you from doing something you knew that you needed to do." Dr. Todd put the pen down and looked at me again. "It's important for you to try and not focus on the act of cutting, and instead look at the way you were feeling. Identify the triggers and figure out an alternate response. Let's review your self-harm plan and see if there's anything you could change or add."

We spent the next ten minutes going over the plan we had devised together in my first week of treatment. It outlined ways for me to cope that didn't involve self-harming behaviors. Okay, so I had been a bit of a shit when I had first written it. Because there was no way in hell I'd "pick flowers" or "hum a Mamas and Papas song." I was also pretty sure that Dr. Todd knew I had been mocking the whole process when we had compiled the list, because he wouldn't let me take things away, only add to it. It was damn embarrassing to see some of the crap I had put down because I was being a confrontational jackass. But I guess that was the reason I couldn't remove them. Touché, Dr. Todd. Touché.

"Thanks, Doc," I said sincerely, realizing we were at the end of our session. I picked up my journal and headed for the door. Dr. Todd followed me out. He clasped my shoulder, a first for him.

"I'm proud of you, Clay." And the validation was something I needed so desperately that I could have cried with the relief of it. I nodded my head and tucked my journal under my arm as I headed back to my room, feeling like things were clicking into place. Just the way they should be.

chapter
seven

i sat on the cold ground stretching out my legs, bending low over my knees until I could touch my skin with my nose. Maybe I was weird, but I loved to feel the burn in the back of my calves and thighs as my muscles were pulled taut. The late March afternoon was uncharacteristically cold. I could see my air puffing out in front of my lips as I tried to loosen up my body for track practice.

"Hey, Mags!" I looked up to see Daniel and the rest of the soccer team heading into the gym for their conditioning. I gave my friend a distracted wave as I got to my feet. I leaned down between my legs, resting my palms flat on the track surface, and counted to ten before raising my arms up over my head.

"Need any help?" Jake stopped in front of me, giving his signature flirty grin. I cocked an eyebrow but didn't respond. "I can get you to stretch muscles you didn't even know you had," he teased and I snorted.

"Please save your witty charm for someone it will actually work on." I shot him a pointed look and reached down to get my water bottle. Jake laughed. He was never put off by my abrasive attitude. I wasn't sure if that was comforting or just really obnoxious.

Jake came up beside me and took the bottle out of my hand and put it to his lips, taking a drink. He really had a problem with personal boundaries. Eating my food, drinking from my bottle—it was a habit I needed to break. Before I started breaking other things—like his kneecaps. "You wound me, Maggie," Jake teased, clutching his shirt over his heart.

I didn't bother to say anything, knowing that if I encouraged him he'd never stop and I had to start my training. There were some days I enjoyed the playful banter, but today wasn't one of them. I'd been in a horrible mood since last week.

Well, since Clay's out-of-the-blue phone call to be exact. I still couldn't believe he had actually called me after all this time. Though wasn't that what I was hoping would happen when I gave Ruby the present? Didn't I want that to elicit a response from him in some way?

Whatever my subconscious reasons, I still had been pissed by his attempt at casual. I had found it extremely insulting that he could call me after months. After everything we had been through together and ask me how I was doing! If he had been within smacking distance I would have done just that. My rage switch had been flipped and the only thing I wanted to do was hurt him. To wound him as deeply as he had wounded me.

Clay had always made me act irrationally.

So I had been bitchy and dismissive. And after I had hung up the phone I felt horrible all over again. I spent the rest of the night beating myself up for not trying to have a conversation with him. I had missed out on the opportunity to talk to him, to see how he was doing. How many times had I moaned about the fact that I just wanted to know he was okay?

But in those five minutes we had been on the phone, my pride had gotten the better of me and I had ruined my chance to restart a dialogue. To try and repair some of what had been broken.

It was too late now, though. Because I was damn sure Clay wouldn't bother calling me again. I mean why would he?

I was such a jerk.

"My mom called me a few minutes ago and told me I got my admission letter from the University of Virginia. It was thick," Jake was saying. I pulled myself out of my Clay obsession. Okay, I needed to come up with a friendly and supportive response here. But I was feeling anything but friendly and supportive. Maggie "bitch face" Young was out to play and I didn't see her taking a nap anytime soon.

"That's great, Jake," I said, cringing at how fake I sounded. Jake didn't seem to notice anything off about me. He just smiled and nodded. His good mood was sort of infectious. And I found myself smiling a bit more naturally this time.

"Have you heard back from JMU yet?" he asked me as I finished up my stretching. I had applied to James Madison University and then a handful of other in-state colleges as backup. JMU had a great track team and I was really hoping to get a sport scholarship.

But I hadn't heard back from them yet and I wouldn't be getting news from the other schools until sometime in April. I knew I should be a bit more anxious about the whole thing. But I just couldn't summon the energy to care. Sure, I played the part with my parents, engaging in endless discussions about SATs and campus tours. But the truth was my enthusiasm was sorely lacking. It didn't change the fact that I had a big decision to make in a few months.

It was just hard to talk about a future without the one thing I wanted most.

"Not yet," I said shortly, looking over my shoulder at Coach Kline, who was starting to round up the track team for a quick powwow before practice. "I've gotta go, Jake. Otherwise, Coach will make me run laps." I pulled my hair up into a ponytail and straightened my track shorts.

Jake nodded. "Yeah, I've got to get into the weight room. But before I go . . ." His voice trailed off and he seemed suddenly interested in his shoes. I looked at him impatiently.

"What is it, Jake? Seriously, I've got to get going," I said sharply. I didn't mean to be rude, but I didn't have time for his nervous rambling.

Jake sighed heavily. "Damn, Maggie, you really know how to cut a guy's balls off." He laughed uncomfortably. I chuckled but started to tap my foot, letting him know his time was running short.

"Okay, shit, I guess I'll just spit it out. You wanna go out this weekend?" Jake asked in a rush. His question was like a punch to the gut. Crap! Crap, crap! I should have seen this coming. I had taken his patient understanding for granted, it seemed. I knew he liked me; I had just really hoped I wouldn't have to turn him down. I liked Jake. A lot. I just wasn't prepared to like him as anything more than a friend.

Jake instantly took my silence as a rejection, and the look of hurt on his face made me feel horrible. "It's okay, Maggie. I get it. I just wish . . . never mind." He ran his hand over his short red hair.

"You just wish what, Jake?" I asked, trying not to be irritated with him for putting us both in the awkward situation we found ourselves in. But I was mostly irritated with myself. Maybe I had been leading him on. Being too flirty. Yeah, this was probably my fault. Crap, crap, crap!

"You need to get over that guy, Maggie. It's been months. He's not coming back. But you're acting like he's the only one out there. I mean, even if you don't want to date me, you shouldn't rule out every other guy who isn't Clay Fucking Reed!" Jake said in frustration and I clenched my teeth. Okay, so now he was pissing me off.

"Wow, thanks for your support. Glad to know what you really think of me. Sorry if I'm not moving on at a pace that is agreeable to you. Look, I've got to go. I don't have time for this." I started to turn away but Jake grabbed my arm, stopping me.

I snatched my arm back and glared at him. Jake grimaced and dropped his hand. "Damn it, Maggie, I'm not trying to be a dick here. I just want to see you happy. It's time to let yourself— Fuck it, never mind. Forget I said anything. See you around." Jake hefted his gym bag onto his shoulder and started toward the school.

I don't know what made me do it, but I yelled out, "Fine, Jake! I'll go out with you." What was I saying? I felt possessed by the impulse to prove him wrong. To show him and everyone else that I wasn't going to spend my life moping over a boy who had thrown me away. It was humiliating and I was sick and tired of being the pathetic girl who had been dumped by her crazy boyfriend.

Jake shook his head. "Forget it, Maggie. I don't want you going because you feel bad for me or something. I just thought we could go out and have a good time, that's all." I closed the distance between us and put my hand on his arm.

"No, really, Jake, I'd like to go. You're right. I'm done with the sad-girl act. But you'd better plan something good," I warned good-naturedly, smiling. Jake smiled back at me.

"You got it, Mags." And then he leaned down and kissed my cheek, his lips lingering on my skin. I flushed and backed away, not sure how I felt about all of this. "I'll call you tonight, okay?" Jake said as I headed back to the track.

I only nodded and waved good-bye. I couldn't let myself think about what I had just agreed to and what that meant for me. I threw myself into track practice. I was running the sixteen-hundred- and thirty-two-hundred-meter this year. After flaking out so much during cross country, I was determined to show Coach Kline that I really did kick ass.

So I ran. Not fast, but I ran far. I was pleased at how my endurance had increased and I found that I was able to run the thirty-two-hundred-meter in a record eleven minutes. That was incredible! I had beaten my best time by a minute. I felt good and the closest to happy I had been in a while.

Coach Kline was pleased and made sure to heap praise on me before I left. As I walked out to my car, I saw Daniel and Jake headed to Danny's truck. "Mags!" Daniel called out, waiting for me to catch up.

I smiled at him and then gave Jake a shy grin. I felt a little strange around him, now that he had asked me out and I had agreed. But he simply tugged on my ponytail and grinned as though nothing had changed between us.

"We're headed to Bubbles, you wanna come?" Daniel asked. I tensed up at the suggestion. I hadn't been to Bubbles since . . .

You know what? Fuck this. "Yeah, I could use a banana split," I said almost defiantly. Though who I was defying I wasn't entirely sure. Was I defying Clay? Myself? The memory of the hundreds of banana splits I had shared with my ex-boyfriend? God, how ridiculous was that?

So I followed them to the restaurant and I ordered the banana split with extra whipped cream. And I ate every last bite. "Jeesh, girl, you were hungry," Jake teased as I scooped up the last bit of ice cream and put it into my mouth.

I felt faintly nauseous with the amount of food I had just consumed. I had never finished one of Bubbles' banana splits by myself before. But damned if I hadn't made it my mission to eat that entire one. It was like I was proving something to myself. Like if I could do this, I could really start to move on with my life.

Though I think all I got out of it was feeling like I needed to puke all over the table.

Daniel only shook his head as I dropped the spoon into the bowl with a loud clang. I met his eyes and dared him to say anything about my gross display of overeating. But he just smirked and finished his hamburger.

Jake tapped my foot with his under the table. I looked at him and grinned sheepishly. "I think I might have overdone it," I admitted, feeling my stomach roll in revolt.

"That was pretty impressive," Jake said, pushing his half-eaten sundae aside. "So what do you think about going to see a movie on Saturday? We could hit the IMAX in Charlottesville," Jake suggested, and I wanted to groan as Danny's head popped up.

"You guys have plans this weekend?" Daniel asked, raising his eyebrows at me. I'd be interrogated about this later. If not by Daniel, then by Rachel. Separate they were dangerous; now, as a unified team, they were darn near lethal.

"Yeah, we do," I told him sharply, shooting daggers in his direction with my eyes. If he embarrassed me, I'd flipping kill him.

"That's cool. Can Rachel and I join you? Make it a group thing?" Daniel asked, and my irritation dissolved at my relief at not having to sit awkwardly through a datelike situation with Jake.

Daniel raised his eyebrows at me and I knew his suggestion wasn't a spur-of-the-moment idea. My best friend knew me so well. And I too often underestimated what he would do to make me happy. He really was a good guy, even if he tried to hide it under douchey armor way too often.

Jake shrugged his shoulders, though I could tell he was less than thrilled with our date crashers. But Jake too was a decent guy and would never let on to his disappointment. "Sounds good. We can figure out what we want to do at lunchtime. Cool?" Jake looked at me and I gave him a thumbs-up.

"I'm sure Rach and I can find some sappy chick flick to drag you guys to. I'm thinking Zac Efron or, oh, I know, what about the movie with Robert Pattinson! A theater full of squealing women will be awesome!" I clapped my hands. Daniel laughed, knowing I was full of it. There was no way I could subject *myself* to a chick flick, let alone anyone else.

"Whatever, we'll discuss tomorrow. I've got to pick Rachel up from work. Come on, Jake." We each slid out of the booth and paid our tickets. Jake tried to pay for mine but I staunchly refused. We were not a couple, and even though we were going on a quasi-date this weekend, it didn't mean I had to throw myself headfirst into coupledom. I was so *not* ready for that.

"See you guys tomorrow," I called out as I made my way to my car. For the first time in as long as I could remember, I was feeling pretty good. The funk I had found myself in after Clay's phone call was finally receding. And while I was nervous about where things were headed with Jake, I wasn't overly freaked out about it either. Even the sound of my engine struggling to turn over couldn't darken my mood.

This could only mean that things were finally looking up for me. The clouds were parting and I could finally see the sun again. I took a deep breath, feeling the cold air burn my lungs, and I felt like smiling. Just because.

I was surprised to see both Mom and Dad's cars in the driveway when I got home. Mom typically worked crazy hours and it was Dad's bowling night. He and a few of the other librarians had formed a league a few months ago, complete with shirts with their team name, The Bookish Bowlers, embroidered on the back. I had blown snot balls when he had shown them to me. My dad hadn't been amused when I begged for a T-shirt of my own. He knew it wasn't for my love of bowling or librarians, that's for sure.

I dropped my keys on the table inside the front door. "Hello?" I said, walking into the living room.

"In the kitchen, Maggie. Can you come in here, please?" my mom called out. I didn't like the sound of her voice and my good mood evaporated instantly and anxious nerves took its place in the pit of my stomach.

I walked into my brightly lit kitchen that seemed in such contrast to the dark looks my parents wore. They both sat at the kitchen table, hands folded in an almost identical way. If they hadn't looked so serious, I would have laughed.

"Uh, is everything okay?" I asked, moving to sit in the vacant chair at the table. My dad looked to my mother, who gave me what I'm sure was meant to be a reassuring smile. Instead it looked strained and uncomfortable.

"Well, honey, I heard some bad news a little while ago," Mom said uncertainly. I took a deep breath.

"Well, what was it?" I asked, feeling the sick sense of dread thick in my throat. My mother sighed and covered my hand with hers.

"It's about Lisa McCabe," she began and I blinked at the unexpected direction of the conversation. Ruby's Lisa? I frowned in confusion.

"What's up with Lisa?" I asked with some hesitation, knowing on an instinctual level that I wouldn't like what she had to tell me.

My mom squeezed my hand. "Lisa was involved in a car crash on I-81 early this morning," she said softly. I stiffened.

"Is she okay?" I asked quietly, already knowing by the looks on both her and my father's faces exactly what her next words would be.

Dad shook his head. "Lisa ran her own media production company out of Charlottesville, right?" my dad asked me and I nodded. "Apparently she was headed home after working most of the night and fell asleep behind the wheel. She hit a guardrail and flipped her vehicle. She died on impact." I sucked in a breath and closed my eyes. God, how awful!

I instantly felt guilty for letting my relationship with Lisa and Ruby dissolve. I had been trying so hard to put distance between me and everything and everyone Clay-related. But that hadn't been fair of me. Particularly when Lisa and Ruby had done nothing but love and support me. And Lisa had cared deeply about Clay. She had wanted to help him so badly.

I thought about her visit to the coffee shop just a few weeks ago. I couldn't wrap my mind around the fact that that was the last time I would ever see her.

"I should call Ruby. Go see her. Something," I said. This would kill Ruby. I had always thought her relationship with Lisa had been beautiful. Theirs was a love that would last forever. It was so wrong that their forever hadn't lasted nearly long enough.

I got to my feet. I knew I had to do something. I just wasn't sure what. My grief for Lisa was a heavy thing. My mom and dad came quickly to my side, both putting their arms around my shoulders, holding me up from either side. "We can go see her together, Maggie. See if there's anything we can do to help. Ruby is such a lovely woman," my mom said, and I leaned into her, grateful for the comfort.

And then I thought of the other person who would be affected by this sudden tragedy. A person who couldn't afford to be blindsided by the pain this would cause. Someone who I knew was barely holding it together as it was. The knife in my gut this time wasn't for me, or for Ruby. It belonged entirely to Clay, who I knew would be hurting beyond anything I could imagine.

"Thanks, Mom, Dad," I whispered, unable to find my voice. My dad kissed the top of my head and went over to the electric kettle, pulling out my favorite chamomile tea to make me a cup. My mom went to the cupboard and started pulling ingredients out and putting them on the counter. I recognized the items needed for her seven-cheese casserole. What was it about death that ignited the need to cook? It seemed so trivial in the face of such a terrible thing. But I supposed it was more about feeling useful. Even if that filled our own needs more than anyone else's.

"I'm gonna get some air," was all I could say, and I found myself pushing through the back door and out into the yard. I swept the bangs off my forehead and dropped my head back, staring at the sky. All I could think of was Clay. Clay. Clay. Clay.

He never seemed to catch a break. My heart broke all over again for the boy I loved deeply and with every fiber of my being. I couldn't stop myself from obsessing about how he would handle the news. Would it undo all of the progress he'd made? Would he be able to come back from the grief? He loved Lisa like a mother. She and Ruby had been all that he had in the way of supportive and caring family. This had the potential to destroy him all over again.

And then my mind ground to a halt at a sudden realization. He would be coming back to Davidson. Shit, of course he would be. I shook my head, gripping my hair at the scalp. I couldn't think about that. *Wouldn't* think about what that would mean for me when I saw him again. Because it was supremely selfish to worry about my own feelings when Ruby and Clay had lost so much.

I pulled out my phone and dialed Ruby's number. I didn't know what I would say. Words seemed useless at the moment. And I hated how relieved I was when I got her voice mail. My eyes burned with tears at the sound of the silly message she and Lisa used as their greeting. I sniffled and wiped my eyes just as the beep ended.

"Ruby. It's Maggie. I, uh, I just wanted to call and tell you how . . . *sorry* I am. God, I'm so very sorry." I choked on the words and had to stop. I tried to calm down so I could get out the rest of what I wanted to say.

"I just wanted you to know if you need anything. Please call. I loved Lisa. She was such a wonderful person. I'm just so sorry," I ended on a whisper. And I couldn't speak anymore so I just hung up.

My head dropped, my chin hitting my chest. My phone fell from my hand to the ground and I was lost in my feelings of sadness for a life cut short and for the impact it would have on the person I loved the most.

chapter
eight

clay

The day began like any other. My alarm went off at seven. I got out of bed and took a shower. After eating a barely edible breakfast, I headed for my first group session. Today's topic was on building your support systems. I was engaged and focused. Because I was Clayton Reed, Super Patient!

Then I attended school for two hours. I completed my biology paper and started working on an essay on the short story "A Rose for Emily" for my American lit assignment. I had never particularly enjoyed school. I hated the crowded hallways and people way too up in your business. But now, having a seven-hour school day crammed into two, I missed the luxury of going from class to class. I hated the breakneck pace of reading and writing, trying to shove an entire education into such a short time.

But I was kicking ass. I had never cared about doing well. Do my homework? Fuck that. Pay attention to my teachers' lectures? No way. But now, with my head more in the game than it used to be, I was finally taking the whole education thing seriously.

I was determined to be the poster child for a postbreakdown lifestyle. Look at me, I can go to school, talk about my feelings, *and* be a productive member of society. Suck that, Mom and Dad!

I finished my assignments and had lunch. Maria and Tyler were still in group and Susan was in her therapy session. So it was only Greg and me. Which was cool. Greg was a pretty funny guy, giving new meaning to the word *crazy*. Because, man, did Greg fit the stereotype of a mental patient. Or maybe he was channeling someone from *One Flew Over the Cuckoo's Nest*.

You'd think he had Tourette's with the stuff that came out of his mouth. But nope, he just had zero filter. He could tell someone to fuck off right after explaining why the global economy was failing. You could be scared of him or just roll with it. I had to admit I did a bit of both.

So, like I said, the day was like every other since I had come to Grayson. I should have known that the moment things started to resemble normal the floor was going to drop out from underneath me.

I was in my room. Tyler was still at lunch, having come in as I was leaving. So I was trying to enjoy this rare piece of solitude by taking a nap before my next support group. I was just about to nod off when there was a knock at my door.

I tried not to growl as I said, "Come in." Jonathan entered and I could tell instantly that something was wrong. I sat up and put my feet on the floor.

"Dr. Todd needs to see you," he said, giving me a smile that held too much sympathy for my peace of mind.

"Why? What's going on?" I asked combatively. I hated secrets. They were dangerous, with way too much potential for fallout. Being called to your therapist's office outside of your normal meetings didn't bode well.

I thought back over my behavior in the last week and a half but came up short. Surely I wasn't about to be punished for something.

After my freak-out over calling Maggie, I had tried really hard to get my shit back under control. And I thought I had done a damn good job of it. So why was the good doc calling me in for a special meeting?

Jonathan only shrugged but didn't say anything. That pissed me off. Mostly because I was starting to lose it. Because I could tell by the look on his face that he *did* know what this was about. And that whatever it was, was best heard from my shrink.

This *was not* good.

So I followed Jonathan to Dr. Todd's office and waited while he knocked on the door. He poked his head inside and I could hear him tell Dr. Todd that I was here. Jonathan put a hand on my shoulder after turning back to me. "Head on in. I'll come by and see you later." Fuck me, this was bad. Really, really bad.

I didn't acknowledge Jonathan's words in any way, just moved past him to go into Dr. Todd's office. I closed the door behind me and faced my therapist, surprised to see Julie, Sabrina, and Matt, the other therapists at the center, also in the room. Dr. Todd pulled his chair from behind the desk so that he was sitting in front of it. He then motioned for me to have a seat on the couch.

Matt moved over to make room for me and I tried not to get defensive in reaction to the obvious concern on each of their faces. But self-control was not my strong suit.

"Enough already. Just tell me what the fuck is going on," I bit out sharply, sitting down heavily and crossing my arms over my chest. I was mad. And worried. So that made me even angrier.

Dr. Todd's neutral expression didn't seem to change, though I did notice a tightening around his eyes, as though he were steeling himself to say something he knew I wouldn't like. God, if I wasn't already crazy, the endless speculation in my head of what I was about to hear would most definitely make me that way.

"Clay, we received a call from Ruby a little while ago." I *hated* it when people started a statement by saying my name. I know I looked surprised, because Dr. Todd's placid face broke into an uncharacteristic grimace.

I shot looks at the other therapists and they all looked at me expectantly. Shit, what did they think I was going to do?

"There was an accident yesterday morning," Sabrina said softly, as though trying to soothe a wild animal. I got to my feet in a panic.

"Is Ruby okay? What the hell happened?" I could hear the rising hysteria in my voice. If they didn't start giving me some answers, I was going to rip the place apart. Dr. Todd must have seen the panic on my face, because he got to his feet and was by my side in an instant. He put his hands heavily on my shoulders, pressing down slightly.

"Take a deep breath, Clay." His voice carried just enough authority that I listened without wanting to punch him in the face. I tried to breathe in through my nose and out through my mouth, but my thoughts were getting in the way of it.

"Just tell me, please," I begged, figuring if rage wasn't getting them talking, then pleading would. Dr. Todd continued to press down on my shoulders. I knew he was trying to "ground" me. It was meant to create the "chill" effect, triggering the body's ability to relax and calm down. Right now it wasn't doing shit.

"It's about Lisa. She was involved in a car accident," Dr. Todd said softly, steadily. My whole body tensed up, as if bracing myself for a blow.

"Is she all right?" I croaked out. My eyes became blurry and the doc's next words seemed to reach me through a thick fog.

"Lisa didn't make it . . . I'm so sorry, Clay," Dr. Todd said, his voice clear and strong. I blinked a few times, not sure I heard him correctly.

"Lisa didn't make it?" I asked for clarification. No, that couldn't be right. I had just spoken to Lisa this past weekend. She had given me a bunch of crap about watching *The Notebook*, even though I had very little choice in the movies the center showed. But Lisa had loved every minute of teasing me about it. And then I had made fun of her new biker boots. It had been a great conversation, with her promising to come down with Ruby when I was discharged from Grayson in two weeks.

Dr. Todd nodded, his hands still firm on my shoulders. "No, Clay. She didn't," he confirmed. My heart bottomed out and I felt sick. What the fuck? Matt appeared beside me, not touching me, but the act was meant to be supportive.

What I felt was freaking smothered. "Back the hell off. Please." I tried to sound threatening, but instead I only sounded weak and broken. Matt tentatively took me by the elbow and tried to steer me to the couch.

"Have a seat, Clay. We can talk if you want." I wrenched my arm away and backed up. I dug my fingers into my hair and started to pull. The familiar sensation of falling apart tickled the edges of my consciousness.

"Clayton. Sit down now." Dr. Todd's words were perhaps more harsh than the situation warranted, but he knew that I responded to his authority on a basic level. I don't know why, but his firm voice cut through the noise in my head. The man didn't have MD after his name for nothing.

I sat down heavily and vaguely heard Sabrina direct me to focus on my breathing. Fuck that! They could take their breathing and shove it up their asses. Who the hell were they to tell me to calm down when I had just found out one of the only three people I had ever loved was dead?

Fuck . . . Lisa was dead. That was the kind of forever I wanted nothing to do with. I just wanted to wake up and realize this was a bad dream. I started to pinch my arm, liking the pain but knowing it meant that, yep, I was definitely awake.

I covered my face with my hands and leaned my elbows on my knees, trying to stop the invading panic attack. No one touched me. Nobody spoke. The only sound was from the constant ticking of Dr. Todd's clock on the wall.

I don't know how long I stayed like that. It could have been minutes. Hours, even. Who the fuck knows? But I finally looked up and saw that the four other people in the room hadn't moved. They all looked ready, poised, and waiting for my inevitable meltdown.

Well, I hated to disappoint them, because that just wasn't going to happen. "I want to call Ruby," I said, proud of how steady I was. Matt and Sabrina got up.

"We'll come by and see you in a little while," Matt assured me. I didn't nod. I didn't do shit. I just wanted them to leave. Sabrina squeezed my shoulder and I wanted to smack her hand away. I had never felt condescended to at Grayson. But right now, I felt like the epitome of the mental patient. Everyone was walking on eggshells around me and it made me want to scream.

Once the other therapists left the room, Dr. Todd picked up the phone on his desk and held out the receiver for me to take. "Clay, Ruby is going to be grieving. She is in a horrible place right now. Be prepared for what that will do to you. Be aware of your own triggers and I'll help you deal with them, all right?" He stared me straight in the eye and I took the phone from his hand.

"Yeah. Okay," I muttered. I quickly dialed Ruby's cell phone number and waited. I heard it ring. And ring. And ring. Finally, when I was just about to hang up, I heard the click of the call connecting. Ruby's hello sounded hollow.

"Aunt Ruby," I got out, my voice cracking. I heard her broken sob on the other end.

"Clay, honey. I'm so glad you called," Ruby said through gasping breaths. And then she started crying. I was paralyzed. I didn't know what to do. I wasn't used to playing the role of comforter. My entire life, these roles had been reversed. It was Ruby picking up the pieces and trying to put me together again.

I didn't know how to do the same for her. And I felt horrible because of it. I felt useless. So I did the only thing I could. I let her cry while I let out my own tears. "I don't know what I'm going to do, Clay," Ruby whispered, her voice hoarse.

My head was a mess. I couldn't get my thoughts together. I was in shock, I knew that. My body felt numb and I couldn't focus. But I needed to say something. "I'm coming home," was all I said.

"I . . . Clay . . . no, you have to think about yourself right now. Lisa wouldn't want you to compromise your treatment," Ruby argued and I immediately cut her off.

"Stop it, Ruby, I'm coming home. I need to be there." My throat constricted and I put my head on the top of the desk. I wasn't sure it was the best decision for me. But there was no other choice to make. Of course I'd go.

"Thank you. So much. I just don't know what to do . . . so many things to think about." Ruby started crying again and I hated being a thousand miles away.

"I'll be there soon," I promised before we got off the phone. I told Ruby I'd call her when I'd arranged a flight. After hanging up I turned to Dr. Todd, not sure if I was going to get into a fight about my leaving. But the truth was I didn't care. Nothing would stop me from getting on a plane to Virginia.

"I want to buy a plane ticket," I said shortly. Dr. Todd looked at me steadily and simply nodded.

"I can arrange for you to do that," he replied, getting on the phone and calling Louis, the daytime administrator, giving me permission to use the Internet to secure a flight.

"I need to go back to my room and get my wallet. I need my credit card," I said, knowing how wobbly I sounded.

"This is a lot to take in, Clay. After you make your flight reservation, go to your room, take the afternoon off. Get some rest. Give Louis your itinerary and he'll make sure it gets to me. But I'd like to meet first thing in the morning." I only nodded. There was nothing else to say.

So I went through the motions. I was able to get a flight from Miami International to Dulles for tomorrow evening. Twenty-four hours and I would be back in Virginia. I couldn't allow myself to think about what that would mean for me. I was only focused on the new gaping hole in my heart.

Because Lisa, my aunt's girlfriend—tough as nails but with a heart of gold—was dead. Christ. I had never been able to handle grief and change in any sort of healthy way. My first instinct was to hurt myself. Dig deep into my skin and watch myself bleed. Or get so wasted that thinking wasn't an option. It would be so easy to lose myself in something like that. I wet my lips with my tongue, practically salivating at the thought.

No! Goddamn it, no! I started to pace the floor of my room. As though wearing a hole in my floor would do something. After that accomplished absolutely nothing, I tried to lie down and close my eyes. Nothing was helping. I tried to remember those super awesome coping skills that were supposed to get me through the hard stuff.

Squeezing my eyes shut, I tried to reframe. When that didn't help I started to feel pretty desperate. I needed something to distract me from finding something either sharp and pointy or pharmaceutical. Opening my eyes, I saw the bag of birthday stuff in the corner. I had yet to put my gifts away, so they still sat in the same spot where I had left them.

I stuck my hand inside and purposefully made myself move past the scrapbook to grab ahold of my sketch pad and pencils. I sat down at my desk and turned on the lamp. Popping in my earbuds, I scrolled through my music until I found some Apocalyptica and cranked it. Then I started drawing. Sketch after sketch, I poured everything out of me through my fingers and onto the paper.

Hours passed and I was still drawing. Tyler had come in and tried to talk to me but I ignored him. He knew me well enough to leave it alone. Maria had stopped by, obviously having heard about Lisa, but I ignored her as well. I didn't drop my pencil for a moment. I was like a man possessed.

I stopped sometime around midnight. Pictures littered the surface of my desk and the only light came from the soft glow of my lamp. I could hear Tyler's steady breathing and knew the aide on duty would soon be coming around to check on everyone.

I started to leaf through the sketches and realized I couldn't even remember what I had been drawing. I had let my emotions take over, and it worked. I had been able to channel my self-destructive needs into something *else*.

There were drawings of trees and fields. A few of the ocean and more than a dozen of Lisa. Lisa with Ruby. Lisa reading a book. Lisa cooking dinner. I took these and bundled them together. I would give them to Ruby.

I started to pile up the rest when I realized what else I had drawn in my frenzy. Of course, I should have known that when I put pencil to paper, her face would materialize. It always did.

I touched the curve of Maggie's cheek that I had carefully and precisely depicted. Her eyes were closed, as if in pain. And I couldn't ignore what going back to Davidson would mean for me. I would be ripping open the wound that I had worked really hard to stitch closed. Even if the sutures were only now starting to heal.

I sighed and shoved the pictures into my desk drawer and turned off the lamp. Crawling into bed, I curled in on myself and fought against the personal demons that threatened to ruin my life.

chapter
nine

clay

I stuffed clothes into my suitcase. I'm not sure why, but I started putting everything inside. My pictures, my books, everything. I had every intention of coming back after the funeral, but something inside me told me to be prepared.

"So you're leaving, huh?" I looked over my shoulder to see Maria standing in the doorway, hands shoved into the pockets of her hoodie. Her smile was hesitant and I could tell she was unhappy.

"Yeah, my plane leaves at six thirty," I answered her, turning back to the pile on my bed. Maria didn't say anything else and she didn't come any farther into my room. When I was finished, I closed the lid to my suitcase and zipped it. I heaved it off the bed, and it fell to the floor with a thud. I ran my hands through my hair and knew it was sticking up all over the place, but I didn't give a shit.

I had slept like crap. My eyes were gritty and tired. My mind was fuzzy and my mouth felt dry. I felt like I had been run over. Maria leaned against the jamb and watched me quietly. "You coming back?" she asked, looking around my now very bare room. Tyler's side was still a wreck, but mine was devoid of any sign that I had ever occupied it.

"I plan on it," I said unconvincingly. Because I knew, even then, that it would be hard to leave once I got home. Not when Ruby needed me. But I had promised myself that I still had to make my treatment a priority, for the remaining time I had. Priorities had a way of changing, though.

"Yeah, but that doesn't mean you will," Maria said with a sad resignation.

"Maria. Look . . ." I started, but she held up her hand, stopping me.

"I get it, Clay. You don't have to explain. I just wanted to let you know how sorry I am about Lisa. She was really cool. I'm glad I got to hang out with her when she came down here. I wish I could be there for you. We all do. We'll be thinking of you," Maria said softly, smiling wistfully.

"Thanks. I really needed to hear that," I told her truthfully. I was running on autopilot right now, not sure what the hell I was going to do when my plane touched down in Virginia. I had called Ruby that morning to let her know I would be flying in tonight. She insisted on coming to get me, even when I argued that I could take a bus. She wouldn't hear of it, saying she needed to be the one to do it. I didn't try to talk her out of it. There was no point. She'd be there to get me, no matter what. She had always been there for me. And that wouldn't stop just because her life had detonated.

Maria came over to me and wrapped her arms around my waist. I slowly brought my arms up to hug her back. She rested her cheek on my chest and I lowered my chin to the top of her head. We stood that way for a while until I pulled away.

Maria took my hand between hers and held on. "I'll miss you," she confessed, looking embarrassed for some reason. I squeezed her hands before pulling away.

"You too." I smiled at her and she tried to smile back. I looked at the clock on the wall and realized I had to get to my meeting with Dr. Todd. "I've got to get going. You want to meet up for lunch?" I asked her, feeling strange with the tension in the room. I wasn't exactly sure what this was, but I just knew I had to get away from it.

Maria meant well, but I knew how much she had come to depend on our friendship. And I just couldn't handle worrying about what that would mean for her when I left. I didn't like having anyone dependent on me for their happiness. Because that hadn't worked out so well the last time it had happened.

"Sure," she said, taking note of the way I moved away from her. She respected my need for space and let me walk away. I hurried to Dr. Todd's office and he was already waiting for me.

"Clay. How are you?" he asked after I closed the door behind me. I only shrugged as I sat down.

"I'm not really sure," I answered. Dr. Todd nodded.

"That's understandable. You've gone through a lot in the last twelve hours." Dr. Todd crossed his arms over his chest. "How long are you planning to be in Virginia?" he asked me.

I knew the question was coming, I just wish I knew how to answer him. "I don't know. I don't think Ruby has even started making funeral arrangements yet. I planned on getting there and then I guess I'll just have to see." I was being purposefully vague. Because the truth was I had no idea what to expect.

"I get that. I really do. But Clay, I'm okay with this visit because I know how important it is for you and your healing to be there for Ruby. I *am* concerned about how this will impact your ongoing progress, though. I can't lie." I rubbed the space between my eyebrows, feeling the beginnings of a headache.

"I know, Dr. Todd. But last night, instead of cutting, I spent hours drawing. Even with everything going on. So that's something, right? But regardless, I need to go." My statement left no room for argument. I was getting on that plane at six thirty, and there was nothing Dr. Todd or anyone else could say to change my mind.

Dr. Todd lifted his hands in a placating gesture. "I know, Clay. But we still need to make some plans, should things get difficult for you while you're there. You've worked too hard and come too far. This trip will test you in every possible way. Given the circumstances you find yourself in, anticipate old patterns to start becoming extremely appealing. We have only started examining the way your mind reacts to stressors. The nature of this visit will be mentally and emotionally taxing. Being here at Grayson is like living in a bubble. Once leaving it, a lot of people have a hard time with the adjustment. And I expect that to be magnified exponentially given your situation."

Shit, he wasn't pulling any punches. "I know! You're not telling me anything I haven't already thought about." I wasn't going into this thing blind. For the first time in my life I was entering a situation with my blinders off. Sure, I was freaked out a bit. I'd be an idiot not to be. But I wasn't going to let my fear stop me from being there for Ruby.

"Good, being prepared is essential. But, Clay, I'd like you to check in with me daily while you're in Davidson. That way if things come up, you have a means of processing them." I tried not to feel insulted by the suggestion. I didn't need a goddamned babysitter.

I ran my hand over my arms in agitation, feeling the ridges of old scars. Okay, so maybe a babysitter wasn't such a bad idea.

"Sure, I'll call you." Dr. Todd picked up a file on his desk, pulled a paper out, and handed it to me. It was my no-harm contract.

"Take this with you, read it, remember it." I folded up the sheet and put it into my back pocket. He was really covering all the bases here.

"Thanks, Doc, I appreciate it. I honestly don't know how long I would have lasted if I hadn't come here." I hadn't really expressed my gratitude for the staff at Grayson. But it seemed important that I say it now.

"It's what we're here for," was all Dr. Todd said in reply. I got to my feet. "Jacqui will give you your medications before you leave this evening. And if you need anything, Clay, anything at all, know that you can call either me or the other staff here, day or night. Someone will always be here." His words were reassuring and it made me feel less alone.

"Thanks," I said again before leaving.

The rest of the day was spent going to group and finishing up the homework I had yet to complete. I hung out with Tyler and Greg. Had lunch with Maria. I was trying to work up the courage to leave the place that had provided the safety and security I had so desperately needed for the last three months.

Even though I had imagined what it would be like to finally leave the center, the reality was a hell of a lot different from what I thought it would be. This is not the way I wanted to be leaving. Even with my intentions of coming back, it didn't change that I was walking out the door into a world that was vastly different from when I'd left it.

✦

Thirty minutes before I was due to head to the airport to catch my flight, Sabrina came to get me. "Your mother is on the phone and is asking to speak to you," she informed me, leading me to her office. I closed my eyes and clenched my fists. What the fuck did she want? Though deep down, I knew exactly what she wanted.

I picked up the phone and gritted my teeth. "Hi, Mom," I said shortly. Sabrina had left her office but kept the door open. I had a feeling she was listening carefully to this particular conversation. It was no secret that my parents were like an emotional bomb for me. There was no telling how I'd react.

"What's this I hear about you flying to Virginia? That is completely unacceptable!" her frosty voice cut through the line.

"Nice to hear from you, Mom," I replied sarcastically. She completely ignored my statement.

"You are not going to Virginia. How could you even think of doing something so stupid? After everything you put your father and I through with your little suicide attempt! And now you're trying to ruin everything all over again! Do you have no self-respect?" She sounded disgusted. And I'm sure she was. I wish I didn't care. And some part of me had learned to stop being so hung up in my desire for her approval.

But that didn't completely drown out that small part of me that did still care. And that part of me needed to be cut the hell out. Forcibly if necessary.

"Ruby needs me. I'm sure you've heard about Lisa. Aren't you planning on attending the funeral?" I don't know why I bothered to ask such a ridiculous question. Neither of my parents had ever approved of Lisa's or Ruby's "lifestyle." But I guess I had some bizarre hope that family ties would mean more than misplaced morals. That my mother would care enough about her sister's grief to put aside her judgments and to be supportive.

"I don't think that would be appropriate. Not with your father running for Congress this year. What would it look like if the conservative candidate attended the funeral of . . . a *homosexual*?" She said the word as though it were something dirty. God, what a bitch.

"It would look like the two of you had a heart. Even if it was a lie," I said angrily, hating that I allowed her to get under my skin like that.

"Enough with the dramatics, Clayton. You will not be going anywhere. You are in treatment. You cannot afford to leave right now. You could relapse. Because I can assure you if there is another embarrassing *incident*, your father and I will not be there to help you this time."

I barked out a harsh laugh. "Help me? Are you fucking high? When have you *ever* helped me?"

I heard my mother's sharp intake of breath. "Don't you dare speak to me that way." Her voice was dangerously low and I knew I had overstepped a line. The one that demanded total and complete compliance. Too bad for her that I had kicked the obedient fool out on his ass.

"You will not be leaving the Grayson Center, Clay. Your father and I admitted you and if you refuse to stay in treatment, we will be forced to take drastic measures to make sure you aren't posing a risk to *yourself*." I could almost see the derisive curl of her lip as her threat spewed from her mouth.

"You do that, *Mother*. Just try and lock me up again and you will find a very *disobedient* son. And I don't think that's something you or Dad can afford right now. Particularly with it being an election year and all." My mother went quiet. I could hear her silently fuming. The thing she didn't realize was that I had learned a thing or two from my manipulative parents. And that was knowing how to get what I wanted. Because I had hit her Achilles' heel: her fear of public disclosure. And I meant every word of what I had said. If she and my father fought me on this, I would be a thorn in their fucking side.

Finally, my mother said, "If that's how you want it, fine. But don't expect any further assistance from your father or me. That includes financially. You want to defy us and self-destruct, do it on your own."

I snorted, not remotely bothered by her statement. "I've been on my own most of my life," I muttered and then hung up.

Wow, that felt . . . good. I left the office to find Sabrina working on her laptop. She looked up and gave me a reassuring smile. "All finished up?" she asked.

I nodded. Yeah, I was finished. And it was about fucking time.

After that, I got my stuff together, including my meds, said my good-byes, and headed to the airport with Jonathan. I boarded the plane and we took off ten minutes early. That had to be a positive sign, right?

I tried not to fixate on what would be waiting for me when I landed. Instead I watched a couple of TV shows, ate some pretzels, and stared out the window. The flight was short, only two and a half hours. I checked the time on my cell phone after we landed. It was only a little after nine.

I hung back, letting everyone else get off of the plane before I did. I didn't want to keep Ruby waiting, but being here, my feet on Virginia soil, made all of this way too real. It wasn't some horrible dream I could wake up from.

I pushed my way through the crowded airport and headed toward the baggage claim. I started to look around for Ruby, knowing this was where we were supposed to meet up. I felt sick to my stomach. My nerves were a wreck and already my body craved the worst kind of release.

Three hours away from the center and I was already losing it. I cut across the sea of people and practically ran into the restroom. Thank God it was mercifully empty. I ran water in the sink and splashed my face, then pulled my hands through my hair and along the back of my neck in an effort to calm down.

I needed to control my breathing. I realized I hadn't taken my medication yet. My inability to stay on my meds had already caused me a lot of heartache. Having bipolar disorder didn't leave room for forgetfulness.

I dug through my laptop bag and pulled out the small brown bottle. Popping the top, I shook two pills into my palm. I swallowed them quickly, without water.

I thought about taking some of my anxiety medication but had been hesitant to do so. So instead I chose the pep talk route and waited for the Tegretol to kick in, hoping that had the desired effect.

I fished my cell phone out of my pocket and realized I had

been in the bathroom for almost fifteen minutes. Ruby was prob-ably starting to worry. I picked up my bag and headed back toward the baggage carousel.

I saw Ruby before she saw me. She was sitting on a bench, watching people as they walked by, obviously looking for me. She looked like shit. I know that's a messed-up thing to say, but, God, it was true. She looked like she had lost ten pounds; her clothes were practically swimming on her.

Her long red hair was dull and lifeless and I saw the beginnings of gray around her temples and scalp. She looked . . . old. And that freaked me out. Ruby had always been strong and capable. She was the rock I had always needed. Staring at my aunt, I realized she wasn't my rock anymore. And that I was going to have to suck it up and be the rock for her.

"Ruby," I called out. She turned her head in the direction of my voice and I was relieved to see some of the old sparkle come back into her listless eyes. She got to her feet and held her arms out for me.

I walked into them and hugged her. "I'm so glad you're here," she breathed out as she held me. I let her hold on, knowing she wasn't ready to let go yet. She felt smaller, almost as though she had shrunk in on herself. It worried me.

Finally I pulled back and she tried to give me a smile. It didn't come close to reaching her eyes. But I took what I could get. I found my suitcase quickly and followed her out of the airport.

Once outside I shivered. Goddamn, it was cold. I had gotten too used to southern Florida and the days that never dipped below seventy degrees. Shit, this was like walking into a freezer.

"I hope you remembered to bring a coat. We've had an unsea-sonable cold snap. They're actually calling for snow tonight. The seasons are all messed up. And some people have the audacity to say that global warming is a myth," Ruby said, clearly trying her hardest to make things normal.

But there was no such thing as normal. *That* was the myth. I had fought long and hard for something that I now realized didn't exist. And boy, was that depressing. I took a deep breath. I swear the air just smelled different in Virginia. I wasn't sure what it was, but it just felt like . . . well, home.

I put my arm around my aunt's shoulders and walked quietly with her to the car. "Why don't you let me drive?" I suggested, holding my hand out for the car keys. Ruby looked exhausted and I didn't want to admit to her that on a good day her driving scared the piss out of me. But seeing her like this, barely able to put one foot in front of the other, there was no way I was letting her behind the wheel.

Ruby didn't argue as she dropped the two-pound key ring into my palm. I sorted through the mess of spare keys and random trinkets until I found the one for her Volvo. I got into the driver's side and looked over to see that Ruby was standing in the open door, not moving.

"Ruby?" I said her name more as a question. Mostly because I hated to see my aunt, who used to be so full of life, reduced to this shell of a person. It pissed me off that life could be so cruel. Ruby didn't deserve the grief she was feeling. There were millions of people who lived their fucked-up lives, never lifting a finger to help anyone else. But a woman who had put her life on hold to save mine was suffering. It made me want to hit something.

"Sorry," Ruby murmured, finally getting into the car. She sat numbly, looking out of the window as I pulled into beltway traffic. We didn't talk. Not a word. I knew there was nowhere else I'd rather be than with Ruby right now. But, God, that selfish part of me wanted to run for the hills.

The weight of our mutual grief was suffocating. "Have you eaten any dinner?" I asked, trying to prod some sort of conversation out of my silent aunt. She shook her head.

"I'm not hungry," she said, her voice deadened. I was starving but I thought it was a better idea to just get to Davidson and start dealing with everything that was waiting for me there. I wanted to ask how she was doing. But I could see exactly how she was doing, and it wasn't good.

Ruby was hollow and I wasn't sure how well I was going to handle all of this. I merged onto I-66 and headed south. I tried several times to start a conversation, and even though Ruby attempted to engage, we ended up dropping off into silence. After a while, I gave up and turned on the radio.

Two hours later, I drove into Davidson and it was like my entire world shuddered around me. I drove down the familiar streets and felt intense and overwhelming panic. I couldn't do this! I needed to get the fuck out of here!

The mellow edge brought on from my medication blurred into the freak-out rising inside me. The roads were pretty empty. Not surprising, considering it was almost midnight on a Wednesday evening. And what did I expect as I rolled into town? A mob greeting me with pitchforks and torches, shouting, "Get the nut job!"?

I fought an internal battle that urged me to drop Ruby off at home and run away as fast as I could. I pulled into the driveway at Ruby's and parked behind my car. It still sat there as though waiting for me.

"You didn't have to hang on to it, you know. I told you to sell it and to keep the money," I said to Ruby as we climbed out of the car. Ruby shook her head and gave me a ghost of a smile.

"There was no way we were going to sell it. It's yours," was all she said as we walked to the front door. Turning on the hallway light, I dropped my suitcase in the living room and froze.

Lisa's glasses and book still lay on the coffee table. Her favorite mug half full of cold coffee sat beside them. Lisa's slippers kicked half under the couch as though she had just taken them off.

The air in here was oppressive. Lisa had always been the housekeeper and that was very obvious. The place was a wreck. Going into the kitchen, I saw dishes piled up in the sink, the trash over-flowing onto the floor. The counters were sticky with spilled tea.

There were flowers everywhere. The sickeningly sweet smell of decaying food mixed with the scent of flowers made me want to puke. One particularly huge arrangement sat on the kitchen table. I noticed distractedly that someone had to have spent a lot of money on that particular bouquet.

The rest of the house wasn't any better. And worse than that, Lisa's things had all been left just as they were. Like she could be expected to walk in the door at any moment.

"Sorry everything is such a mess," Ruby said. "Lisa was the one . . . she always . . ." Ruby choked up and covered her mouth with her hand.

I hugged her and rubbed her back. I felt like I couldn't breathe. The tightness in my chest was too much. But I tried, for my aunt's sake, to hide my discomfort. "It's okay. I'll take care of it in the morning," I assured her.

Ruby nodded, and without another word walked up the stairs. Her shoulders drooped, and her head hung low. She looked years older as she made her way up those steps. And I felt powerless to do anything about it.

I stood in the middle of the filthy kitchen not sure what I should do. I guess I could go upstairs and get some sleep. But the truth was I was terrified to go in my room. Too many memories. Too many triggers. I just wasn't ready for that.

Instead, I rolled up my sleeves and filled the sink with soapy water. I started to wash the dishes. Then I moved on to cleaning the counters and taking out the trash. I found the broom in the closet and swept the floor.

After I was finished in the kitchen, I moved onto the living room. Straightening couch cushions and throwing out mail. But I didn't touch Lisa's stuff. I just couldn't do that. I knew that Ruby wasn't ready.

By the time I had straightened up the downstairs, it was two thirty in the morning. I stood at the base of the stairs, debating whether I should go up to my old bedroom or not. But I wasn't in any sort of emotional state to handle the feelings that would create in me.

I pulled off my shirt and made myself comfortable on the couch. Staring up at the ceiling, I wondered how I would survive being back here. I forced myself away from all Maggie-related thoughts and tried to get some sleep.

I finally nodded off with her eyes burning in my mind.

chapter
ten

I pulled a black dress out of my closet and held it up in front of me. Yuck, no way. I hated black. And I knew Ruby hated black. So I pulled out my dark green dress and decided to wear that one instead.

Lisa's funeral was at two. It was only ten in the morning. But I couldn't stay in bed. I felt restless and antsy. The last few days had passed in a bit of a blur. Mom and I had tried to go by and see Ruby a few times. But every time we attempted to do so, she wasn't home. Or didn't answer the door.

We left the casserole on her front porch and when I drove by later, I saw that it was gone. I hoped Ruby had gotten it. Otherwise some jackass had stolen it and was enjoying some of my mother's fantastic cooking. Which was completely fucked up.

I had sent a bouquet of flowers to Ruby's house. I had spent a long time picking out the most beautiful arrangement possible. Which was sort of ridiculous. Who really gave a shit about flowers when they were putting the love of their life in the ground?

Rachel and Daniel would be going to the funeral with my parents and me later today. They hadn't really known Lisa, but they were going to support me. I spent an inordinate amount of time putting together my outfit. Brushing out my hair and applying my makeup. I hated how obsessive I was acting over my appearance.

This was a funeral, not a beauty pageant.

But today I would see *him*. And even if I somehow convinced myself that I didn't care, that what *he* thought about the way I looked was insignificant, it would be a freaking lie.

Unfortunately I cared way too much about what he thought. What he felt. How he was handling things now that he was back in Davidson. I had to talk myself out of driving to Ruby's yesterday after I had learned he was back in town.

His arrival had caused quite the stir at school. I had overheard a number of people talking about how they had seen him around. It was confirmed that he had gone into the flower shop to order arrangements. Then he had taken Ruby to Grandy's Steak House for dinner. His every move was catalogued and dissected as though he were a damn celebrity.

It wasn't every day that the town crazy came home. Because that's what everyone was really talking about. How good he looked. He was even acting social. Apparently a few brave souls had attempted conversation with him. And, oh my gosh, he had talked to them! How amazing was that? This wasn't the same guy who had refused to talk to anyone when he had lived here before. The social outcast who had become the guy with suicidal tendencies.

The gossip pissed me off. It unearthed my need to protect and defend him. But I was also unabashedly thankful for it. I clung to every tiny shred of news I could hear about him.

Because Clayton Reed was back in Davidson and I was prepared for him to blow my world apart . . . again.

Rachel and Daniel were driving me a little insane. They wouldn't let me out of their sight. They insisted on staying at my house last night so we could watch movies and "hang out."

Whatever. That was best-friend code for eliminating all possibilities for stupid decision making. Which included calling, visiting, or otherwise stalking my former boyfriend. Not that I would do such a thing. I mean, I was so past all that. So says the girl who fell to sleep last night staring at a picture of said former boyfriend that I secretly stowed away in the back of my closet.

All right, so I was sickeningly excited to see Clay. How fucked up was that? To be happy to see him in light of what he was here for. It was beyond selfish and beyond wrong. But it was there nonetheless.

And Rachel, in her all-seeing best-friendy ways, saw it right away. "Mags, don't make this into something more than it is. He's here for Lisa's funeral. He's not here to reunite and whisk you away in some romantic happily-ever-after. You've moved on. You're actually starting to live your life again. You have a future to look forward to. So don't expect something he damn sure can't give you. He made himself very clear with that letter. Remember that," Rachel had warned me last night as she waited for Daniel, who had gone out to start the car so he could drive her home.

Her words were pretty mean and I sucked in a painful breath in response. Shit, this girl was ruthless. But also annoyingly accurate. "Damn, Rach, that was harsh. When did you become a mega bitch?" I griped, trying to cover up how bothered I was by her words.

She arched her eyebrow and leveled the *look* in my direction. The look that said she was about to throw off the gloves and smack some shit into me. "I watched you self-destruct once over Clayton Reed and I won't see you do it again. It's cool that you're going to the funeral out of respect for Ruby and for Lisa. I get that you want to be there for that. But just don't go tomorrow thinking it's going to herald the new age of Maggie and Clay. You've been down that path before and it only brought about depression and significant weight loss," Rachel said with more snark than I thought her capable of.

"You've been hanging out with me way too long, Rachel Brad-field," I complained, trying to change the subject. Clay would always be a bone of contention between us. Rachel and Daniel, while endlessly supportive, had expressed their opinions (however gently) on the matter. He was bad news. Even though they under-stood on some level why he had acted the way he had, it didn't change the outcome. He had pulled me into his darkness and I had almost lost myself there. It was only now, after all these months, that I was starting to find my way back from it.

The front door had opened before Rachel could say anything else, bringing with it a blast of cold March air. "Am I missing out on some girl talk? Come on, fill me in, ladies." Daniel rubbed his hands together, trying to warm them up.

I shook my head at Rachel, warning her to keep her mouth shut. I didn't need to hear the same shit over again from Daniel. One best friend nagging me was enough. But even though her de-livery annoyed me, I took her words to heart. And whether she realized it or not, I truly had no plans to ever walk down that road again.

I could be perversely excited to see Clay again. I could want to know how he was holding up and whether he was all right. But that didn't change the fact that my life needed to go on without him in it. He had his treatment and I had my future. And those two things didn't coincide. They never would.

So here I was, the next morning, staring at the reflection of a girl who had changed so much in the last three months. I wasn't the same person who had naively believed that she could help her sick boyfriend. That she was the only medicine he needed. What an idiot that girl had been.

I wasn't sure I was ready for this, but I didn't have a choice. I was scared that I'd see Clay and all of my resolve would take a flying leap. I didn't think I could handle seeing his grief and not want to take care of him. It was in my nature to want to comfort him. The broken inside of him called out to the nurturer in me, something I had never been until he had stumbled into my life.

There was a knock at my door and my dad poked his head inside my room. "You're dressed already?" He looked at me as though I had grown another head. Given that I didn't normally get out of bed on a Saturday before noon, I understood his disbelief.

I shrugged, putting on some silver stud earrings. My dad came in and sat down on the edge of my bed. "You ready for today?" he asked with concern.

"Stop worrying about me, Dad. It makes you twitchy," I teased, trying to lighten the mood. My dad shook his head and scratched at his beard.

"I'm not twitchy, it's just that tic of mine," he joked. I smirked and smoothed my dress. "Mom has breakfast cooking. Come downstairs and eat something," he urged, giving me a placating smile.

"Sure, I'll be down in a bit. Save some bacon for me, will ya?" I called out as my dad left.

"No promises," he said, and I had to laugh.

My phone began ringing from my dresser and I picked it up, seeing Jake's name flash across the screen. I sighed and thought about ignoring it but instead put it to my ear.

"Hey, Jake," I said.

"Good morning, Maggie. I'm just calling to figure out what time I should come and get you today. I figured maybe we could grab some lunch or something and then get with Rachel and Daniel later." He sounded so eager and I tried not to groan. We had made plans just a few days ago, but with everything that had happened since then, I had to say it had completely slipped my mind.

I wanted to cancel; today would leave me emotionally exhausted. I didn't know what would happen when I saw Clay again and I didn't want to go into it knowing I'd have to spend my evening with someone else.

"Jake, about tonight—" I started but Jake's humorless laugh cut me off.

"You're not rain checking on me, are you?" He was clearly trying to sound blasé, but I could hear the hurt. Well, shit.

"It's just today I have a funeral to go to and I'm just not sure what that's going to mean for the rest of the day," I explained, omitting some key details from the excuse. All I knew was that I did not want to go on this date tonight. Things had changed considerably in a short amount of time, and I wasn't sure where I was headed.

"A funeral? What happened, Maggie?" Jake asked with concern. He was such a nice guy and I felt like the world's worst person for leading him on the way that I had. What in the hell had I been thinking? When did Maggie Young become the kind of girl to mess with people's emotions like this?

"It's Lisa McCabe," I answered, steeling myself for the explanation that would make Jake feel even worse.

"Lisa McCabe? Who's that?" he asked.

"She was Clay's aunt Ruby's partner. I, um . . . I just really need to go," I said hurriedly. There was absolute silence on the other end.

Finally, after a few moments, Jake cleared his throat. "Oh, I see. Then I'm guessing Clay's in town then, huh?" His voice had turned cold. I knew Jake wasn't happy with it, but then I shouldn't have to explain myself to anyone, least of all him. Jake wasn't my boyfriend. He was a friend, nothing more.

"Yeah, he is. But I haven't seen him yet. The funeral is at two and then there's a gathering at Ruby's house. I just don't know when it's going to be over," I said shortly, a little irritated by Jake's attitude. It was a freaking funeral. I shouldn't feel guilty for backing out of our plans because of it.

"Well. Okay then. I guess if you finish up early enough, give me a call. Otherwise, I'll see you on Monday." Yeah, he was pissed.

Well, he was just going to have to simmer in his juvenile behavior, because I wasn't biting.

"Sure," I bit out and hung up. Screw Jake Fitzsimmons. I tossed my phone onto the bed and stood there with my hands on my hips, feeling edgy and annoyed.

The smell of bacon wafted up the stairs and my stomach rumbled. I hadn't eaten much the night before and my belly was letting me know. I headed down into the kitchen. My mom glanced up and smiled at me. She looked stunning in her black pencil skirt and gray silk blouse. She had pulled her blond hair into a neat bun at the base of her neck. My mother looked graceful and perfect. Just like she always did.

But what I loved even more was the way she looked at me with understanding and compassion. She knew how hard this day would be for me. "Come eat, honey. I made banana pancakes, just for you." She loaded up a plate and brought it over to the table. My dad was drinking his coffee and reading the paper.

"You look lovely," my mom said, kissing the top of my head. I smiled up at her, picking up a piece of bacon.

"Thanks, Mom," I replied, grabbing the maple syrup and drenching my pancakes with it. Mom poured herself a cup of coffee and came to sit beside me. She watched me silently as I ate.

"How are you feeling?" she asked as I chewed slowly and thought of how to respond. I had to be careful how I answered. I knew my parents were going to be watching me very closely. They were worried about my seeing Clay again. They had only just started to relax their hypervigilant hovering and I didn't want them to start helicoptering again.

I understood why they were concerned. I'd be coming face-to-face with the boy who had ripped my heart out and left me a broken mess. They understood my compulsive need to help him. And seeing him in mourning was sure to bring out all of those feelings again.

But that didn't mean I would act on any of those instincts. I would be there to pay my respects to a woman I had come to love and admire. That was the priority today. Clay was in my past. And while I could offer my condolences, I would leave it at that.

"I'm sad, you know? I hadn't really talked to Lisa in months, but she was such a wonderful person," I said honestly. My mom nodded, sipping on her coffee. My dad looked at me over the top of the newspaper, his brows furrowed.

"I'm not sure going to Ruby's house afterward is the best idea. We'll go to the funeral and then I think we should head home," my father said. I stopped chewing and dropped my fork onto my plate.

"Dad, of course we should go to Ruby's. It would be rude not to," I argued. Honestly, I was terrified at the prospect of walking into Ruby's house again. But I needed to go. It seemed irrationally important that I be there.

"I'm sure there will be enough people there, we won't be missed. I just think it would be uncomfortable. And that's the last thing Ruby needs today," my dad said, closing the newspaper and setting it down on the table.

"Uncomfortable for whom, Dad? Is this about Ruby or more about you?" I asked sharply.

My dad's face flushed and I instantly regretted snapping at him. Time to try a different approach.

"Please, Dad. I need to be there for Ruby," I pleaded. My mom watched me closely.

"And Clay?" she asked casually. Too casually.

I took a deep breath. "Of course, Clay too. But today is about Lisa. Nothing else," I hurried on. My parents shared a look but didn't say anything else. I ate the rest of my breakfast in a thick silence. The bacon and pancakes sat like lead in my stomach.

It was eleven by the time I finished. I got up to rinse my dishes in the sink. My parents each gave me a kiss before heading out to run some errands before the funeral. They hadn't brought up going to Ruby's house again and I still wasn't sure whether I would be permitted to go or not. But I knew if they nixed the idea, I couldn't argue. I wouldn't go down that road again, defying my parents for Clay.

Rachel and Daniel showed up around noon and I was thankful for the distraction. Rachel looked pretty in her black, knee-length dress. Daniel cleaned up nicely in a gray suit and dark blue tie. He was letting his blond hair grow out and it fell in curls over his forehead.

They came in and we made our way up to my room. "So, I heard from Jake that you canceled our plans for tonight," Daniel commented, taking his jacket off and laying it over my desk chair.

"We're not going out tonight?" Rachel asked, looking at me in surprise. I clenched my teeth together.

"I just didn't think I'd be up to it after this afternoon, all right?" I said defensively, sitting down on the edge of my bed, careful not to crease my skirt. Rachel and Daniel looked at one another and I could interpret all too well their silent communication.

"Mags, come on, I think it will be good for you to get out tonight," Daniel said gently, moving clothes off of my vanity stool so Rachel could sit down. I sighed, really hoping that they would just let it drop. But seeing the firm set of Danny's jaw, I knew they wouldn't.

"Is this about Jake? Because I only agreed to go with him because he sort of wore me down. I don't really like him like that—" I started and Danny shook his head.

"This has absolutely nothing to do with Jake and absolutely fucking everything to do with Clay," he bit out angrily. Whoa, where was this coming from?

"Danny," Rachel warned quietly. I looked between the two of them, getting frustrated by their complete lack of faith in me.

"Look, you two, stop freaking out about this. I will tell you the same thing I told my parents: it's a funeral. I will be going to pay my respects to Lisa. Who happens to be someone I had come to care a lot about. Stop making this all about Clay. It's ridiculous and more than a little disrespectful," I scolded them.

Rachel had the decency to look contrite. Daniel on the other hand simply stared back at me belligerently. "Don't act like seeing Clay won't fuck with your head, Mags. You forget it was Rachel and I who sat here day after day while you totally fell apart over that guy. I feel bad for him. I know this is hard on him. But I wish like hell he wasn't here. Because I'm worried what this will do to you." I bit my tongue on the hateful comment that wanted to fly out of my mouth.

"Jeez, give me a little credit here. You're making me feel really pathetic," I mumbled. Rachel shot a dark look at her boyfriend before turning to me.

"We don't mean to make you feel that way. And what Daniel was so ineloquently trying to say was that we're just worried."

I threw my hands up in the air in frustration. "Stop worrying!" I said louder than I meant to.

Daniel crossed the room and put his arm around my shoulders. He stooped down to kiss my cheek. "Not possible, babe. We love you," he said warmly, and any irritation I was feeling melted away. Damn Daniel Lowe and his stupid considerate ass.

"I love you too, you fuckwad," I grumbled, elbowing him in the side. And I knew that I was lucky to have so many people who loved me. I just wished Clay was so lucky.

chapter
eleven

clay

The couch was starting to kill my back. Three nights of sleeping on the lumpy cushions and I would be walking hunched over all day. Okay, I had a perfectly good bed upstairs in my room, but I had yet to go up there.

So maybe I was a coward, but I just wasn't ready to open the door and be confronted with the thousands of memories within those four walls. Being back in Davidson was hard enough. Every street, every shop, every stupid tree carried with it a dozen memories of the person I left behind. And it seriously sucked. I really wanted to leave. This was much harder than I had thought it would be.

I had known it was going to be tough. Ruby's grief was hard to watch. She was barely eating and I knew she wasn't sleeping. I could hear her pacing the floors upstairs all night. It seemed to take everything out of her to get dressed in the morning.

My exuberant aunt had been reduced to this person completely devoid of life. And if she wasn't handling Lisa's death well, what chance did I have?

I had spoken to Dr. Todd every day, just as promised. He didn't sound particularly concerned when I mentioned how difficult this trip was turning out to be. He just let me process and reviewed my coping skills with me. Though yesterday he suggested calling twice a day instead of once. He had also encouraged me to talk to Jean, my substance abuse counselor at the center.

I hadn't done that yet. I was feeling overly shrinked as it was. And today I needed to focus on Ruby and the funeral and getting through it without doing something stupid.

Because every night I lay on the couch, listening to the sounds of Ruby's footsteps, and I wanted to scream. I was just so fucking angry. Angry with Lisa for falling asleep behind the wheel. Angry with Ruby for falling apart like she was. Angry with myself for feeling all the above.

I wanted to cut myself so badly that I could taste it. There were times I'd find myself in the kitchen, my fingers aching to reach for a knife or the pair of scissors. Forcing myself to leave the room and get away from what taunted me was getting harder and harder to do. I usually ended up pulling out my journal and spending hours writing in it. Okay, so maybe it wasn't a completely useless exercise because it *did* help; something I would never say aloud.

But I was exhausted and feeling a little sick. I had so much to do today. I needed to get down to the church in a few hours to make sure everything was set up. The funeral director would be handling most of the arrangements, but I wanted to make sure it was all as it needed to be. After the church, there would be a graveside service, followed by a gathering of friends and family here.

I had worked my ass off to clean the place up. A caterer would be here later to drop off food. I had planned it all down to the tiniest detail. Keeping myself busy helped some. I was able to turn off the emotions that otherwise would have flayed me alive. I was flying on autopilot for now and I was happy to do so.

I'd have time later to deal with my own grief. Right now it was all about taking care of Ruby and getting through the day.

I got to my feet, rolling my head to try to loosen up the kinks in my neck. The couch had become a form of torture. I accidentally knocked Lisa's glasses to the floor from their spot on the coffee table.

They were still there. The half-full coffee cup as well. It was starting to grow mold on the rim, but when I had tried to move it, Ruby had freaked out. So I had left it alone. Picking up my phone, I checked the time.

Shit, it was already eleven thirty. I needed to get a move on. I opened my suitcase and pulled out my gray slacks and a black button-down shirt. I hung them on the kitchen door and got out the ironing board.

I was busy ironing when Ruby finally emerged. She was still in her robe; her red hair looked as though it hadn't seen a brush in a year. Dark circles ringed her eyes and her lips were cracked and chapped from her gnawing at them.

"Morning," I said, watching her open the cabinet and pull down a mug. She gave me a tiny smile as she started to grind coffee beans. "You want me to make you some breakfast?" I asked after I finished ironing my shirt.

Ruby shook her head and waited for her coffee to brew. The silence in the kitchen made me antsy. I watched my aunt, who seemed to be barely functioning, and I just couldn't handle it anymore.

I left her staring at the coffeepot and went out into the backyard. It was cold and had started to drizzle. I drew the frigid air into my lungs and held it there until my chest burned with the need to breathe.

Letting my breath out slowly I wished I had developed a taste for nicotine, because I needed something to do with my itchy hands. I couldn't do this. Fuck me, I just couldn't.

God, I wished I was back in Florida. I pulled my phone out and dialed Dr. Todd's direct line. It rang and rang. On the eleventh ring, I hung up. It was Saturday; of course he wasn't in his office. I had his personal number somewhere in my suitcase but didn't have the energy to go looking for it. I guess I could call the main number and talk to another staff person on duty, but I wasn't entirely comfortable with that.

I stood there warring with myself when I felt a hand on my shoulder. I looked down in surprise to see Ruby staring out into the yard, her hand clutching my sleeve. "Thank you, Clay. For everything you've done," she whispered, her voice sounding hoarse.

I closed my eyes. I could do this. Ruby needed me. I had to stop being so goddamned weak. I brought my hand up to cover hers and we stood that way, in the cold. Two people barely holding on but trying desperately to keep each other going.

"We should start getting ready," Ruby said, squeezing my fingers before letting go. She seemed to be trying to pull herself together and I was unfairly grateful for that. Because again, that horribly selfish part of me needed her strength for myself. I was scared as hell that if she depended too much on mine I'd only let her down.

"Okay. We should probably get over to the church soon. See if there's any last-minute details we need to go over," I said. Ruby nodded and went back inside. I stood out there for another few minutes, finally focusing on my own feelings of sadness and grief.

This sadness was painfully familiar. The silent, openmouthed suffering was something I had felt entirely too much of in my life. The barely controllable urge to purge my grief with the slice of a razor was overwhelming, its kiss sweet on my skin. I could almost hear the darkness whisper in my ear, a taunting tease of potential relief.

I had known this was the risk of coming back here. I knew that it resurrected a thousand instincts to hurt, to maim, and to destroy everything inside of me. Everything that I had worked so hard to rebuild. But progress was a flimsy thing. And the need to tear it all down was a much stronger adversary.

Leaving the center was like leaving a warm and safe cocoon and being thrown headfirst into complete and utter chaos. From the moment my plane had touched down in Virginia, I struggled to remember that I was in control of these traitorous feelings. That it was my choice to cope in a healthier way. That was what Dr. Todd kept drilling into my head. It's my choice. *Mine!*

But returning to Davidson, particularly under these circumstances, was proving a true test of my newfound resolve. The meds helped. I was taking them as scheduled. So I could tick that off my Responsible Clayton Reed list.

The stuff I had learned in therapy rattled around in my head, reminding me to breathe. To reframe. To talk myself back from the edge I was already in danger of toppling over.

But like I said before, Ruby needed me. And even though it made my anxiety that much more acute, I needed to remember that. But I had always been the needy one. The truth was I needed Ruby. Maggie. Lisa. Even as I had always denied needing anyone.

And now I was the one being leaned on and I wasn't so sure I could handle the pressure. The longer it went on, the harder it became. I was brittle and raw and I knew that Dr. Todd's concerns about me coming back were legitimate ones.

I was on a precariously slippery slope. The wrong move, the wrong thought, and I would be sliding down on my ass. And the landing would be hard.

But that didn't change the fact that I had responsibilities. And that trumped everything else. It had to.

◆

I was making it through the day. Barely. The light drizzle from earlier had changed into a steady downpour. Even the weather was in mourning. Everything felt dark. I focused on my damn breathing even as my guts knotted up inside of me.

Breathe in. Breathe out. I swear I could write my own book on all the different ways to freaking breathe.

I needed to pull it together. I needed to be the man Ruby could count on, not just someone to rely on everyone else's strength. They say it's in times of crisis that your merit is proven. Well, I had a hell of a lot to prove right now. To myself and to everyone who doubted I could be anything more than the crazy kid who had already lost it once.

I was engaged in this furious internal dialogue. Jumping back and forth between giving myself a perky little pep talk and mentally screaming at myself to man up. I was totally absorbed in it, trying to get up the nerve to go to the front of the church and sit with Ruby in the pew where she sat quietly sobbing.

I had been able to lose myself in the final arrangements when we had arrived, but now the start of the service drew closer and I was cracking up a bit. Okay, not a bit . . . a lot.

I watched as people stopped by Ruby to talk to her. She was trying to be polite but she was so consumed by her grief that she could do little more than nod. I should get up there and help her out, but I felt paralyzed.

It was all almost too much to bear. But I really needed to get over that. It wasn't fair to leave her alone. Not now. Not when she had never abandoned me when I needed her. But there was that part of me that fought for self-preservation and I knew this whole scene had the makings of my own personal disaster.

I was very close to running out the side door and never looking back. Drive straight to the airport and jump on the first available flight out of fucking Virginia.

I had almost talked myself into it when I felt a stirring in the air. It was an intense humming that took my body completely by surprise. The hairs rose up on the back of my neck and I just knew.

She was here.

Maggie.

And just like that, the fuzzy black faded away and everything clicked into place. My heart thudded into overdrive and my palms started to sweat, so I shoved them into the pockets of my slacks.

Of course she came. I knew she'd be here. And though I tried not to allow myself the hope of seeing her, I couldn't deny that I had longed for it all the same.

And here she was, looking the same, only *better*. Her dark hair looked shorter and was pulled back in a low ponytail. She wore a black wool coat over a dark green dress. She looked beautiful and perfect and the embodiment of everything I had always craved.

She walked into the church, flanked by her parents. I barely noticed them or the fact that Rachel and Daniel followed close behind. My eyes were only for her. I knew I should go to Ruby. But I couldn't make myself move. I stood there, rooted to the spot, not sure if I wanted Maggie to see me or not, even as I screamed at her in my head to look at me.

Please.

As much as I missed her and dreamed of this moment, I was scared of it. Too much had changed. Yet after I saw her, my heart and body reacted the same as they always had. She had been my crutch and now she was something else entirely, a painful reminder of all the ways I screwed up. But watching my gorgeous girl move through the crowd of people, I only saw the person I had pinned my future on. And that was both exhilarating and terrifying.

But God, I *loved* her. She was the piece I had been missing for the last three months. She was everything I wanted in my life but was still unsure I deserved. And this was why I wasn't any good for her. My feelings about Maggie May Young were too intense, too consuming, and they always threatened to swallow me whole.

Then she lifted her eyes and met mine and everything else disappeared. Her eyes were bright and I could see the way her chest started to rise and fall more rapidly. Before I realized what I was doing, I was moving toward her at the same instant that she began to make her journey down the aisle of the church.

I saw Rachel over her shoulder, her eyes wide, her hand reaching out to possibly stop Maggie. But there was no detaining her. Our eyes never left each other as we worked to bridge the physical distance between us.

It was like every time we were together. Our bodies orbited around each other as if pulled by an invisible force that we had no control over.

I wanted this. And I wanted to run from it. I wanted to pull her in and never let go. And I wanted to push her away.

Two minutes. That's all it took for my head to short-circuit.

Maggie stopped five feet away and we stood there, staring at each other. I didn't know what to say. What worked as appropriate chitchat when you saw the love of your life again after breaking her heart? And at a funeral, no less.

I could see she was struggling as much as I was. And I hated that. Her face was flushed and I could see her pulse fluttering in her neck. I wanted to taste her skin and feel her heartbeat beneath my lips.

So instead, I went for the anticlimactic.

"Hi," I said softly. Maggie closed her eyes as if in pain, and when she opened them again, they were wet with tears.

"Hi," she said, barely loud enough for anyone to hear. But I could hear her. I could always hear her. I wanted to reach out and touch her; my fingers tingled with anticipation, as if they were already plotting ways to do so. My breathing became shallow and I felt light-headed.

The emotional punch to the gut was enough to leave me reeling. And apparently Maggie was feeling the same way. We stood there, staring at each other, unconcerned by the rest of the people in the room.

My eyes drank in the sight of her after so long. I was drowning and parched all at the same time. My senses were desperate to see, smell, taste, touch every inch of Maggie May Young. But I was also overwhelmed by her presence. Because with her came a deluge of memories that I wasn't prepared to deal with. Ones that left me shattered and torn apart.

The last time I had seen her I had been lying in a hospital bed and her face had been red and splotchy from crying. The ringing of what I thought was her betrayal was loud in my ears. I had turned on her. Turned on myself. And I had almost taken us both down in my delusions.

"Clay, I'm so sorry for your loss," Maggie said after a few heartbeats. The way she said my name made me tremble inside. I was acting like a little girl. *Man up!* I told myself harshly. *Don't let her see you crumble.*

But her voice, smooth and full of emotion, hit me straight in the center of my chest. The soft cadence of her voice as it tumbled out of her mouth both scared and soothed me. Looking at her, I didn't see a girl who had moved on. I saw someone who ached for me just as I did for her.

I couldn't take it anymore. I reached out and grabbed ahold of her hand, slightly tugging her forward. She moved, as if without her volition. The tips of our shoes touched and we were so close I could smell the mint on her breath. Her eyes widened at my presumption, but I noticed she didn't back away.

I held her hand tightly in mine and she tentatively squeezed. And everything inside of me started to unravel. My fear, my panic, it all just faded into the background. She was all I saw. She was all I needed. Just like always.

"Clay. I'm so sorry about Lisa." A voice brought me out of the moment. Maggie blinked a few times and seemed to suddenly realize how close we were standing. She pulled her hand away and

I was left clutching only air. She took a few steps backward and looked at the ground sheepishly.

My heart squeezed painfully and I ran my hands through my hair. I looked at the person who had interrupted us and tried not to bite their fucking head off.

"Thanks, Rachel. It's good to see you, even under the circumstances," I offered politely, my eyes moving back to Maggie, who had refused to look at me again.

"We're thinking of you, man." Daniel Lowe had come up beside Rachel and I noticed the way his hand fell possessively to the small of her back. Wow, glad to see that they were still going strong. That some relationships could survive. It made my generally pessimistic outlook a little brighter.

"Thank you," I told him genuinely, sparing Maggie's best friends a look. I tried to give them my attention, but my focus was only for the dark-haired girl who was now looking everywhere but at me.

The four of us stood awkwardly just inside the church entryway. I knew I was being a little intense with the way I was staring at Maggie. But I couldn't look away. I had spent way too many days fantasizing about seeing her face again. I didn't think I had it in me to look anywhere else ever again.

Maggie moved back even farther and I felt the separation like a physical ache. She seemed nervous all of a sudden and I didn't have to wonder too long what had put the anxiety on her face.

"Hi, Clayton." A warm hand came down on my arm and I looked away from my girl to see her mother standing beside me, wearing a worried but sympathetic expression. She looked between Maggie and me and I knew that she was concerned about what my unexpected reemergence meant for her daughter.

And not for the first time I hated myself for being the guy who would make them worry. I didn't want to be someone they feared.

But I was and I knew that wasn't likely to change, no matter how much I tried to be different.

Mrs. Young gave me a hug and I tried not to act surprised by it. But Maggie's mom had always been a lot easier to be around than her dad. As if on cue, Mr. Young flanked his wife's side and watched me warily.

"We were sorry to hear about Lisa," he said gruffly, scratching at his beard uncomfortably. I didn't say anything. Mr. Young had a way of making me feel two years old and two feet tall. Like I was being examined and coming up short.

Mrs. Young took Maggie by the elbow and led her away. Her father followed behind, leaving me standing with the protective best friends. I shoved my hands into my pockets, feeling the need to flee all over again.

"So, Clay, how long are you in town for?" Daniel asked, trying to make the question sound informal, but I knew he was really digging for information. He didn't want me here, that was obvious. Daniel and I had been close to being friends *before*. But we had never quite gotten there. And then I had taken off with Maggie and he had been there to clean up my mess after I had left.

So I knew without a doubt I wasn't one of his favorite people.

"Uh, I'm not really sure. I guess I'll just see how Ruby gets on. I don't want to just leave her, you know?" I forced myself to meet his eyes and pressed my lips together. I sort of wanted to tell him it was none of his damn business. I didn't need his approval.

But for the sake of harmony, I kept my mouth shut. It was Rachel who nodded in understanding. "Well, you can only take it one day at a time." She spoke as though from experience and it made me wonder what more there was to Maggie's unassuming best friend. I had never paid much attention to her except as an extension of Maggie. But her eyes glowed with their own hidden pain, and I knew she got it.

"Yeah," I murmured, not knowing what else to say. And apparently they didn't either, so they moved on down the aisle, finding their place beside Maggie. I watched them huddle together, Daniel and Rachel on one side, her parents on the other. They circled her in their support and love and I found that I was unreasonably jealous.

Not for the unconditional affection she was receiving, but for the fact that I wasn't the one to give it to her. She should be by my side. *With me.* We should be holding up and leaning on each other. But I had given up that right when I had left her. When I had written that fucking letter that at the time seemed like the right thing to do.

Now I was seeing it was a huge mistake. Because I had effectively robbed myself of the one thing that had ever made me happy.

I finally understood all too well what people meant when they say the path to hell is paved with good intentions. Because I was stuck in the middle of my own personal purgatory.

People started to find their seats and I realized the service was about to begin. So I went to join Ruby and Lisa's parents at the front of the church. She reached over and grabbed ahold of my hand when I sat down and we held on to each other as the minister began his sermon about the beauty of heaven and Lisa entering God's Kingdom. What a bunch of sanctimonious bullshit. Lisa would have hated every minute of this overindulgent, trite nonsense.

But funerals were for the living and really had nothing to do with the person who died. They were meant to give those left behind some sort of solace. But I found none. I just felt empty.

Looking over at Ruby, with her head bowed low, her hair obscuring her face, I knew she was feeling the exact same way. How do you go on living when the love of your life is gone?

I looked over my shoulder, taking in row after row of people who had come to pay their respects. Lisa's family, her friends, her coworkers. And my eyes rested on Maggie. She was listening to the minister with an unreadable expression on her face.

As though she could feel me looking, her gaze met mine. Her eyes were wet; I could see it from here. But one thing was for certain: those eyes of hers had always been my undoing.

I had to look away. My heart felt too full in my chest and I could barely breathe. So I tried to focus on the rest of the service. Before I knew it, it was over and people were filing out of the church. Ruby clutched my arm as I led her out the side door and toward my car.

"How are you holding up?" I asked quietly as I opened up the passenger-side door. Ruby shook her head, letting out a muffled sob as she sank into the leather seat. I closed the door behind her with a soft click and went around to the driver's side.

And then we made our way to the cemetery to put Lisa into the ground. Ruby said nothing, lost in her own world. And I had never felt more alone.

chapter
twelve

god, that was horrible.

The crying, the misery. It was like a knife to my heart. Ruby's grief had torn me apart. Once infectiously happy, she had now been reduced to the blank woman standing beside an open hole in the earth.

And Clay. He had his arm around his aunt, holding her up as they slowly lowered Lisa's casket into the ground. People were singing "Amazing Grace" as the box descended and finally disappeared.

Death was an unfeeling bitch. It didn't matter who you were, who loved you—it struck mercilessly and without discrimination. I had never really experienced death. I was lucky in that respect. I wasn't able to fully understand how gut-wrenching it was.

But watching Ruby and Clay, I felt for the first time how terrifying and lonely it was. I hadn't known Lisa nearly as long as they had, but I felt her death deeply. And knowing how it would affect the two people across from me trying so hard to hold it together, I wasn't sure there was any coming back from that.

After dirt was tossed down into the hole, everyone began to

disperse. I wanted to go over to Clay again. I wanted to be there for him so badly. I couldn't stand the look of anguish on his face. It broke my heart all over again.

"Come on, Maggie." Rachel tugged on my arm and I tore my eyes away from Clay, who still stood with Ruby, staring at the ground where Lisa now rested.

"Yeah, okay," I said, walking with them down the rows of headstones. Each step took me farther and farther from Clay, yet again. Why did I feel this separation even greater than the last one? I had barely spoken to him, but it felt fundamentally wrong to leave him when he was hurting like that.

I had been so sure I could come here today, give my condolences, and be strong enough not to be affected by him and his pain. I really should have known better. Because when it came to Clay, there was never a choice but to be with him.

"Your dad and I have to run to the grocery store. We'll meet you at home, okay?" my mom said, pulling me into a hug.

"Okay. I'll see you later," I said as she touched my cheek lovingly.

"You are such an amazing girl, Maggie May Young. And I'm so proud to be your mom," she told me gently. I smiled.

"Thanks, Mom. I think I'm pretty amazing too," I quipped. My dad laughed beside me and ruffled my hair.

"Always so modest," he teased, moving in for his hug.

After they left I turned to Rachel and Daniel, who were talking quietly by Rachel's car. "Do you have any plans this afternoon?" We climbed into Rachel's car. Once we were settle, she turned around in her seat.

"Nope, we're all yours, girl. What do you have in mind? You want to give Jake a call and see that movie? It might be good for you," Rachel suggested and I grimaced. That was *not* what I had in mind at all. I wondered if they'd be cool with the plans I had decided on.

"Uh, no. I was thinking we could head over to Ruby's. You

know, for the family and friends thing," I said quickly. Daniel ran his hand through his hair and looked at me with obvious frustration.

"Do you think that's really a good idea, Mags? I mean, come on. That's just opening up a load of bullshit." I tensed at his tone and dug my nails into my palm. It was either that or slap his face.

But then Rachel surprised me. "Give it a rest, Danny. She knows how we feel about things. But if this is what she needs to do, then that's where we're going." She turned in her seat and put the key into the ignition.

Daniel stared at his girlfriend openmouthed. "Rach, I thought we were on the same page about all this," he said under his breath. As if I couldn't hear him. Nice to know I was the topic of conversation.

"I'm not trying to be an asshole, Mags. I'm just not sure I can handle seeing you like that again," Daniel said. He didn't turn around to look at me. He continued to stare out the window in front of him.

I didn't know what to say to that. His honesty took the wind out of my self-righteous sails. I couldn't be irritated with him, not when he was only looking out for me. I would have been hurt if he did anything less.

I guess I could tell him that he didn't need to worry. That I had no intention of being that girl. That I would never allow myself to become so consumed by Clay again that I lost sight of everything else. The older and wiser Maggie should definitely be saying all of those things.

But I stayed quiet. Because even I knew that the hold Clay had on my heart wasn't rational and it wasn't gentle. It was a vicious tug that threatened to rip the beating organ straight out of my chest.

Seeing him again had only confirmed what my subconscious already knew. I would never move on from Clay. My soul belonged with him, was so entangled in him that I was no longer a single being.

I had at one time wondered whether it was a good thing. Whether loving someone like that was healthy for either of us. I still wasn't entirely sure, but I was tired of trying to deny something that was as natural to me as breathing. I loved Clayton Reed and no amount of time or distance would ever take that away from me.

That didn't change the reality of where we found ourselves. Our relationship had been toxic and detrimental to both of us. I had learned that you could love someone entirely but not necessarily be *with* them. And that's where the new Maggie came out to play. Because for once I wasn't letting my feelings rule me. I was trying to let my head have as much of a say as my heart.

We pulled up in front of Ruby's house five minutes later. There were several cars there already and I felt a bit strange walking up to the house. Rachel was close behind me, Daniel purposefully trailing after her. I knocked on the door and waited. I could hear people talking inside.

Finally the door was opened by someone I didn't recognize. "Hi, I'm Maggie. And this is Rachel and Daniel. We're . . . uh, Clay's friends," I stuttered out. The older woman smiled and held the screen door open, motioning us to come inside.

"I'm glad you could come. I'm Darla, Lisa's sister." Looking at her, I could see the same straight nose and square jaw. I gave her a tight smile and followed her into the kitchen. I looked around but didn't see anyone I knew. I saw an older couple surrounded by a group of people and assumed they were Lisa's parents. But Ruby and Clay were conspicuously absent from the gathering.

"Well, what should we do? We don't know any of these people," Rachel said nervously. I picked up a few paper plates and handed them to my friends.

"I say we eat first. That's usually a good place to start," I remarked dryly. Daniel and Rachel took their plates and loaded up with food. I kept looking around the room, trying to locate either Ruby or Clay. It was strange that neither was anywhere around.

After filling up our plates, we found a spot in the living room. Sitting on the couch, I noticed a pair of glasses and a coffee mug sitting on the table in front of me. My throat closed up when I realized they were Lisa's.

A few of Lisa's family members came over and introduced themselves. I asked where Ruby and Clay were but no one seemed to know. After we ate our food, I got to my feet. Daniel and Rachel looked extremely uncomfortable and I felt bad for dragging them here.

"Guys, I'm going to go see if I can find Ruby. Then we can go, all right?" I gave them credit for trying to hide their relief, but I saw it all the same.

I tossed our plates into the trash and then started to look for Ruby. Her house wasn't that big, so there weren't many places for her to go. I headed upstairs, looking in her bedroom. She wasn't there. I stopped outside the door at the end of the hallway and froze.

I put my hand on the doorknob but didn't turn it. It felt cool in my hand and I tightened my grip around it. I wasn't sure I could go in. But without giving myself time to think about it too much I pushed open the door and was hit by a wave of stale air.

It was exactly the same as the last time I was in here. Clay's bed was made and untouched. Was he not staying in here then? I stepped inside and looked around. The blinds were drawn and it was so dark I could barely see. I walked across the room and turned on the lamp that sat on his desk.

Light flooded the room and I blinked as my eyes adjusted. A thin layer of dust sat on everything, as though no one had been inside since he left. Aside from the pictures that were missing on his wall, the ones I had taken *after*, everything was the same.

I sat down on the bed and let my hands drop limply between my knees. What was I doing here? I felt like I was chasing a ghost. Looking for something that I had lost a long time ago. But my earlier revelations held true. I couldn't let go of him. I *wouldn't* let go of him.

I felt him before I saw him. "What are you doing in here?" I looked up at the sharp tone of his voice. Clay stood in the doorway, not moving. His face was pale and drawn; his dark hair wildly tussled from his anxious fingers. His eyes were tired as they watched me warily. He looked at me as though I were invading his privacy.

Which sort of pissed me off. When had we become strangers? When had we stopped being able to read each other? Because now, staring at him, I wasn't sure what to expect. And the way he was looking at me set me on edge.

I didn't get to my feet. Maybe I should get out, but I was feeling defiant and I kept my butt right where it was. "Looking for you," I told him honestly. Clay frowned, still not moving into the room.

He seemed hesitant to step into the space that had once been his. "Are you not staying in here?" I asked, swiping my finger along the bedside table, and then wiping the dust away.

"No, I've been sleeping on the couch," Clay admitted, watching me as I ran my hand down the blue comforter, touching his pillows, smoothing the sheets.

"Why?" I asked him, turning to look at him. Clay shook his head and crossed his arms over his chest as though shielding himself. From me? That was crazy. If anyone should be protecting themselves, it should be me.

"I didn't think I could sleep in here." He looked around the room, clearly taking it all in for the first time since he had left. "Too many memories," he whispered, more to himself than to me.

"I understand about wanting to hide from memories," I said bitterly. I turned my back to him and picked up the sketchbook still on the table. I leafed through the pages leisurely, taking my time. Trying not to get choked up by the pictures inside. So many of them I remembered him drawing. Back when our lives were infinitely more complicated but in some twisted way, much happier.

I hadn't realized Clay had come into the room until the bed dipped. I felt the heat of his body beside me. We weren't touching; the space between us was much wider than it ever would have been *before*. But it was still the closest we had been in three months. I bit down on my lip to stop myself from sobbing at the relief of seeing him again. Of being near him.

The silence spread out in front of us, neither of us doing anything to break it. As though words would ruin this perfect piece of time we were being blessed with. In our reality, it could be over in an instant. And I wanted to prolong the inevitable, forever.

But like everything, the silence had to end. Clay reached out and took the sketch pad from my hands and closed it, leaning over me to put it back on the bedside table. I could smell the musky scent of his cologne and willed myself to not lean into him.

"I should get downstairs," Clay said quietly, though he didn't get to his feet. I laced my hands in my lap and kept my head down.

"I'm sorry, Clay. I know how much you loved Lisa." I wanted to hold him while I said it, but that's not where we were. Not where we'd ever be again. Hadn't I told him just last week that love had stopped being enough? So why did I want to throw my resolve straight out the window?

"Thanks, Maggie. It's been . . . rough," he admitted, plucking at the skin around his fingernail. I looked at his hands and noticed that all of the nails had been bitten to the quick. I wondered whether there would be any fresh cuts on his arms. Any healing scabs. Or had he defeated that particular demon?

But there was no way I could ask him. "How's Ruby holding up?" I asked, chancing a look at him up through my hair. I saw his body rise and fall with his deep sigh. He chewed at his bottom lip until it started to bleed. The picking around his fingers became almost frantic.

"Not good. She's barely keeping it together. I'm scared to leave her. I'm not sure what will happen when I go back." I think I stopped breathing then.

"So you *are* going back then?" I asked. I had suspected this was only a temporary visit, but hearing it confirmed definitely hurt. Which was ridiculous. We weren't together anymore. But my feelings hadn't changed. And even though I didn't trust him with my heart, it was his nonetheless.

Clay looked at me, smoothing his raw lip with his tongue. "I had planned on it. I still have things I need to do in Florida. But I just feel like I'd be abandoning Ruby. I'm not sure she'll be able to handle living in this house alone." He was scared, I could see that. And while part of me wanted to drag more information out of him about where he'd been for the last few months, a bigger part of me just wanted to let it go. There was no point in dredging it up right now. It would accomplish absolutely nothing.

"I wish I could tell you what to do, but that's a decision you have to make for yourself. Only you can decide where you need to be," I said, sounding way wiser than I actually was.

Clay's lip quirked into a half smile. "Wow, when did you get so deep?" he joked. I laughed.

"You have no idea how deep I've become," I teased back, though I wished I could take back my words when I saw Clay's face fall.

"No, I guess I don't know much about you anymore." He sounded so sad and I hated it. I grabbed his hand and held it between mine. My thumb rubbed his skin in purposeful circles.

"There is no one that knows me better," I said firmly, needing him to believe that. As though he couldn't help himself, Clay dropped his head to my shoulder and pressed his nose into my hair.

My heart began to beat wildly in my chest but there was nothing sexual in this. It was just two people who loved each other, trying to make some sense in a world where there was none.

I felt the wetness of his tears on my neck as he moved his face farther into my hair. I lifted my arm and wrapped it around his back. His body shook with silent sobs and I just held him. Like I had done a thousand times before.

We didn't say anything else. We really didn't need to. But after a while I realized it was growing late as the shadows deepened in the room.

"I think we should go downstairs," I said softly, rubbing the back of his head, letting his hair slide between my fingers, perhaps for the last time.

Clay reluctantly sat up and rubbed at his face with his hands. "Thank you, Maggie. You're always here to save me, aren't you?" He touched my face, his eyes dropping to my mouth as if by compulsion. I wondered briefly if he would try and kiss me. And if he did, would I let him?

Turns out I didn't have to think about that too much, because without another word, Clay got to his feet and left the room. I sat there, not sure what to do. After sharing such an intense moment together, it felt strange for me to go. But Clay leaving me alone spoke volumes.

I turned off the light and closed the bedroom door behind me. Going down the stairs I finally saw Ruby. She was talking to Lisa's sister and I recognized Tilly from the shop. The same Tilly who had openly lusted after Clay, who I noticed was once again missing in action.

So I used the time to pay Ruby my respects. She hugged me tightly and thanked me for coming. I ignored Tilly. So, maybe that was rude, but I never liked the girl. And I didn't want to think about her being here to comfort Clay. It made me want to bring the claws out and make her my bitch.

I returned to Rachel and Daniel, who asked me where I had disappeared to. "I was around." No sense in trying to come up with a lie, they'd see through it anyway. We got our things and left. And even though I looked for him, I didn't see Clay again.

chapter
thirteen

clay

I had decided to stay in Davidson. After the get-together was over and I had cleaned up the mess, I sat with Ruby for a long while. She was going through picture albums, stopping periodically to cry. It killed me to see her like this and I knew then I couldn't leave her. She had never left me and I was determined to return the favor.

Okay, so part of me was motivated by something else as well. And that something was more like a *someone* with brown hair and beautiful eyes.

Even though I thought I was ready, I had been ill prepared to see Maggie again. Lord knows I had imagined it enough times. But still coming face-to-face with her had thrown me.

And then there was that moment up in my bedroom. Finding her there had given me instant déjà vu. I felt like I had been sucked into a time warp, as I had walked up the steps to find the door to my room wide open. She was sitting on my bed, as though she were waiting for me. Like she had done so many times before.

And it was easy to get pulled back into that pattern of letting her take care of me. For a moment, we had drifted back into our old roles. Me the broken one and Maggie the girl piecing me back together.

But that was beyond screwed up. I was trying really hard to get rid of the person that I was. But being around Maggie made it hard to leave him in my past. And as fucked up as it was, I realized I missed the old Clay. Because the old Clay belonged with Maggie. The Clay that I was now didn't seem to belong anywhere.

I hadn't told Ruby my plans yet; I was still considering the complete upheaval it would create in my world. The first three days back in Davidson had been spent with total, overwhelming anxiety. I had wanted to run, to get my ass back to Grayson. But here I was, Saturday night, knowing deep in my bones that I wouldn't be going anywhere.

Dr. Todd would not be happy. He had warned me that coming back to a place that carried so much baggage would be opening myself up to old wounds. I was supposed to be prepared for this. Hadn't that been what I'd spent the last three months doing? But the pull I felt in Davidson, Virginia, was too strong to resist.

Plus, it was *my* life. I could do with it what I wanted. Okay, even I recognized how counterproductive that statement was, but I was feeling testy and defensive. And I knew I'd be letting people down back in Florida. But the people who mattered the most were right here, and that's what was important.

After Ruby went to bed, I spent a long time sitting up, going through the same photo albums. I propped my feet up on the coffee table and accidentally knocked over Lisa's coffee mug. It fell to the hardwood floor and broke into pieces.

Shit! I leaned down and picked up the mess. Then, on an impulse, I picked up Lisa's glasses, gathered her slippers that still lay where she had kicked them off beside the couch. I grabbed her gray sweater that lay over the back of the chair and took them into the kitchen. I was suddenly very, very angry.

I found a black trash bag and dumped the painful reminders

inside. I tied it shut and dropped it at the foot of the stairs. When I was done, I stood there, bracing myself against the wall, breathing quickly.

Now that my spurt of anger had disappeared, I realized Ruby would have my head for messing with Lisa's stuff like that. But I just couldn't handle sitting around while her shit lay about like she would walk through the door at any moment.

Like today was just any other day and not the day we had put her in the ground. It wasn't right. And I was sick and tired of living in a delusion. Sure, life was tough to deal with and some days it took everything in me to even put my feet on the floor. But that was better than living a lie, with unrealistic expectations that would never be realized.

I picked up the bag and quietly took it upstairs. I opened up the door to Ruby's bedroom. She was finally asleep, curled under a blanket. Trying to be as silent as possible, I opened the bag and took out Lisa's stuff. I gently laid them out on the dresser just inside the entryway.

When I was done, I took a final look at Ruby, who hadn't moved, and closed the door behind me. Standing in the hallway, I made another decision. I strode across the floorboards and flung my bedroom door open, wincing when it hit the wall with a bang.

I turned on the light and went inside. I could still see the indentation on the bedspread from where Maggie was sitting earlier. Looking around, I wondered why I had been so scared to come in here.

It was just a room, like any other. Only this one seemed to whisper with a hundred memories. Some I wanted to remember, others I didn't. But whatever, this was my room and I had to start learning to exorcise the ghosts of my past. There was no way I could move forward, in whatever direction my future decided to take me, unless I faced things.

I was done with being a weak coward. And staying in this room, even if it seemed a small thing to do, was a start.

I went downstairs and turned off the lights, then grabbed my suitcase and lugged it up the stairs. I placed it on the bed and opened it, pulled out my clothes, and then dumped them into my chest of drawers. When I was finished, I stuffed my now empty suitcase into the closet.

Then curling up on my bed, I fell into a fitful sleep.

◆

The next morning, I spent a long time putting off the inevitable; calling Dr. Todd and explaining that I wouldn't be returning to Grayson. Ruby was still in her room. I wasn't sure if she was sleeping or not but I made sure to be quiet, just in case.

I sat down in the living room and pulled out my cell phone and dialed Dr. Todd's personal number before I lost my nerve. It rang twice before he answered.

"Hey, Doc, how's it goin'?" I asked lightly. I picked up the pen and started doodling on a pad of paper.

"Clayton, it's nice to hear from you. How were things yesterday?" he asked. I gave him the quick rundown about the service, the get-together afterward. I told him about Ruby and how hard this was on her. And then I told him about Maggie, seeing her again and how tough that had been for me.

Just like always, unloading felt really good. It was unbelievable that I had fought sharing my feelings for so long. I really was such a fool. It was amazing how knowing someone would listen patiently made it so easy to open up.

"That's a lot for someone to handle, Clay. How are you dealing with everything?" His question was loaded with a million tiny subtexts. Was I cutting? Was I drinking? Was there a hypodermic needle poking out of my arm as we spoke? Was I falling face-first in a pile of my own shit?

"I'm dealing. Some minutes are easier than others, but so far so good." And that was the truth. I hadn't fallen off the wagon just yet. Though the temptation was pretty damn great.

"That's wonderful, Clay. I'm glad to hear that. Now, why don't you tell me the reason for your call?" said Dr. Todd, the all-seeing psychic. The man was good, too good. And here I thought I was hiding my true intentions so well. I was clearly losing my touch.

I took a deep breath and laid it all out there. Like ripping off a Band-Aid, it was better to do it quickly. "I'm staying in Davidson." I sounded belligerent, as though daring him to argue with me.

"I suspected this would happen. I know how hard it is to leave home, once you're there," Dr. Todd said patiently, making me feel unreasonably guilty. It wasn't as though he were trying to shame me. In fact, he sounded totally understanding, but I felt the disappointment a thousand miles away.

"I just can't leave Ruby. Not like this. She's going through a lot and I would hate myself if I took off again," I explained.

"I understand, Clay, I really do. But as your therapist, I have to remind you of the fact that you have at least one more week left in your treatment contract. Three months may seem like a long time, but when it comes to getting a handle on your issues, it's not nearly long enough. Don't become complacent in your treatment," Dr. Todd told me firmly. He was using his principal voice, the one that let me know I needed to listen to what he was telling me.

And I was listening, honestly. But that wouldn't change my decision. My mind was set.

"Does that mean I *have* to come back? Because I was under the impression that I could make those decisions for myself now," I said sharply, not liking the fact that I was now starting to second-guess myself.

"You are 100 percent right. You control where you go and what you do. You are an adult now, Clay. You are not a direct danger to yourself or others, so I can't force you to re-admit yourself. But I won't lie to you; I'm very concerned about you leaving treatment without proper planning and discharge arrangements, whatever the reason. Time and attention need to be given to your outpatient care plan and solidifying your supports. Given the severity of your illness, you can't take that lightly. But if you are set against returning to Grayson, I think we need to put some things into place to ensure you won't relapse. Which includes continuing your medication regimen. No ifs, ands, or buts, Clayton," Dr. Todd explained.

"I know that, Doc. I won't forget to take my medicine like a good little boy," I spat out, taking my frustration out on the person I knew could take it.

Dr. Todd didn't address my surly attitude. "And you need to continue with your therapy, but on an outpatient basis now. I want you to call the counselor I told you about. Shaemus Laughtry is one of the best licensed professional counselors in the field. I have worked with him in the past and I'm more than comfortable with transferring your case to him. He and I can work together to ensure your treatment is seamless. I'm serious about this, Clay. You can't afford to quit now. You've come a long way, but you still have a lot ahead of you."

I had every intention of reaching out to the other therapist, but hearing Dr. Todd put it like that, I felt scared. Was I ready to try this whole living-on-my-own-terms thing? I had wanted the ability to call the shots, to do this my way. But now that I was being handed the keys to the kingdom, I sort of wanted to give them back.

I started to pick at the skin around my fingernail again. The area was already raw, but that didn't stop me from digging a little deeper. "Yeah, I will. I'll call him first thing tomorrow and set up an appointment," I agreed.

"Good. I'm glad to hear that. And I would still like you to call and check in with me until you start seeing Shaemus regularly. It's important you start building your support systems there. I know that Ruby and Lisa have always been your primary supports, but that system is no longer in place. So, Clay, you need to start building a new one. Shaemus can help you do that. Without that foundation, it makes the rest so much more difficult." Dr. Todd was right; I couldn't exactly depend on Ruby right now. And that freaked me out.

I swallowed thickly, trying not to panic at how alone I suddenly felt. "Okay," I said quietly.

"You can do this, Clay. But when you think you can't, please call if you need me," he urged and I nodded, though he couldn't see me. I felt like the floor was opening up beneath me and I was about to be sucked in. This was not a good way for me to feel.

"What if I do it again? What if I fuck it all up? I'm not good at the whole good-decision-making thing. Am I making a huge mistake staying here?" I hated the pleading in my voice. But I needed to hear total and complete honesty, at whatever the cost.

I heard Dr. Todd let out a sigh. "I can't answer that, Clay. I can't predict what will happen. All I can say is that you are a smart young man and if you remember the things you've been learning— how to reframe, how to step back and look at your choices before you act on them—you can make this work for you. And if you feel like you can't do it, that's when you need to ask for help. Never be ashamed to admit you can't handle it. There's nothing weak in acknowledging when things are greater than you."

I wish I had Dr. Todd's ability to say exactly the right thing. It was a skill I could get a hell of a lot of mileage out of right now.

"Thanks, Doc. I'll call Mr. Laughtry in the morning and then let you know what I can work out. I appreciate everything, really."

"As I've always told you, Clayton, it's what I'm here for. I look forward to hearing from you." And with that, we disconnected the call. Now that that was out of the way, I had an entire day left in order to figure out what the hell I was going to do.

Ruby hadn't been to her shop in over a week. I knew there had to be inventory and shelving to be done. I went up the stairs and lightly knocked on her bedroom door. When there was no answer I looked inside to find her still asleep. So I left her to it, leaving her a note telling her where I was.

Then I grabbed my keys and my wallet and went to my car. I headed down the familiar streets until I saw a sign for the coffee shop, Java Madness. I seemed to remember Ruby telling me this was where Maggie worked.

So what did I do? I pulled into the small parking lot and then went inside. I looked around noticing that it was pretty quiet. I approached the counter to place my order. I didn't see Maggie anywhere. Maybe she wasn't working. But I was already there, so I might as well get something.

"What can I get ya?" a tall guy with red hair who was working the industrial espresso machine asked without looking at me. I glanced up at the menu.

"Uh, just a coffee, black. And one of those chocolate croissant things. To go, please." I pulled my wallet out and got some cash. When I looked back up, Mr. Red Head was staring at me with a peculiar look on his face. Did I know this guy? I looked at him a little closer. He did seem familiar, but I couldn't place him. I assumed he went to Jackson; he was about my age. But that didn't explain why he seemed almost pissed to see me. Did I have some altercation with this dude that I couldn't remember? It was highly likely, given how much of a dick I was during my last go-around in Davidson.

"Clay Reed. I heard you were back in town," he said as though I had made it my mission to fuck up his morning. What the hell was this guy's problem?

"And you are?" I asked acidly, narrowing my eyes a bit as he tried to mad-dog me. Was he seriously trying to play macho man while wearing a fucking apron with a smiling coffeepot on it?

"Jake Fitzsimmons," he answered as if that explained everything. Jake Fitzsimmons? I arched my eyebrow.

"Sorry, buddy, I don't know who the hell you are." I was way past caring how rude I sounded. This guy was rubbing me the wrong way.

Jake smirked as though he knew he was getting to me. "Maggie's friend," he expanded and then it all clicked. Jake Fitzsimmons. Daniel's friend who spent way too much time sniffing around my girl. Now I knew why my appearance had him looking as though he had swallowed glass. He had always had a hard-on for Maggie. And it was pretty apparent that hadn't changed. Had this fucking douche moved in as soon as I was out of the picture? Shit, was Maggie *with* this guy now?

She hadn't said anything about a boyfriend, but that didn't mean anything. We hadn't exactly exchanged full details about the last three months. I felt like punching the redheaded coffee-slinging monkey straight in his obnoxious face.

"Ah, okay. You're the guy who's all about the sloppy seconds, right?" Yeah, that was a messed-up thing to say, but he was flicking my rage switch with his bony finger.

Jake snorted. "Sloppy seconds, huh? No, there's nothing sloppy about it."

Okay, that was it, I was going to come across the counter and pound his skull into the floor. I had tucked my wallet back into my pocket and braced my hands on the counter when a hand grabbed me by the upper arm.

"Cool it, Jake. Just get the man his coffee and stop being an ass about it." I gritted my teeth, pissed that it looked as though I would have to reschedule kicking the shit out of Jake Fucking Fitzsimmons for another day.

"He's not getting any, Clay, sloppy or otherwise, so just calm the fuck down, all right?" I wrenched my arm out of Daniel's grip and took a deep, steadying breath. I didn't say anything, just waited for my coffee.

Jake came back and shoved the Styrofoam cup across the counter, sloshing hot liquid all over the surface. "And that's on the house, right?" Daniel said, clearly irritated with his buddy. Jake gave a curt nod and walked away to help another customer. He hadn't given me my damn croissant but I decided I'd made enough of a scene for one day.

I picked up the drink and took a sip, the bitter coffee soothing my jangled nerves. I looked at Daniel and he was watching me as though waiting for me to pounce or something. I held up my free hand in a placating gesture. "I'll keep my hands to myself, I promise," I said begrudgingly.

Daniel shrugged. "I wouldn't blame you for beating his face in. Jake was being a prick. But he's wanted in Maggie's pants for years. And with you out of the picture he thought he had a shot. Now you've shown back up and he has to get all girly about it. Don't take anything he says seriously. He's just got a bad case of PMS going on."

Huh. This was the most Daniel and I had said to each other . . . well, ever. He had never hidden the fact that he didn't trust me, so him coming to my defense was surprising.

"Thanks for the assist and all," I said, ready to get the hell out of there. Coming to Java Madness was a massive mistake. All I had ended up with was high blood pressure and a shitty cup of coffee.

"Clay, you got a minute?" Daniel called out just before I walked out the door. I should have seen that one coming. It was time for the *you hurt my friend and I break your legs* conversation. We'd had that same talk several times in the past. I guess Daniel felt it necessary to have a refresher course.

"Sure." I went and sat down at a table near the window, trying to force down more coffee. It really was crap. I bet Jake I've-got-my-panties-in-a-bunch Fitzsimmons spit in it. Asshole. I pushed the cup away from me and crossed my arms over my chest. Daniel flipped his cell phone over and over again in his hand.

"First of all, I really am sorry about Lisa. She was really nice and all. Even though I only met her the one time, she seemed cool," Daniel said directly. One thing I had always respected about Daniel Lowe was the fact that he told things like they were. He didn't dance around a subject, he just bulldozed through it. Maggie would get pissed about it at times, thinking he was an insensitive ass. But you couldn't help but admire someone who never bothered with pretense.

"Thanks, man," I said, tapping my fingers on the table.

"So how long are you in town for?" Daniel asked me, furrowing his eyebrows as he waited for my answer. We had already been over this once at the funeral, but clearly he needed a more definitive response this time.

"You gonna try and kick my ass if I tell you I'm staying?" I asked him a bit belligerently. I stopped tapping my fingers and laid my hand flat on the table, meeting Daniel's stare head-on. There was a moment when I wasn't entirely sure what he was going to do. He didn't seem particularly happy with my announcement.

"You gonna give me a reason to kick your ass, Clay?" he asked me pointedly.

I blew out a breath and ran my hand through my hair. "I sure as hell hope not," I answered honestly. Because I really hoped I wouldn't be making the same mistakes as before. And if I did, then I deserved whatever ass kicking Daniel dished out.

Daniel frowned. "Does Maggie know?"

I shook my head. "Nope. And just so you know, this decision has nothing to do with Maggie, all right?" I tried to say it like I meant it. Daniel rolled his eyes.

"Give me a fucking break. Everything you do seems to be about Maggie in some way or another. But I'm telling you right now, Clay, she's been through hell. *You* put her through fucking hell. I don't know everything that went down when you guys were in North Carolina. She'd never tell me. And I don't want to fucking know. But what I *do* know is you left. I don't care what your reasons were. You left her. You don't call her. You don't write. You just cut her out of your life. And that is all sorts of wrong. Look, I don't want to bring up ancient history here. I'm just warning you that if you fuck with my girl again, I won't be so forgiving next time." Daniel's blue eyes were icy cold, and even though we were pretty even physically, I knew he'd fight to the death for Maggie.

The thing I didn't think Daniel realized, even now, is that so would I.

"I hear you, Daniel. I really do. But I'm not trying to open up a book that is better off closed, okay?" I really wish I meant what I said. Because I still believed Maggie was better off without me. Not that she was better off with some douche like Jake Fitzsimmons (who was still glaring at me from behind the counter, fucking pussy), but I wanted more for her than what I had ever been able to give.

But Daniel only laughed. Like I had just said the funniest joke he had ever heard. And it ticked me off. I clenched my fist, my knuckles turning white. "What's so damn funny?" I asked in a low voice. My urge to pummel people was out of control today.

Daniel shook his head. "You're what's funny. Do you really expect me to believe you won't be sniffing around Mags' skirt the first chance you get? You can't stay away from her. And I get it, okay. All I'm saying is be a bit more . . . careful with her this time. She's just now getting her crap together. And you can't come blowing back into her life and shitting all over it." He leveled his eyes at me in warning and I wanted to deny what he said. But the man spoke truth.

We watched each other warily for a few more moments. "Fair enough," I said finally. Daniel nodded, seeming to accept my response.

"So, you gonna come back to Jackson?" he asked me, changing the subject. I was left in a bit of recoil by the switch. Daniel crossed his arms on top of the table and waited for me to answer him as though he had all time in the world to sit here and chat.

"I'd planned on it. I probably won't start until the end of the week. I've got to help Ruby out at the shop, make sure she's doing all right before I go back to school," I explained.

"Understandable. Well, if there's anything you need, Rachel and I are around," he offered offhandedly, and I couldn't really tell if he meant it or not. Then he got to his feet. Clearly our conversation was over.

I grabbed the full coffee cup and threw it into the trash. Daniel called out a good-bye to Jake, who was still watching us, looking pissy, which gave me immense satisfaction. We headed out to the parking lot.

"Okay, well, I guess I'll see you around," Daniel said, throwing me a wave as he got into his truck. I waved back. I got into my car and started it up, not sure if I had just experienced a thinly veiled threat or unexpected support. Either way, Daniel Lowe had given me something to think about.

chapter
fourteen

"You'll never guess who I just saw in the office, filling out paperwork," Claire said, sitting down at our lunch table. Daniel and Rachel looked up as she started to unwrap her sandwich. Daniel seemed wary, as though he knew something the rest of us didn't know. I narrowed my eyes at him, but he seemed reluctant to make any sort of eye contact.

"Who?" Rachel asked, taking a sip of her soda.

"Clay Reed," Claire said in a whisper. My head jerked in her direction. What did she just say?

"Huh?" Rachel asked, looking confused. She shot me a look as if to ask *Do you know anything about this?* I shook my head. I was currently the last person on the planet to be in the know when it came to Clayton Reed.

"Yeah, rumor has it, he's reenrolling at Jackson. He was talking to the secretary when I saw him. I tried to hang around outside the door for a while, hoping I'd catch him. But the bell rang and I had to get to class," Claire said conspiratorially.

Clay was back in school? That must mean he had decided to stay in Davidson. When we had spoken after the funeral, he had seemed set on returning to Florida. I wondered what had changed. And there went my stomach flip-flopping all over the place.

"Interesting," I muttered, pushing my lunch away. I had suddenly lost my appetite.

Daniel cleared his throat, drawing my attention. Rachel gave him a look. "What do you know, Danny? Spill it," his girlfriend demanded. He looked uncomfortable.

"Well, I *may* have run into him on Sunday. And he *may* have mentioned he was planning on sticking around," Daniel mumbled, stuffing a few french fries into his mouth.

Rachel smacked his arm. "And you didn't say anything? What the hell, Danny?" she shrieked, glaring at him. Daniel hunched his shoulders up, clearly feeling the stink eye hitting him from all directions.

"I wasn't sure he would actually do it. I didn't want to say anything if he ended up leaving again," Daniel defended himself. I gritted my teeth together in frustration. Nothing like being blindsided to make me feel punchy.

"Way to keep secrets, asshole," I threw at him, though I couldn't summon up a whole lot of anger. Mostly because I was annoyingly thrilled that I would be seeing Clay again. Not that that changed *anything*.

Sure, sweetie, you keep telling yourself that, I goaded myself. Yep, the full-on internal conversations had begun.

"What's with the angry faces, guys?" Jake asked, plopping down beside me. Claire looked from him to me as he put his hand on the small of my back briefly before digging into his lunch. When did Jake start feeling like it was his place to touch me? He and I were definitely not on the same page. In fact, he was a good twenty chapters ahead of me. It made me want to rip out the freaking pages and shove them down his throat.

See? . . . Punchy.

"Oh, just dishing out the gossip. You know with Clay back, that's all anyone is talking about." Claire grinned, licking pudding off the back of her spoon, her eyes twinkling devilishly.

Jake went instantly tense beside me and he shifted uncomfortably in his seat. "Well, that's cool, I guess." It was very obvious that it was anything *but* cool as far as he was concerned. Rachel was staring at me, trying to send me Morse code through her eyeballs. But clearly I wasn't up to receiving encrypted messages.

"Yep, cool," I said dryly, getting to my feet. I was definitely finished with this conversation and I had homework to complete before my next class. "Later, guys," I tossed out as casually as possible before heading to the trash can.

I was shaking the food off my tray before putting it on the counter when Daniel's ex-girlfriend, Kylie, joined me. She flipped her hair over her shoulder. "Wow, so Clay's moved back to Davidson. That's so awesome. I hope he's okay. I mean after trying to kill himself and all," she said with false brightness. I shot her a look over my shoulder and then walked out of the cafeteria, deciding no response was better than going all kung-fu ninja on her ass. Fuck that bitch.

The rest of the day was spent fielding a million and one questions about Clay. You'd think this was the only newsworthy event happening at Jackson. Had everyone already forgotten about the junior girl who had gotten knocked up by her thirty-year-old boyfriend? That seemed a hell of a lot more interesting than the fact that Clayton Reed had returned.

By the end of the day I was ready to bash my head in. "Have you talked to him at all?" Lila Casteel asked me as I headed toward the gym for track practice. I hefted the bag up onto my shoulder and gave her my frostiest smile.

"Nope, but I'll get right on that, Lila. It's right behind learning to tap dance and translating *The Odyssey* into Pig Latin." Lila looked taken aback but I just didn't give a shit. I stormed away from her and was glad to have track to keep my mind distracted.

✦

After practice, I grabbed my bag and left before anyone else could stop me, asking questions I didn't have answers for. If one more person asked me if I had seen Clay and whether he was *really* coming back to Jackson, I would profess temporary insanity and go UFC fighter on their faces.

I dug through my bag for my keys as I got into the parking lot. When I glanced up, the sight of who was waiting by my car made me stumble. There went my plans for plausible deniability.

"Damn it," I muttered under my breath, righting myself, feeling the sting of embarrassment color my cheeks.

"You okay?" Clay asked, coming to my side, making the flash of humiliation even more acute.

I waved him away. "I'm fine."

He jammed his hands into his pockets and fell into step beside me.

"This thing still lives, huh?" he asked, poking the tire of my car with his shoe. I snorted as I opened the door to throw my bag inside.

"Still kickin'. She'll outlive your fancy ride over there, I have no doubt," I said, nodding toward his BMW that was parked beside mine. Clay laughed.

"I'm pretty sure your car could take mine in a cage fight. I bet she fights dirty." I tried not to get lost in his eyes as they twinkled in amusement. It was way too easy to fall into our old banter. But too much water had run under that particular bridge.

"As great as it is to stand here and discuss the finer points of our respective cars, I'm feeling smelly and sweaty and would really like a shower. I'm assuming there is a reason for your random stalking?" I asked, trying to sound annoyed, when in actuality I was entirely too excited to see him.

Clay's smile faltered and then disappeared altogether. Jeesh, I hadn't meant to be so testy. He looked as though I had just told him his favorite dog had run away. But my overly fluttery heart set me on edge. It reminded me of how simple it would be to lose myself in that place where he was my entire world. The world he had decimated.

"Yeah. Okay. Well, I just wanted to tell you that I've decided to stay in Davidson. At least for a while—" he began, but I cut him off.

"I've already heard." I made a show of checking my imaginary wristwatch. "About six and a half hours ago, to be precise."

Clay groaned. "God, don't these people have anything better to talk about?" he growled.

I lifted my shoulders in a shrug. "This is Davidson, Virginia. You sneeze in the woods and everyone knows about it five minutes later and then talks about it until you're forty. It's nothing personal. You just gave these people something to talk about. Be flattered," I said shortly, closing my car door and leaning against it.

Clay rolled his eyes toward the sky. "I just wish they'd talk about someone who wasn't me," he said softly and I felt bad for making light of it. I knew it was hard for him to be the center of attention. He had always preferred to blend into the background. But that was difficult to do after our stint as teenagers on the run. The town would be hard-pressed to forget something like that anytime soon. And now that he was back, it only served to fan the flames that had only just started to die down.

"Yeah, it sucks," I agreed, crossing my arms over my chest. Clay looked at me. I mean really looked at me, and something flickered in his dark eyes that made my heart race. Annoying heart!

Slowly, he leaned against my car beside me. Our elbows

rubbed together and the familiar tingles of electricity flickered across my skin.

"I just wanted to tell you myself. I know I've made things . . . difficult for you and I'm sure my showing up here makes it even worse." I wanted to stay angry with him. I wanted to yell and scream about the way he had left me. But it was hard to summon up anything other than stone-cold relief that he was here at all. But as always, I was able to hide my more vulnerable emotions under a hefty pile of sarcasm and snark.

"Nah. You give yourself too much credit," I teased, knocking his shoulder with mine. Clay glanced at me through his lashes, the look on his face leaving me breathless.

"Probably. But all the same, I don't want to make things harder for you." His voice dropped as his eyes fell to my lips.

I found myself leaning into him, my eyes searching his and not letting go. And I let the rough edges I had honed into sharp points soften a bit. "It was harder for me when you were gone," I admitted, surprising myself by laying such honesty at the feet of the one person who could stomp all over me. Something lit in Clay's eyes and flared to life. Reaching up, he pushed my hair back off of my shoulder and placed his hand on the side of my neck.

"Maggie, there's so much I need to tell you. To explain. I want you to understand why I never called. Why I needed to write that letter. Everything I did was done for what I *thought* were really good reasons. But right now it just feels like wasted time." His thumb caressed the skin under my ear and I had to tamp down on the urge to shiver, at both his touch and his words. The chemistry began to build between us, just the way it always had. This felt so reminiscent of a time, not too long ago, when the next logical step would be to fall into each other's arms. And I saw that Clay recognized that as well. Then it all changed and the smoldering fire in his eyes flickered out.

Clay dropped his hand and stepped away, looking apologetic. "I, uh, I really need to get home. I have to check on Ruby. I just wanted you to hear the news from me. I don't expect this to change things between us. I only wanted you to know." The shift in his demeanor left me confused and then irritated. Again, this was classic Clay. Hot and cold. Yes and no. Up and down.

"How typical," I said under my breath. Though not softly enough, as became apparent by Clay's frown.

"What's that supposed to mean?" he asked in confusion. I threw my hands up in the air.

"This is so stereotypically Clay Reed! So predictable. You track me down after practice, because you *had* to see me. We have this little moment; you stare into my eyes, make some lame point to touch me. And just when we're getting somewhere, you turn around and leave. Because it's all so *difficult* for you. Whatever, Clay! I rode that roller coaster once. And I want a fucking refund! If you're going to be living here, fine! But don't yank me around. I don't have the time or patience to go another round of will-he-won't-he with you." My voice petered out and I wasn't sure whether I wanted to kiss his stupid, perfect lips or throw my water bottle at his head.

Clay's face went pale. "I never meant . . . No, you're right, Maggie. You didn't deserve it then, and you sure as hell don't deserve it now. But I'm trying, I swear. I'm working really hard to pull it together. I wish you could trust that." Trust. There was no way I was gift wrapping *that* and handing it over to him anytime soon. It would take more than puppy dog eyes and a velvet tongue, that's for sure.

"I guess only time will tell, Clay," I said, getting into my car. I didn't wait for his response. I started the engine and left before I ended up making a fool of myself by chucking in all of my self-respect for a momentary taste of Clayton Reed heaven.

When I got home, compelled by motives I wasn't entirely sure

I wanted to identify, I dug the butterfly necklace out from the bottom of my jewelry box. I hadn't worn it since I had taken it off after getting Clay's kiss-off letter.

But here I was, carefully clasping the delicate chain around my neck, letting the thin silver butterfly lie hidden beneath my shirt.

It rested cold against my skin, but I felt the truth of why I was wearing it again burn through me. Clay was in my heart and in my head. It was exhausting, continually pushing him out.

But was I ready to let him in?

chapter
fifteen

I had started seeing my new therapist a few weeks ago. Shaemus Laughtry was about as different from Dr. Todd as you could get. Whereas my Grayson therapist was calm and collected, Shaemus was energetic and fervent. He was a likable guy, I'd give him that, but I was still on the fence as to whether he would be a good fit for me.

Our sessions had included teleconferencing with Dr. Todd, in order to "ease my transition." Shaemus had me sign a new no-harm contract and we went over what I wanted to get out of therapy. It was hard for me to open up to someone new, but I was determined to give it the good ol' college try.

I met with Shaemus two times a week, Tuesdays and Thursdays. I would go to his office in Staunton right after school and stayed until six. So in all I was meeting with my new shrink four hours a week. This was significantly less than what I was getting at Grayson, but it was still a lot of time to be spending in counseling every week. I was bitter. Of course I was bitter. What eighteen-year-old guy wanted to be stuck talking to a balding, middle-aged dude who smelled like stale coffee and cigarettes instead of doing, oh I don't know, anything else?

I felt like a freak, needing to spend that much time talking about my feelings. *How does that make you feel? Let's process that. Draw a picture of your happiest memory.* Fucking hell, what a pain in the ass! I could have blown it off; conveniently forgotten to show up. But then where would that leave me? And the truth was, I was too scared to find out.

Things at home with Ruby weren't getting any better. It was like *Night of the Living Dead* around there. And not in the cool George Romero kind of way. More like the crappy remake.

She barely spoke to me and I felt like I was taking care of a child. She had yet to return to the shop. Tilly was running things for now, which was fine for the interim, but couldn't be a long-term solution. I was beginning to think that Ruby would never bounce back. But then wasn't it messed up of me to expect her to be right as rain after only a few weeks? What did that say about me that I couldn't let the poor woman grieve? That I was so set on helping her *move on.*

The vibe in the house was miserable. For the first time in my life, I didn't want to be there. But I couldn't leave. I *wouldn't* leave. Even if it did trigger every self-destructive impulse I had.

"You need to find a hobby, Clay. Or a job. Something," Shaemus announced as our session was coming to a close. I blinked slowly. Huh?

"I have a hobby. I draw. A lot," I replied, swearing that if he told me to take up macramé I was out of there.

Shaemus rubbed at his graying goatee thoughtfully. I started fixating on his sweater. It was a loud teal and neon green. Who woke up in the morning and thought *Today I'm going to wear a sweater that will make everyone that looks at me want to gouge their eyes out?*

Just when I was going to ask where he bought his wardrobe because I think I might want one of those sweaters, he snapped his fingers. I waited for him to shout out "Aha!" and the moment would be complete.

"Not drawing. Your art is wonderful, but it's become too tied up in the angsty stuff. I'm talking about something that would force you out of your house and to interact more with other people. You self-isolate entirely too much."

Oh, God, he was going to tell me to sign up to coach Little League, wasn't he? I had a flash of screaming children and I shuddered in revulsion. Interacting with people, in my opinion, was entirely overrated. I shared my assessment with Shaemus, who raised his bushy eyebrows as though I had just proven his point. "That's exactly why you should do it. You fall into old patterns when things get hard. That's a natural, human response. But the point of all this is for you to break those patterns. To make yourself bust out of the mold you've created. So that is why you need some sort of activity that keeps your mind active and focused on something positive." He gave me several brochures on volunteering. Wow, I could spend my free time emptying bedpans as a Candy Striper. What the hell did you call a guy Candy Striper? Shit, it was going to drive me nuts.

Or I could join the litter patrol and get up at six every Saturday morning to walk up and down the road picking up garbage like some sort of chain gang.

Not liking any of those options, I decided on something a bit more productive. And that's how I found myself Thursday evening after my therapy session filling out an application at Bubbles, home of gluttonous banana splits and hamburgers with a side of heartburn.

I had never worked before, unless I could list illegal sales on my job history. But now that my parents had cut me off and Ruby's shop was floundering, I figured it was time for me to roll up my sleeves and pitch in. And this would get me "interacting." Mark your calendars, folks, Clay Reed was gettin' a job!

"You're here to schlepp in with the rest of us?" I looked up to see Rachel smiling at me a little warily.

I put down the pen and turned to face her. "I thought you worked at the movie store in town," I said, indicating her Bubbles apron. She smoothed down the purple fabric strapped to her front and looked sheepish.

"I do. This is my second job. My car and insurance don't pay for themselves. Though I really wish they would." Her lopsided smile was a bit warmer this time. I laughed and nodded in agreement.

"Yeah, I understand that." I tapped the pen on the paper, feeling a bit awkward. What did I have to talk about with Rachel Bradfield? Should I start off with *Hey! So remember that time I tried to off myself? Good times, right?* Yeah, my sense of humor was seriously messed up.

Discomfort aside, I needed the job. And I needed to prove to my therapist that I was capable of mingling in general society. No more playing scary shut-in for me.

"Well, cool. I'll leave you to it. Nice seeing you again." Rachel's head bobbed a few times and I watched her with amusement. I was definitely making her uncomfortable. Which I found inappropriately funny. See, messed-up sense of humor over here!

Before she got too far away, she turned back around and cocked her head sideways. "You know, I'm glad to see you're doing okay. You had a lot of people worried about you. Maybe we could all get together sometime, you, Maggie, Daniel, and me." Okay, that was not what I was expecting her to say. Well, crap, I had nothing sarcastic or droll to say to that.

"Uh, yeah, that sounds g-good," I stumbled pathetically over my words. Yep, I had been reduced to a stuttering simpleton. I had never exactly been welcomed into the fold before. If you're looking for the black sheep of Jackson High School, then search no further. Rachel had been nicer than most, but it was a barely tolerant politeness. This offer not only surprised the shit out of me, but left me feeling almost . . . included.

"Fabulous. I'll see you at school." Rachel went back to her tables and I went back to filling out my application, actually looking forward to having the job.

The manager offered to give me a few shifts to start, just to see how things went. I had been surprised that he gave me the job so quickly, but I didn't ask him what the hell he was thinking. My first one would be next week. Now that I had accomplished what I had set out to do, I was left with an entire weekend full of nothingness. And having nothing to do was a big no-no.

I jingled my keys in my hand, debating whether I should head over to Ruby's shop to check in with Tilly, when the sound of a sputtering engine caught my attention.

I couldn't help but laugh as I watched Maggie pull into the parking lot, smoke billowing out of the car's tailpipe. Then it stuttered to a stop, the air ringing with its death knell. Luckily she was able to coast into an empty parking spot. I could hear her cursing from twenty feet away and I couldn't get rid of the goofy smile on my face as I watched her smack the steering wheel over and over again. An angry Maggie was a tiny bit scary, but I was a masochist by nature.

I walked over and tapped on her window. She looked up in surprise that turned into embarrassment once she recognized me. Her face was flushed and her neck was splotchy. She got out of the car and slammed the door shut.

"What was I just saying about your car taking my car in a cage fight?" I leaned back to examine it. "I take it back." Maggie groaned and rolled her eyes.

"She put up a good fight, but you're right, it's time to put her to pasture." Maggie patted the hood. She reached into the backseat and grabbed her purse and a plastic grocery bag, then turned around to look at me.

"What are you doing here?" she asked, looking over my shoulder toward Bubbles.

"Putting in an application. You are now looking at the newest addition of the Bubbles waitstaff. Don't get too hot and bothered by the purple apron." I held my hands out to keep her back and she reluctantly laughed.

"I'll work on keeping my hands to myself." Her smile fell and she scuffed her shoe into the asphalt, looking away from me. "Well, I'd better get inside and see if Rachel can give me a ride home. And she'd better, considering I was only driving around in my death trap because she *needed* these shoes she left at my house. You know, because the other forty pairs she owns just wouldn't do for her date with Daniel later." She held up a bag by way of explanation. "So I'd better get in there. See ya around."

She started to walk around me when I reached out to grab her arm. *Come on, Clay, seize the moment*, I yelled at myself. My life had become all about second chances. So why not jump at this one?

"What do you say you come with me to Ruby's shop and then I can give you a ride home? I could use some help with the inventory. Ruby hasn't been in for a while and the place is a mess." I didn't drop her arm; instead, I slid my hand down her skin until I took ahold of her hand. I felt like a bit of a manipulator. I was using her need to help to get her to spend time with me. Well, whatever worked, right?

Maggie looked at my hand holding hers and I realized I was seriously overstepping here. I moved my fingers from her skin and curled them into a fist before jamming them into my pocket. I instantly understood her anger during our last conversation. I was sending some seriously messed-up mixed messages.

But it's like I couldn't help myself. Being around her was more intoxicating than any drug. My body seemed to move of its own volition, seeking out any means to touch her. She was and always would be my weakness.

My heart and mind were in a constant battle where Maggie was concerned. The near panic I felt when I was around her made it difficult to see anything else. But my heart needed her. And that's where we always had our problems. Because I couldn't *need* her, not anymore. I could *want* her, *long* for her, but never *need*. Because that spelled disaster for both of us. And I had had more than enough disaster in my life.

I was determined to do right by her and I had sworn that meant staying the fuck away from her. But being near her again made doing the *right* thing nearly impossible. In fact, I was thinking the *right* thing needed to take a hike. I was ready to do the *what felt good* thing for a couple of hours.

For a guy who struggled with finding his place in the world, standing next to Maggie, I understood one thing on a very fundamental level. Wherever she went, whatever she did, that is where I belonged.

Maggie chewed on her bottom lip for a moment and then gave me a small smile. "Just give me a minute. Let me take Rachel her hooker shoes." She glanced over her shoulder as she made her way into the restaurant, as though to make sure I was still waiting for her.

You crazy girl, don't you know I'd wait for you forever?

Maggie came back a few minutes later, this time wearing a large smile. Could that be for me? I sure freaking hoped so.

"Let's go." She went around to the passenger side of my car and I followed her to unlock the door, just as I had a thousand times before. I held the door for her, and she climbed in with a soft "Thanks."

I couldn't control the huge grin that spread across my face. My heart beat wildly in my chest, a reminder that this could still end very badly. That my screwed-up head was still capable of fucking it all up. But for right now, I was letting my heart do the leading.

Maggie reached down into the pocket of the door and pulled out my CDs. They were the same ones that I had always had. Thumbing through them, she chose one and put it into the player. The familiar strains of Placebo came out of the speakers and I tapped my fingers on the steering wheel. "Nice choice," I said, shooting her a sideways smile. We always had shared a common love of alternative glam rock. Okay, so I'm a closet Davie Bowie fan, what of it?

"Of course," she quipped as she started to bob her head up and down to the music. We pulled into the shop's parking lot a short time later. "Ruby hasn't been here in a while then?" she asked. I shook my head.

"Nope, Tilly's been covering things, but I'm trying to pitch in and help when I can." We walked through the front door, the bells tingling above us. "Hey, Tilly!" I called out in greeting.

Tilly was reading a book behind the counter but jumped to her feet when she saw me. "Clay! Hi! I didn't know you were coming in today."

"Yeah, I wanted to get a head start on the shipment we got in yesterday. Ruby would have come . . ." Tilly nodded in understanding so I didn't bother to come up with an excuse.

"Of course. I can help you if you want . . ." she offered, but I noticed she was now staring over my shoulder. She looked strangely irritated. Hmm, Tilly was usually too busy meditating or focusing her chi or whatever to get pissed about anything.

Maggie was hanging back and I waved her up. "You remember Maggie, right? She's gonna help me with the boxes. So if you need anything, we'll be in the back." Tilly's smile had disappeared and I noticed some weird communication going on between her and Maggie. There was a full-blown chick showdown going on. I just wish I knew why.

I never knew they had a problem with each other. I couldn't remember them ever having interacted before.

"Sure. I'll be up here." Tilly's voice was decidedly cooler and I took that as our cue to vacate. Girls were such a head fuck sometimes.

"Wonder what her problem is," I mused as I took in the huge pile of boxes lining the storeroom. Damn, this would take forever. Maggie snickered as she went to one and opened it.

"I forgot how oblivious you were," she commented, though it was clearly more to herself than to me.

"What's that supposed to mean?" I asked her. Me oblivious? Purposefully in denial, maybe. But oblivious? Maggie simply shook her head and started unpacking the box. Grabbing the inventory sheet, she started checking off items as I came to sit down beside her.

"Seriously, Mags. What am I so oblivious about? Don't leave me hanging," I dug. Maggie nudged me with her shoulder.

"Tilly. She likes you, you idiot."

"Well, of course she likes me, we're friends." This wasn't the news of the century. What was the big deal? And to be honest, I didn't want to spend time talking about Tilly. There were about a million other things I'd rather be doing than talking at all. Yes, my mind went there. Of course it went there. Maggie was beautiful and her jeans fit her ass really well.

"No, you dork. She *likes* you."

I snorted and shook my head. "Whatever, Mags." I didn't know what the hell she was talking about. But I really didn't care. Being here, with my girl, teasing and joking in a way that was almost . . . normal, that's what I cared about.

"See . . . oblivious," she muttered, turning back to the box in front of her. I didn't say anything else, just got down to our task. We worked quietly, taking out items and placing them on the floor.

When we were done with one box, we moved on to the next. After a while, we started to talk again. Nothing serious, just random conversation about nothing in particular. It was the best useless conversation I had ever had.

Maggie did this for me. She made it all matter. Even the insignificant stuff.

"Crap, Clay, I really have to get home. I told my parents I'd be back in time for dinner," Maggie said, getting to her feet. I closed up the box I had been working on and stood up, pulling my keys out of my pocket.

My bubble had burst. Knowing that this was over, whatever it had been, left me completely bereft. What if I never got an opportunity like this again? What if Maggie went home and realized our spending time together had been a huge mistake? I knew I couldn't live with that. Not when I had only just gotten a taste of what I had been missing.

"I'm glad we hung out, Clay. This was nice," Maggie said, tugging on her coat. And like that, I was okay again. And I knew that Dr. Todd had been right all along, that there was something so fundamentally wrong about my moods and feelings being dictated by another person like this. But when it was good, it was so freaking good.

"Bye, Tilly," I said as we were leaving and Maggie smirked at me.

"Oblivious," she mouthed.

I rolled my eyes. "Whatever," I muttered, though I could play oblivious all day long if it meant she kept teasing me like this.

Maggie's phone started to ring and she pulled it out to check the caller ID. I noticed the way her eyes darted to me before she answered.

I unlocked my car doors as Maggie began to talk to the person on the other line. I could tell instantly that she wasn't speaking to either Daniel or Rachel. There was something about her voice that I couldn't quite place.

She turned her face away as she spoke quietly and I tried to respect her privacy and not eavesdrop. But that possessive animal inside of me had me listening all the same. And when I heard her say, "I don't know, Jake. I promised my parents I'd be home for dinner," I wanted to snarl.

Fucking Jake. Apparently they were close enough to talk on the phone now. And yeah, that pissed the hell out of me. A voice inside me growled *She's mine.* And then my head became consumed by dark, twisted thoughts of Maggie with Jake, and I couldn't handle it.

I pulled out into traffic and hauled ass to her house. Maggie looked over at me in concern when I cut a sharp turn, causing my tires to squeal. I didn't even spare her a glance. I couldn't look at her. This was killing me.

"I've gotta go, Jake. I'll call you later," Maggie said and hung up. My teeth were clenched and I was equal parts relieved and devastated when I pulled up in front of Maggie's house.

I didn't turn off the car. I just needed her to go, even as I dreaded her getting out of the vehicle and leaving me. But I was fuming. I was mad at her, mad at me, mad at that fucking tool Jake. I couldn't deal with this right now. The dark need to take care of this horrible pain was becoming overwhelming.

"Clay. About Jake—" Maggie started and I held up my hand, cutting her off.

"You don't need to explain shit to me. We're not together. End of story." I sounded bitter and cold and I saw the way Maggie flinched. I felt the flicker of regret but it was quickly drowned out by the noise in my head.

"No, we're not together, Clay. But I'm not *with* Jake either. We're just friends. Not that I should have to tell you anything." She sounded irritated but even still she reached out, placing her hand on my arm.

I tensed and thought about pulling away. But I was rendered motionless, too needy for her touch. "You're right, it's your life. Spend it with who you want," I said, my words strangled in my throat. It was such a lie. I didn't want her spending it with anyone but me. That scary part of me wanted me to claim her, force her to see that I was all she wanted because she was all I *needed*.

Maggie sighed and removed her hand, leaving me aching and alone. "God, Clay. Why can't anything ever be simple between us? Jake's a friend. And let me remind you that it was *you* who ended us. Because I wouldn't have done that. There is nothing in this world that would have made me leave you." Maggie got out of my car and shut the door. Without a backward glance she went into her house.

I slammed my palms down onto the steering wheel several times and let out a deep, guttural scream. I threw the car into drive and got the hell out of there. I couldn't think. I couldn't focus. I just wanted to go somewhere. Find something to take it all away. This was too fucking much. I couldn't deal with the pain that fizzled in my gut. I needed it to disappear.

I got on the interstate and drove. And drove. And drove. With no purpose other than putting distance between me and the girl who was ripping my insides out. After an hour, I pulled into a rest stop to try to figure out what the hell I was going to do.

I got out of my car, grabbed the glass juice bottle that had been left in my center console, and headed toward some picnic tables in the middle of a grove of trees. I smashed the bottle on the ground and picked up the largest shard of glass and held it tightly in my fist.

It bit into my skin but not enough to draw blood. If I squeezed just a little harder it would cut me. Just a bit more and this buzzing in my head would go away. I wanted the quiet. For a little while at least.

"Fuck," I breathed out and dropped the glass onto the grass. And then I lost it. I dropped my head into the cover of my arms and cried. I hated myself for almost giving in to the self-destructive craving. I hated that I couldn't be stronger. And I really hated that in that moment, the life I wanted so desperately seemed miserably out of reach.

chapter
sixteen

maggie

To say things had been . . . intense since Clay had shown back up in my life would be a vast understatement. The truth was I didn't know how I was supposed to feel or act. Or what the hell I was supposed to say to him when he looked at me like I held the answers to the most important questions.

Last Thursday had been completely surreal. It was like the past and the present had gotten all mixed up and I was somehow transported back in time. It had been too easy, too natural, to fall back into that place in my life where Clay fit.

And it was just as easy to remember why he could so easily tear me apart. I could tell that he was trying to change. I could practically see the struggle in him to show me that *See, I'm different.* And in some ways he was.

Gone was the paranoid, hypersensitive recluse. Since returning to school, he seemed to make it a point to talk to people. He didn't skirt the edges of the hallway, hoping no one would notice him. He walked straight down the middle with his head held high. And I felt my heart swell in my chest every time I saw him because I was so proud of him.

He seemed to be doing his best to ignore the insatiable gossip that still swirled around him. More power to him, because that was something I had yet to master.

I knew he was working at Bubbles. The fact he was working where he would be forced to interact with people on a regular basis absolutely floored me.

He was trying to paint a new picture of himself, that was clear. But it didn't change what I had glimpsed when he dropped me off at my house last week. The anger and jealousy when he realized it was Jake on the phone. The way he had instantly shut me out. I had seen the wall come down. And I had been devastated and disappointed. Because I had hoped we were past that particular ugliness. But apparently not. Because that *other* Clay was still there. At least when he was around me. And *that* Clay still scared the hell out of me. And I wasn't sure if this new and improved Clayton Reed would ever be able to eradicate him.

There were times during the week when I would see him in the hallway or in the cafeteria and our eyes would meet and I could believe that we would find our way back to each other. That no matter what, Clay and I belonged together.

But then he would look away, move on, and I just knew he was avoiding me. Because he had made no effort to talk to me since being at Ruby's shop. And, for the first time in my entire life, I didn't do what was in my nature. Barge in, demand an explanation. Take control of things until I was satisfied with the result. It was as though I were waiting for a sign that read Safe to Proceed.

But so far, I was looking for something that remained hidden.

And Jake. Well, I felt like a real bitch for the way I had treated him. He had been such a good friend, even if I knew he had been biding his time, waiting for me to realize he was the guy I wanted to be with.

And for one whole moment, I thought that, yeah, maybe I

could move on and be with someone else. And why couldn't that someone be Jake Fitzsimmons?

But then Clay had blown back into my world and I realized I was deluding myself. Because I couldn't stomach the thought of sharing my life with anyone else.

"Why don't we order a pizza and catch up on *CSI*? I won't tell your mom that we watched TV during dinner," my dad joked, dropping his keys down onto the counter after coming in from work.

It was Thursday, Mom's Bunco night. Dad and I had proclaimed it Pizza Thursday years ago and it was a routine we rarely deviated from. I looked up from my English homework and grinned as my dad started rooting through the junk drawer, trying to find the coupons for Papa John's.

"Sounds like a plan," I agreed. My dad opened the refrigerator to get a drink and pulled out a Pyrex dish covered in foil with a note attached to the top. My dad read it and let out an audible groan.

"What is it?" I asked, coming over to grab the note. It was from my mom. She was asking my dad to run the casserole over to Ruby. A knot suddenly formed in my stomach.

"Well, that was nice of her," I said, peeking up at my dad hesitantly. His mouth was set in a firm line and he looked anything but pleased with my mother's thoughtfulness.

"I wish she'd just leave well enough alone," he grumbled, putting the casserole down on the counter with a hard slam.

"What's that supposed to mean?" I asked, getting annoyed by my dad's rudeness. Whatever his feelings for Clay, how he could be less than friendly to Ruby after all that she had been through seemed callous.

My dad sighed. "I feel horrible for Ruby. She's a sweet woman, always has been. But it doesn't change the fact that her nephew caused you a lot of anguish. Anguish I don't want to see repeated.

And I think prolonging our contact with that family, whatever the reason, is just asking for more heartache." I understood his hesitance about putting Clay and me in close proximity. That didn't change the fact that Clay and Ruby had lost someone they loved and needed as much support as we could give them.

But I understood where my dad was coming from. He had to watch his only child waste away in the middle of a severe depression brought on by a destructive relationship with Ruby's very sick nephew. I could get why he wanted us to keep our distance.

But that just wasn't realistic.

"Dad, Clay lives here now. You can't expect me to avoid him altogether. It takes you all of ten minutes to drive from one side of Davidson to the next," I teased, trying to lighten the mood.

My dad gave me a look that saw entirely too much. "Look, Maggie May. I won't tell you to stay away from him. We did that once and it didn't end very well." I cringed at his assessment.

"I can only hope you've learned something from what you went through with that boy. That maybe you've figured out what works in your life and what doesn't." He watched me closely, and I tried to keep my face neutral.

When I didn't respond, he sighed again and held out the casserole dish. "Here, run this over to Ruby's for me. I'll order the pizza." He didn't look at me and I blinked in surprise. Was he serious? He was actually suggesting that I go to Clay's house?

I slowly took the dish out of his hands and went to grab my purse. My dad was standing at the counter, staring down at the phone book, though I wasn't sure he was seeing it. I got the sense that he felt he was releasing me into the lion's den.

Right then I loved him so much. For letting me make my own choices and not trying to control my potential mistakes. And I swore that I wouldn't let him or Mom down again. That I *would* do things differently.

How that would pan out, I didn't know. But my resolve was ironclad.

For the moment.

✦

"Maggie! What are you doing here?" Ruby asked, opening the door to me. I tried not to recoil at the sight of the shrunken woman in front of me. Ruby's shoulders were hunched over, her normally happy face lined with grief and pain. Her skin held a sallow sheen and her hair was dull and lifeless. She was a shadow of the person she was before and this image of her shocked me to the core.

"Uh . . . well, my mom made you another one of her casseroles. I thought I'd drop it off." I held out the foil-covered glass dish. Ruby's smile was a sad caricature and I tried not to grimace.

"She really is such a lovely woman. Tell your mother thank you for me." She took the dish out of my hands and slightly tugged on my arm. "Do you have a moment for a cup of tea? I would love to spend time with you, sweetheart."

I looked over my shoulder, looking for Clay's car. Part of me wanted to see him. Part of me wanted to avoid him. I was in a serious quandary. But Ruby solved my internal debate for me.

Ruby patted my cheek. "He's not here, love. He won't be home for a while. So please come in and spend some time with me." Damn, she'd seen right through me. I pulled out my cell phone to double-check the time. I probably had some time before Dad called out the cavalry. So I followed her into the house.

I hung up my coat and joined Ruby in the kitchen. I noticed that the tiny bits of Lisa that had been everywhere the last time I was here were slowly disappearing. Peeking into the living room, I noticed that the coffee cup was no longer there, though the slippers remained. In the kitchen, Lisa's laptop still sat untouched on the table, but the newspaper she had been reading was gone.

Ruby opened up a cabinet and pulled out an ordinary box of Earl Grey tea. I was relieved I wouldn't have to force down one of her questionable herbal mixtures. We were silent as she put the kettle on and found two mugs and placed them on the counter.

When our tea was steeping, she brought me my cup and set it down in front of me at the kitchen table. She joined me and started dumping sugar and milk into her drink. I wondered how long we would sit there, drinking our tea, without talking. Ruby watched me as I sipped on the hot liquid. She appeared as though she wanted to say something, but was in no rush to do so. It made me a little uncomfortable.

"How's the shop?" I asked, though I could answer that question myself, having just been there last week. Ruby lifted her shoulders in a tired shrug.

"Fine. Tilly has been running things for me. I'm hoping I'll feel up to going in next week." Her voice was soft and she ran her finger around the rim of her cup. "Thank you for helping Clay with the deliveries last week. He mentioned you had come by and unloaded some things. I really appreciate it, Maggie."

"I didn't do much, honestly," I said offhandedly. Ruby put her mug down and covered my hand that lay on the table.

"Thank you all the same." She let out a soft sigh. "I just haven't been able to do it. I hate making Clay do so much. I know it's not fair to him, given how much he's gone through himself . . ." Her words trailed off and I swallowed thickly.

"I think he's just happy to help you. He loves you so much, Ruby," I told her, hating the sound of her guilt heavy in her voice. This woman was dealing with so much. Ruby's answering smile was sad.

"I know he does. I know that's why he's still here when he should be back in Florida. I should have made him go back. He's not ready to be here, to deal with all this." Her voice caught and she covered her mouth with the back of her hand, closing her eyes tightly on the tears that started to drip down her cheeks.

I got up and moved to sit beside her. Wrapping my arm around the smaller woman's shoulders, I squeezed her tightly. "You know that Clay would never leave you when you needed him," I said quietly, rubbing her arm soothingly.

Ruby's body shuddered as she tried to pull herself together. She reached up and held the hand that was wrapped around her arm. "You're such a good girl, Maggie. Clay and I are so lucky to have you in our lives," she said sincerely. I tensed a bit.

"I just wish I could do more," I replied, mostly to myself. Because it was true. I felt like I wasn't doing nearly enough.

"Just don't waste your life on regrets, Maggie. That's what you can do." I pulled back slightly, surprised by the vehemence in Ruby's tone.

"I know Clay hurt you. He's a difficult boy. But he loves you. As much as you love him. I see the way you look at each other. And it's a beautiful thing." Ruby looked at me and her pale green eyes seared into mine with an intensity that made me take pause.

"Whatever your hesitations, don't let them get in the way of living your life with the person you love. Lisa and I wasted too much time in the beginning worrying about what everyone else thought." A quiet sob escaped from Ruby and she bit down on her bottom lip.

She stood up, taking our mugs to the sink. She braced herself on the counter, her head bowed. This was a woman who I wasn't so sure would be able to come back from losing the love of her life. I think the person who said *it's better to have loved and lost than to never have loved at all* was full of shit. This much pain wasn't good for anyone, no matter that it came from something as amazing as the love for another person.

As if reading my thoughts, Ruby turned around to face me.

"Promise me, Maggie, to follow your heart and not your head. Our heads have a nasty habit of ruining what can make us happiest. And there are times in our lives when we have to put aside what we *think* is best and go with what we *feel* is best." I could barely breathe. Her advice hit me right where she meant it to, straight into my heart.

"Regret is a bitter bedfellow, Maggie," she whispered.

The sound of a throat being cleared made me squeak in surprise. Clay stood in the doorway, his form filling the small space. His dark hair hung down over his forehead and ears in loose waves. His eyes were hooded and concerned. His hands were characteristically jammed into his pockets as he looked between Ruby and me.

My heart constricted tightly at the sight of him. I was full of love and pain and, yes . . . regret. And Ruby was right, it was a horrible waste of emotion.

"Maggie just came by to drop off her mother's casserole," Ruby said tiredly, walking over to Clay and touching him on the cheek. "Why don't you two visit for a while, I'm going to go lie down." Ruby turned to me as she left the kitchen.

"It was nice seeing you, Maggie. I hope to see you again soon." For the first time I saw something *alive* flare in her eyes. They seemed to almost twinkle as she looked at me, a million messages being communicated. Her gaze drifted to her nephew and then back to me, an almost contented smile on her face. Then she left, leaving me feeling strangely at peace.

Looking at my phone, I knew I should be heading home but I was in no rush to leave the warm kitchen. Clay hadn't moved from the doorway. He watched me hesitantly and I could tell he was nervous.

"You got anything with chocolate around here? I'm sort of hungry," I said lightly. And even though I had dinner waiting for me, I needed something to break the tension.

"Yeah, I think we have some cookies or something," Clay said, finally coming into the room. He went rooting through the cabinets until he found a tin of chocolate chip cookies. Opening it up, he took one before handing it to me. I took my own cookie and put the tin down.

"Thanks for bringing the food. Ruby hasn't been up to cooking and I'm pretty sure I could burn water." Clay smirked and I felt my lips twitch into a smile.

"No problem. My mom goes through these compulsive cooking phases. Figure this way food isn't going to waste." I chewed on the cookie, trying not to be obvious in the way I stared at the boy who seemed ready to crawl out of his skin. Ruby's words still rang in my ears. Regret. When I looked at Clay that's definitely what I felt. Mostly for everything we never got to be. For everything I wanted so much to experience with him.

But he still seemed so vulnerable. Fragile even. And I was scared to let myself get close to him again. I didn't trust him with my heart. He'd broken it once already.

"Well, tell her thank you, from both of us. Ramen noodles were getting old." Clay wiped crumbs from his fingers and hooked his thumbs into his belt loops. I could tell he was winding down this nonexistent conversation in order to retreat. Even then his eyes clung to mine in a way that said he didn't want to be anywhere else.

He was clearly as conflicted as I felt. "I should get upstairs and start on my homework." Clay bobbed his head toward the hallway and I nodded.

"Sure thing," I replied and watched him turn around and leave. His broad back looked tense as he disappeared up the stairs. I reached up to touch the butterfly necklace. It lay hidden beneath my shirt and I was pretty sure that Clay hadn't noticed it. But since I'd put it back on, it hadn't left my neck.

That unconscious reluctance to part with it spoke volumes.

My fingers traced the delicate curves and I remembered the look on Clay's face when he had given it to me.

You make me feel free.

Tears pricked my eyes and then before I knew what I was doing, I was heading up the stairs two at a time.

I hurried down to the end of the hallway, pausing only briefly before pushing open Clay's door. It bounced off the wall with a loud thud. Clay sat on his bed and he looked up in shock. I was breathing heavily, my face flushed.

"Maggie, is everything—" Clay began but stopped as I crossed the room and sank to the floor at his feet. I went up on my knees and grabbed his face between my hands. His gorgeous brown eyes widened and his lips parted in surprise.

"I don't want to wake up ten years from now regretting that I let this slip through my fingers. I don't want to waste another *moment* without you in my life," I let out in a rush. Clay's hands came up and covered mine, his fingers slipping between the ones that held him. His eyes closed briefly and when he opened them they were wet with barely contained emotion.

"God, Maggie. How can you say that after everything I put you through?" His voice cracked and my heart nearly split in two. I gripped his face tightly and pulled him toward me. Our noses brushed against one another and we looked at each other as if for the first time.

"It's because of everything we've been through that I can say it. I love you, Clayton Reed. God, I love you so damn much." My strangled words came out in a whisper as I waited for him to hear me. To either accept or reject what I was giving him. I was taking the hugest risk handing him my heart and soul like this. Especially when they were still bruised from the last time he held them. I had agonized about not trusting him. About my fears of being ripped apart all over again.

But that didn't change the gut-wrenching response I had whenever I saw him. The way my heart beat just for him. I wasn't sure I could live my life having turned my back on the person who made me feel truly alive. And I was sick of being a coward. My love for this beautifully broken, yet slowly healing boy made me strong.

Clay took a deep breath and carefully yet purposefully rubbed his nose along the side of my cheek. I closed my eyes as his lips gently touched the corner of my mouth and then made their way along my jaw. He was breathing deeply, inhaling me in.

My hands, still cradling his face, began to tremble with the intense anticipation. Clay uncurled his fingers from around mine and moved them into my hair, digging them into the thick waves and holding tight.

"You are everything good in my life. Even when I thought all I had was the darkness, you were there. And you gave me something to live for. I couldn't let you go. No matter how hard I tried. I know now that's because to lose you would be losing the very best part of myself." I opened my eyes to see Clay staring back at me, tears sliding down his face. He leaned in, his lips inching closer to mine.

"I love you, Maggie. More than you could ever possibly understand." Clay tightened his grip in my hair and slammed his mouth over mine. I rose up on my knees and pressed my chest into his. His tongue plunged past my lips. Not a gentle probing. This was a passionate invasion and my body quivered with desire.

I let go of Clay's face so I could wrap my arms around him, holding him as tightly as he held me. Our mouths slanted over each other time and again, our breathing heavy and erratic. My heart beat wildly behind my rib cage.

When Clay's mouth moved away from mine to start a tortuous path of light kisses and loving nips along the side of my neck, I let out a deep and guttural groan. I should have been mortified with the way I responded to him. But we were way past embarrassment.

Clay's hands left my hair and clutched at the back of my shirt, pulling it up to find bare skin. And then we were touching and tasting. There was not one ounce of hesitation or reticence in our actions. This was the culmination of months of desperate longing.

When we finally came up for air, our lips tender and swollen, we could only stare at each other. Clay ran his hand along the side of my face. "How could I ever think life without you would be worth living?" he asked, seemingly mystified.

I grinned, brimming with the delicious high of Clay's kisses. "Stop trying to find out." I kissed him lightly on the mouth again. I couldn't tear myself away. Now that I had allowed myself to climb over the wall, there was no way I was turning back.

Because right then, in the heat of the moment, it was so easy to forget the mountain of issues that had nearly destroyed us the last time. But when we finally separated and Clay pulled me into his arms and back onto his bed, I knew I couldn't go into this blind again. My eyes needed to be open and aware. We had come too far, lost too much, and I wouldn't make the same mistakes again.

Clay's fingers made lazy trails through the thick heaviness of my hair and the quiet comfort was just as intoxicating as our moment of passion. "We have a lot to talk about, Maggie. A lot that needs to be said. We can't pick up where we left off, because that was a place I never want to be again." Clay's words were hard and bitter, but I understood where he was coming from.

I propped up on my elbow and looked down at him. "I know. We have to do it right this time," I said, tracing the line of his eyebrows with my fingertip. Clay grabbed my hand and placed a kiss into the open palm.

"We will. We have to. Because the alternative isn't one I can live with. Not anymore." I started to kiss him again when my phone buzzed in my pocket. We groaned simultaneously and then gave each other silly smiles.

I had received a new text message. It was from my dad, asking where I was. I didn't have much time before he came over here, guns blazing. Particularly when I was engaging in the very behavior he didn't want for me. "Shit." I jumped up and straightened my clothes and ran my fingers through my hair.

"I've got to get home. Dad ordered pizza," I explained lamely as Clay sat up. He grabbed me by the back of the knees and tugged me forward until I stood between his legs. He looked up at me and the grin on his face made being late for dinner so completely worth it.

"Can I call you? Later?" he asked me and I giggled at his adorable insecurity.

I bent over and captured his mouth with mine again, pulling back before we could deepen it, knowing my dad was waiting impatiently for me to get home. "You damn well better," I warned him, poking him lightly in the chest.

Clay ran his hands up the back of my thighs, sending a jolt straight between my legs. "Well, then, I'll call you this evening." His voice sounded husky as his hands inched higher up my legs. I stopped their slow ascent just shy of my butt and pulled them away.

"I have to go," I groaned, putting distance between us. Wearing a satisfied smile, Clay followed me out into the hallway. I noticed Ruby's door was closed. "Tell her I said good-bye, okay?" I told Clay.

"Of course," he said, twining his hand with mine as we walked down the stairs and out to my dad's minivan.

"Nice wheels," he joked and I elbowed him playfully in the ribs. I opened the driver-side door but turned around to kiss him lightly on the lips one last time. I was an addict and Clay was my crack. Crappy analogy, I know, but it was the truth.

The thought of losing him again was a very real and legitimate fear. Clay was right, we needed to talk. My distrust and insecurity still reigned supreme and if we were going to have a future, these issues needed to be addressed.

But for this moment, I could simply enjoy being with him again. Being granted something I had wished for but never hoped to have. It made me a believer in second chances.

Clay's eyes darkened and he ran his thumb along my bottom lip. "Thanks for coming by, Maggie. And thank you for . . . well . . . you." He smiled and dropped his eyes almost bashfully. I chuckled.

"You don't have to thank me for something that was always yours," I told him. Yuck, I was such a sap. His eyes came immediately back to mine and I forgot about my saccharin-induced mortification. We didn't kiss again, but Clay's hand cupped my cheek and I grasped his arm. My phone buzzed in my pocket again.

My dad, the cock-blocker. He would probably love that title.

"Gotta go before Dad blows a gasket," I said, climbing behind the wheel. Clay closed the door, slowly backing away from the van. I felt his eyes on me until I knew he could no longer see me. And there was nothing in this world, not even the threat of my parents' disapproval, that could wipe the hard-earned smile from my face.

chapter
seventeen

clay

So here I was, living my dream. My hand wrapped around Maggie's smaller one as we walked into the school together. It was like déjà vu and writing a whole new chapter all at the same time.

This was familiar but *new*. I still couldn't believe that we were here. In this place I hadn't dared to think about. But this beautiful reality I found myself in was laced with that *other* thing. The weight of our past and the heaviness of our future.

I was so happy. But fucking terrified at the same time. Because my brain still worked against me, trying to twist this amazing thing into that something ugly. And that is why I still took my medication. Still went to therapy religiously. I would not ruin us this time. I had miraculously been given another chance. Another opportunity to live my life the way I was meant to.

Maggie and I still needed to talk. To lay so many things out on the table. But it was as though we were both scared to shatter this tentative peace we had created. Which was stupid. If there was one thing both of us had learned, it was that ignoring things didn't make them go away. It only made it harder to face them when they finally came around to beat the shit out of you.

But for now we were going with plausible deniability and blissful ignorance wrapped up together in a blend of perfect delusion.

And for now that wasn't a bad thing.

Last year had been about me and my crap. This time, I wanted to focus on Maggie.

My fingers flexed around hers as we walked through the front doors of the school. I swear to God, it was like everyone within a twenty-foot radius ground to a halt and watched our progress down the hall.

I caught the firm lift of Maggie's chin as though she were defying everyone. Daring them to say something. And God help them if they did. Because my girl was fierce and I would place my money on her any day.

I tried not to give a shit. What did these people mean in the grand scheme of my life? Not when the girl I would walk over burning hot coals for was holding my hand. It really was all about the simple stuff. The bigger things, like my crazy, fucked-up head shit, could be put on hold for a little while longer.

We stopped at her locker while she twisted the dial. I could see the tremors in her hand and I knew this was taking a lot out of her. And I realized that I didn't know what she had to endure while I was in Florida. How much bullshit she had to swallow on a daily basis. But by the tension in her shoulders and the clench of her jaw, I could tell it had been a lot. And I felt even more like an ass for abandoning her the way that I had.

Here I was, the king of abandonment issues, dishing it out with the worst of them. I had to make this better if it was the last thing I did.

"Do you have any plans for Friday night?" I asked her, shoving my hands into the pockets of my coat. The old green army jacket that I had worn like a second skin had long been lost. Left in that hotel room in North Carolina with the rest of the stuff I would never see again. Getting my shit out of the place where I had nearly destroyed everything hadn't been high on my list of priorities. But damned if I didn't miss the stupid thing. It was just a coat, but for some reason it was like leaving a piece of me behind.

It really was ridiculous how sentimental I became about the most inconsequential objects.

Maggie gave me a shy smile. This new, more reserved Maggie Young was hard to get used to at times. The Maggie I had met all those months ago was in your face. She didn't hesitate to tell you what she was thinking, even if it hurt. She wasn't ever cruel; she just lacked any patience for games. And that's one of the million things I loved about her.

This Maggie was different. She seemed unsure and hesitant. She appeared to think before she spoke as though worried about the way her words would be received.

This Maggie made it her mission to disappear. And I hated that. Because I knew deep down that it was because of me. I had changed Maggie May Young in ways I had yet to understand.

I didn't love her any less for it. In fact I loved her more than I thought my heart was capable of. But it didn't stop the all-too-familiar sting of regret deep in my gut.

I reached out and tucked a flyaway strand of dark brown hair behind her ear. Her shorter hair took some getting used to. Just another example of how much my girl had changed in the three months we had been apart.

But they might as well have been three years and I had a lot to make up for.

"No plans," she said quietly, stuffing her bag into the locker and grabbing her books for class.

I cupped the side of her neck and tugged her closer. I kissed the tip of her nose, making her blush. It was beautiful the way her skin flushed when I touched her. "I'd like to take you out," I said, grinning at her.

"Like a date?" Maggie asked incredulously. I felt that jab of regret again, her surprise hitting me like a slap in the face. Regret was quickly replaced by guilt. I suddenly realized that we had never exactly gone out on a date. *Before*, we had spent most of our time at my house or Ruby's shop. Sure, we went to Bubbles for sundaes and we'd rent movies. But I had not once taken her on a proper date.

Dinner, movie, walking her to the door, and stealing a kiss good night.

Fuck! I really was an asshole. No, not just an asshole, but a selfish asshole.

My smile was a bit more pained after that but I held it all the same. "Yeah, like a date. I want to take you out to dinner. Then you can drag me to whatever lame-ass chick flick is playing." Maggie's smile grew wider and if I could punch myself in the nuts, I would. Yep, I was a selfish asshole.

"That sounds good. Um. Though, I haven't . . . well . . ." Maggie stumbled and my eyebrows knit together.

"Spit it out," I teased, tugging on her ponytail. Maggie bit her bottom lip and I wanted to pull it free with my teeth. I felt a stirring in my jeans and had to tamp down the urge to maul her in the hallway.

"Well, my parents don't know about you and me. I haven't told them." Well, that was like a bucket of cold water on my burgeoning hard-on.

"Oh. Okay. If you want to meet me somewhere, that's cool." No, it wasn't cool. It was the farthest thing from cool I could think of. This brought me perilously close to the way I felt *before*. When one of my greatest fears was never being the guy Mr. and Mrs. Young felt their only child deserved.

And I had proven their worries were completely founded.

I didn't blame Maggie for not telling them. I wasn't convinced I could ever be what they wanted for their daughter. But I was trying my fucking hardest.

But hearing her hesitance to share our relationship with her mom and dad made me feel like shit. As though I was again the shameful secret. A role I thought was singularly reserved for me as the son of Mr. and Mrs. Reed.

I never thought I'd have to feel this way as the boyfriend of Maggie Young.

Pain. Hurt. Betrayal. They were all there, jumping up and down, waiting for me to acknowledge them.

I wasn't worth it.

I'll never be enough for anyone.

There's only one thing that will help it all go away.

No! I stared into Maggie's eyes and tried to focus on my breathing. I could see them cloud with concern and I tried like hell not to show her how much her statement had wounded me.

Maggie grabbed my hand and squeezed. I winced at the strength of her grip. "I just haven't had a chance to really tell anyone. This is so new and I didn't want to jinx it. I *will* tell them. I'll tell everyone!" she said emphatically, and I didn't know if she was trying to convince me or herself.

"So, pick me up at seven," she said, giving my hand a shake, pulling me out of the decidedly dark turn my thoughts had taken. My smile this time was a replica of the genuine one I had worn only minutes before.

"Sure," I said, but I didn't really mean it. My mind was trying to work its way through the nasty urges that whispered dangerously. Shame, guilt, anger. All waiting for me to do what I had to do in order for them to leave me alone.

I clenched my hands into tight fists.

"Clay," Maggie said softly, clearly recognizing the look that had settled onto my face.

"Maggie! There you are! I waited for you at Java Madness this morning! I thought we were meeting there for coffee before school." An indescribable emotion crossed Maggie's face before she turned to Rachel, who had yet to notice me standing there.

"Girl, that was not cool. I had to drink my latte alone. And you know I don't do alone," Rachel chided teasingly. Then she realized I was there and I didn't miss the shocked expression that she tried to hide. Maggie's friend acknowledged our close proximity with her eyes but didn't comment on it.

"Hey, Clay," Rachel said in greeting, though it was far from the jovial tone she had used with Maggie. Her eyes darted between us. Maggie moved in closer to my side. It was a small movement, but it spoke volumes. And fuck if it didn't make all of the earlier bad stuff that was still floating around in my head recede just a bit.

"Sorry, Rach. Clay picked me up. It was a last-minute thing and I forgot to text you the change in plans." Maggie's voice was sharp, as though daring her friend to question her.

Rachel must have picked up on Maggie's mood, because she stayed resolutely quiet, only lifting her shoulder in an offhanded shrug. "I guess I'll see you later then." Rachel held her hand up in a wave and went on down the hallway.

"Well, that was . . . awkward," I mused sarcastically. Maggie slammed her locker shut and turned to face me.

"Yeah, it was." She gave me a weak smile and I reached down and grabbed her hand. I refused to let anything—not Maggie's friends, not the gossip-obsessed jackasses at school, and certainly not my insane paranoia and self-doubt—piss on my cornflakes.

"I've got track practice after school. But do you want to do some-thing after?" Maggie asked as we came to a stop in front of her class-room. I noticed the way everyone stared as they moved past us. Shit, did they really have nothing better to do than worry about what we were talking about? I didn't do fishbowl living. I was already feeling the strain of being the focus of way too much attention.

"Uh, I can't. I have an appointment right after school, and then I have to work," I said distractedly, trying not to get annoyed as I saw a group of girls stop and whisper behind their hands as they watched us.

"An appointment?" Maggie asked. I nodded, still too fixated on the gossiping going on around us. I felt cool fingers on my chin, pulling my face around so that I was looking down into Maggie's beautiful brown eyes. Eyes that made me forget my own name.

"Don't look at them. Look at me, Clay," she commanded and I was powerless to resist her. A smile danced on her lips as I ran my hand through my hair. "What appointment do you have?" she asked.

"Therapy," I said shortly, dropping my voice so that only she could hear me. No sense in announcing it to half the student body.

Maggie's face lit up, which took me aback. "Really? I'm so glad to hear that." My shoulders relaxed at her easy acceptance. I finally returned her smile.

"I go twice a week on Tuesdays and Thursdays," I admitted as Maggie squeezed my hand.

"Have I told you yet that I'm so proud of you?" she whispered, stepping in closer so that our chests brushed against one another. I wanted to grab her and kiss her right there. And I would have if Daniel hadn't picked that exact moment to come on the scene.

"The bell's about to ring, Mags. Hurry it up." Daniel stood to our side and seemed ready to wait for Maggie to follow him. I met Daniel's eyes and caught the unspoken communication he broadcast my way. *Don't fuck her over again.*

Reading you loud and clear, buddy, I communicated back.

I backed away from Maggie and gave her a last smile. "I'll see you later," I said, trying not to get irritated as Daniel began to shepherd her away. He was so fucking transparent. But I grudgingly appreciated how he looked after her.

After all, he had been the one to make sure she was okay after all I had done to her. I don't think I was in any position to be annoyed with him. Not where Maggie was concerned.

"Lunch?" Maggie said and I darted another glance at Daniel. Yeah, I didn't think he'd be joining the Maggie and Clay bandwagon anytime soon. But I'd have to deal with that. For Maggie. Because Daniel would have to see eventually that I meant to do right by his friend. I knew I had a lot of proving to do and I was determined to do it.

"Not today, I have to meet with the guidance counselor to go over some stuff," I said and she tried to cover up her disappointment.

"Okay then. I guess I'll talk to you later." I inclined my head in agreement and waited until she was inside her classroom before turning to Daniel, who still stood there, arms crossed over his chest.

"So much for not opening that book again, huh?" he asked me and for once there wasn't any anger in his tone. He seemed almost resigned.

"Yeah, well. You know how it goes." Okay, that didn't answer shit. But I really didn't feel like getting into the touchy-feely saga with Daniel Lowe. That would go over like a lead balloon.

Daniel leaned against the door frame and cocked an eyebrow. "Yeah, actually I do know how it goes." Surprisingly, we had a moment of understanding flicker between us and for the first time ever, I felt like Daniel and I got each other on some level. Maybe being with Rachel had mellowed him out more than I thought.

Daniel pushed himself off the wall. "Guess I'll be seeing you around then," was all he said before joining Maggie and the rest of the students in their English class.

Huh. That was the most normal conversation I'd ever had with the guy.

The rest of the day passed without issue or drama. Which was an amazing feat in high school. My meeting with the guidance counselor at lunchtime proved to be a bit more anxiety inducing. I was happy to learn I wasn't as behind in school as I originally thought, thanks mostly to the hefty amount of work I completed while at the Grayson Center.

The problem began when Mr. Hunt started to ask what my plans were for after graduation. I had sat there, my mouth hanging open, with no way of answering him. Because I wasn't in the habit of thinking much beyond tomorrow, let alone putting on paper what I wanted out of my life.

For the longest time, all I cared about was getting through the day. When your every breath was an effort, that quickly became the extent of your expectations. But now, with the end of my high school career looming in front of me like a giant neon sign, I realized I had never taken the time to develop . . . well . . . actual goals.

I did decently in school, when I was paying attention and focused. My GPA wasn't anything fantastic, but it didn't suck either. So when Mr. Hunt started to throw out words like *community college* and *university*, I felt blindsided.

For a guy with no thoughts for the future, it was expected that I started figuring some shit out.

I left the guidance department with my bag stuffed full of brochures. Crap. College. Then I realized I didn't know what Maggie's plans were for after we graduated. Of course she would be going away somewhere, but we hadn't discussed it.

And there was the panic again. It overtook me so quickly I barely had time to register the full-blown attack that swept through my body. I pushed my way into the bathroom at the end of the corridor. It was thankfully empty.

The one time I might consider taking one of the anxiety pills Dr. Todd had prescribed and I had left the damn things at home.

I braced myself on the edge of the sink and tried to get my breathing under control. I looked up at my reflection and winced at the white pallor of my skin. I turned the tap on and splashed my face with ice-cold water. My heart slammed with force inside my chest and my throat constricted painfully.

Reframe, focus, go to my calm place. Goddamn it! Don't do this! Not here!

"Fuck, man, are you okay?" I had the shittiest luck on the planet.

Daniel stood just inside the door to the guys' bathroom and I knew he was staring at me. I clenched my eyes shut and willed him away. Maybe if I ignore him, he'll take the hint. Or maybe I should just advertise my fresh round of crazy with Maggie's best friend and get it over with.

I felt light-headed and even though I tried like hell to calm myself down, having Daniel in here with me at such a vulnerable moment made it one hundred times worse. "Just get out." My words came out of my mouth in a distorted hush.

"Like hell. You look like you're going to keel over and I don't need that on my conscience." I heard Daniel move across the bathroom and he was suddenly beside me. Just freaking great, he was going to play hero to the nut job. Not what I needed right now.

"I'm fine. Just leave," I growled.

I heard Daniel turn on the water followed by a cold, wet paper towel thrust into my hand. "Just put it on your face. It might help." I was sweating like a pig and shaking like I was having a seizure. But I took his advice and pressed the cloth to my face.

"You just need to breathe. One at a time." Daniel's voice became calm and direct and I found myself responding to it.

It could have been ten minutes or an hour later, but I finally felt my heart slow down and my head clear. When I opened my eyes, Daniel was still standing there. And I didn't see any judgment on his face. This was not the Daniel Lowe I was used to dealing with.

"You cool?" he asked, taking the paper towel from my hand and tossing it into the trash.

"Yeah, I'm cool," I replied. Good ol' shame and embarrassment were quickly making an appearance. Of all people to see me at my worst, it had to be Daniel Fucking Lowe.

"I used to get those. Panic attacks, I mean. After my parents split up and my mom moved me in with her and her fuckwad of a boyfriend. They can be pretty intense." I shot Daniel a look from the corner of my eye. Was he being for real right now? Sharing personal stories and all that kumbaya crap?

"Yeah, they can be," I admitted, still reluctant to share anything with the guy who had never hidden the fact that he didn't trust me or even particularly like me. Daniel reached down and picked up the bag that I had thrown onto the floor.

He handed it to me and I took it, slinging it over my shoulder. I jammed my hands into my pockets and met Daniel's stare head-on. No sense in being a pussy about it.

"Thanks," I said begrudgingly. Maybe I shouldn't be such a dick to the guy who had just helped me out. But the last thing I wanted was to acknowledge what had happened to Maggie's best friend and the leader of the anti-Clay club. Because I know if there was one, this dude would be the president.

Daniel ran his hand over his head and darted his eyes around the restroom. "Look, man. I know I haven't been the most . . . uh . . . supportive of you and Maggie. And I'm still not sure how I feel seeing the two of you all up in each other's stuff again. But, I know you're a decent guy. So for now, I'm reserving judgment."

I snorted. "Wow, that's really big of you," I said sarcastically. Daniel smiled sheepishly.

"Okay, so that sounded way assier than I meant it to. What I'm trying to say is, I know you're dealing with shit. A lot of shit by the looks of it. And for Maggie's sake . . . well . . . and yours too, I won't be the speed bump on your road to the candy castle or whatever."

His metaphors were confusing the hell out of me, but I guess I got what he was trying to say. "I don't know about any candy castle. Whatever the hell that's supposed to mean. But I appreciate where you're trying to go with that." My lips quirked in a grin and Daniel took my cue and laughed. The tension that had been building popped like a bubble.

We left the bathroom and walked down the quiet hallway. We were already twenty minutes late for class. Shit. "So, if you don't mind me asking, what the hell brought all that on back there?" Daniel asked and I clamped down immediately. It was an age-old response to people digging into my crap.

"Yeah, no offense, but I'm really not into talking about it with people." I probably sounded harsher than I meant to. But I was trying not to hash out my crazy psyche for Daniel to analyze. My insurance paid a professional to do that twice a week.

"I get it. Sorry for sticking my nose in. Just, you know . . . If you ever want to talk about stuff. I mean, I'm here if you want. And I don't mean for that to sound as douchey as it came out. I swear to God, I did not just grow a vagina." I barked out a laugh and Daniel grinned.

"Glad to hear it, otherwise Rachel's in for one hell of a surprise," I joked. Wow. It was like I had entered a parallel universe. I was joking around with Daniel of all people. Almost like we were friends. I hadn't had many of those over the years. At least not ones that I wasn't forced into spending time with out of therapeutic necessity.

"All right. Well, I've got to get to class. Mrs. Bowan is going to castrate me for being late again. I'll catch you later," Daniel said, heading up the stairs.

"Hey, Daniel," I called out before he disappeared. Daniel turned around.

"I just want you to know that all that shit, well, I'm working on it." I just really needed him to know that I was going to do my damnedest to make this right for Maggie. That I wasn't the selfish jackass I was three months ago. That I was going to do what I needed to do for the girl we both loved.

Daniel gave me a curt nod. "Glad to hear it. Check you later." And with that, he disappeared up the stairs.

✦

Therapy went well. After my minimeltdown in the bathroom at school, I was in a surprisingly good place. I talked to Shaemus about Maggie. And unlike with Dr. Todd, he didn't immediately launch into all of the reasons it wasn't a good idea. Though he did remind me that it perhaps wasn't a good idea to put so much energy into a relationship while I was working on getting myself in order.

He then suggested I bring Maggie in for a session or two. This blew my mind. Why in the hell would I bring Maggie to therapy? But when Shaemus explained that it could be a way for both of us to break the patterns we had developed in our relationship and learn better ways to communicate, I couldn't deny that it sounded really good.

But how to broach the subject with Maggie? *Hey, you wanna go hang out at my shrink's office for some superintense couples' therapy?* Now there was a date to remember.

After leaving Shaemus's office, I headed home to change for my shift at Bubbles. Ruby's car was parked by the house, but when I went inside, it was quiet. Not wanting to disturb her, I hurried to change, then headed to work.

Checking my phone after I pulled into the parking lot I saw that I had a text from Maggie.

Just finished practice. Thinking of you. Call me when your shift is over. We have some date planning to do.

My phone rang in my hand and I frowned at the unfamiliar number that flashed across the screen. "Hello?" I said, answering it.

"Clay?" a female voice said on the other end.

"Maria?" I asked, and heard her familiar giggle through the line.

"Yep, it's me! How are you? I miss you so much!" Her voice was high-pitched, as though she was nervous. I instantly felt guilty for not contacting her or my other friends from the center since I had been back in Virginia. The truth was I hadn't much thought about them. And that made me a really crappy friend.

"Wow! Maria, I'm good actually. Much better than I thought I'd be. How are you?" I figured I'd leave the whole I-miss-you thing alone for now.

I heard Maria take a deep breath. "Well, that's actually why I called. I've been discharged from Grayson." I frowned at her statement.

"You've been discharged? I thought you were going to do another six months." Maria and I had both talked about staying on for the six-month program before I left. But then I had up and left. I really hoped her decision had nothing to do with my leaving. But I had a bad feeling that it did. Maria's attachment had become borderline dependent. Dr. Todd and I had discussed it a few times. He had mentioned that it was normal for people in treatment to come to rely on other patients as a means of emotional support. That it wasn't unusual for people to transfer their intense feelings on to those around them.

Dr. Todd had warned me that it could quickly become unhealthy and counterproductive. Which is why staff closely monitored interactions between patients. Though I knew for a fact quite a few had entered into romantic relationships with each other while in treatment.

Maria and I were just friends, but I knew my leaving would be hard for her. So hearing that she had left had me worried.

"Yeah, well, I was sort of sick of being there. I didn't really feel like I was going to get any more out of it, you know?" I guess I could understand that, but I wasn't convinced that was Maria's reason for leaving.

"So, where are you then? Back with your grandma?" Maria lived with her grandmother in Boca Raton before she went to the Grayson Center. Her biological father was in jail for abusing her when she was a child and Maria hadn't heard from her mother since she was ten. So she had gone to live with her mother's mother, who happened to be a cosmetic executive and had more money than God. But thus had very little time for her emotionally scarred granddaughter. This had created the perfect environment for self-destructive behavior. Maria and I had more in common in ways that neither of us liked to acknowledge.

"Yeah, for now. I'm finishing up the last few credits for school. Blah, blah, blah. That's not why I'm calling, Clay!" Maria squealed and I couldn't help but laugh at her boisterous excitement.

"Okay, okay. Spill already before you have an aneurysm." Maria's girlish laugh filled the other end of the phone and I found that I really did miss her and all of our friends back at Grayson. Even though I was there to deal with some heavy shit, in a way it was a hell of a lot simpler. Sure, I was only living half a life, but it was an uncomplicated half a life.

"I'm coming to Virginia!" she rushed out and I stilled in surprise.

"You're coming to Virginia? Why?" Okay, so I hadn't meant to sound so unhappy about the idea. But hadn't I just been thinking how uncomplicated my life was at Grayson? That didn't mean I wanted that life to follow me on the outside. Compartmentalization was key.

"Wow, don't sound so thrilled," Maria said, clearly hurt by my lack of enthusiasm.

"Sorry. No, that's cool. What brings you north of the Florida state line?" I asked, rubbing the piece of skin between my eyebrows. I was getting a headache.

"Well, I'm only going to be there for a few days. I'm actually heading to Alexandria, to see my older brother, Hector. I haven't seen him in years. And we started talking again while I was in treatment, so I figured it was a good time to come up and see him. Plus, I thought it would be the perfect excuse to visit with my best friend." Way to lay on the guilt. Sheesh.

"No, that's cool. I'd love to see you. So when will you be coming to Virginia? You know I could come up to Alexandria to see you. Save you the hassle of driving to Davidson." Please, please, please.

I wasn't sure why this was stressing me out so badly. But I just knew that Maria being here would push my two worlds uncomfortably together.

"And miss out on seeing all the sights of Davidson, Virginia? There is no way I'm missing out on that. I'll be up next weekend. I'll call you when I get to Alexandria and we can sort out a time for me to come down. Eeee! I'm so excited!" Maria's giddiness was hard to ignore. Yeah, this was fine. Maria was cool. No weirdness necessary.

"I can't wait to hear all about your life on the outside. Is it everything you hoped it would be?" she asked. I needed to get inside Bubbles and start my shift.

"I can fill you in next weekend. I've got to get to work," I explained. Maria gave a mock gasp.

"You're working? Look at you, being a productive member of society."

"That's me, productive society guy." I chuckled.

"Before you go, have you seen that girl? Maggie?" Maria asked and I knew there was more to her direction of questioning than simple curiosity.

"Yeah. Actually, she and I are, well . . . we got back together," I admitted.

"Oh. That's great, Clay. I hope you're happy." She sounded sincere, if a little crestfallen. I tried to ignore the disappointment and jealousy in her voice.

"I'd better get going. I'll talk to you next week," I said, ready to conclude the phone call.

I wasn't entirely sure how to feel about Maria's upcoming visit. But my gut, or was it my deep-seated paranoia, couldn't help but feel this was a disaster waiting to happen.

chapter
eighteen

I was nervous. Screw it, I was really, *really* nervous. I stared at my reflection in the mirror and smoothed the skirt of my gray sweater dress for the millionth time since I had put it on. I looked cute. But was I trying to be cute? Sexy, amazing, or drop-dead gorgeous would have been so much better.

But I was stuck with *cute.*

I had never been one to obsess about my looks like most teenage girls. I went with what God gave me and was okay with that. But for some reason, tonight I was freaking the hell out.

Which was beyond ridiculous. Because the person I was dressing up for already thought I was the most beautiful girl on the planet.

Poor deluded sap that he was.

Tonight was the "date." Clay and I had talked a few times during the week and we hadn't been able to agree on what we wanted to do. I didn't want him to go to a lot of trouble. But he wanted to make it special.

And I could appreciate that. Because this felt like the beginning for us. Our first step toward a future that we had always wanted to have. Our chance to take things one step at a time, in the right order. Lord knows we skipped a whole bunch of pivotal moments the last time.

But now was about walking, not sprinting to the finish line. And I was happy to stroll.

Part of me wished this was the first time for us. That we didn't have a butt load of baggage that always tickled the back of our minds with unwanted memories. I hated the twinge of distrust I continued to feel in Clay's presence and I absolutely *loathed* the hypervigilant anxiousness that I often felt from him.

I had been so lost in the blissful throes of reunion that it had taken a few days before the reality started to set in. I tried not to watch him and monitor his behavior. But it was habit. And I couldn't help but look for any indication that he had veered off the course to recovery and was lying to me all over again.

This was not the friendly feeling of déjà vu, but a smack-a-bitch-in-the-face remembrance of how things used to be. And I didn't like it one bit.

But I would have been the worst kind of naïve if I dusted off my rose-colored glasses again. I could tell Clay was making every effort to show me things were different. But how different could they really be? Not that much time had passed. And given all that he had gone through, relapse almost seemed preordained.

Which was a shitty way of thinking.

But for tonight, I wanted to walk the road Clay was trying so hard to pave for us.

"You look lovely. Big plans tonight?" My mom peered into my room, a soft smile on her face. I tensed, ready to launch over hurdle number one.

I took a brush to my hair and tugged it through with enough force to make me wince. Just because I was nervous didn't mean I had to inflict bodily harm. What had my poor hair ever done to me?

"Yeah. Actually, you got a minute, Mom?" I asked, trying to control the wobble in my voice. My mom seemed to pick up on my apprehension and came in to sit down on my bed.

"You really need to clean this room. You can barely see the floor, Maggie May," my mom scolded, picking up a pile of clothes and absently beginning to fold them.

I swallowed around the thick lump in my throat. "I'm going out with Clay tonight," I let out in a rush. My mom's hands stilled and she laid them on the clothes in her lap. I could see by the way her neck tensed up that she was not happy with my news.

But I refused to hide things from my parents ever again. I had played the part of the secretive teenager and it only served to demolish the trust they had in me. And that was not a place I wished to revisit anytime soon.

"Mom?" I ventured, wanting her to respond in some way. Her silence only served to increase the nervous flutter in my stomach.

My mom took a deep breath and looked up at me. She seemed tired and much older than I ever remembered her being. Had I done this to her? Was I responsible for the new wrinkles around her eyes and the tired droop of her mouth?

"Okay," she said slowly, and I know my eyes popped out of my head.

"Okay?" I clarified, not sure I had heard her correctly.

My mom's smile was tight. "Not the response you were expecting?" she asked me, moving the pile of clothes off to the side and folding her hands in her lap.

"Well, no. I was expecting something a bit more . . . explosive," I admitted, eyeing her warily. Who was this woman and what had she done with my mother?

My mom patted the bed beside her and I quickly joined her. She brushed my bangs out of my face and rubbed my cheek. She seemed sad and tired, and just like my dad several weeks ago, she appeared resigned.

"What would be the point of yelling and telling you not to go? Would you stay home? Would you forget about Clay?" she inquired, taking my hands and holding them lightly in hers.

I shook my head. "No. I wouldn't," I answered her honestly. My mom's eyes began to glisten. I knew tears were imminent. I hated it when my mother cried. I felt helpless and guilty.

"I don't want to lose all that we've worked so hard to rebuild between us. Your father and I love you. Before, with Clay, we were so scared for you. We knew what you had with him could only end in a broken heart. And I hate it that we were right." I found it hard to breathe and my mom wrapped her arm around my shoulders.

"I know that if your dad and I had been more open-minded, if we had listened instead of judging, things could have turned out very differently. But we were so terrified that our baby girl would get hurt that we went into shutdown. You resented us. We were so angry. That was a horrible place to be." She laid her cheek on the top of my head and I felt myself relax against her.

"You're not the only one who can change, Maggie May. Even us old folks can learn a lesson or two. And the main one we've learned is we have to trust you to live your life. You're going to make your own choices and I just hope that you know you can talk to us. About anything." She pulled me up by my shoulders so I was looking at her again.

"And I'm still scared for you, baby girl. Because I'm not sure how much has really changed for Clayton. I know he's getting help now and that maybe he's heading in the right direction. But it has been a very short time. You can't expect miracles overnight. And given his struggles, I wouldn't set yourself up for another round of disappointment and misery. If you're really set on doing this with Clay again, then just make sure you remember the lessons *you've* learned." Her advice was sound and I listened intently.

Before, I would have gotten defensive. Become angry at her insinuations. But after the events of last year, I could only take in her words and heed them. What else could I do? Denial hadn't worked so well for me in the past.

"I will, Mom. I promise." She kissed my cheek and got to her feet.

"What time will he be picking you up?" she asked. I looked at the clock on my bedside table and realized how late it was.

"He's supposed to be here in an hour." My mom made a clucking noise with her tongue.

"Your dad and I were heading out to dinner. But maybe we'll wait until after the two of you leave." I could tell she was extremely uncomfortable with the idea of me going out with Clay. But I also felt such an amazing love for my parents that they were being so reasonable about it.

"No, you guys go on. But I think maybe I should bring Clay over. So you can spend some time together, get to know each other properly. I know there wasn't much chance for that the last time."

My mom nodded. "I'd like that. Well, if you're okay with us leaving. We should get going. But be home by midnight and not a minute later." I smiled, feeling us slip back into the more comfortable role of mother and daughter.

"Yes, ma'am," I said. My mom tried to hide her grin as she pointed her finger at me.

"Not a minute later," she warned again and I gave her a salute.

I sagged down onto my bed. Had that really happened? I was again reminded how truly lucky I was and I swore to myself I wouldn't let them down again. How easy it was to say that now. But deep down, I was all too aware of how a beautiful pair of brown eyes and messy dark hair could ruin everything.

◆

By the time seven rolled around, I was a pacing, palms-sweating, hair-pulling mess. I had practically worn a hole in the carpet from my endless walking. You'd think I had never been out with a guy before. It was sort of ludicrous the way I was fretting about dinner and a movie.

But I knew so much hinged on this evening. This would decide for me whether Clay and I were capable of a relationship not defined by his mental illness. When we were together before, I was swept up in the tumultuous emotions that he was living in. It was easy to get lost in the ups and downs, the side ways and back ways and all the other ways in between.

I had spent so much time thinking of ways to *save* him that everything else took a backseat. But here we were, months later, and I wasn't sure what we were left with. How did we create a new relationship built on something other than his mood swings?

Was it masochistic of me to almost miss the turmoil? Because I knew, even in the middle of our crazy dysfunction, that he needed me. That he loved me. That I was all he wanted. Now, I wasn't so sure. Were we fooling ourselves into thinking anything was left to build from?

Sure, the attraction was still there. But I worried that the depth of love we felt for one another was merely a symptom of the crisis we had found ourselves in.

And would I ever be able to look at him as just a boy? And not someone I had to watch like a hawk just to make sure he was taking his medicine? Would we ever be able to have the easy, relaxed way of being together that other couples had?

I would watch Rachel and Daniel and long for what they had deep in my bones. A love that was unquestionable and unwavering.

I just needed to give us time. Time to navigate through the uncharted waters we now found ourselves in. And I had to remember that nothing with Clayton Reed would ever be simple. I just had to decide if I was okay with that.

I was so deep in my thoughts that I barely heard the doorbell.

It was only when a loud knock sounded on the door that I snapped out of it. There would be enough time later for over-analysis. Tonight was about Clay and me rediscovering everything we loved about one another.

"Um . . . wow. Thanks," I said in absolute and utter amazement. Clay stood at my doorstep wearing dark jeans, a pressed blue collared shirt, and a black jacket, and holding the largest bouquet of roses I had ever seen. It was obvious he had checked all of the required boxes for this date. Down to his perfectly-slicked-back hair and overeager expression.

In the previous incarnation of our relationship we sort of skipped the whole "dating" thing. Somewhere between saying hello and diving headfirst into the drama, we had forgotten the basics. Our love hadn't been typically teenage in any way. We had gone from zero to a million without so much as a trip to the movies or an uncomfortable dinner at Applebee's while we chatted about favorite bands and most embarrassing moments.

Looking at Clay all dolled up and standing almost timidly in front of me, I realized how much we had missed. How in the heat of our intense and crazy love we had forgotten the most important step in any relationship . . . the first date.

I felt a resurgence of my earlier sadness at those tiny moments that we hadn't experienced together. I took a deep breath and reached out for the roses. Clay's smile was shy and uncertain, showing me that he was as clueless as I was when it came to rewriting our history.

Was it possible to go back to the beginning? To try and change a past that had already come to define us? To change the direction of fate and see where it took us?

I gripped the bundle of overpriced flowers in my hands and gasped in surprise. I lifted my finger and saw a bright red blob on the tip. Shit, I should have realized there were thorns. The bite of pain reminded me that we had a long way to go. That no matter how beautiful the package, the hurt was still there.

And I wasn't sure how long it would take for it to go away. Or if it ever would. But I reminded myself that now was not the time. The hurt would be there for me to think about . . . later.

"Are you all right?" Clay asked, moving toward me. I stuck my finger into my mouth. The tang of copper was sharp on my tongue. I nodded my head and moved away before Clay could touch me.

I dropped the flowers onto the table inside the door and grabbed my purse. I joined him on the porch and zipped up my coat.

"Are your parents here? I should say hi." Clay peered into the house.

"No, they're out. But I've been given a very strict curfew of midnight. Otherwise I'll turn into a pumpkin or something," I teased. Clay laughed, clearly relieved that the parental meet and greet would be postponed for another time.

"You ready, then?" Clay asked, his smile less painful and much more heart wrenching. That was the kind of smile that could make a girl forget everything else. And at one time I had.

Was I ready?

Hell if I knew.

But looking at his hopeful expression, I knew that I could only try.

I placed my hand in his outstretched one and squeezed lightly. "Lead on, kind sir. I'm entirely at your disposal," I said as Clay pulled me toward his car. His demeanor seemed to change once we were in the car and headed down the road.

He was happy and carefree and, yes . . . hopeful. And I knew then that I really liked the look of it on his face. I only wished it could stay there forever.

"So where are you taking me?" I asked, fiddling with his radio until I found a rock station playing the Dandy Warhols.

Clay grinned. "Oh, we're going total high school cliché tonight, baby. Full-on dinner, a movie, then maybe a little making out in the backseat." I enjoyed his teasing as well as his excitement.

"Wow," I breathed out. I looked over at him coyly. "That sounds just about perfect." Clay's hand reached out to rest on my upper thigh and my entire body clenched under his touch. My earlier insecurities aside, one thing was for sure, the attraction we felt toward one another was alive and well.

"We're not going to Red Lobster, are we?" I joked, reminding him of our silly dinner the night of the Fall Formal. The same night he had lost it and declared his feelings for me. It had been a beautiful night. And a scary one. That was the way with Clay and me. The good had always been so intertwined with the bad, it was hard to have one without the other.

Clay's face fell at the memory and I knew mentioning the night that was so full of turmoil for both of us wasn't the best idea. But then he seemed to shake himself out of whatever dark place he had started to go and smiled again. And I let out a breath I didn't even realize I was holding and felt relief that the moment had passed without incident.

"Nope, no Red Lobster. I'm doin' it right. We're going to Ruby Tuesday." I laughed then, deep and genuine. Clay joined in and this felt good. The two of us, together, enjoying each other's company.

The restaurant was packed, but we were seated almost immediately in a booth in the atrium. "Awesome! Easy access to the salad bar!" I enthused. Clay winked at me as he slid onto the bench seat across from me.

"What, you're not going to sit beside me, like that old couple over there? We can listen to each other chew and stare at the wall." I patted the seat beside me and Clay chuckled. We both looked over at an elderly couple one booth over. And, yep, they were sitting on the same side of the booth. Neither of them spoke to each other, more focused on their food. Clay and I looked at each other again and broke into laughter.

When we finally calmed down, Clay reached across the table and grabbed my hand. "This feels really good, Mags," he said softly, his eyes sparkling. I swallowed thickly, feeling overcome with a different kind of emotion. One that could only be described as borderline euphoria. I was feeling high on being here with him. On knowing he wasn't going anywhere. The gift of that wasn't lost on me.

The waitress came and took our drink orders and we were left alone again. Clay seemed content to look at me. With anyone else, that would have made me supremely uncomfortable. With Clay it just made me warm all over.

"How's Ruby doing?" I asked, taking a sip of my soda. Clay swirled the ice in his water, poking the lemon with his finger.

"Ah, well, she's the same. She did go into the shop this morning. So, that's something, I guess." He sounded sad and I thought hard about something helpful to say.

"You just have to give her time. You can't get over losing someone overnight. These things are a process," I said with a tone that spoke of experience. Clay's eyes rested on me.

And there it was, the giant tap-dancing, tutu-wearing elephant in the room. It demanded for us to acknowledge it, but I was scared once that box was opened, it would reveal things I would rather not know. But that was my need for denial again. It was like a comfortable pair of slippers that I wanted to put back on. Crazy how being with Clay brought out those impulses.

"No, I guess not," Clay replied heavily. We were saved from continuing the entirely too serious conversation by the reappearance of our waitress. After we gave her our food orders, I was desperate to move on to something a bit easier to stomach before eating.

"So, I've been thinking about getting a tattoo," I told him shyly. Clay's eyebrows rose.

"Really? What would you get?" he asked me. I rooted through my purse and found a pen. Pulling the cap off with my teeth, I grabbed one of the beverage napkins and quickly drew a symbol. It looked like a lopsided upside-down U.

Clay pulled the napkin closer and studied it. "What is it?" He traced his finger over the groove from my pen.

"It's the rune Uruz. It's for healing, endurance, courage. I found it in one of the books Ruby gave me a few weeks back. It just, I don't know, made sense. I like what it stands for." I flipped my hand over and touched the sensitive skin on the underside of my wrist. "Just a small one, right here."

Clay slid his finger along the curve of my wrist, rubbing the spot I had indicated. I hoped he wouldn't think I was stupid. But there was something empowering about the symbol. As though branding it on my body would remind me that I possessed those qualities, even when they were hard to find.

"I like it. In fact, it sounds perfect." His fingers dropped from my skin and I pulled my hand back into my lap. Clay's lips quirked into a grin. "Ruby would love it. You should tell her about it. Hell, she'll probably want to go with you to get it." The seriousness of the moment passed and I felt myself back on even footing.

"Yeah, maybe I'll ask her. I was actually thinking of getting it for my birthday."

Clay's smile spread. "Was that a hint? Trying to make sure I don't forget your birthday?" he joked and I felt my face flush.

"No, really. I was just saying," I sputtered, feeling like an idiot.

Clay nudged my foot with his. "As if I could forget your birthday," he said quietly, and my insides quivered at the soft look in his eyes.

We ate our dinner and talked. About everything and nothing at all. We seemed to reach an unspoken understanding to leave the heavier stuff for later. Right now, we simply enjoyed each other's company. After Clay paid the bill, we slid out of the booth and he helped me into my coat, his hands lingering as he pulled it up over my arms.

"Ready for part two of our stereotypically normal date?" Clay asked me after we were buckled up in his car.

"Lead on! I'm ready for some more clichéd date madness."

And that's what we did. We watched a movie, choosing a lighthearted comedy that had us both cracking up. We shared a tub of popcorn and we playfully fought over the carton of Milk Duds. Clay held my hand the whole time, slowly rubbing the pad of his thumb along the skin between my thumb and forefinger. It was so thankfully simple.

We saw a few people from school and I knew they were watching us like we were animals at the zoo. But even that couldn't ruin our good time.

After the movie, we still had an hour until I had to be at home, so Clay drove us outside of town. It wasn't until he pulled down a small dirt road that I knew where he was taking us. He killed the engine once we got to our destination, and I turned to him, poking my finger into his chest.

"No swimming tonight, we'll freeze our butts off," I warned, and Clay brought my finger up to his lips.

"No swimming. Hypothermia wasn't part of my plans for you tonight," he said, his voice taking on a decidedly seductive tone. Hmm, what exactly did he have planned for me tonight? If it involved his hands and tongue, then I was ready to put said plan into action. He opened his car door and came around to the other side to open mine. Climbing out, I rubbed my arms, feeling the night's chill.

Clay got a thick quilt out of the trunk and laid it on the ground. He pulled me down beside him and I tried not to shiver as the cold seeped through the blanket. "It's not exactly warm out, you know." I tried not to whine, but I was starting to shiver.

Clay wrapped me in his arms and pulled the blanket up around us. He nuzzled his cold nose into the side of my neck. "Is that better?" he whispered and I nodded. I wasn't feeling the cold anymore. As long as he held me like this, there would be no complaining out of me.

"Thank you for a wonderful night," Clay said into my hair, kissing the corner of my eye. I relaxed into him, leaning my head back to look up at the clear night sky.

"I never thought we'd get here," I remarked quietly. Clay's grip tightened.

"Me either. But we are. And it makes me feel like just maybe everything else was worth it, if it brought us to this point." I felt his fingers in my hair, and when I shivered this time it had more to do with my whacked-out hormones than with the cold air.

"I've really missed you. It killed me not being able to talk to you. To not know how you were doing." I turned to look at Clay. "I want to be able to ask how things are with you. If you're still taking your medication. If therapy is working. I want to know about your time in treatment. I want to ask you a million and one questions, but I'll be honest with you, I'm scared to. I suppose it's because I worry that I won't necessarily like the answers. That probably sounds horribly unsupportive, but I just wanted you to know how I felt."

I couldn't believe I had just said all that. But there was something about being here with him like this that hit my honesty button and I couldn't sit quietly and pretend that these thoughts weren't swirling around in my head.

Clay ran his hand through his hair, a total giveaway that he was nervous and unsure. "I want to answer your questions. I really do. I want to put these fears of yours to rest. But at the same time, I'm worried I'll bring us back to that place we were before. When everything was about me and my stuff. I don't want that for us this time. It wasn't fair to you."

Gripping the blanket around me, I slithered onto his lap, my legs straddling him, and I put my arms around his chest. Resting my cheek over his heart, I could hear how fast it was beating. Past experience told me that talking about this could bring about a potential meltdown. Clay didn't have a history of being very receptive to discussing his mental illness. But if we were both serious about being totally open, then I couldn't tiptoe around the bigger issues.

"But, Clay, if we don't talk about it, things won't change. You and I spent way too much time ignoring what was going on. We can't do that again," I pleaded.

I felt Clay take a deep breath, my body rising and falling with his. His fingers curled into tight fists as he held me. This was an important moment. For both of us. Denial and mistrust had characterized our relationship for so long. Nothing but total honesty would be welcome from here on out.

"It's hard. Every day, every minute, is a struggle," he began. I sat up so that I could look at him. He stared off to the side, his jaw tense.

"When I was admitted to the Grayson Center, I was a mess. After everything that happened in North Carolina, I wasn't thinking clearly. I was so screwed up in the head that on my first night there, I tried to climb out of my window." I wish I could have been surprised by his revelation but I wasn't. I remembered all too well the state he was in when I had left him in that hospital room in the hands of the two people who loved him the least, even when it was their job to support him.

"I was caught, of course. And I spent five days on some heavy-duty tranquilizers. I was kept numb and emotionless until I was able to start dealing with things. You know you're in a bad place when drool starts to crust over on your face because it's been there for so long." Clay grimaced and I blanched.

"Well, that's a really gross image," I muttered. All I could think about was the movie *Shutter Island* and the electroshock therapy and patients wandering around in long white gowns.

Clay gave a humorless laugh before returning to his story. "I was poked and prodded so much that I felt like some sort of science experiment gone bad, but I just didn't care. I was past worrying about myself. I hated my parents, I hated myself, I hated the staff—my only thought was biding my time until I could leave. And I knew once that happened, I would make sure to finish what I had started in that motel room."

My heart was hammering in my chest. This was exactly what I was afraid of. This was everything I had feared for him when his parents took him away. To know that he had been alone and suffering was like a knife to my gut.

I discreetly brushed away the tears that had silently made their way down my cheeks, making sure that he didn't see how much his words were hurting me. I knew that if he saw, he might shut down and not talk about it at all. And I didn't want that, even though his story was tearing me apart.

"But at some point, it all changed. I'm not sure what did it, exactly. Maybe it was the new medication. Once I was off the lithium and started taking the Tegretol, I started to feel . . . well, not better, exactly, but I wasn't experiencing the out-of-control swings anymore. The fucked-up thing was I missed the mania. I still miss it. I liked the person I was when I was feeling that high." He sounded almost wistful when talking about his manic swings. I didn't understand how he could ever want to feel like that, but I didn't say anything. The truth was I'd never understand any of this. I could only listen and support him.

"But you're still taking your meds, right?" I had to ask. His refusal to take his medication had been our biggest problem. He needed them. He couldn't function without them. I wasn't sure there would ever be a day I didn't worry whether he was taking them or not.

Clay met my eyes, and they burned straight into mine. "Yes,

Maggie. I haven't missed a pill since I started the Tegretol. I swear to you, I won't do that to myself again," he said firmly and with total conviction. My belly uncoiled a bit.

Clay ran his hands up and down my back, as though the action comforted him. I knew this was hard for him to talk about.

"I know that stopping my medication isn't an option. I'll have to take them every day for the rest of my life. It's just how it is. I think I've come to terms with that. Or at least, I'm trying." The rhythmic movement of his hands continued and I tried to relax. But I was wound too tight.

"I'm glad to hear that," I told him and he gave me a small smile but didn't respond to my statement.

"Dr. Todd said sometimes it takes changing your medication multiple times until you find something that works with your body chemistry. I was lucky that I found what worked for me so quickly. Because the trial-and-error period is horrible. I saw it firsthand in some of the other patients. They were miserable."

"Dr. Todd?" I asked.

Clay nodded. "Yeah, Dr. Todd. He was my therapist at Grayson. He's pretty cool. He's the first shrink I've had that made me feel like I had a chance at dealing with everything. He just . . . got me, you know?"

"And your new therapist, what's he like?"

Clay shrugged. "He's nice. I like him. He and Dr. Todd are working closely together right now, so that's cool. He's different, but I think we'll get on fine." I was relieved to hear that. Clay smirked at me and I raised my eyebrows at him in question.

"Actually, he's suggested I bring you in for one of my sessions," he said, surprising me.

"Me? Why would he want to see me?" I squeaked. I knew this took a lot for Clay to say, but I was sort of weirded out by the thought of going to therapy. Weren't we too young for couples' counseling?

Clay laughed. "That's what I said. But he told me it would be good for us to talk about our relationship, to make sure we don't fall back into old patterns. Both Shaemus and Dr. Todd are very aware of how important you are to me and they just want to make sure what we have is healthy. For both of us. It's easy to put your feelings in the backseat. I know you got sucked under by what I was going through. But we have to go into this as equals. It can't just be about me."

What could I say to that? He had always been amazingly insightful and self-aware. But his inability to change or control his behaviors caused immeasurable damage. Yet here he was, one institution stay later, saying things that I never thought I'd hear. I wasn't delusional enough to think he was all fixed now. I knew this was an ongoing process. But what he was laying at my feet was the opportunity to share with him in his healing. Something he had denied me when he went away.

Something I knew I would jump at the chance to do.

"Of course I'll go with you. I'll do whatever I can to make sure you're happy and healthy. I want us to work. I want this to last. You just let me know when and I'm there," I promised.

Clay cupped my face between his hands and the look in his eyes made me feel all gooey. "You are the most selfless and amazing person I've ever met, Maggie May Young. I don't know what I did to deserve you. I will try every single day to make sure I'm worthy of the faith you put in me."

I leaned forward and touched my lips ever so gently against his. He hummed in approval and moved one hand to cup the back of my neck while the other snaked around my middle, pulling me closer. I was pressed up against him, our mouths moving against one another, and I couldn't ignore the tingling heat that was creeping its way through my body.

When his tongue touched the seam of my lips, I opened them without hesitation. Our tongues tangled together as we devoured one another. I gripped at his shirt, the blanket falling away from my shoulders, and his hands moved down my body.

His fingers stopped just shy of the hem of my dress, which had hiked up my thighs and was barely covering my bottom half. How easy it would be to jump back into the physical side of our relationship. When everything else had been so crazy, that was one thing that had always made sense. When our bodies came together, it had been the most beautiful thing I had ever known.

I could feel how much Clay wanted me. It was pressed intimately against the valley between my legs as I squirmed in his lap. He groaned, rich and raw in the back of his throat, his fingers digging into my flesh, the only barrier being my thin tights.

But just as soon as we were moving to where I wanted to go, Clay pulled away. His eyes were tightly closed and his breathing ragged. My heart hammered in my chest and I had to fight myself for control. I wanted him. More than anything.

"Maggie," he said, my name coming out as a moan, and it was such a turn-on. I pressed against him again, ready to pick up where we had so abruptly left off.

Clay put his hands on my shoulders and I thought he was going to pull me closer, but instead he held me away from his body. "We can't. Not yet." He opened eyes that were heavy with desire and I knew that he only half meant his words.

I blinked in confusion. "What? Why?" I hated how whiny I sounded. My body was buzzing and I wanted so desperately to be with him. In every way that mattered.

"I want you. I want this. So much. But we can't. Not while things are still so unstable. Please, just give me some time. I want everything to be perfect for you. I want to be the guy you deserve. Just understand that when we're together again, it will be amazing and wonderful and my head will be in a place where I know I can give you everything you ever wanted." I slithered off his lap trying not to act like a petulant child.

"I get it. It's fine." What a lie. I was feeling absurdly rejected. I had always been the aggressor in the physical side of our relationship. I suppose I was hoping this once I wouldn't have to be. It was stupid and immature, but when you're in the heat of the moment, only to be denied what your body wants so badly, it's hard to see things logically.

"Maggie. Please don't look like that. I love you. There is nothing in this world I want more than to make love to you. But let's just take this slow. It will be better in the long run. For both of us." His pleading made it difficult to stay miffed.

I laid my head down on his shoulder, turning my face into his shirt, and kissed the spot just above his heart. "Okay," I said quietly. Clay held me tightly to his side and we were quiet. And for the time being, it was enough.

chapter
nineteen

clay

trying to fit years of work into a few short months was daunting, if not impossible. Here I was, a month out of treatment, and I was attempting to run before I had even learned to walk. Sure, I was doing better. I was making strides to do things different, to break preexisting patterns. But I was a fool in thinking I was okay.

Every day was a testimonial to how far I had come. But there were a thousand moments that reminded me of how stupid I was being for trying to promise Maggie, Ruby, myself, anything when I was in no position to do so.

The dark voice in my head, while not as loud, still taunted me. It tried to tell me that I wasn't ever going to get better. The urge to hurt myself was overwhelming. And for every smile I forced onto my face, it was followed by the fight to keep it all together.

But I was sticking to my treatment plan. I never missed a therapy appointment. I made sure to take my medication twice a day as prescribed. But the niggling doubts began to resurface the longer I was in Davidson.

Did I really need the medicine?

Come on, wouldn't I feel so much better if I was just able to live without it? Remember how awesome it was? How I felt on top of the world?

What could it hurt? Missing a day or two? No one would have to know.

I was fighting an enemy every single day. And his name was Clayton Reed.

The only difference this time was I refused to bottle it up inside and hope it would go away. Or even worse, cave into the demands of the voice inside me. I spoke with Shaemus about how scared I was. About the urges that at times seemed to eat me alive.

He started having me journal again—just freaking fantastic. He wanted me to write down every time I wanted to hurt myself. I was supposed to focus on what I was feeling, what triggered it. He didn't try to hide from me the fact that he was worried. He shared that the likelihood of relapse for someone with borderline personality disorder was huge. He suggested that the Tegretol might need to be adjusted to combat my manic symptoms.

And then we would talk about voluntary readmission to a mental health facility. Sometimes that sounded like a good idea. Other times, not so much.

Every day I came home to an aunt who was barely able to get out of bed in the morning. The house that had once felt warm and safe was now an empty shell. Ruby had started to see a grief counselor, at my insistence, but I wasn't noticing any change yet. But just like my own progress, it would happen over time.

And there was Maggie, who was both the brightest part of my day and the darkest. Because with all the journaling I was doing, it was clear my trigger hadn't changed. It seemed that my most negative emotions were somehow still tied to the girl who loved me.

I had lost it during my last therapy session. I had ripped the pages out of my journal and thrown them away. I had wanted to grab the pair of scissors on Shaemus's desk and cut myself wide. The tears had been furious and intense.

Shaemus didn't bat an eyelash. Thankfully he was like Dr. Todd in that way. He had simply told me to take deep breaths, to focus on something else, and walked me through pulling myself together. It had taken a while and I had gone over my session time by twenty minutes.

When my tirade was finished, he started talking about my returning to Grayson. He had spoken with Dr. Todd and they could arrange for a place for me in two weeks.

"I know you want to be here, for Ruby, for Maggie. But what good are you to either of them when you are in pain?" Shaemus had asked me gently. "They wouldn't want you to sacrifice your health for them." I hadn't been able to argue with that.

I had left my therapy appointment feeling defeated. I was a failure, convinced that I couldn't be in this town a moment longer. But I had gone home to find Ruby curled up on the couch, fast asleep, clutching Lisa's coat in her hands, evidence of her drying tears on her worn face.

How could I leave her? Not when she was like this.

I hadn't called Maggie that night. I was worried that just the sound of her voice would either reinforce my desire to stay or make me want to get the hell out of there. How could my love for her be so fucking conflicted? It wasn't fair to her. Not after everything.

But when I had woken up in the morning, I felt good. Happy, even. The events from the day before were a hazy memory. And I had picked up Maggie for school, and just being around her put any thoughts of leaving firmly out of my mind.

How many times in my life had I convinced myself that everything would be fine? It seemed that some things really hadn't changed.

Particularly where Maggie was concerned. Becoming consumed by her was dangerous territory. One that I had traversed before with horrific results. But it was such a beautiful way to fall.

Maybe it was time to get Maggie to come with me to therapy. I was sure that this was a proactive way of taking control of my life.

"Do you think you could come with me to Shaemus's office tomorrow after school?" I asked Maggie as we walked into the cafeteria for lunch. I had started eating with her, Rachel, and Daniel again. And so far, it hadn't been completely awkward.

Rachel and I had developed a bond of tentative respect since working together at Bubbles. She no longer avoided me and even tried to engage in conversation when we had our breaks. I knew her efforts had more to do with Maggie than with me, but I appreciated it nonetheless.

And Daniel. His antagonism had surprisingly died down. I knew he still watched me, waiting for the moment he had to intervene. But thankfully there hadn't been a need. Despite my inner craziness, outwardly I was working my ass off to show the world I was a changed man.

It was exhausting being two separate people. I was beginning to wonder which was the "real" Clayton Reed.

Maggie stopped just inside the doorway to the overly loud lunchroom and looked up at me. Her eyes were soft and I knew she understood how hard it was for me to open this part of myself to her. I hadn't been able to do it the last time, but this time I would.

"Sure," she said when I asked her to come to therapy. "I'll just switch my shift at the coffee shop with someone."

"If it's too much of a hassle, we can do it another time," I assured her. Maggie gripped my forearm, her fingers digging into my skin.

"No, I'll be there," she said emphatically, and I leaned down to kiss the top of her head. I felt the sensation of eyes on me. When I looked up, I saw that fuckwad Jake Fitzsimmons staring at us. He looked extremely unhappy about seeing Maggie and me together.

Maybe it was juvenile, but I couldn't help but sling my arm around Maggie's shoulders and smirk at Jake, who had yet to look away. I felt a flash of sadistic satisfaction at the way his jaw tensed up right before he broke eye contact. That's right, asshole, she's mine. Get that through your thick fucking head.

"Clay?" I realized that Maggie had been talking but I had been so fixated on my testosterone showdown that I hadn't heard her. She followed my line of sight and gave a frustrated snort.

"Really, Clay? Do you want me to hold my leg out so you can pee on it? How about tattoo your name on my forehead? Leave Jake alone, okay?" She moved out from underneath my arm and I felt my paranoid anger resurface.

Why was she defending him? Was there more to their relationship than I realized? It was irrational but I became suspicious. I grabbed her arm. Not hard, just firmly, so that she couldn't move away from me. She looked down at my hand gripping her arm and I saw her face go pale.

I quickly realized what I was doing and dropped my hand. Shit. What was wrong with me?

"Sorry," I muttered, running my hand over the spot I had just held, maybe too harshly. Maggie's arm was tense and I moved back a fraction. "I don't have any reason to be jealous. I'm being dumb," I said quietly, feeling ashamed and embarrassed.

"Yeah, you were. I'm not having this conversation about Jake again. It's stupid." Maggie hurried off toward our normal table and I wasn't so sure I should follow. I watched as Daniel and Rachel greeted her and I was relieved that neither of her friends had witnessed our confrontation.

I clenched my hand into a fist and felt like smashing it into the concrete wall beside me.

See, this was what I was afraid of. The longer I was in Davidson, the closer I came to being that other Clay. It was as though everything I had learned in treatment was being lost in the day-to-day effort to be normal. Maggie glanced up and caught my eye. She didn't look happy. I couldn't blame her. I had been a certifiable asshole. A crazy jealous boyfriend. And over what? Because some dude was staring at my girl? How insecure was I that I couldn't handle that?

I made a conscious choice then to not run from my gigantic fuckup. I bought my lunch and walked with purpose to the lunch table shared by Maggie and her friends. She didn't look at me as I sat down beside her. Rachel and Daniel wore similar expressions of distrustful wariness.

"I'm sorry, Maggie," I said sincerely, loud enough for her friends to hear. I wasn't going to hide what I had done. I wasn't going to act like nothing had happened. I wouldn't manipulate her into forgiving my shitty behavior. I would own up and hope that she forgave me.

"I got jealous. I know you and Jake have been close. Especially since I was gone. And he's always looking at you. And, yeah, it pisses me off. But that never gives me the right to put my hands on you. To restrain you or to make you afraid. My feelings have to do with me, not you." I sucked in a breath and waited for the crucifixion.

I looked from Rachel to Daniel, ready to accept the stones they wanted to throw. Daniel's eyes were cool as he assessed me. Rachel looked sad.

"Do I need to remind you of the fact I will take you out at the kneecaps if you fuck with her, man? Seriously. We are not going to sit around and watch you do this shit again," Daniel growled and Rachel put a hand on his arm in an effort to calm him down.

I met his hard gaze and nodded. "No, I don't need the reminder. I know damn well what you will do. And I'm okay with that. I was a jerk." My voice cracked and I felt my throat tighten up.

Maggie shook her head and didn't say anything. We ate our lunch in uncomfortable silence and I was sure I had screwed everything up all over again. But when Maggie got to her feet she looked down at me, her face heavy with emotion.

"I'll meet you after school tomorrow for your appointment. But I've got to go." And with that she left. I didn't say anything more to Daniel or Rachel. I picked up my tray and left the cafeteria. I didn't follow Maggie. I thought about leaving her a note in her locker, the way I had done way too many times before.

But that was something the old Clay would have done. The new Clay had to break the pattern. Even if it was reaching out to strangle me.

◆

I waited by my car after school on Thursday. I hadn't talked to Maggie since yesterday. I knew she was taking a step back. And for once I gave her space. I didn't stalk her like a psychopath. Though I had tried to call her last night. When she didn't answer, I simply left her a message telling her that I loved her and left it at that.

I had met with the guidance counselor again at lunchtime. He was really pressing me to make some decisions about after graduation. I was really uncomfortable doing that. I wanted to throw caution to the wind and commit to some idealization of what I wanted for my life. But right now, with things being held together by a thread, I didn't think that was the smartest idea.

Goals were important, and in fact therapy encouraged them, but I just wasn't ready to put them to paper. Right now I had to try and get through this vicious backslide I was finding myself in.

When I saw Maggie walk across the parking lot toward me, I felt like I could breathe again. My heart went into overdrive and I felt almost weak with relief. I had been terrified that she wouldn't meet me. Not that I would have blamed her if she had turned her back and run as far away from me as she could get.

But yet here she was. And it reminded me that I had love and support and I was damn lucky. I pushed my hair back off of my forehead, my palms sweating.

"I wasn't sure you'd show," I admitted as she stopped in front of me. She looked beautiful in jeans that fit her narrow hips in a way that put very inappropriate but very hot thoughts in my head. Her teal sweater was low cut and I tried not to be a total pig and peek down her shirt.

I was a guy, after all. I'd have to be dead not to notice how amazing she looked.

She pulled her hair out of the collar of her jacket and gave me an unreadable look. "I wasn't so sure I'd show either." I swallowed thickly.

"Look, if you don't want to go, I understand. What I did was fucked up," I started, but she cut me off.

"Stop it, Clay. I've thought about this long and hard. That's all I've done for the last twenty-four hours. I'm sick and tired of obsessing over you. I was really hoping we'd be past this. But I think I'm just being naïve and a little unfair to you. I can't expect you to morph into super Clay so quickly. It's only setting you up to fail. While what you did was not cool, I committed to taking this journey with you. And I won't go back on that. If there's anything I can do to make this easier on you, then I'll do it."

She stepped closer and narrowed her eyes. "But if you ever touch me like that again, you're going to find yourself missing a few fingers. Are we clear?"

I nodded, finding any words inadequate. Maggie took a step back and her face relaxed.

"Let's get going," she said, and went around to the passenger-side door.

I hurried so I could open the door for her. I know it was old-fashioned, but opening her car door was the very least I could do.

I went through a few of those super-duper, handy calming tech-niques as I made my way to my side of the car.

The air in the vehicle felt thick with tension and I didn't know what to do to get rid of it. I had always been ill equipped to handle uncomfortable situations, because they were usually a result of something I had done. And now was no exception.

For once, Maggie didn't put on any music, so we rode to Shae-mus's office in silence. The rumble of the engine seemed loud in the quiet. I pulled up out front of the nondescript two-story brick house with the sign reading Blue Ridge Mental Health Services.

I jumped out of the car and went around to open Maggie's door. She looked up at the building that held Shaemus's office. And without saying a word, she reached out and took my hand. Squeezing lightly, she walked with me to the front door.

We walked into the brightly lit waiting room. His receptionist, Holly, sat at her desk, typing on her computer. She looked up and smiled when she saw us. "Hi, Clay. Just have a seat. Shaemus is running a few minutes late." Holly had to be in her midforties and at least seventy pounds overweight. But she was nice enough. I gave her a slight smile and led Maggie to a small couch in the corner.

"This is . . . nice," Maggie offered, looking around at the worn furniture and off-color walls.

"Not what you were expecting?" I asked her.

She shook her head. "No, I was picturing something more . . . clinical, I guess. You know, hospital white walls and chairs that make your back ache. More like an emergency room. This is almost like being in someone's house." Her observation was spot on. In fact, there was even a small TV off to the side and fish tank by the window. Sure, the furnishings were a little shabby, but it was anything but cold and impersonal.

We hadn't been there long when the door in front of us opened and a girl close to our age came out. She was heroin-addict skinny, with straggly blond hair and sunken eyes. I knew Maggie was trying not to stare, but I could practically hear the wheels turning in her head. She was asking herself the standard questions: *I wonder what she's doing here? She looks like a drug addict. Is she? Or is she just crazy?*

By now I had long since given up trying to figure out anyone else's issues. I had enough of my own. The girl's eyes stayed fixed to the floor as she shuffled out of the office, giving Holly a wave as the receptionist called out good-bye.

Shaemus came over and I got to my feet. Maggie seemed suddenly apprehensive and I was reminded that this was a lot for her to agree to. Therapy is daunting even for those who do it regularly. I should have prepared her more for what this would be like. But I had forgotten to in the wake of our argument. Yet another shitty thing to add to the growing list of shitty things I had done.

"Clay! Hello! This must be Maggie." Shaemus held out his hand for Maggie to shake. She gave him a wan smile and Shaemus looked between the two of us with a jovial grin. He really did look like someone's balding uncle. When you saw him for the first time, you didn't see shrink. I could imagine him playing bingo instead of dishing out therapy.

"Come on back." He waved us toward his office and I took Maggie's hand again as we headed inside. I watched Maggie take in her surroundings again before she sat down in one of the overstuffed armchairs in front of a walled-up fireplace. Shaemus didn't have a desk, like Dr. Todd had. There was a small worktable off to the side, but he preferred to sit in the middle of the room with his clients. He said that desks were too easy to hide behind, and if he expected his clients to be open and forthcoming, then he should do the same.

"You are my last appointment of the day, so we're in no rush. We're going to take all the time that we need. Have a seat, Clay.

You make me nervous when you stand about like that," Shaemus joked, waving his hands in the direction of another chair. Maggie looked at my therapist in surprise, clearly taken aback by his candor. It was true that Shaemus took some getting used to. I was still adjusting to his personality. But he hadn't set off the bitch-slap reflex yet, so I suppose we were doing pretty well.

I met Maggie's eyes and gave her what I hoped was a reassuring smile. Hers was unsure, but genuine, as she made herself comfortable. Shameus took his place in the love seat across from us. He picked up a pad of paper and clicked his pen a few times.

"Have the two of you had a chance to discuss what you hope to get out of the session together?" Shaemus asked, getting right to the point. Maggie and I shared a glance and I grimaced.

"No, not really," I said. Shaemus nodded, obviously not surprised. He clicked his pen again.

"Maggie, have you ever been to therapy before?" he asked her. Maggie cleared her throat and shook her head.

"No, I haven't. My parents wanted me to . . . uh . . . see someone a few months ago. But I never did." I looked at her in surprise. This was news to me. I started to chew the inside of my lip. God, how bad had things been for her if her parents were suggesting therapy?

Shaemus looked between the two of us again. "This was after Clay left?" he asked for clarification. Maggie's face began to flush and I knew this was hard for her to admit.

"Yes," she said quietly. I wanted to reach out for her hand again. Should I touch her? Would she let me? I didn't know what to do. This new information had thrown me.

Shaemus made a noise in his throat. "Can you tell me a little bit about why your parents would think you needed to see someone? Just so I can get an idea of how things were for you." He didn't look at me once; his entire focus was on Maggie.

She squirmed in her seat and shot me another look. This one

seemed full of apology and this time I took her hand. Doubts be damned, I needed the physical connection. *We* needed it.

Maggie cleared her throat again. "I was depressed. After . . . everything—" Shaemus interrupted her.

"It's okay to say what happened. One of the things Clay and I are working on is facing his choices, his behaviors, head-on. We don't have to dance around them in here. This is a safe place. It's important that you feel comfortable in voicing your feelings and concerns. These four walls are meant as a sanctuary. But if at any time you are unable to talk about something, you just need to say so. Communication is essential." I watched Maggie's throat move up and down as she swallowed. Her fingers gripped mine painfully.

"Yeah, so I was depressed. Really depressed after I came home from North Carolina. After Clay had tried to kill himself." My gut twisted at the reminder of my actions that came from her lips. It wasn't an easy thing to talk about but to hear her say it made me want to hide under my chair.

"I wouldn't leave my room. I had a hard time sleeping. I lost weight. I was pretty pathetic. Anyway, my parents talked about me getting counseling. I knew they were worried. I hated that they were worried, but I couldn't snap out of it." A betraying tear slipped down her cheek and I had to look away.

"What changed for you then? Since you never sought out professional help, I can only assume something did." Shaemus lifted his pen and made some notes on his pad.

"I don't know. I guess I just got sick of feeling sorry for myself. I told myself that Clay wasn't coming back, that he was trying to get better. And me moping around wouldn't help him or me." She looked over at me and her eyes were glassy from tears.

"And then I got this letter from Clay telling me to move on. That he didn't want me to wait around for him. Something inside me snapped and I became angry, not sad. So I suppose that helped." I started gnawing the inside of my lip again. Hearing this was more difficult than I imagined. I bit down hard enough to draw blood, the copper taste oddly soothing.

Shaemus stopped writing and looked at me, obviously picking up on my anxiety. "And how does this make you feel, Clay? To hear how hard things were for Maggie after your suicide attempt?" Shaemus asked matter-of-factly.

Wow, dude wasn't pulling any punches.

I stared down into my lap, the hand that held Maggie's feeling foreign and disconnected. I could barely compute that she was still there with me. I was left alone with my guilt.

"I feel like shit, all right? I was a selfish dick, is that what you want to hear?" I was getting angry. I wished I wasn't because anger had never helped me.

Maggie squeezed my hand and I tried to calm down. I took several deep breaths. "I feel angry. At myself for doing that to her. I feel sad and regretful for all the time I missed. I feel guilty for causing her pain. And mostly I feel like a failure. Because I failed Maggie. And I failed myself," I whispered.

I heard Maggie's soft intake of breath and I looked up at her. Tears fell steadily down her cheeks and her lower lip trembled. Shaemus handed her a box of tissues and she took several, wiping her face.

"Maggie, what do you feel, hearing about Clay's pain?" Shaemus urged. Maggie never took her eyes from mine as she answered.

"I feel sad. But I also don't want him to feel guilty, or ashamed, or any of those things. He's not responsible for what happened. He was sick." I closed my eyes and shook my head.

"You don't think Clay is responsible for his behavior? That he isn't ultimately culpable for what happened to him?" Shaemus asked her curiously.

When I opened my eyes it was to find Maggie glaring at my

therapist. Her chest heaved with her erratic breathing. "How can you blame him? He couldn't control himself! He has been suffering from bipolar and borderline personality disorder most of his life! What kind of person would that make me if I blamed him for something that wasn't his fault?" Maggie's voice was getting loud, but Shaemus's neutral expression never faltered. I recognized the look. He was getting ready to shrink her.

"I'd think you were normal. Human. How can you not blame him for putting you through that? What I'm hearing right now is a young girl who was put in a horrible situation. That's a lot for someone so young to deal with. No one would blame you for being angry with Clay."

Fuck me; this was like ripping your fingernails off. I felt like interjecting something. Perhaps defend myself. But I realized that this session was just as much about Maggie as it was about me. That it was about the fundamental dysfunction of the relationship we had had. Getting Maggie to identify those things was important. Even if it hurt like hell to hear.

Maggie dropped my hand and covered her face. I shot Shaemus a look but he just held up his hand, watching Maggie closely. Her shoulders shook and I felt horrible for bringing her here. This was beyond messed up. How could I put her through this shit all over again? Making her relive one of the most gut-wrenchingly painful periods of both of our lives.

"Yes, I'm mad at him. I'm furious at him for hurting himself. For leaving me behind and cutting off all contact. But more than that, I love him. And I think . . . no I know that outweighs everything else." Maggie wiped the tears from her face and I could see the determined set of her jaw.

Shaemus smiled. "And that, we can work with. But don't make excuses for him or for yourself. Denial hurts more than it helps," he warned.

We spent the next hour talking about how we communicated

with each other. We talked about my jealousy issues and Maggie's insecurities. I was shocked to hear how little she really thought about herself. And I recognized that I hadn't done anything to make that better for her. In fact, I had made it ten times worse.

We discussed what had occurred in the cafeteria yesterday. Shaemus proved to be an excellent sounding board to deal with the way we were treating each other. I felt mostly to blame for the problems between us, but Shaemus pointed out the ways both of us could work on communicating better.

By the time our session was winding down, I felt like I had run a marathon. I was exhausted. Looking at Maggie, I knew she was drained as well. Shaemus handed Maggie a notebook.

"I recommend you start journaling. It's great in helping to identify feelings and motivations you perhaps didn't know you had." I tried not to roll my eyes. Therapists and their fucking journals.

Shaemus followed us out of his office. "You both did well today. That was a lot to share. I'd really like for you both to meet with me again. Clay comes twice a week. Maggie, perhaps you could come every other week. What are your thoughts?" Shaemus said.

Maggie was holding my hand again and she peered up at me and my heart stopped. There was real happiness in her eyes.

"I think I'd like that," she said. Shaemus smiled at the both of us.

"Wonderful. Well, then, you two, have a good evening. Clay, I will see you next Tuesday, and Maggie, I'll see you in two weeks. It was wonderful to meet such an amazing young woman." He shook her hand again and Maggie flushed at the compliment.

Walking outside, it felt like we had spent days inside the office. We had entered one way and left as something completely different.

Once we were both buckled in our seats and I was pulling out into traffic, Maggie popped a CD into the player. "Wow. That was intense. Is that how it always is?" she asked.

I laughed, relieved that she didn't hate me for dragging her there.

"No, it's not always like that. Sometimes it's actually pretty chill. But usually the first few times can be rough," I told her.

Maggie tapped her fingers on the dashboard in time to the music. She stopped abruptly and pressed her hands down on the plastic.

"I'm glad I went. I feel like this could be good for us," she said seriously.

I reached over and placed my hand on her thigh, just needing to touch her. I always needed to touch her.

"Me too, Mags," I agreed softly and then fell silent. Neither of us spoke again, letting our newfound contentment do all the talking for us.

chapter
twenty

maggie

things were pretty freaking fantastic. Better than I could have ever dared to hope for. After that horrible day in the cafeteria and then accompanying Clay to therapy, I felt like we had entered a new chapter. I was done with waiting for the next bad thing to happen. Now that I was hearing how Clay struggled, about how hard things still were for him, I didn't obsess so much about being blindsided. I felt like finally we were being honest.

I still worried about him. It was damn near impossible to listen to him tell Shaemus about how he thought of cutting himself, and how I unwittingly triggered these responses because of his deep-seated feelings of shame and guilt.

I would stare at Rachel and Daniel and wish like hell Clay and I could get to that point where we were past the bullshit and just living our lives, with each other. Like any other normal couple.

But that wasn't our lot and I was learning to accept it. Life with Clayton Reed would never be sunshine and roses. It would be lots of shadows with intermittent light. And I was beginning to figure out ways to appreciate the light when I saw it. Because that darkness was still there. It most likely would always be there.

We were working on it, though, together. And that was saying something.

So we slipped into a much better place than we had ever been before. Everyone could see the change in not only Clay but in me as well. Rachel commented on it after school one day.

"You seem happy, Mags. So does Clay. It makes me feel good to know you're feeling good." Rachel was simplistic like that. I had given her a hug, which again was totally unlike me. But she had taken it in stride.

Daniel was less convinced, but for the time being he kept his mouth shut about it. If I was okay, then he was okay, and that's what I loved about him.

My parents were barely concealing their very serious anxiety about the situation. They didn't interrogate me, which I appreciated. But they had become sneakier in getting information. Clay had been insistent in coming to see them. I knew that he felt he needed to make the effort with them. So I had facilitated their reintroduction.

Clay brought me home after a shift at Java Madness. I knew both of my parents were home, so I impulsively asked Clay to come inside. It was probably best not to prepare him for the meeting with my parents. I knew he would have only worked himself up unnecessarily. Mom and Dad would either accept him or not. Either way, this was Clay's chance to prove that he wanted to make amends and that he was trying to change.

"You ready for this?" I asked him, noticing he had gone a little pale. Clay didn't say anything, only nodded his head. Going inside I found my dad reading the newspaper and my mom working on her laptop in the living room.

They both looked up as we came into the room. They weren't surprised to see Clay; I had told them I'd be bringing him by.

While I didn't want to put undue pressure on Clay by preparing him for the visit, my parents needed to be told ahead of time. It gave them a chance to sort out how they would respond to seeing the boy they blamed for their daughter's shutdown months before.

Clay dropped my hand and stuffed his into his jeans, a sure sign of his discomfort. "Hello, Mr. Young. Mrs. Young." He tentatively walked farther into the room as though he were approaching a firing squad.

My dad looked at him over the top of his glasses and put the paper on the couch beside him before getting to his feet. My mother's smile, while a little forced, was at least firmly in place as she met Clay halfway to greet him.

"Hello, Clay." My dad shook his hand and I was relieved at the lack of posturing on his part. Mom shook his hand as well and I was pleased at how civil they were being. Score one for the parental units.

"How's Ruby?" my mother asked, squeezing Clay's forearm in sympathy. Clay rubbed the back of his neck, his eyes darting to me as though reaffirming that I hadn't left him to face my parents alone.

"She has her good and bad days. Well, actually, her bad days and not-so-bad days. It's been tough," Clay answered truthfully. My dad's face softened a bit and I knew that Clay's honesty had gotten to him. My mom made a tsking sound.

"If there's anything either of you need, please don't hesitate to ask," my mom told him, and I could see that Clay was blown away by her offer.

"Thank you, Mrs. Young. Ruby and I appreciate all of the food you've given us. It's been nice to eat something that didn't come out of a box from the freezer." Clay's mouth quirked up in a painful smile. It was the smile of someone who didn't know whether he was about to be eaten alive or not.

"You are very welcome," Mom said and waved him toward the couch. "Have a seat. I was just getting ready to make some tea. Can I get you anything?" she asked both of us. Clay shook his head.

"No, thank you," he responded with such forced politeness that I wished I could tell him to relax. But my dad had already honed in. He sat down across from Clay, his arms crossed over his chest. My dad had always been the harder sell. Particularly where Clayton Reed was concerned.

When my mother asked me to help her in the kitchen I had declined initially. I was more than a little worried about leaving Clay alone with my dad for any amount of time. But my mom insisted, and I could tell by the look she was throwing my way that I needed to make myself scarce.

Clay's expression was bordering on panic and I could only grimace in return as I followed my mom into the kitchen. "Do you think it's smart leaving those two alone?" I asked my mom, casting nervous looks down the hallway toward the living room. I could hear the nondescript murmur of their voices but nothing else.

My mom went about getting things together for tea. She pulled out a box of peanut butter cookies and put them onto a plate. "Your dad needs to talk to Clay, Maggie. I think it's best to let them speak privately for a moment." That made my stomach flutter nervously.

Mom gave me a reassuring hug. "He's not going to threaten him with a shotgun. But there are things he needs to say. Things Clay needs to hear. If you plan on having a relationship with him, then your father and I are going to make certain things very clear." I felt the overwhelming urge to throw up and then run into the living room and whisk Clay out of the house. What the hell had I been thinking in bringing him here? I wasn't so sure Clay was emotionally ready to deal with whatever my dad decided to dish out.

Five minutes—that actually felt like five hours—later, we took the cups of tea and plate of cookies back into the living room. I felt the tension as soon as we entered the room and my eyes fastened on Clay in apprehension. I was surprised to see that he appeared . . . well . . . okay. Both he and my dad looked up when we placed the stuff on the coffee table. I chanced a glance at my dad and he seemed rigid, but at least he wasn't angry.

I was dying to know what was said, but I figured I'd have to wait until later. For the time being, conversation drifted into how Ruby's shop was doing. Whether it had been hard for Clay readjusting to life in a small town. My parents asked him questions about Florida without outright demanding information concerning the facility where he had lived for three months.

Their questions instead consisted of that sneaky, underhanded method of information gathering that they had recently adopted. I realized this because Clay began to offer tidbits about his time at the Grayson Center that he hadn't even told me. He shared about how difficult it had been to keep up with school, having only two hours a day to cram it all in. He talked a bit about the people he met there, speaking at length about his roommate, Tyler, who had been there for heroin abuse and paranoid schizophrenia.

I tried not to sit there with my mouth hanging open. Here we were, a little over a month after Clay had returned to Davidson, and I barely knew a thing about Grayson or the people he had befriended there. I felt like the world's worst girlfriend. But my parents respectfully listened and asked their own questions.

"I'm glad Maggie is seeing your therapist. That was a wonderful thing to suggest," my mom said, again flooring me with her understanding. Clay smiled at me, a soft look on his face as he answered my mother.

"I'm completely invested in making this work. I want Maggie and me to have the kind of relationship that is built totally on trust and support for each other. I'll do whatever I have to do to make sure I'm the best person I can be for her. And for me." My parents seemed to appreciate his words, though I noticed they still watched the two of us closely.

When it was time for Clay to leave, my mother hugged him and my dad had patted his shoulder. "We'll see you soon," Dad said as I walked Clay out to his car.

"Yes, sir. And thank you, for everything," Clay told my dad, who only nodded. I waited until my parents closed the front door and we were walking down the front path to his car before asking him about his earlier conversation with my dad.

Clay laughed. "That was killing you, wasn't it?" I playfully punched him in the shoulder.

"Tell me! Please!" I whined, making Clay laugh harder.

He tapped the end of my nose with his finger. "So nosy." I rolled my eyes.

Clay unlocked his car and turned to lean against it, pulling me between his legs, his arms wrapped around my middle. "He was giving me the dad warning. Letting me know he didn't want me hurting you again. Threatened bodily harm, you know how it goes," Clay said lightly, and I pinched his side, knowing he was messing with me.

"Ouch, okay." Clay sobered and pulled me tightly against his chest. He looked down into my upturned face and kissed me on the lips. "He told me that what happened before had hurt you deeply. That they had been terrified for you and it had been the most helpless he has ever felt as your father. I knew my leaving you would be hard, Maggie. I just thought I was doing the right thing. For you. For me. For both of us. I had no idea you were going through as rough a time as I was. Your dad told me that he wouldn't watch you go through that again, even if that meant being the bad guy and keeping us apart." I sucked in a breath, scared and shocked by my father's candor with Clay. Though I should have expected it.

Clay kissed the top of my head. "I told him that I understood and that is why I hadn't contacted you while I was in treatment. I was convinced that staying away was the best thing for you. That you needed to live your life without me in it." His grip around my body became tighter and his voice broke.

"But I then told your dad that I now knew living my life without you wasn't an option. And that is why I was taking my medication, going to therapy, doing whatever I had to do to make sure the life we have together is a good one and that it makes you happy. Because there is nothing more important to me than your happiness." My eyes stung with tears and I pulled up on my tiptoes, pressing a kiss to his mouth.

He held me for a long time, tasting me, caressing my lips with his. Our tongues tangled in a dance of total love. When we pulled away he ran his hand down the side of my face.

"I love you, Maggie May Young," he whispered.

"And I love you, Clayton Reed," I responded with equal ardor.

After Clay had left and I went back inside, my parents didn't discuss Clay's visit. But I felt the ice thaw and I knew that while they didn't necessarily trust Clay, they at least respected where he was coming from.

Saturday night dates quickly became a regular occurrence. It was as though Clay was making up for lost time. Sometimes he took me to dinner. Sometimes it was a movie. Sometimes we went hiking in the afternoon and had a picnic. Other times we met up with Rachel and Daniel and went to the mall.

It was all so normal. So teenage. I felt better knowing that Clay was consistently taking his medications. He had to take them at lunchtime and he did so every day without fail. He didn't make a show of it, but he never hid it from me either.

How did we ever get so lucky as to be in this place together? It was like a dream. I was terrified that I would wake up and find everything had popped like a bubble. Clay would be gone and I would be alone and all of this would be nothing more than a massive delusion.

But while I was deliriously happy, some people, or should I say person, wasn't so thrilled with my relationship. My friendship with Jake had significantly cooled. Gone was our easy banter while we worked. In fact, we hadn't shared a shift in over two weeks and I couldn't help but wonder if he had requested a different schedule.

My heart hurt a little at the thought that I had callously led him on, only to drop him in a red hot minute the second Clay gave me the time of day again. I felt like a total asshole. I had tried to talk to Jake, to make it right in some way, but he either was too pissed or just not ready to talk to me. So any attempts at making myself feel better where he was concerned would just have to wait, if it ever happened at all.

But Clay and I were pretty close to perfect.

I tried not to stare at him as he sat on his bed after school, sketching in a notebook while I tried to finish my homework. I was horribly distracted by the fact that his shirt had ridden up on his stomach, revealing smooth skin and drool-worthy muscles.

"Do your homework," he scolded me with a smirk. I flushed at being caught. I looked down at the illegible words on my paper and tried to focus.

"I am doing my homework," I muttered, tapping my pencil against my book. Clay's chuckle made my stomach knot up. Yeah, I was so not doing my homework. I closed my American history book with a bang and moved across the room slowly until I was beside the bed.

Clay grinned as I sat down and leaned in to kiss the side of his neck. "Whatcha workin' on?" I purred, rubbing my nose along the joint of his shoulder.

"You should be doing your work. I feel bad for distracting you." Clay's voice was husky as I started to kiss the line of his jaw. I loved the taste of him, salty and sweet all at the same time. While the emotional side of our relationship was going strong, the physical aspects had come to an unfortunate stall. I wasn't sure what the hang-up was. Because I knew Clay wanted me. I could feel it in the way he kissed me, the way he held me. But it was as though he was scared to take that step back into that place that used to be so familiar.

"Don't feel bad. I'd rather be doing this anyway," I said, lightly nipping at the skin below his ear. When I threw my leg over him and straddled his lap, I felt him weaken. Finally! I almost did a victory dance, but then I was sucked under by something else entirely. Oh yeah, it was my raging hormones.

Clay tossed his sketchbook off to the side and grabbed ahold of my hips and pulled me up against him, his fingers digging into the sensitive skin. My tongue traced a line from his earlobe to the corner of his mouth. When I pressed my lips to his, he flipped me onto my back and began to devour me. Our teeth banged together with the force of his mouth against mine and I opened up for his tongue.

Clay groaned as my hands worked up the back of his shirt, desperate for the feel of his bare skin. And then his shirt was up and over his head, landing on the floor. I ran my fingers lightly over the ridged scars on his chest and he shivered. Even in the heat of that moment, I couldn't stop myself from making sure there were no new cuts on his body. I was relieved to touch only old wounds.

His hands followed my example and began their own exploration up my shirt. This was the furthest we had gone since we were together in North Carolina. I eagerly anticipated the feel of his hands on my breasts and arched my back when he finally palmed my bra-covered flesh.

When he started to roll my aching nipples between his forefinger and thumb I thought I would come undone right then and there. Like a man possessed, Clay ripped my shirt and my bra off in record time. If there was a world record for bra removal, Clay Reed would have broken it.

His mouth left my lips and attached to my waiting breasts. He tasted and teased with his tongue until he pulled a nipple into his mouth. "Ahh!" I called out, too lost in the moment to worry about the fact that Ruby was in the house somewhere. Classy, huh?

Clay's fingers found the button of my jeans and deftly unbuttoned them and brought the zipper down. His mouth still on my breast, his hand slipped down the front of my pants, touching me over my panties. I started to tremble, my head thrown back on the pillow as Clay worked my body.

It had been so long since I had felt this. Entirely too long if you ask me. I wasn't one for regular self-pleasuring, so I had been sadly neglected on the orgasm front. That was clearly about to be remedied.

"Clay," I moaned as his fingers pushed past the edge of my underwear and found my wet core. In one perfect thrust, he slipped his finger inside me and started the slow, torturous rhythm that had me falling apart in 10.2 seconds flat.

He continued to rub and thrust as his mouth claimed mine and his tongue fell into rhythm with his finger. Maybe I should be returning the favor, but I was way too caught up in my orgasmic haze.

After my body skyrocketed again, only to come crashing down, Clay withdrew his finger, his lips slowing in their aggressive assault of my mouth. I was breathing like I had just run a mile in four minutes. My heart beat so fast I was worried I might pass out.

Clay fixed my panties and zipped up my pants. He then pulled me onto my side so that he was cradling my back to his front. He nuzzled into my hair and pressed a hand to my belly.

"Uh, wow. Thank you," I said lamely.

Clay snorted in my ear. "You don't need to thank me for that. It was my pleasure, baby." My toes curled at the sensual way he voiced the endearment. I wanted to rub against him like a cat. I was such a girl sometimes. A squealing, pink-ribbon-and-sequins girl. And that was a side of me that only Clay could bring out.

My eyes caught sight of the discarded sketch pad and I pulled it closer. I rolled onto my back and brought the paper up to my face. My lips split into a smile as I saw the detailed drawing Clay had done of my profile while I had been sitting at his desk doing my homework.

"I do not look like that, Clay. You have some biases in the way that you see me," I scoffed, taken aback as I always was by the depth of his talent. He really was an amazing artist.

Clay kissed my cheek and brought his hand up to run down my nose. "No, I think you're the one who doesn't see things clearly. How you can look in the mirror every single day and not see the beautiful girl that I do is beyond me." His words made me flush. Not in embarrassment but in complete contentment. A feeling I was becoming slightly addicted to.

I propped myself up on my elbow and looked at Clay, who arched his eyebrow at me. "That look makes me nervous. Makes me wonder what you have going on in that head of yours," Clay teased, tapping the middle of my forehead.

"You should go to art school or something. You're really good. You should be able to get into a program somewhere," I said, and was more than a little disappointed by the way Clay tensed up. We hadn't really talked about the future much beyond the fact that we wanted to spend it together.

But how would that work when I went off to school? I had gotten my acceptance letter to James Madison University several weeks ago. My parents were thrilled, and Rachel and Daniel were stoked. But I hadn't told Clay yet. Mostly because I was terrified of ruining what we had with talk of separation and long-distance relationships.

Clay sat up and tossed his sketch pad on the bedside table. It was getting dark and he turned on the small lamp. I could see the strain my suggestion had caused. Which was ridiculous. I hadn't been blowing smoke up his ass when I complimented his artistic abilities. He really was awesome.

"So what do you think?" I asked, scooting along the bed until I sat beside him, our legs pressed against each other.

"Yeah, I don't know," Clay said shortly, which kind of irritated me.

"Why don't you look into it? What could it hurt? Have you thought at all about what you're going to do after graduation? Are you planning to stay here with Ruby? Or are you going to school?" I knew I was pressing. But the unanswered questions between us were starting to suffocate me.

Clay gritted his teeth. "Look, Maggie. I appreciate what you're trying to do, but I just don't know what I'm going to do. I mean, I just got out of fucking treatment. My aunt's girlfriend was killed in a car accident and I'm trying to do the right thing by Ruby. I haven't exactly had the luxury of thinking too much about my goals." He sneered at me and I recoiled a bit, not happy to see this old and all too familiar Clay.

"I was just—" I began but Clay cut me off.

"You were just sticking your nose in where it's not wanted. That's what you were doing. I don't want to talk about it. Why can't we just enjoy right now without fucking it up with talk about what you think I should be doing?" All right, he was getting pissed, and the way he started pacing around made all of this way too reminiscent of before.

But unlike before I didn't start backpedaling and trying to make this situation better for him. I didn't placate Clay and soothe his wounded psyche. This time I decided laying it out there was better for him and for me.

"Well, I'm going off to college in a few months. Months, Clay! That's it! And I don't want to go away without knowing you're doing something with your life too," I said firmly, crossing my arms over my chest.

Clay's laugh was dark and bitter and made me cringe. "Don't worry about me, Mags. I won't interfere with your life. You'll get your pretty little future and I won't stand in your way," he spit out.

I jumped to my feet. "Enough with the self-pity. I was just trying to point out that you are an amazing artist and that would be a constructive use of your talents. You know, find a career doing something you love. I was just trying to be helpful," I retorted. I eyed the brown bottle of pills on his dresser and I wondered whether he was taking them or not. Because the erratic mood swing was scaring me.

Clay must have seen the direction of my gaze because he sighed and shook his head. "Are you going to start thinking I'm lying about taking my meds every time we get into a fight?" he asked me wearily.

I felt my lips start to tremble. "Can you blame me?" I asked, and that seemed to take the wind right out of Clay's anger. His shoulders drooped and he dropped his head.

"No, I guess I can't," he said. Then the only sound was our heavy breathing. I didn't know what to say to get us back to that beautiful moment we had shared minutes earlier. The whiplash change was unfortunately not unexpected. And that made me more than a little sad. I wanted so much to be past this, but I knew we had such a long way to go.

The coward in me wondered if I had it in me to tough it out, to ride this roller coaster for as long as it lasted. But that part inside me was very, very small.

I slowly moved until I stood in front of him and put my hands up so that my fingers smoothed their way through his thick, dark hair. "I suppose that was my less-than-tactful way of asking about our future. Sorry if I was bitchy about it," I said. Because I really was sorry for taking this important conversation and becoming combative about it.

Clay shook his head. "You have nothing to be sorry for. It's not like I haven't been thinking about what I'm going to do . . . after. That's part of the reason I meet with the stupid guidance counselor so damn much. Mr. Hunt is trying to personally shape my life." He smirked, finally meeting my eyes, and I knew we were over that frightening hump.

"Oh yeah? How's that going?" I asked, my fingers still combing through his hair. I knew he loved it when I did that and I was rewarded with the softness that started to overtake his face.

"Well, if you couldn't tell by my shitty attitude a few minutes ago, the whole thing is pretty crappy. I have no idea what I want to do after I graduate. I wish I had some sort of plan. But I just don't," he said tiredly. I grasped the back of his neck and pulled him to my lips, kissing him soundly.

"Well, I'll help you figure it out. And we can make sure that whatever you do will involve the both of us," I promised, and Clay's small smile made our earlier argument fade into the background.

The sound of Clay's phone ringing broke the mood and he grabbed it and answered without looking at the screen to see who it was.

"Hello?" he said, still smiling at me. I cocked my head to the side when I saw the way his face blanked. "Hey, no, that's cool. I didn't forget." Clay darted a look my way, which made me feel kind of weird. Who was he talking to?

"This weekend? Sure. No, honestly, Ruby won't care. I'll text you directions on Friday." Clay looked at me again and I couldn't read his expression. Okay, so it sounded like someone was coming for a visit. Why did that make his entire demeanor change?

"Okay. I'll talk to you then, Maria." Maria? Who the fuck was Maria?

Clay hung up a few seconds later and dropped the phone back to his desk. Okay, Maggie, don't pounce. Wait for him to explain about Maria and why she was coming for a visit. Don't play the part of the jealous shrew. Easier said than done.

Clay jammed his hands into his pockets. *Dead giveaway there, buddy,* I thought.

"Maria?" I said impatiently, tired of waiting for him to grow some balls and give me an explanation.

Clay grimaced, never a good sign. "Uh, yeah. Maria is a friend of mine from Grayson. She's visiting her brother in Alexandria and wants to come down for the night," he said. A friend from treatment. Okay, that didn't sound so bad. Then why was Clay acting so strangely?

"I've never heard you mention Maria. Were you close?" I asked, watching him carefully. One point for Clay, he not once looked away guiltily. He met my eyes steadily and I knew that this girl, whoever she was, wasn't some girlfriend he acquired in the short time we were apart. Because for all of Clay's faults, he wasn't a cheater. Even though we hadn't technically been together while he was in Florida. But I knew him well enough to know that he would never have hooked up with someone that soon after ending things with me. He just wasn't wired that way.

"Yeah, we got pretty tight. She and Tyler were my closest friends there. I was surprised when she called not too long ago and told me she had been discharged. But I guess she was ready. Anyway, she'll only be here for the day. She asked to stay over and I hope that's cool with you," Clay said, and I knew that if I had told him it wasn't, he would have called his friend Maria and told her she would have to make other arrangements.

And that reassurance went a long way in squelching the beginning tinges of jealousy in my gut. "Yeah, that's fine. I look forward to meeting her." Okay, so I was lying my ass off. But I didn't want to admit that this faceless Maria freaked me out a bit. Mostly because she was close to my boyfriend when I had been completely shut out and I wasn't sure how to process that. If it had been a guy, I wouldn't have batted an eyelash. But a girl . . . Well, let's just say I knew how potent the Clay Reed effect was, having been a victim myself on a regular basis.

Clay's eyebrows rose and it was obvious he saw straight through my fakeness. "Sure you do," he deadpanned and I smirked.

"In the spirit of total honesty, I should probably tell you that Maria had a bit of a . . . crush on me while we were in treatment." Of course she did. She had been in treatment, not a coma.

"But she never acted on it and I made it very clear that I loved you and wasn't interested. So there has never been anything but friendship between us," he went on in a rush. I reached out and pulled his hand from his jeans pocket, lacing our fingers together.

"Chill out, Clay. I believe you. And while I had a momentary brush with the green-eyed monster, I assure you I'm over it. Don't stress yourself about it," I assured him. Clay's lopsided grin was breathtaking.

"Have I told you recently how much I love you?" he asked, pulling our joined hands to his lips and kissing the back of my hand.

"Not in at least five minutes. You're slacking, Mr. Reed," I joked. He kissed my hand again.

"I. Love. You," he said, punctuating each word with a sloppy kiss to my skin. I giggled like a schoolgirl and blushed. Yep, I was a pink, sparkly girl all right. I just hoped I didn't have to morph into a fist-throwing, claw-your-eyes-out girl around this Maria. Because I wouldn't think twice about unleashing my inner She-Ra if she pissed me off.

chapter
twenty-one

clay

Maria had been here for all of ten minutes and I was already regretting my decision to let her stay at Ruby's for the night. I sensed the change in her the moment she showed up at my house Friday evening. It could have been the inch-thick layer of makeup on her face or the fact that her skirt barely covered her ass. I felt like I was staring at a stranger. This was not the Maria Cruz from Grayson.

"Clay!" she squealed after I had opened the door. Yeah, I noticed that she rubbed her tits against my chest as she squeezed me. And I wasn't blind to the fact that she stared a little too long at my mouth as I greeted her. I didn't know who the fuck this girl was, but she was not my friend. She looked and sounded a lot like the girl Maria had been trying to get rid of. The one that fucked any guy who would give her an ounce of attention. The girl who used sex the same way I had used drugs and cutting.

"Hey, Maria," I said less enthusiastically, letting her into the house. Ruby wasn't home; she was at the store, having thrown herself back into keeping the shop in order. I was glad she was getting herself out of the house, but right now I would have given anything for the Ruby buffer.

Maria tugged in an overnight bag that looked as though she had packed for a damn week. "Here, let me get that," I offered, picking it up. Jesus Christ, did she think she was moving in?

"What the hell do you have in here? Bowling balls?" I grunted, bringing it into the living room. Maria giggled, making my skin crawl a bit.

"No, silly. A girl just needs plenty of clothing options. And shoes aren't light," she teased. I rolled my eyes.

"Shoes. Sure," I said, trying not to be annoyed by the already shitty beginning to this visit. I was instantly on guard around Maria and I had never felt that way before. Not even when it was apparent she had feelings for me. She had always been unassuming, shy even. Nothing like the Maria who stood in the middle of my living room with her cleavage on full display and a hand on her hip giving me fuck-me eyes.

"How was the drive?" I asked, trying to find a way into comfortable territory. Asinine small talk seemed the way to go. Maria pulled a tube of lip gloss from her purse and started to liberally apply it, rubbing it in with her finger.

"Fine. Hit some traffic on the beltway, but that was to be expected on a Friday," she said, shrugging, the action causing her shirt to fall dangerously low on her shoulder. Crap, I could see the top of her boobs. This was not cool. Maggie was going to be pissed when she got a load of Maria. I knew she was feeling insecure about my friendship with Maria. She had never come right out and admitted it, but I knew my girlfriend well enough to recognize the signs of her self-esteem taking a nosedive. I hadn't been sure how to handle that, because Maggie's feelings were completely unfounded.

So seeing Maria dressed like this, making it obvious that this visit was more about seeing the inside of my bedroom than about hanging out, would not go over well. And Maggie was supposed to be here any minute.

I looked away and gestured with my head toward the kitchen. "Want something to drink?" I asked. Maria grinned and nodded.

"Sure, I am pretty thirsty," she purred, the innuendo obvious. *Just get through the next twenty-four hours without having to break up a chick fight,* I thought. Because if Maggie didn't go ballistic on this overly sexualized Maria, then Rachel would definitely have something to say.

I needed a serious reminder as to why I thought hanging out with Maria, Maggie, Rachel, and Daniel would be a good idea. Oh that's right, because I wasn't expecting Maria "Sex Fiend" Cruz to arrive on my doorstep like she was deep-throating my cock in her head.

"Water okay?" I asked, flipping on the light as we entered the kitchen.

"Sounds perfect," Maria answered, making herself at home at the kitchen table. "So, things seem good for you since you've gotten out," she said, taking the glass I handed her.

"You make it sound like I busted out of prison," I commented, sitting down across from her at the table, though making sure to keep a healthy distance. One that would make any sort of touching impossible. I knew Maria to be touchy-feely anyway, and I didn't know what to expect with her acting like this.

Maria laughed. "Well, it kind of was like prison, don't you think?" she said, taking a sip of water.

"Not really. There are days I wish I could go back, actually," I found myself admitting. Despite how weird Maria was being, there was something reassuring about talking to someone who had been in the trenches with me. That maybe she of all people would understand how hard it was to be out of treatment.

Or maybe not.

"That's just crazy, Clay! I would never go back there. Not in a

million years!" she said emphatically and I looked at her in surprise. I had no idea she had hated it there so badly. I had always
gotten the impression that she felt the same way I did about treatment. That it was a necessary evil. Not one that we would have
originally chosen for ourselves, but an essential one.

"Really? You don't find it hard being on the outside? Trying to
get through the day?" I asked.

Maria looked at me levelly. "No, Clay. I much prefer the person
I am off the medication."

Well, shit. She wasn't medicated anymore. That explained a lot.
Maria had been on heavy-duty antidepressants. I was more than a
little shocked that she had stopped taking them. But then didn't I
have moments myself where I thought about chucking mine into
the toilet? Maria reminded me of how easy it was to forget why
you took them in the first place.

But one thing was for sure: Maria was officially a ticking time
bomb and not one that I particularly wanted around Maggie and
her friends. But I was stuck now. I just had to temper the situation
as much as possible.

"How long have you been off your meds, Maria?" I asked softly.

She tapped her hand on the table in agitation, clearly not liking
my question. "I don't know, awhile. Why does it matter, anyway?
You aren't still taking that crap, are you?" she scoffed. Wow, okay.

"Yeah, I am. I don't particularly feel like having a visit with a
straitjacket, all right?" I said testily.

Maria rolled her eyes. "Don't be such a drama queen, Clay.
Look at me, I'm fine." She held her arms out as if that proved her
point.

"You don't seem fine, Maria. In fact, you seem about the furthest from fine I've ever seen," I told her firmly. Her eyes widened
and her mouth gaped in shock at my blunt assessment. Before she
could respond, I heard the doorbell ring and I groaned inwardly.

Here we go, I thought.

"Hang on a sec. That's Maggie," I told Maria, whose mouth tightened at the mention of my girlfriend.

"Well, come on, let me meet this famous Maggie," Maria said overly brightly, following me into the foyer. I had hoped to have a moment alone with Maggie to prepare her for my good ol' friend from treatment. So much for that. Time to witness the train wreck about to happen and just hope like hell I could fix it all later.

Maggie stood on my stoop looking the complete opposite of Maria in every way that counted. She wore jeans that fit her perfectly and a long-sleeved cotton top that didn't show an excess amount of skin but made my mouth water all the same. Her shoulder-length brown hair was pulled back in a ponytail and she wore next to no makeup. She was gorgeous.

"Hi, baby," I said in genuine happiness to see her. I pulled her into my arms and kissed her on the mouth, loving the taste of her cherry lip gloss. The sound of Maria clearing her throat made Maggie pull back, looking slightly mortified by our overt public display of affection.

The moment she saw Maria and her streetwalker getup, I knew I'd hear about it later. Her eyes widened slightly and she gave Maria the quick girl once-over. Not something I had ever seen Maggie do before, but I could see how insecure she was about Maria's presence in my house.

"Hi, I'm Maggie," she said politely, holding out her hand for Maria to take. Maria laughed.

"What are we, fifty? Who shakes hands anymore?" Maria said snidely. Maggie stiffened and dropped her hand.

"People who have enough sense not to be rude to someone they just met?" Maggie stated, cocking her head to the side and giving Maria a smile that was both sickeningly sweet and full of bitch-slapping condescension.

Maria snorted and turned on her heel and walked back into

the living room. Maggie narrowed her eyes at me. "What the hell is that?" she whispered angrily.

"I have no freaking clue! She was nothing like that while we were at Grayson. But she has a history of . . . sexual issues. So, I don't know," I answered weakly. Maggie stood there fuming.

"And Miss Fuck Me Please is staying overnight under the same roof as you? Yeah, I feel really great about that, Clay!" Maggie hissed, trying to keep her voice low.

I ushered her into the house and closed the door behind her. "You have nothing to worry about," I told her, grabbing her hand.

Maggie sighed. "It's not you I worry about. That bitch has her claws out and she's ready to sink them into your flesh. So you'd better watch out," she warned, stomping off into the living room, where Maria was flipping through channels on the television.

We had around twenty minutes before we had to meet Rachel and Daniel for dinner. And they proved to be the longest twenty minutes in the history of awkwardness.

Maggie tried to talk to Maria but the other girl was having none of it. Maria directed all of her attention my way and I felt like a bone being fought over by two dogs. I know this is probably every other guy's dream come true, to have good-looking chicks fighting over him. But I didn't feel lucky. I just wished I could kick Maria's ass out of my house and pretend this crappy night had never happened.

But I couldn't. Even if I wanted to, I wasn't that much of a dick.

When Maggie excused herself to go to the bathroom I turned on Maria. "What the fuck is your problem?" I asked her angrily.

Maria could tell I was pissed and she tried to dial down the witchiness. "Sorry, I don't mean to be a brat. I guess I was just so used to having your attention all to myself when we were at Grayson, I just don't like to share." Her response threw me off balance. And if I hadn't been sure before, I knew now that Maria had developed an unhealthy attachment to me.

"Look, Maria, I'll remind you of what I said to you at the center. We are friends. Only friends. Maggie is who I love. If you can't be in my house and be respectful to my girlfriend, then I'm sorry, I'm going to have to ask you to leave," I told her firmly.

And just like that, the vampy sex kitten cracked and I could start to see Maria, my friend, underneath. "I'm sorry, Clay. I'll stop it. You're right, I'm being rude," she said.

When Maggie returned from the bathroom, Maria tried to talk to her. Maggie looked surprised, but she went with it, and I felt I could let out a sigh of relief that maybe it was a crisis averted.

◆

"How long do we have until it's time to leave?" Maria asked. I looked at my phone.

"Ten minutes or so," I said.

"I'm going to go change," Maria said, looking suddenly self-conscious.

"The guest room is upstairs, the first door on the right. The bathroom is at the end of the hall," I told her. Maria picked up her bag and gave Maggie and me a small smile before heading up the stairs.

"She's . . . something," Maggie said in feigned politeness. I sighed deeply and sat down on the couch.

"Sorry about earlier. I don't know what her deal is," I replied tiredly, already wishing the night was over.

Maggie snorted and sat down beside me, laying her head against my shoulder. "She likes you, Clay. It's not that hard to figure out. Between the outfit from Tramps 'R' Us and the I-hate-you glare I've been getting since I showed up, I'd think that was pretty obvious," Maggie said. I didn't say anything. No point, really. I didn't want to try to explain Maria's brand of fucked-upness just now.

Maria reappeared a few minutes later, this time dressed in a simple pair of jeans and red blouse. She had scrubbed off most of the makeup and I was relieved to see her looking more like herself.

"Okay, ladies. Let's get this show on the road," I said, grabbing my keys. Maria and Maggie followed me out to my car.

"You can take the front, Maria," Maggie offered magnanimously. Maria thanked her and climbed up front with me. I gave Maggie an appreciative kiss on the lips and got into the driver's seat.

"Do you mind?" Maria asked, messing with the radio. I shrugged and almost took back my agreement when Maria picked a rap station and turned it up. I caught Maggie's eye in the rearview mirror and she stuck her tongue out at me.

I grinned and turned onto Davidson's main street. "Wow, it's so small," Maria commented, looking out her window as we drove past the string of shops that lined the center of town. "How do you guys not lose your minds?" she joked.

"Cow tipping and making moonshine fills the free time," Maggie replied blandly and Maria blinked in confusion, as though she were trying to figure out whether Maggie was being serious or not. Maggie's sarcasm took some getting used to, that's for sure.

We pulled into the local diner and I noticed Daniel's truck was already parked. "Places like this make me gain ten pounds. Just super," Maria complained, and I tried not to get irritated by her whining. How had I never noticed this unappealing side of my friend during all the months we had spent together?

"That's okay, the average American is ten to fifteen pounds overweight anyway. You'll just be fitting in with the general population," Maggie quipped, sliding out of the car after I opened the door for her. I shot her a look and she returned my stare with wide-eyed innocence. Maggie clearly hadn't forgotten Maria's earlier bitchiness. This night had awesome written all over it. Obviously I was sporting my own level of sarcasm this evening.

We found Rachel and Daniel at a corner booth and headed

toward them. "Yummy," Maria purred, catching sight of Daniel. Maggie stiffened beside her.

"Yeah, and he's very taken," she warned, cutting Maria off so she could slide into the booth beside Daniel. Maria grinned like a cat on the prowl and I groaned inwardly for the hundredth time since she had shown up.

"Hi, guys! Took you long enough," Rachel teased, giving me a smile. Rachel and I had definitely become something close to friends. She was a cool girl and I knew it made Maggie happy to have us getting along.

"Hey, this is Maria Cruz, my friend from Florida. Maria, this is Rachel Bradfield and Daniel Lowe." I waved my hand between them in introduction. Rachel gave Maria a wide smile.

"Hi, Maria! Nice to meet you," she said, leaning around me as she spoke. Maria smiled tightly.

"You guys up for a dude movie tonight? I've had my fill of chick flicks lately," Daniel said, grabbing some menus and passing them around to everyone.

"I'm up for anything," Maria said, batting her eyelashes. Daniel looked at her as though she had three heads and Rachel tried to cover up her laughter. Maggie gritted her teeth and I just wanted to cover my head with my arms and pretend this night wasn't happening.

"Okay, then, I vote for shit being blown up. Rachel is not allowed to suggest that movie about the two best friends where one of them has cancer. I didn't bring enough tissues for that crap," Daniel griped.

Maggie smacked his arm. "Spoiler alert, you ass! I wanted to see that!"

Daniel laughed and dodged another punch.

Rachel rolled her eyes and turned back to Maria. "So, Maria, you're from Florida? Did you go to school with Clay?" Ah, fuck. Clearly Maggie's friends weren't clued in to the fact that I knew Maria from the treatment center.

Maria shot me a look before answering. "Not exactly. I was a patient at the Grayson Center while Clay was there. We had a lot of groups together," she answered, not shy in the least about announcing to complete strangers that she had been in a psychiatric facility for three months.

Rachel paled and looked embarrassed. "Oh, that's n-nice," she stuttered, looking away.

Maria, seeming to revel in Rachel's mortification, kept on going. "Yeah, I wasn't there for trying to off myself like our good buddy, Clay, here. I have a bad habit of fucking anything that moves. Of course that's because of my abusive asshole of a father. So consider me the stereotypical slut with a bad case of Daddy issues." I choked on my soda and Rachel's pale face went bright red.

"Cool it, Maria," I bit out under my breath. Maria snickered and looked down at her menu. She seemed entirely too pleased with herself.

"So how long are you visiting for?" Maggie asked, obviously wanting to know how long we'd have to put up with Maria's fantastic personality.

"Just for the night. I have to head back to Alexandria in the morning. My brother lives there and I'm supposed to stay with him for a few days before flying back to Florida. But I think I kind of like Virginia. I may have to extend my stay." Maria smiled at me and I looked away.

Yeah, that was the last thing I needed.

The waitress came and took our orders. Maria complained about the greasy food on the menu and took forever to decide finally on a salad.

While we waited for our food, Rachel attempted more small talk. She asked Maria questions about Florida. Maria gave short, one-word answers. After several conversation nonstarters, Rachel gave up and sat quietly drinking her milk shake. Daniel and Maggie were engaged in their own discussion about soccer.

"I thought you were going to try to be nice. Enough with the Cruella De Vil act!" I whispered. Maria narrowed her eyes at me but didn't say anything.

Once our food arrived, everyone seemed to be in complete agreement and we inhaled our meals. No one seemed particularly keen on spending any more time sitting there in awkward silence. Maggie looked pissed and I didn't blame her. Maria was causing some serious drama and I would be giving her a piece of my mind about this later. Maria's unmedicated self was not particularly likable. And I was able to see for the first time how horrible it must have been to be around me when I refused to take my meds.

I felt like shit for putting Maggie, Ruby, and Lisa through that for so long.

Daniel and Rachel followed us to the movie theater in the next town. Maggie didn't even bother trying to talk to Maria: the line in the dirt was drawn and neither girl was going to step over it. These two were definitely not destined to be best friends anytime soon.

Maria was acting like a jealous girlfriend. And my actual girlfriend simply ignored me. Super fucking fantastic.

I bought tickets for Maggie and myself. Maybe I should have offered to pay for Maria but at this point, I didn't want to give her any ideas. While Maggie went to the restroom and Maria went to get some popcorn, Rachel and I waited for Daniel, who was talking to a few guys from school.

"So you were in treatment with Maria?" Rachel asked. I looked down at the much shorter girl and she seemed really uncomfortable. We didn't have the type of relationship that allowed for deep discussion. And I had never contemplated talking about my time in Florida with her.

"Yeah," I answered briefly. Rachel shuffled her feet on the ground.

"I don't mean to be rude or anything, but what's her deal? She seems, I don't know, weird, I guess." That was the understatement of the year.

I looked over at the women's restroom, hoping Maggie would come out and save me from this conversation. No such luck.

"She's not taking her medication, for starters. I had no idea she'd be like this when I said she could come for a visit. Maria wasn't like this in treatment. Trust me, I'd never have been friends with someone who acts the way she is acting tonight. She really is a nice girl. A screwed-up girl. But she means well, deep down." I found myself defending Maria.

Rachel chewed on her lip thoughtfully. "I believe you. That just sucks she's not taking care of herself. I can tell she's probably pretty cool underneath all that other stuff." Rachel surprised me with her astuteness.

"Yeah, she is. I'm really sorry about all of this, though," I said.

Rachel gave me a smile. "Don't apologize. It's fine. I just feel for Maggie. She hides her insecurity well, but I know this whole thing has to be bothering her," Rachel said, meeting my eyes.

"We both have some issues to sort out with the whole jealousy thing, I suppose," I said. Rachel and I stood there quietly and I noticed a girl with long blond hair approach Daniel and put her hand on his arm. The guys he was talking to all exchanged looks and I wondered who the hell that was and why Rachel wasn't marching over there and pulling the other girl's hair out.

Rachel was watching them and she did seem a bit tenser, but she didn't move. "Who's that?" I asked, indicating the girl. Daniel had purposefully moved away from her and seemed to be extremely unhappy with the chick trying to touch him.

"That's Kylie Good," Rachel said, and it all made sense. Daniel's ex-girlfriend tried to say something to him but he wasn't having it. He turned to the guys and said something, his back to Kylie in clear dismissal.

"Does that bother you? Seeing some other girl hit on him like that?" I asked, honestly curious as to how she was staying in check. Fuck, if that was Maggie and Jake, I would be losing my freaking mind about now. I was beyond impressed with Rachel's self-control.

Rachel shrugged. "It bothers me. But there's no point in getting upset about it. Daniel isn't interested in Kylie. She can play her stupid little games and it doesn't change the fact that he's with me. So what's the point of getting jealous? Either you trust someone or you don't." My mouth fell open in disbelief.

"Man, I could use some of your logical thinking the next time Jake eye-fucks my girlfriend," I joked, but I was deadly serious. I wished I could get to where Rachel was at. I just didn't know if I had it in me right now to be so levelheaded.

Rachel put her hand on my arm. "You have nothing to worry about where Jake is concerned. Maggie has always had eyes only for you. That jealousy crap is about you, not her," she said sagely. And I wondered whether my insurance company should be paying her instead of Shaemus. This chick was wise.

Maria joined us then, a box of Milk Duds and a small bucket of popcorn in her hands. "I thought you didn't eat junk food, Maria," I commented. Maria smiled sheepishly.

"Ah, well, you know. When in Rome," she said. Maggie came out of the bathroom and Daniel headed back to our group without saying another word to Kylie. Rachel was right not to worry about Daniel. That dude was so whipped, if I wasn't in the same boat with Maggie, I'd give him shit about it.

After the movie, I drove Maggie and Maria back to my house. Ruby was home so we sat with her and watched TV for a while. Maggie's frostiness thawed a bit once she was around my aunt. Ruby seemed more like her old self. She talked about things at the shop and even pulled out her tarot cards to give Maria a reading.

When it was time for Maggie to leave, I left Maria with Ruby and walked her out to her car. Maria had called out a good-bye but didn't say anything else. "Mags, I'm so sorry about Maria this evening. I know that had to be hard for you," I said once we got to her car.

"Well, a day at Disney World it wasn't, but that's not your fault. I just don't like leaving, knowing she'll be under the same roof as you all night. She could try to crawl into your bed while you're sleeping or something," she teased, but I could tell she was barely containing her jealousy.

I pulled her into my arms. "If she does that shit, I'll kick her ass out. Friend or not. There's only one girl allowed in my bed." I kissed her deeply, feeling instant relief as she parted her lips and let my tongue slide into her mouth. My hand snaked up her back and tangled in her hair.

"Sorry if I wasn't Miss Molly Sunshine. I guess I could have tried harder to be nice," Maggie said after breaking away. I hugged her tightly to my chest.

"You were perfect, you always are," I assured her and she snorted.

"And you are ridiculous. But thank you. I'll see you tomorrow." Maggie gave me another kiss and I waited until her car disappeared before I returned to the house.

Ruby had gone up to bed and Maria was thumbing through a magazine. "Girlfriend gone?" she asked without looking up.

"Yeah, *Maggie* left. And I'm going to tell you right now, Maria, your behavior tonight was really fucking shitty. I don't care what reasons you had, you don't come to my home, my town, around my friends and act like a bitch. This person I see right now, she isn't the Maria I became friends with at Grayson," I told her, feeling myself get angry.

Maria dropped the magazine on the table. "I know. But being who I was at Grayson doesn't work for me out here. Who I am now doesn't get hurt. She makes her own rules. It's the only way I can survive," she admitted softly, her face more open and vulnerable than it had been since she had arrived.

I sat down beside her on the couch. "Yeah, but at least you were being honest with yourself while you were at the center. This whole I'm-a-bitch-don't-fuck-with-me act will only leave you miserable and alone. I should know. I've spent way too much time pushing people away," I said, seeing way too much of myself in the girl who sat beside me.

Her brokenness covered by rough defiance was entirely too familiar. "And you need to get back on your medication," I told her sternly and she rolled her eyes to the ceiling.

"Jeesh, Clay, you're not my parent. Because if you were, you wouldn't be giving a shit about anything I do." Maria tried to hide the tears in her eyes by looking away.

"We really are a fucked-up pair, you and me," I said. "Way too many Mommy and Daddy issues and way too much self-loathing. You're heading into a bad place. I can see it; I've been there enough times myself." I hated to see my friend like this and it was unfortunately triggering something else in me.

A reminder of how much I had screwed up in my own life. Of the person I still was deep down. And I felt the all-too-familiar pain in my gut. Maria didn't respond. I don't know if it was because I had made her think about her behavior or whether she had just shut down.

"I'm tired. I'm going to bed. I have to get up and leave early. So I'll see you in the morning," Maria said abruptly, getting to her feet.

And I was left in the wake of it all, feeling like I had come face-to-face with a person who was more like me than I wanted to admit.

chapter
twenty-two

clay

Maria left the following morning without saying good-bye. There wasn't a phone call, a note, nothing. I sent her a text, just to make sure she had gotten back to Alexandria safely, but she never responded. A week later and I still hadn't heard from her. I thought about reaching out but had decided not to.

When I brought up Maria's whacked-out visit during my next session with Shaemus, he said it was best to let it go. We had processed how I had been triggered by Maria's erratic behavior and it had called into question my own mental stability. The truth was I had seen way too much of myself in Maria Cruz. It was like looking into one of those messed-up mirrors in a fun house, offering a warped, distorted view of who I was.

School started to ramp up toward graduation and I felt like I was hurtling through space toward some unknown destination. I was no closer to knowing what the fuck I was going to do with my life than I ever was. Maggie and her friends were excited about college. Daniel had gotten accepted to VCU and Rachel would be going to the University of Richmond. They'd be less than fifteen minutes apart.

Maggie had tried on numerous occasions to bring up college but I shut it down every time. I felt like everyone was sprinting past me and I was falling farther and farther behind. I wasn't sure I was ready for college and everything that entailed, and Maggie wouldn't contemplate a future that held anything else.

We loved each other so much, but I felt like we were starting to head in two very different directions. Every day I felt the crushing weight of my fear and anxiety pressing in. I couldn't breathe, I couldn't think. I only wanted the sweet oblivion of physical pain or a syringe full of mind-erasing drugs. The need was all I could think about.

Shaemus insisted I start going to Narcotics Anonymous meetings. He could see how close I was coming to a relapse. I knew it too, but some sadistic part of me relished it. Craved the total meltdown. Because right now I couldn't handle the effort of working through a normal life. It was completely beyond me.

And pretending was proving next to impossible.

Maggie could see something was wrong. She confronted me and I couldn't deny it. I wanted to tell her she had nothing to worry about, but I was way past lying to her. If I couldn't give her the future she wanted, I could at least be honest.

Even if I downplayed it a bit.

"Maybe we could go visit Piedmont Community College. I've heard they have an excellent art program. You know, just to have a look. You don't have to make a decision," Maggie suggested as we sat in her backyard on a Sunday afternoon. It was hot, the start of summer a little over a month away. It was already May and I just wished I could share in her enthusiasm for graduation. But it seemed to loom in front of me like a warning sign: Caution, Rough Road Ahead.

"Yeah, maybe," I said dismissively, already knowing I wouldn't do any such thing. The wedge had been firmly inserted between us and I wasn't sure what to do to get past it. Or whether I wanted to. Maggie continued to come to therapy every other week. And I was trying the whole healthy communication thing, but I was starting to feel like it was all a freaking waste of time.

Why would I continue to ask her to devote energy to something that hadn't a hope of going anywhere? She would go to the university and I would what? Work at Bubbles for seven dollars an hour until I felt like ending it all just to escape the mind-numbing misery my life would become?

Why couldn't I just indulge Maggie? Who knows, maybe I could see myself in one of these colleges and the road would be laid out for me. But my self-defeating thoughts were too loud in my head. It wasn't the highs and lows of mania anymore, just the constant drone of pessimism that was making it hard to focus on anything else.

Shaemus had again brought up the fact that I could return to Grayson. That an extended stay in the facility could be extremely beneficial for me. I rebelled against the thought, feeling like returning at this point would be a huge failure. Not that I was doing a bang-up job anywhere else in my life.

Plus, financially I couldn't afford it. Grayson Center was a secluded and very expensive facility. My parents had completely cut me off. I hadn't received any money from them from the moment I discharged myself from the center. I wasn't sure whether my mother had been in contact with Ruby, and if she had, I didn't know about it. It was like I no longer existed for them. Their emotional negligence was both freeing and crushing.

"Come on, Clay. It won't kill you to go on the tour. Who knows, you may actually like it," Maggie said lightly, leaning back on her elbows in the middle of her yard. I looked up from my sketchbook. I had been drawing the birdbath in the corner of the garden. Not the most amazing subject to draw but it kept my hands busy. And I needed them to be occupied, with the direction my thoughts were going lately.

The sun was hot and I could see sweat pebble along Maggie's collarbone. She really was perfect in every way. I was such a fucking fool for not seizing the future she was handing me. Isn't this what I had wanted? The possibility of a life with her? Why did the thought scare me to death?

I had been doing everything right. Taking my meds, going to therapy, playing the responsible guy, and getting a job to contribute financially at home. I had ticked every goddamned box and yet here I was, still stuck in the same bullshit mind fuck that had always sucked me in.

"I don't know, Maggie. I just don't want to think about it right now," I said tersely, sick of talking about it. Maggie was like a dog with a bone, though, and she wasn't going to give up that easily.

"Clay, you have to start thinking about it. Graduation is less than a month away. The deadline for applications to Piedmont is next week for the fall semester," she said, and I shot her a look. She shrugged her shoulders. "I've been doing my research, okay? But seriously, why can't we ever talk about it? I feel like you're not even trying to figure stuff out," she said in frustration, which in turn triggered my own.

I closed my sketchbook and got to my feet, wiping the grass from my shorts. "I told you I don't want to talk about it, Maggie. I know you want me to jump on the college bandwagon, get my sweatshirt and all that shit, but I just can't. I don't know what's going to happen with Ruby. Hell, I don't know what's going to happen with me. Just please, back off." I was practically yelling by the time I finished and Maggie just stared at me.

Damn it, I was being a dick again. Maggie stared down at her hands. "You're doing it again. You're shutting me out. Even when you promised you wouldn't," she said quietly, and it just made me feel even guiltier. I sat back down beside her and took her hand.

"I'm sorry. Really. It just freaks me out talking about all these plans for my future. Because I can barely plan tomorrow, let alone the rest of my life," I said, being honest. Her hand shook slightly in mine and I tried to reassure her with my touch. I ran my hand up the side of her arm and leaned in to kiss below her ear, her favorite spot.

She pulled away, still not looking at me. "Are you still taking them?" she whispered, and I froze. Oh fuck no. I was not going there again. I felt the anger sweep through me like a forest fire and I dropped my hand from her skin.

"Are you really asking me that? What the hell, Maggie?" I asked, trying to control the ugly emotions starting to bubble to the surface.

"It's just you've been so distant and off lately. I just wanted to make sure," she replied, her voice cracking. I was torn between feeling horrible for being the source of her doubt and being royally pissed off at her lack of trust.

"I'm taking them, I told you I would never do that again, and I'm working hard on keeping those promises. Give me a little fucking credit here," I said harshly. Would we have this argument for the rest of our lives? Would she ever just be able to trust that I was trying? Logically I understood where she was coming from, but it didn't stop the hurt.

"I know you are, Clay. I'm sorry," Maggie said, still not looking at me. We were at a standstill and I knew that if I stayed there, the situation would only deteriorate more.

"I'm gonna go. I don't want to do this right now. I'll call you later." I kissed her on the cheek and went to leave.

"Just think about the tour, Clay. I want you happy, that's all," Maggie called out before I left. Some of the anger left as I took in her sincerity. But there was nothing more to say.

I was in a horrible mood when I got home. I wanted nothing more than to go up to my room, turn on some music, and figure out a way to wash off all of the bad feelings. The only ways I could think of to do that were not good ones. And even though I knew I should pull out my healthy coping skills, they just didn't appeal to me the way the unhealthy ones did.

"Clay, you're home early," Ruby said, startling me. I had been so lost in my thoughts that I didn't even realize she was home. She had been spending most of her days at the shop. While I was glad she was getting out of the house and trying to get on with her life, I worried she was instead suppressing her grief by working herself to death.

"Hey, yeah, I was tired so I thought I'd take a nap," I said, just wanting to head to my room and be alone.

"Do you have a minute? I was going to talk with you this evening, but since you're here, no sense in putting it off. Come into the kitchen and I'll make you some tea." Ruby waved me down the hall and all I could do was follow her.

Ruby and her freaking tea. I wasn't sure what herbal number she'd force my way this time. But watching her move around the room, I realized she was nervous. What the hell did she have to be nervous about? Her edginess made me edgy.

"Need any help?" I asked and she shooed me into a seat at the table. When she finally set a cup of god knows what in front of me, she sat down and gave me a look that had my heart racing. She looked sad and worried. And I did not like that at all.

"So, what's up?" I asked, trying to sound calm. She surprised me by reaching over and grabbing an envelope off of a pile of letters and sliding it toward me. I arched my eyebrow questioningly.

"What's this?" I asked.

"Just open it and then I'll explain," she urged and I did just that. Slowly I lifted the tab and pulled out what was inside. It appeared to be a checkbook. I opened it up to the first page and almost swallowed my tongue.

"Ruby, this is a lot of money. Where did you get all of this?" I asked, completely taken aback.

Ruby sipped on her tea before answering. "It's Lisa's life insurance money. It just came through a few days ago. So I went and opened a joint account. The money is yours, Clay. To do what you want with it. You could use it to go to school, or travel, or whatever. I just wanted you to have it. Lisa would have wanted you to have it."

I flipped through the checks, seeing my name and Ruby's on the top. This was unbelievable. I tried to push it back into her hands. "I can't accept this, Ruby. You need this money more than I do. Lisa would have wanted you to use it. Seriously, it feels wrong for me to take it," I said.

Ruby took my hands and pressed the small blue book into my palm. "This isn't open for discussion, Clayton. You need this. You are a bright young man with the world at your feet. This is just a means to get you wherever you want to go. Your parents are useless and I know they have cut you off. I don't want you starting this next chapter of your life struggling. Do this for me, so your old aunt won't worry about how you're keeping yourself. I have always loved you like you were my own. Lisa did too. You were the son we never had. You made our lives—"

"Miserable? Don't blow smoke up my ass, Ruby. I was a fucking nightmare while I lived with you and Lisa. How you can say anything different is beyond me," I muttered around the lump in my throat.

Ruby closed her hands around the one holding the checkbook. "Clay, you made our lives complete. You gave us purpose. Loving and caring for you has been my greatest joy. Lisa saw you for the amazing, complicated, and talented young man that you are. Don't throw this gift back in her face. Use the money and do something with your life. You deserve it," she said emphatically.

Shit, I was going to cry. What was it about this tiny woman that brought me to my knees so quickly? She went straight for the jugular and I couldn't refuse her.

"Thank you, Ruby. I just . . . I don't know what to say." My voice broke and I tried not to sob like a baby. But I hadn't been expecting anything like this. It was all so . . . overwhelming.

"Anything for you, Clay. Anything. But there's something else I need to tell you," she said, and I could detect a wobble in her voice. She was looking nervous again.

"I'm selling the house and the shop. I've already had a real estate agent come by and start the paperwork. It's too hard staying here. I don't need a house to keep my memories and I just think it would be easier to get on with my life if I wasn't drowning in the grief I feel here," Ruby said, tears dripping down her face.

I felt like I had been smacked in the face with a two-by-four. Ruby was selling the house? She was getting rid of the shop? I felt like I was plummeting to the ground without a parachute.

"What? Where will you go?" I demanded.

Ruby dropped my hand and sat back in her chair, picking up her mug and holding it between her palms. "I was thinking of going back to Florida. Lisa and I had talked about retiring to Key West and I think that's where I want to go. I just have to leave Davidson. I feel like I'm suffocating. I used to be so happy here. But now, I just see ghosts," Ruby sobbed and I knew I should probably comfort her. But I was too busy freaking out.

Ruby was selling the house. She was leaving me. The one person in my family who had never abandoned me was leaving me behind. That tiny kid inside of me curled into a ball and started to scream. How could she do this to me?

"What about me?" I rasped out, my voice gone. Ruby's face crumpled and she started crying in earnest.

"My darling Clay. I won't leave until you decide what you're going to do. I wouldn't do that to you. But please, just understand that I need to do this. I just can't . . . move on! If I'm going to live this life without Lisa, it can't be here!" My dependable aunt was fucking flaking out on me.

I stood up so abruptly that I knocked my chair onto the floor. "Well, it seems that what I have to say about it doesn't really matter, then, does it?" I said coldly. Perhaps I was being unfair but I couldn't think much past the turmoil in my head.

Ruby was leaving me. Maggie was leaving me. Everyone leaves me. Because who can love someone who is so completely screwed up?

How could I have ever thought I would be able to live a normal life? I was destined only for loneliness and pain. That's all I deserved.

Ruby hurried to my side, her body shaking with the force of her sobs. "Clay, you can come with me to Florida if you want. I don't ever want you to feel like I'm leaving you! I would never do that!" she implored, but I was past hearing.

I pushed by her and grabbed my car keys. Without another word, I took off, not sure where the hell I was going. Part of me wanted to leave before anyone could leave me. I hated Ruby for doing this to me when I was already feeling vulnerable. She was supposed to be my rock. Well, my rock had just crumbled.

I kept driving, not knowing where I was headed. So I was surprised when I stopped my car in a familiar field. I grabbed my cell phone and walked down the well-worn trail through the woods. Breaking through the trees, I saw the swimming hole. It was late afternoon and hot, but there was no one else there.

I sat down on one of the rocks and stared out into the water. I flipped my phone over and over again in my hands, wondering if I should call Shaemus. Or Dr. Todd. I knew I was at my breaking point. But I didn't make the call. I only sat there, feeling emotional numbness filter into my body.

Abandoned, alone, unloved. The words bounced around in my

head until it was all I heard. Just cut it all away. One slice and you'll feel better. The voice in my head had grown louder and harder to ignore.

No one cares about you. You'd be better off dead.

Ugly, dishonest words that veiled themselves as truths.

My phone started to ring in my hands and I looked down to see Maggie's name flash across the screen. I hit ignore and then turned my phone off. Coming back to Davidson had been such a colossal mistake. I had been an idiot to think it could be anything else.

It only taught me that my life didn't belong here anymore. With these people who didn't want me. It ran like a loop through my brain. I didn't belong. Nobody wanted me. I was cracking up.

"I thought I'd find you here." I looked up sharply at the sound of a voice breaking through my internal tirade. Maggie stomped through the underbrush and made her way toward me.

"Guess I should find a better place to be alone if I'm so easy to find," I said sarcastically. She doesn't want me. She would leave me. Everyone leaves me.

"I'd always be able to find you," she promised, jumping up on the rock to sit beside me. I couldn't look at her, not when I was feeling the way I was. I recognized the beginnings of my very real meltdown. And Maggie, being a huge trigger for me, could make it all so much worse.

She didn't touch me, as though she could sense that would be the wrong thing to do. "Ruby called," she said in explanation.

"Oh yeah? So that's why you're galloping in to the rescue?" I asked nastily. I don't know why I was lashing out at her except that I was hurting and she was here and she had always taken my bullshit without complaint. It wasn't fair to her, but it was a pattern we obviously hadn't broken yet.

"Well, in saying that, you just confirmed you need rescuing then," she observed and I didn't acknowledge it. She sighed heavily and I still refused to look at her. Because looking at her would be my undoing and I was already dangling over the edge, my fingers slipping one at a time.

"So, Ruby's selling the house," she said.

I nodded. "Yep, so I've been told." I sounded bitter. Well, who fucking cares, I *was* bitter.

"And you're feeling like she's leaving you." What the hell was with the on-the-mark analysis?

"Wow, you can read me like a book, huh? Why don't you tell me all about my fucked-up head, Dr. Young," I spat out, feeling angry and raw and ready to take down anyone around me.

Maggie grew quiet again, clearly taken aback by my verbal attack. "You feel like cutting. Or using. Don't you?" she asked in a hush after a few minutes.

My shoulders sagged and I just felt tired. "I don't know. Yes. No. I'm just really messed up right now. You should probably leave. We've been there, done that, and you don't need the front-row seat," I said angrily, wishing for once she'd leave me to my hell. Why did she insist on riding this train wreck with me?

"I'm not going anywhere. Because no one is abandoning you. People can move on and live their lives but that doesn't mean you're not a part of it anymore. I love you, Clay. Ruby loves you. Because you, Clay, are worthy of that love. You deserve it. All of it. And Ruby and I just want you to find the place where you'll be okay and healthy. You can get angry with me, tell me to leave. But not once have I ever turned my back on you and I won't start now," she told me, putting her hands on me for the first time.

Her fingers gripped my chin and pulled my face around to her. The sight of her in my confused state of mind was like striking a match. And I lost it. I just fucking lost it. I started to sob and I couldn't stop. I don't know exactly what I was crying for, except that everything that had been dammed up inside of me was pouring out.

I had always believed I was irredeemable. That I couldn't expect others to love me when I didn't even love myself. But Maggie's words hit me exactly when I so desperately needed to hear them. I needed to believe that she was right, that I was worthy.

Because I was so angry at myself right now. This had been my chance to do things over. Leaving Grayson had been my new lease on life and I had ruined it. I had deluded myself into thinking I was ready for all of this. Even with the therapy and the meds, I couldn't do this.

So I cried for the man I couldn't be. At least not right now. And I felt like in some ways I had been transported back to all those months ago when I had made this same realization. Only then it had come with much harsher consequences.

This time, I didn't cut. I didn't think of some way to end things so I'd never have to feel this way again. Instead, I clung to my girlfriend. The person who had always been my light in the shadows and who continued to love me even at my worst. Who reminded me that everyone deserved love, even me.

"It's okay, Clay. We'll figure it out. Together," she crooned, with my head buried into the soft skin of her neck. Together. That was a word I could live with.

✦

I don't know how long I was at the swimming hole. But being there, with Maggie, crying like a little kid, was strangely cathartic. By the time we headed back to Ruby's, it was getting dark. I was more exhausted than I could ever remember being. But that nastiness inside me was thankfully quiet. And I couldn't help but feel like I had turned some sort of corner. I had been given the opportunity to make a choice and I was proud that I hadn't made the one that ended in blood.

Maggie followed me in her car. I knew I had scared the shit out of her, but she hadn't shown it. It was only because I knew her so well that I was able to see the terror in her eyes. I knew how hard it was for her to see me like that, perilously close to that edge I had fallen off before. Not knowing whether I would take her back down the dark road again.

I wish I could say that I would never do that. But the truth was, I just couldn't be sure, and there lied the crux of the problem. The last few months had been more of a holding pattern. I was existing, thinking I was making progress, but in reality I still had such a long way to go.

On the drive home, I finally made a decision about my future. I knew it wasn't the one everyone wanted me to make, but it was mine. I had made it. Me. And I felt a measure of pride at that.

Ruby was pacing the living room when Maggie and I walked through the door. "Clay!" she called out, rushing over to me. I was enveloped in her patchouli-scented arms and I felt guilty for making her worry.

Maggie stood in the doorway until Ruby waved her into our hug. My aunt held us both, crying. "If you don't want me to sell the house, I won't. Clay, I'm so sorry, I had no idea it meant so much to you," Ruby said through her tears of relief that I was home and in one piece. No life-threatening self-mutilations. No drug-and-alcohol-induced benders. Those were Maggie's and Ruby's fears when I lost it like that. And that made the choice I had made in the car all the more clear.

I stepped out of Ruby's hold. "No, Ruby. You can't make a decision based on me. I'm an adult, not a little kid. I shouldn't have taken off like that. I didn't mean to scare you." I kissed the top of her graying head.

"If you need to sell the house and shop, then you sell the house and shop. You need to do what's right for you," I assured her. Maggie wrapped her arm around my waist and I leaned into her body.

"But if this makes you unhappy, I can't be okay with it," Ruby argued, and I held up my hand, stopping her.

"You've always done what's right for me, for Lisa, for the shop. This time, do what's right for you." And I realized I really meant it. It didn't take away the pain and the deep-rooted fear that I was being abandoned, but feeling Maggie's arm around me I knew it would all be okay.

I looked down at my girlfriend, who stared up at me with tears in her eyes. Would there ever be a day when I didn't make her cry? I used the pad of my thumb and wiped the wetness from her cheeks.

But she was right. We were in this together. And that made it all okay.

chapter
twenty-three

five more days and I would officially be a high school graduate. I had finished up my English lit exam and was ready to start my last weekend as a senior. The feeling of it was bittersweet. I was a jumbled mixture of excited and scared.

My parents had taken me up to JMU two weeks ago for a tour of the campus. I filled out the pile of paperwork and submitted it. Things were set in motion and I felt like it all was going as it was supposed to.

Well, most things.

Clay had changed. You would think I would have become accustomed to the multitude of Clayton Reed fluctuations. I had seen him at his highest and at his lowest and every facet in between. I had loved the Clay in the throes of his mania and I had loved the Clay who had tried to end it all.

And then I had loved the Clay who had come back to me, determined to be a better man and to make a life for the two of us together, whatever form that took.

And I loved this new Clay as well, but it made me nervous. Which was sort of silly. He wasn't freaking out. He wasn't angry and defensive. He wasn't abnormally happy and trying desperately to make things in his world work out.

No, he was just . . . content. Peaceful even. Like he had come to terms with something that he wasn't letting me in on. I hadn't been able to go to therapy since before his breakdown at the swimming hole. My schedule had been so chaotic with track meets and studying for exams and college prep that there hadn't been time for it. Clay was okay with that. He continued to go to his sessions twice a week.

We spent time together as much as possible, but there was a definite undercurrent now that I couldn't quite put my finger on. I would find Clay watching me sometimes, seeming as though he were trying to find a way to say something. But the moment would pass and we'd carry on as though I hadn't noticed the odd look in his eyes.

I hadn't brought up the community college again and neither had Clay. He had told me about the large chunk of money Ruby had given him. When I had delicately asked what he planned to do with it, he hadn't been able to give me a straight answer. But something told me that it didn't include college. I just wish I knew what his plans were, but after his extreme reaction to any questions in that regard, I tried to back off and only hoped he'd share with me when he was ready.

"Hey, birthday girl!" Rachel squealed, running up to me as I was cleaning out my locker. I laughed as she launched herself at me, hugging me as tightly as she was able.

"Hey, you. I'd like to resume the ability to breathe, Rach," I said as she squeezed me. She let me go and beamed up at me with her contagious smile.

"I have presents! So many presents! I can't wait to give them to you!" I often thought Rachel got more excited about other people's birthdays than she did about her own. I flicked her in the arm.

"You don't need to be spending your money on me. I don't

need anything," I complained, not liking my cash-strapped friend blowing her paychecks on me. Not when I knew she had to save up for school.

"Psh, don't be ridiculous. Of course I have to lavish my bestie with gifts on her birthday! It's like a written friendship rule or something," she protested, and I didn't bother to argue. There was no arguing with Rachel about some things, especially all things birthday-related.

I rubbed at the Band-Aid that covered the underside of my wrist and couldn't help but smile. It itched like crazy but it was a discomfort I could handle.

"I can't believe you actually did it. And that your dad took you to get it! You are such a badass, Mags!" Rachel remarked, shaking her head.

Last weekend, my father had gotten me up bright and early on Saturday and taken me to the tattoo parlor in the next town over. I had gotten the rune Uruz, just as I had wanted. My dad had liked what it represented and conceded that it was small and tasteful. "As long as you're not getting a rose on your upper arm or *Mom* on your knuckles, I'm okay with it," he had said when I mentioned the idea.

Uruz represented healing, endurance, and courage. They were qualities that I needed to be reminded of, and I liked having something that symbolized it on my skin.

"So your mom said to be at your place by six for the birthday dinner extravaganza! I'm bringing my world-famous three-cheese and bean dip!" she said excitedly, as though the world's problems could be solved with cheese and bean dip.

"Sounds good. It's just you, Danny, and Clay. Nothing wild and crazy," I said, hoping to calm her down a bit. No sense in her getting her hopes up for some raging party that wasn't going to happen.

Rachel gave me a funny look. "Yeah, okay. Well, I have to get to work. I'll see you tonight!" she said, hurrying down the hallway.

"God, Mags, something could be buried in there! Do you ever clean that thing out?" I looked over my shoulder and grinned as I saw Clay peering into my locker. I turned around to give him a hug and leaned up on my tiptoes to kiss his lips before turning back to the task at hand.

"It's not that bad," I said in mock defense. Clay reached in and tugged on a piece of paper toward the bottom, sending half the contents of my locker careening to the floor. "Way to go, slick," I muttered sarcastically, shooting him a glare as I knelt down to pick everything up.

Clay squatted beside me and gathered up most of the trash, tossing it into the recycling bin. "Sorry I didn't get to see you at lunch. I was roped into a last meeting with Mr. Hunt." Clay rolled his eyes. Mr. Hunt, the guidance counselor, seemed to think Clay was his pet project. The older man was determined to make Clay into what he considered to be a productive high school student. I would never admit this to my boyfriend, but I secretly wished something Mr. Hunt shoved down his throat would stick and he'd realize that college and planning for his future weren't such bad things.

Clay kissed the side of my neck, making me shiver. "I didn't get to spend lunch with the birthday girl; it's totally inexcusable," he said huskily into my ear. Damn, he could make me turn to mush without batting an eye. It was an evil, evil gift and one that he liked to wield frequently, much to my enjoyment and sometimes utter embarrassment.

"The day is still young, you can make it up to me," I replied, trying to sound seductive but feeling like I sounded like I just swallowed a bullfrog. I wasn't cut out for sultry.

"That it is. Do I need to bring anything for the dinner tonight?" he asked as I swiped my hand through the locker one last time, pulling out the few pieces of paper still inside and throwing them away.

"I don't think so; Mom and Dad seem to have it covered." I closed the locker with a bang and gathered up my book bag and water bottle. Clay slung his arm around my shoulders and I felt the same rush of heat I always experienced when we were touching. I wondered if it would ever go away? I sincerely hoped not.

I hopped into Clay's car. I was still without wheels and I had forgone the mortification of driving the grocery getter for the time being. I had a boyfriend with a sweet ride, so I opted to take advantage of that. I opened up the glove compartment and then the center console.

"What are you doing?" Clay laughed, watching me reach under my seat.

"Looking for my birthday present," I huffed out, coming up empty-handed.

"Well, baby, you won't find it in here. So you might as well give up," he teased, smirking as I sat back with a scowl.

"Fine. Just leave me in suspense. You're really cruel, Clayton Reed," I grumped, though I wasn't the least bit annoyed with him. Whatever Clay had gotten was top secret. And no amount of persuasion had made him give up the goods—even after I took off my shirt! He was stronger than I gave him credit for.

I also knew he hadn't shared it with either of my friends because Rachel in particular would never have been able to keep it a secret.

Clay drove me to my house, chuckling at my attempts to get him to spill the big secret. I slithered across the car and pressed my boobs into his arm. "Come on, you know you want to tell me," I purred into his ear, taking his lobe between my teeth and giving it a tug. Clay groaned in the back of his throat.

"You really don't play fair, do you?" he complained just before getting out of the car. I had to brace myself on his seat; otherwise I would have face-planted with the swiftness of his exit. The dude would not budge an inch. Who could resist the lure of the breasts? I was beginning to suspect a cyborg had taken over his body.

"Hurry up and change, I want to go swimming before it rains." Clay swatted my behind and I giggled as I hurried into the house. My parents were already home and I poked my head into the kitchen to greet them both.

"Clay and I are going swimming at the hole. We'll be back before dinner," I said, stealing a carrot stick that Mom had laid out on a platter. She smacked my hand.

"That's fine. Just remember to take your sunscreen, it's bright out there today," she said and I rolled my eyes. It didn't matter that today I was legally an adult; she would always treat me as though I were four.

Clay came in behind me and said hello to my parents. They responded in kind and I left them to chat while I went upstairs to throw on my suit. It was amazing how relaxed my parents had become with Clay. I knew they still harbored some distrust toward him, but he had come a long way in proving himself to them. While I still saw his daily struggles, my parents were finally understanding that he was a good person and really did love and want the best for me.

And if anything could soften their hardened hearts, it was that.

When I came back downstairs, my mom and Clay were laughing over something my dad was saying. One of his horrible jokes, no doubt. "I'm ready," I said, looping my arm with Clay's and pulling him out of the kitchen.

"I'll have her back before six," he told my parents, who thanked him before I could get him out of the house.

"Hurry up; we have two and a half hours for just us. I don't want to waste a minute of it," I urged, hurrying toward the car. It only took us ten minutes to pull into the tall grass. Another five before we were at the water.

I realized, as I watched Clay tug off his shoes and shorts, re-vealing his trunks, that we always came back here. These trees, this water, had witnessed a lot of the Clay and Maggie roller coaster. Whether it was good or bad, we gravitated toward this space as though it were the one spot that was just for us.

Once again we were alone. Over the last year, I had found that fewer people used the old swimming hole, choosing the public pool instead. Fewer young kids even knew about its existence, thus making it feel even more like it belonged to the two of us.

Clay pulled me into the water and I let out a startled scream. I swallowed a mouthful of river water. "You are so going to pay for that!" I yelled, dipping under the water and pulling his feet out from underneath him. He couldn't stay upright on the silt bottom and fell over. Laughing, he grabbed me and dunked me under again.

This went on for quite a while, reminding me so much of the first time I had brought him here, at the beginning of the school year. It was unreal how much had changed but still stayed the same. We were two kids who had been through the fire together, bruised and burned for it, but still going.

"I surrender! No more!" I held up my hands in defeat.

Clay swam over to me and scooped me up in his arms and car-ried me out of the water. He had laid a quilt down on the ground and pulled two towels from his messenger bag. Wrapping me in one, he patted me down until my extremities were dry.

"You hungry?" he asked, pulling out a bag of snacks.

"Sure," I responded, reaching for some chips and a drink.

"So after this, you want to go buy some chewing tobacco and a *Playgirl*? How about some lotto tickets?" Clay suggested and I smirked.

"I'll pass on all of the above. Though I did register to vote a few weeks ago. Woo-hoo for me!" I pumped my fist into the air and took a drink of water.

"Do not underestimate the value of civic duty, Maggie," he taunted me and I went to punch him in the arm. He grabbed my hand and gave me a tug, pulling me into his lap. I dropped the bag of potato chips onto the ground as I bumped my chest into his.

Our noses rubbed against one another and he smirked as I realized how closely I was pressed against him. I was still bundled up in the towel, so Clay slowly reached up and slipped it from my shoulders, his fingers trailing down my back to settle on my hip.

"Happy birthday, Mags," he breathed as his hands gripped my skin, his thumbs playing with the string of my bikini bottom. I was suddenly aware of how alone we were and I knew I needed to capitalize on this opportunity before it slipped through my grasp.

Clay had been keeping the physical intimacy at arm's length. I tried to understand his motives, but it mostly left me feeling extremely unsatisfied and more than a little rejected. But feeling him harden beneath me, I knew instinctively that he wouldn't stop it this time.

I wound my arms behind his neck and leaned into him, our mouths furtively touching. My hands dove into his thick, wet hair and I gave it a little tug, making him chuckle beneath my lips. "Playing rough, huh?" he teased and I gave his hair another pull.

His teeth nipped at my bottom lip and I squirmed in his lap. There was so little fabric between us and his erection was very apparent. Clay's hands came up my sides, causing me to shiver. "Is this what you want for your birthday, Maggie?" he asked breathlessly.

I wrapped my legs around his waist and rocked myself gently against him, causing his eyes to close and his head to fall back. "What do you think?" I asked, kissing the underside of his jaw.

Clay's head snapped up and he grabbed ahold of my face and pulled me, almost roughly, to his mouth, where he attacked me like a drowning man. Our lips and tongues worked furiously at each other.

My hands couldn't touch enough of him. My fingers clawed at his back as he pulled my bikini top down and cupped my breasts. I moaned loudly and began to rock against him again. The friction between my legs was unbelievable.

"My God, Maggie, I need you so badly," he let out in almost tortured anguish. He sounded strangled and afraid but so desperate for me that I could do nothing but comply.

With shaking fingers, Clay loosened the bikini tie around my neck, where it promptly fell to my middle. His hands were back on my breasts, rubbing and kneading until I felt myself start to build toward the inevitable explosion.

I pushed his shoulders until he lay on his back while I still straddled him. He made quick work of my bottoms until I was completely naked above him. He pulled back, resting his head on the ground, and looked up at me with such adoration that it made my heart clench painfully and my lungs squeeze tightly. What had I ever done to deserve this kind of love?

I suddenly remembered Rachel telling me after Clay's parents had come into town and blown his world apart that our love wasn't one she would want. I had agreed at the time, so overwhelmed with the hurt and devastation that had been a constant side effect of loving him not so long ago.

I looked down at Clay, his dark hair slicked back, his eyes radiating warmth and devotion. Our love had taken me to the highest heights and the lowest depths, had terrified me and filled me with hope. And I knew that this love between us was something I wanted to feel for the rest of my life.

"I love you," I whispered, tears filling my eyes. Clay reached up and cradled my face in his hand.

"I'll love you forever," he answered as he pulled me back down to his waiting mouth. He removed his swimming trunks, adding them to the pile of soggy clothing on the ground. When we were completely bare, we held each other tight, needing the press of skin to skin, no barriers.

The next moments moved both too fast and achingly slow. The sound of the foil packet punctuated the air. Our heavy breathing as Clay rolled me over and positioned himself between my legs.

Then the smooth, perfect union as he slid into my body. It was like coming home. I thought my heart would burst with the amazing sensations that overtook me. And as we started to move together, flesh on flesh, our hands touching, lips tasting, the only sounds were the beating of our hearts and our soft whispered *I love you*s.

When we were finished and Clay held me securely in his arms, I felt a sudden shift, as though I had better enjoy this moment because it just might be the last. I didn't understand my sudden bout of doom and gloom but I couldn't shake it.

The afternoon disappeared as twilight took over and with it the cooling of the air, but we were still in no hurry to get dressed. Clay rolled over and pulled a small package out of his bag and handed it to me.

"Happy birthday, Maggie," he said, smiling. I picked up the small box and quirked my eyebrow.

"Why do you always feel the need to give me presents after we've had sex? I'm sensing a pattern here," I joked, referring to the butterfly necklace that still hung around my neck. Clay chuckled and traced a finger along the delicate curves of silver.

"Less smart-ass and more opening," he prompted, picking up the box and wiggling it in front of me. I snatched it from his hand and ripped open the paper. My heart sputtered and nearly stopped when I saw the small, black velvet box hidden beneath the birthday wrapping.

He wouldn't, would he?

"Stop freaking out and just open it," Clay teased, seeing the way my eyes had widened and my hands had stilled. I did as he said and slowly opened the hinged top.

Nestled inside was a ring. Not *that* kind of ring, but a beautiful one nonetheless. It was a thin band of white gold meeting in the middle in a loop. On the sides were tiny, diamond-inlaid butter-flies. They were so small you had to look closely to make them out. Dear Lord, my boyfriend's taste in jewelry was incredible.

I removed the ring from the box and held it in my palm, too awestruck by its beauty to put it on. Clay took the piece of jewelry and grabbed my left hand, slipping it onto the ring finger. It fit perfectly. Of course it did. Had I expected anything less?

"It's gorgeous, Clay. Thank you," I said, feeling another crying jag come on. Clay threaded his fingers through mine and held up the hand adorned with the ring for us both to see.

"It's a promise ring. A long time ago, they would be engraved with the words *Pour toute ma vie, de tout mon coeur.* 'For my whole life, all of my love.' I wanted to give you something that showed my complete and total devotion to you, to us. I have turned your world upside down. First when I tried to kill myself and left you to deal with the aftermath. Then again when I came back and you've been trying to handle my constantly changing life. I know I haven't been easy. I wish I could say that one day things might be simpler. But the truth is I can't say that. I wish I could. I can only say, with 100 percent certainty, that I love you. That I live and breathe for you. That I would lay down my life a million times over for you. And no matter what happens tomor-row, next week, next year, my heart will always be yours."

Oh yeah, I was definitely crying now. How could a girl hear that stuff and not start sobbing her eyes out? I wasn't made of stone, for Pete's sake!

Clay touched his finger to the ring that symbolized his com-mitment to me. "And as long as we're together, I think we can get through anything. I promise to never shut you out of my life again. I was miserable the three months we were apart. I thought I was doing it for you, but call me selfish, I can't do that again. No matter where I go, or what I do, I want you in my life," he concluded, his face soft, his eyes full of love.

Shit, I was done. I gave a strangled sort of sob and threw myself at him, kissing every inch of his beloved face. "I love you, Clay! My God, I love you so much!" I said over and over again. We probably would have gotten lost in each other again if his phone didn't start beeping.

He gave me an apologetic smile and grabbed it and let out an "Oh fuck."

"What is it?" I asked as he got hurriedly to his feet and started pulling on his clothes.

"Baby, you need to get dressed. We're going to be late if we don't get a move on. And your parents have only recently stopped looking at me as though I'm going to abscond with you in the middle of the night again. So come on," he ordered, grabbing my hand.

"All right, all right," I grumbled, not really feeling the need to have a family dinner after what I had just experienced with Clay. That had made my birthday and I wasn't sure anything else could top it.

We touched and laughed and kissed while we got dressed, reveling in a renewed closeness. A closeness that was beyond what we had ever had before.

"Thank you so much for making this the best birthday I've ever had," I said, turning to Clay as he parked in front of my house. We met in a beautiful, soul-melting kiss before Clay broke away.

"We'd better get in there before your dad skins me alive." I huffed and puffed but finally got out of the car. I was so blissed out from the perfect afternoon with Clay that I didn't notice the excess number of cars on the street.

I walked into the house and dozens of voices called out,

"Happy birthday!" I blinked in surprise, looking around at my house now full of friends and acquaintances, and every single one of them was looking at me.

I turned to Clay, who was grinning a Cheshire cat smile, and wagged my finger at him. "You are so going to get it for not warning me!" He gave me a gentle shove forward and I was enveloped by the people who loved me.

chapter
twenty-four

clay

I was being a complete and total coward. Why hadn't I just told Maggie my plans for after graduation? I watched her interact with her party guests, laughing and hugging her friends and family. The smile on her face, the look of complete happiness, was exactly the reason I had chickened out. I didn't want to be the reason she lost that look.

"So what did you guys get into all afternoon?" Daniel asked and I almost choked on my drink.

"Oh, you know, we went swimming and just hung out," I told him vaguely. Daniel raised his eyebrows and gave me a knowing stare.

"I'm sure that was fun, hanging out. Probably the less I know about you guys hanging out, the better. Otherwise I'll have to take out your kneecaps and all. And I was just starting to kind of like you." Daniel smirked and I smirked back.

"Yeah, okay," I agreed, my eyes returning to Maggie as she circulated around her party. I had been surprised when her parents had called me last week and told me their plans for a party. They asked for my help in setting things up and it was the first time I had felt as though Mr. and Mrs. Young had come close to accepting me as a part of Maggie's life.

Which is why I had to tell Maggie about what I was going to do. I was scared. I wasn't sure how she'd react. I couldn't put it off, but it didn't have to happen right now. Right now, Maggie just needed to enjoy herself. My news could wait.

"Are you guys coming to Beach Week with Rachel and me next week? Maggie hasn't said," Daniel said. Fuck, I had forgotten about Beach Week. Maggie had hinted about it, but I hadn't committed to it, knowing that I couldn't.

"I don't know, man," was all I said. Daniel gave me a funny look but didn't press me about it. He called out greetings to different people and I felt a little out of place. It was sad that I had never bothered to get to know many people at Jackson while I had been here. I had been so inwardly focused or obsessed with my relationship with Maggie that I think I had missed out on some key aspects of growing up. Like making friends and going to football games and all that other shit that came with high school.

But then my eyes fell on Maggie again and I couldn't feel regret for anything. Because it all brought me here, to her. And that made up for everything else.

"You know, I'm glad we've gotten to hang out the past few months. I feel bad for never really giving you a chance. I'm sorry if I gave you a hard time. It's just when it comes to my girls, I get a bit overprotective. It was easier for me to judge you before. Because I didn't really get the way you were with Mags. But since Rachel, let's just say I understand now," Daniel offered and I knew his eyes were following his girlfriend just as I was following mine.

"You and Rachel seem good. It's nice to see," I said, noticing the goofy smile that took over his face.

"Yeah, we're good. It took us a while to get here. But it's all worth it in the end. I'm sure you get that," Daniel said looking over at me. I think Daniel and I got each other pretty damn well.

"Yeah, I get that," I responded.

"Hey, Danny," a voice said, coming up behind us. I glanced at the person who now stood on the other side of Daniel and instantly felt my blood pressure rise. Fucking Jake Fitzsimmons. Who the hell had invited that jackass? Though I guess it made sense that he was here. He and Maggie had been friends for a while. But he was also the guy who had tried to take my place in my girl's life and he was not my favorite person.

"Hi, Jake. You just get here?" Daniel asked and even he seemed to tense up a bit at the other guy's appearance.

"Yeah. Though I can't stay long. I just wanted to make sure to give the birthday girl a kiss." Jake smirked, and I felt my head start to buzz and my jaw clench. My teeth started to ache with the way I was gnashing them.

Jake glanced at me and his smirk grew. "Hey there, Clay. Didn't know you'd be here." His voice seemed to taunt me. I knew he was just trying to get under my skin. Jake had never been overt in his aggression toward me. After the one conversation we had at Java Madness, he seemed to avoid me. And that suited me just fine. So I wasn't sure what the hell he was trying to do by purposefully antagonizing me now.

Daniel narrowed his eyes at his friend. "Be cool, Jake. This is Maggie's party," he warned, and even I would have stood down at the underlying threat there. Jake laughed bitterly.

"I am being cool, Danny. I've been nothing but cool. Since this psycho upped and left town, leaving Maggie to fall apart. Who was the one that helped her through that? It certainly wasn't him! It was you and Rachel and me! And what did playing the nice guy get me? Definitely not the girl. It seems being an antisocial asshole is the way to Maggie Young's heart."

Daniel seemed to reach the same conclusion that I did. We both shoved Jake straight toward the door leading into the backyard. The hard look on Daniel's face most likely mirrored my own.

"I told you to drop this shit, Jake! I get that your pride is bruised, but this is not the time or place to be doling this crap out. So you need to either get your act together and enjoy the party or just fucking leave," Daniel ground out, getting into Jake's face. But Jake continued to glare at me.

"I've got your number, man. I know what kind of person you are. *'Look at me, I'm Clay Reed, and I'm so tortured and misunderstood.'* Whatever. You will never make her happy. You will never give her any sort of life. You will only fuck her up and fuck her over every chance you get. If you were any sort of decent individual you'd leave her the hell alone and get out of town. Go ruin someone else's life," Jake yelled, his face flushing red.

This guy was way past pissing me off. He was lucky he was still standing, and if Daniel hadn't been between us, this fucker's ass would be on the floor.

I got as close to Jake as Daniel would allow and when I spoke, I made my words very clear. "I know what it's like to love her. And then to lose her. It sucks. So in a way, I feel bad for you. But that doesn't mean you can come to her house and disrespect her in any way. I love her. I plan to make a life with her. And so sorry for you, but she chose me. She will always choose me. So just fucking live with it and move on."

Jake opened his mouth to say something and then seemed to think better of it. He wrenched himself out of Daniel's grip and left the yard through the gate. "Well, that was pleasant," Daniel said dryly, pounding my back with his hand. "Let's go get something to eat, I'm starving." I nodded in agreement and followed the guy who had somehow become a new friend into Maggie's house.

Jake never reappeared. I guess he had gotten the hint and taken a hike. I spent most of the evening with Daniel and a few of his friends. I mostly just enjoyed seeing Maggie have fun. I'd missed out on this side of her too many times.

"Nice job on the ring, Clay," Rachel enthused later. Daniel groaned and shot me a hateful look.

"Thanks, man. Do you realize you're setting a standard that the rest of us poor schmucks somehow have to live up to? Do the brotherhood a favor and stop being such a pussy!" Daniel punched me in the arm and I tried not to wince. But hell if it didn't hurt.

Rachel glared at her boyfriend. "You need to shut up. Just because Clay actually understands the word *romance* doesn't mean he's a pussy."

Daniel laughed. "Uh, yeah, it does actually."

"Give it up, Daniel, before you get kneed in the junk," I warned, seeing the way Rachel's face darkened dangerously. Daniel struggled to maintain a straight face.

"I'm sorry, babe. You're right, I need to channel some of Clay's douchey, I mean awesome, romantic qualities," Daniel choked out and Rachel finally gave it up and giggled. They were such a functional couple. It was sort of awe-inspiring.

The night started to wind down and Maggie's guests began to leave. Finally there was only Daniel, Rachel, and me left. Mr. and Mrs. Young had ordered some pizza, because most of the food from the party had been eaten early on. We started cleaning up. Rachel and Daniel became comically competitive about it, making the whole process take twice as long as it should have.

"Thanks, Mom and Dad! And Rach, Danny, I just love you guys," Maggie said, clutching a trash bag to her chest. Her parents gave her a hug, followed by her friends. I kissed the top of her head and she looked up at me with an expression that literally took my breath away. I didn't think I'd ever get tired of looking at her.

"And you already know what I think of you." Her eyebrows waggled suggestively and I chuckled. We moved out into the yard to pick up more trash. Rachel and Daniel had given up and were watching television and Maggie's parents were in the kitchen drinking coffee.

"So, I know we haven't really talked about it. But what do you think about Beach Week? Daniel and Rachel rented this amazing house right on the water at Virginia Beach. It would be really fun. My parents would be fine with you going, particularly since I'm a full-grown adult now." Maggie grinned and my stomach knotted up.

I hadn't wanted to do this now, but I couldn't keep putting her off. I had been evasive and vague about my plans for after graduation. It wasn't fair to her.

"I don't think I can do that," I told her, dropping the trash can and sitting heavily on the patio chair. Maggie's face fell and I already hated myself for what I was about to do.

"Oh, okay, that's fine. But maybe we could go away somewhere later in the summer. Just the two of us. That would be really nice, don't you think?" Maggie was starting to ramble now and I knew she was picking up on my unease.

I took ahold of her hand and pulled her into the seat beside me. "Maggie," I started.

"We could go to Ocean City, or even New York. Anywhere as long as we're together!" Maggie was on a roll, as though if she talked fast enough and long enough I would forget about whatever I was trying to tell her. The thing that she feared would break her heart. And I wasn't so sure she wasn't right.

"Maggie," I tried again. She stared straight ahead, not even glancing my way.

"I've always wanted to go to Savannah. I've heard it's beautiful. We could take a week and just drive." She sounded almost desperate and I knew I had to put a stop to it.

"Maggie, stop talking for a minute and please listen to me," I pleaded, and she instantly shut her mouth and lowered her eyes.

"Okay, sorry," Maggie murmured. I cupped her cheeks between my palms and lifted her face to mine. I kissed her slowly and thoroughly. I needed to taste her and savor her before giving her my news.

"I want to do all of those things with you. I really do. There is nothing I want more than to explore this world with you. But it can't happen. At least not for a while. I can't make you any specific promises about my future because right now things have to be put on hold. For me, at least. For us," I said slowly, watching as comprehension dawned on her face.

She looked at me apprehensively. "What are you trying to say?" she asked, her voice trembling, and I hated to do this to her. Not after everything she had already been through because of me. But I honestly felt this was for the best.

"I'm readmitting myself to the Grayson Center for a six-month program. Then after that, I will most likely go into a group home for a while longer. I've already talked with Dr. Todd and I'm set to be checked in next Wednesday," I said, seeing her face pale.

"You're going back to Grayson? To Florida? But why? I thought things were going fine. That you were doing better." Maggie seemed so lost and I wished I had the magic answer for her. So instead I just tried to explain.

"I've tried, Mags. I really have. And while some things are changing, I still have so far to go. The truth is every day is a struggle. Some days I can barely get out of bed."

"But your medication . . ." Maggie started and I shook my head.

"I told you before it wasn't a cure-all. It helps, but it doesn't fix everything. You don't know how many times I've thought about hurting myself. Of ending the pain. It's like there's this voice in my head that tells me to do it. That no one loves me, that I'm nothing but a burden." I could hear the strain in my voice and I couldn't even look at Maggie.

"But that's not true, Clay! You have so many people that love you! You have never been a burden! That's ridiculous!" she implored as she reached for me. Her hands clutched at my shirt and I almost lost my resolve. Almost.

"But don't you see, the fact that I think about it at all means I'm not ready. I'm not ready to plan any sort of future. I need to focus on the present and getting my shit sorted. Otherwise I'm not good to myself or to you. I can't do that to you. I won't do that to you!" My voice started to rise and I had to work on keeping it at a normal volume. Particularly when all I wanted to do was scream.

"What about the ring? All those promises you made just a few hours ago? Was that just a way to butter me up, to soften the blow? I can't believe you!" Maggie's tears were falling in earnest now, and I felt helpless.

"No, Maggie! I meant every word I said. But those promises are for what I hope is our future. I won't leave this time and shut you out. I can't do that again. To either of us. I want you to take this journey with me, wherever it goes. I hope that you'll wait for me to get myself together. I know it's incredibly selfish of me to even ask you to. But knowing you're waiting for me on the other end of all this will make the process that much easier to deal with," I said sincerely. Maggie started hiccuping and heaving.

"I understand if that's asking too much. But I need you to understand that I'm not leaving you this time! I'm going away for a little while to work on my head. But that I hope you will be there every step of the way. I'll support you and you will support me. We'll learn together what a healthy and functional relationship looks like. Because as I am right now, I know I can't give that to you. And I want to give that to you. Because I want my life to begin and end with us together."

My heart was beating hard in my chest and the blood was rushing through my ears so I could barely hear Maggie's whispered response.

I leaned in closer, gripping her hands tightly in my own. "I'll wait for you. I'll always wait for you," she swore. Her tears had stopped and she seemed to have settled down. I cautiously reached out and ran my fingers through her hair, stopping to rest my hand on the back of her neck. I rested my forehead against hers.

"Are you sure?" I asked her. I didn't want her to feel pressured into it. This had to be her choice. If she chose to walk away, I'd let her, even though I knew I'd never move on from her. I would do it for her.

"I'm sure, Clay. I want to be with you. And even if it takes fifty years, I'll be there at the end of it all," she said firmly and I couldn't stop the smile that spread across my face.

"I love you, Maggie May Young. Always and forever." And then my mouth touched hers and I felt my future begin.

maggie

So I graduated high school. And Clay left for Florida. I went to Beach Week with my best friends. Ruby sold her house and moved to Key West. Her shop was bought by a couple that turned it into a natural food store. I refused to go inside.

I spent the summer working and saving money. I spent time with my parents. I went to the movies with Rachel. I helped Daniel clean out his garage.

And I spoke with Clay three times a week. He had kept his promise not to shut me out. He shared every bit of his treatment with me. He told me about his group therapy and his sessions with his counselors. I told him about my college preparations and getting my school schedule.

We stayed a part of each other's lives in every way that we could, even with a thousand miles separating us.

And I firmly believed that this was a new chapter for us. Hell, it was a brand-new freaking book. The Maggie and Clay story was far from over. And we would always be looking for the light . . . together.

epilogue:
six years later

"I'll have her back there by six thirty! Stop freaking out and let us do some shopping. And don't call again!" Rachel barked into the phone before hanging up. I rubbed the raised skin on the underside of my wrist; the scab over my newly inked tattoo was driving me crazy. I couldn't help but smile at the tiny symbol that looked like an off-kilter upside-down U emblazoned on my skin. It was identical in size and location to the one adorning Maggie's arm. I loved what the rune stood for. I remembered when Maggie explained the meaning to me over dinner all those years ago.

Healing and endurance. And most of all, courage. I finally felt, after all this time, that I was mastering these qualities. So I had taken the plunge and marked my body with a permanent reminder of the love I shared with the woman who had saved me in every way possible.

I was pacing around the living room, rubbing my tattoo, when I stubbed my toe on a box that sat strategically in the middle of the floor.

"Goddamn it all to fucking hell!" I yelled at the top of my lungs.

The place was a disaster. Maggie and I had just moved into our new apartment last weekend and we were in the middle of moving chaos. Boxes were everywhere, being systematically unpacked in stages.

So far we had a semifunctional kitchen. Our bed was a mattress on the floor. But none of that mattered because we were here. Together. Finally.

It was almost six years to the day that I flew back to Florida after leaving Virginia and readmitted myself into the Grayson Center, using a big chunk of the money from Lisa's life insurance policy that Ruby had given me.

I had wondered in those first few days if I had made the right decision. I had missed Maggie so much I was tempted to check myself out again and head back to her. But then I would remember that I was doing this for myself. For the future we wanted to have. And I would suck it up and make it through the day.

They say that the third time's a charm and my third go-around in a facility proved that old saying to be true. I was focused and on task. I worked my treatment plan and dealt with my demons, despite the fact that there were days I wanted to forget about all of it. It helped that Maggie and I talked several times a week. She'd tell me about college; her classes, her new friends, the crappy dorms. I'd tell her about group and art therapy.

When I was released into a transitional group home for mental health patients before Christmas she came to Florida and we spent the holidays together. She stayed in a hotel of course, but made sure that Christmas was special.

Ruby had also continued to be a constant and reassuring presence. And her move to Key West went a long way in invigorating her and giving her a new lease on life.

She still grieved for Lisa. We both did. But she was learning to move on as best she could. And really, that was the only thing any of us could do. We saw each other frequently and I did my best to fill the gaping hole left in her heart.

After moving into the group home, I had enrolled in the local community college and took some art and psychology classes. After working my ass off, I was accepted into the University of Miami. I wouldn't live on campus and for the first year I took my classes online.

It took me almost five and a half years to get my bachelor's degree. That may seem like a long time to get a four-year degree but the fact that I had done it all made the time seem insignificant.

I graduated in May with a BS in psychology and a minor in art. I had decided to apply my passion for the thing that had saved my life in so many ways and now I was enrolled for my master's in art therapy at George Washington University.

Before leaving Florida, I had attempted to make amends with my parents. Years had passed and I stopped hearing from them altogether. They didn't know where I was, so I couldn't expect any of the obligatory birthday and Christmas cards. But I strongly doubted they would have even bothered.

When they had cut me out of their lives, I knew it was a quick and decisive severing. I saw my parents on TV now and then. My father eventually won the election and was now the congressman for Florida's Twenty-third District.

They seemed plastic, almost robotic during their public appearances. My mother's flat, emotionless face was most likely a result of Botox. My dad's lack of personality was even more noticeable. It was amazing that a man as devoid of life as my father had been able to sway people to vote for him. It's amazing what a stupid amount of money will buy you, I guess.

So I had stupidly made the trek to Palm Beach to see if my parents were ready to bury the hatchet. To put the past behind us.

All I had gotten was a door slammed in my face and a stern warning to stay away. I remember pulling out of the driveway, waiting for the emotional paralysis. I anticipated some heavy-duty fallout from being rejected once again by the people who had given me life, for whatever that was worth.

But nothing had come. Instead of being devastated, I had called Maggie and then later Ruby. They gave me all of the love and support I could ever need. And I knew without any doubt that I would never desire or need that from my parents. They had no place in the world I was building for myself.

After that, I had thrown myself into my plans for the future. Maggie and I had decided that we would look for an apartment together. Maggie had gotten a job with Fairfax County Schools as a middle-school English teacher. We were both as happy as we could be without being with each other. But we were finally at a point where that could change.

I was in a good place, though I continued to have my setbacks. My therapist in Florida told me I may always have them. There were the moments when I wasn't sure I could put one foot in front of the other. My fear and paranoia about being abandoned, about ruining everything, continued to plague me at times. But I no longer allowed it to rule me either.

Every day I felt myself approaching a semblance of nirvana. And that was what got me out of bed every single morning. I got in contact with a reputable therapist outside of Washington, D.C., and began my weekly appointments soon after arriving in Virginia. I took my medication every day without fail. These small elements of control were hugely important to me. And even though every day was a test, a struggle, I was happy to fight because I had learned to be proud of the person I was. Demons and all.

Maggie had found us an apartment in Arlington. She was thirty minutes from work and I was a short distance from school. But most important we were together.

There was a knock at the door and I hobbled over to open it. "What the hell is wrong with you?" Daniel asked, walking past me with a large, flat object in his hands.

"I think I broke my fucking toe. That's my fucking problem," I growled, unleashing my inner sailor with the F-bombs flying out of my mouth. Daniel rolled his eyes.

"Well, here you go. I had to wade through Saturday traffic. You owe me, man," Daniel said, handing me the thing he had to wade through traffic for.

"I appreciate it. Now help me hang it and stop your bitching." I rooted through a few boxes until I found my hammer and some nails. Daniel held the picture up in the proper spot above the couch. When we were finished, we stood back and took in my handiwork.

Daniel shook his head. "You really need to get the whole pussy thing in check. Rachel will be driving me crazy to up my game, thanks to you. One of these days I will seriously kick your ass," Daniel grumbled. I caught him rubbing the shiny band on his left ring finger and knew he was all talk. He would do anything in the world for his wife and she was way past asking him to "up his game." They already had everything that they wanted.

Daniel and Rachel lived only fifteen minutes from us in Alexandria. Daniel was in medical school at Georgetown and Rachel worked with a catering company in Reston. They had been married for two years now and Rachel was expecting their first child.

If there was such a thing as happily ever after, those two had found it.

And I was determined to have mine.

"Thanks, Daniel. I'm sure we'll call you later," I promised.

"Sure thing. I'm happy to help. We still on for racquetball tomorrow?" he asked before leaving.

"I don't know," I answered and Daniel snorted.

"I guess it all depends on how far into the night the celebrations go, huh?" He pouted his lips in a sad attempt at a seductive face and I shoved him out the door.

"Whatever, man. Later." I closed the door and turned around. There was no way Maggie would miss the new picture. I just hoped she had the response to it that I wanted.

I went about cleaning the apartment as best I could. I worked on a few more boxes, putting things away. I located the rest of my tools and put the bed frame together. Two hours and lots of cursing later, I finally had our mattress off the floor.

The bed looked really inviting and I realized how tired I was. But there was still too much to do before Maggie got home.

At five thirty, I put in an order with our favorite Chinese place and got in the shower. I dressed in jeans and the button-down shirt Maggie had gotten me for my birthday.

She came bursting through the apartment door, arms loaded down with bags. She and Rachel had made a serious dent in their credit cards. "Did you buy an entire store?" I joked, coming out from the kitchen.

I looked behind her to the picture that she had yet to notice. She was too intent on showing me her purchases. "I found these awesome boots that will look killer with my jean skirt! Check them out!" She pulled out a set of knee-high boots that looked exactly like the other pair she had sitting in the closet. Though I didn't dare tell her that.

"They're great, baby," I said, leaning in to kiss her soft lips. Maggie dropped the bags and wrapped her arms around my neck. "Mmm. You taste amazing," she moaned into my mouth, and I forgot momentarily about my big plans for the night.

Before we could get too carried away, there was a knock at the door. "Who the hell is that?" Maggie griped.

I laughed into her downturned mouth. "Food. I ordered from China Chef. Figured your day of consumerism would make you hungry," I said. Maggie rubbed her belly.

"Good thinking. I'm just going to put the bags back in the bedroom," Maggie replied, grabbing her purchases. She still hadn't noticed our new wall art and I didn't say anything. It was important that she saw it on her own.

I gave the delivery guy money and took our dinner into the kitchen. Maggie's shriek from back in the bedroom made me grin. "You put the bed together!" she yelled as she came flying down the hall and leaping into my arms.

"You are so going to get lucky in that thing later," she promised, running her hands up my shirt. I pulled her hands away. As much as I wanted to go in the direction she was heading, I had other plans for her this evening.

"Come and eat your dinner, my little nympho," I told her, getting plates out of the cabinet. Maggie grumbled, but the smell of Chinese food ended any further complaining. We ate our dinner together, laughing, talking, and simply enjoying being with each other.

"I'll clean up; you go into the living room and get comfortable. I'll even watch a chick flick if you want," I said, smiling. I knew what was coming and my stomach flipped over with my nerves.

"Thanks, baby. I love you," Maggie said as she kissed me again. I started piling the dishes into the sink, waiting impatiently for her to call out to me, asking about the new picture above the couch.

By the time I was finished, I realized Maggie was strangely quiet. I went into the living room to find her staring at the matted and framed canvas.

"What is this?" she whispered, her eyes never straying from the new artwork. "Did you paint it?" she asked, looking at me over her shoulder.

I nodded, letting her take the time to absorb what I was trying to tell her through my painting. It was a silhouette of the two of us, darkened in shadow but with a brilliant, bright light behind us revealing the intricate details of our faces bowed in close together.

Butterflies rose in flight around us and it vibrated with the love I felt for the girl standing before it.

On the bottom, in neat script, I had carefully written: *And he asked her to share his forever.*

While she stared at the picture, I pulled out the small velvet box I had kept in my pocket all day and got down on one knee. When Maggie turned around and saw what I was doing, she gasped, her hands flying to her mouth. And then she did the craziest thing. She fell down to her knees in front of me.

"I'm the one who's supposed to be on my knees here. You're ruining the moment," I teased her. She held her hands to my cheeks and gave me one of her earth-shattering smiles. It was a smile that could cure cancer. It told me that I was responsible for this perfect slice of happiness in her life.

As tears rolled down her face, I tried to tell her, with words that could express everything I felt for her, everything she was to me. But words could never be enough to explain the way she had completely filled me.

"Over seven years ago I met a girl who saved me. I didn't realize at the time, mostly because her attitude pissed me off, that she would become the most important thing in my life." Maggie playfully punched my shoulder as I wiped the wetness from her cheeks with my thumbs.

"But then I got to know her, and when I was drowning, she became my air. In the cold, she became my warmth." I cupped her face in my hands as she quietly sobbed, and for once I didn't feel any guilt for her tears. Because these tears were filled with nothing but joy. And those were tears I was glad to give her.

"In the dark, she became my light," I whispered, my voice breaking and my own tears starting to fall.

"Our road hasn't been an easy one. But good things rarely are. You taught me that the person I am is worth loving, worth fighting for. You gave me strength when I had none. You held me up when I wanted to fall. And now I want to give you everything. I want to give you the world. Because, Maggie, you've given me mine. And it's you. It will always, forever, be you," I said, the lump in my throat making my voice a harsh whisper.

"Clay," Maggie sobbed and she fell against me, pressing her forehead into my shoulder.

Holding her tight against my body, I whispered in her ear, "Will you marry me, Maggie?" She tilted her face up and her smile was absolutely radiant.

"I think you already know the answer to that," she said as I slid the diamond ring onto her finger, above the promise ring I had given her all those years ago. Even in the middle of this intense, emotion-filled moment, her sarcasm was ever present. And I loved that about her. I kissed every inch of her face, over and over again. "And just so you know, I already have the world. You're just expanding my universe a little bit," Maggie added, touching the side of my face, and I captured her mouth, kissing her with every ounce of love and adoration I felt for her.

And I held her, this girl who had saved me and continued to save me every day. Our path would never be smooth, but I hadn't lied when I said good things were never easy. And I was okay with going the hard way. Because as long as she was beside me, as long as we were together, I knew we could face anything.

So together we walked into our future. One that *we* had mapped out. And that future held nothing but light.

important resources

Depression, suicide, and cutting are serious issues. Statistics show that two million to three million people in the United States and 13 percent of fifteen- and sixteen-year-olds in the United Kingdom cut every year. Self-injurious behavior is often a way people cope with bigger issues.

If you or someone you know is dealing with cutting or depression, it's important to talk about it, get help, and find a way to stop!

There are so many great resources out there; taking the first step and reaching out is the place to start.

Depression and Bipolar Support Alliance (DBSA):
www.dbsalliance.org

Teen Self-Injury Hotline:
1-800-DONT-CUT

Teen Suicide Hotline:
1-800-SUICIDE

Great source and information about self-injury:
www.selfinjury.com

acknowledgments

Thank you to every one of my readers who have loved Maggie and Clay from the very start. Without your support, I wouldn't be doing this at all!

Thank you to my amazing husband, who always gave me the motivation to keep writing, even when I became discouraged. You are the butter to my bread, the sprinkles to my ice cream, the ketchup to my fries . . . Okay, you get the point. Love you!

Thank you to my gorgeous daughter, who can always make me smile. You are who I want to be when I grow up.

To my fantastic editor, Tanya, for working so fast it makes my head spin. Your enthusiasm for my stories is such a huge motivator! Love ya!

To Sarah Hansen at Okay Creations for finding the amazing photograph that graces the cover. You perfectly captured the feel of this story. Your talent is phenomenal!

To Claire, my numero uno beta reader. Your feedback was essential and you gave me confidence when I felt like the whole story sucked. You are amazing. I can't wait to do some ghost hunting with you.

To Kim Box Person, Denise Tung, Kristy Louise, and all of the other amazing bloggers who have championed my stories. Your endless pimping and total support have helped me to make a career out of something I had only ever dreamed I could do.

And most important, thank you to the beautiful and strong clients I have had the absolute privilege to work with over the years. Your fight and resilience is awe-inspiring and will always remind me to look for the light in the dark.

Don't miss the next powerful love story from

A. MEREDITH WALTERS

lead me not

August 2014 from Gallery Books

Sex and drugs. Love and addiction.
Destruction and salvation.

For a girl trying desperately to do the right thing, Aubrey finds it hard to resist the pull of an unfamiliar tempta- tion. A craving to walk a dark road that both scares and thrills her. Particularly when the man leading her into the darkness is the person who owns her heart. . . .